THE WRONG VICTIM

The gun barked three times. Two of the bullets flew harmlessly through the open door, but the last one cut a deep crease in Cyrus's shoulder. He lunged headfirst over the sofa, landed on his shoulders and rolled. Halfway through the somersault, his body began to change, and by the time he came to his feet, he no longer resembled anything human.

The gunman took one look at the snarling, wolflike creature, then one look at the gun and turned to run. Cyrus grabbed the man's head like he was palming a basketball, twisted, and his neck popped like a dry carrot snapping in two.

The other guy was dragging his body across the floor toward the pistol. Cyrus cleared the distance between them and snatched the man up like a G.I. Joe doll.

Another time Cyrus might have let him go—not this time. He wasn't in a forgiving mood. There was blood on the man's arm and blood on his face—the very air in the penthouse reeked of blood and that destroyed any chance the man might have had. Cyrus tore a massive chunk of flesh from the side of the gunman's neck with his fangs and then raised him high overhead and heaved him through the open balcony door and over the railing. The man was still screaming when he smashed through the windshield of a two-seater Mercedes, thirty-five stories below.

Other *Leisure Books* by Gary Holleman:
DEMON FIRE

HOWL-O-WEEN

Gary L. Holleman

LEISURE BOOKS   NEW YORK CITY

To Kathleen, my wife, partner, and
part-time pit bull.

A LEISURE BOOK®

September, 1999

Published by

Dorchester Publishing Co., Inc.
276 Fifth Avenue
New York, NY 10001

ISBN 0-8439-4639-3

HOWL-O-WEEN

Chapter One

Friday, October 13

It was a typical Indian-summer Memphis morning: seventy-eight degrees and blue skies. But by ten o'clock the temperature would be up somewhere between dehydration and heatstroke. Cyrus had done his five miles early and was sitting on the top step in front of his apartment untying his sneakers when the woman climbed out of the little red Miata. He tried not to stare, but she was the kind of woman a man could not avoid staring at. Pixie-cut hair the color of red autumn leaves, turned-up nose, dressed in cool green silks and dark hose. She had a diamond on her right hand as big as his knuckle, dagger-red nails and a lot of Southwestern turquoise and silver on both wrists. At first glance he thought she was in her mid twenties. But as the woman crossed the parking lot, he saw the fine lines at the corners of her eyes and revised his estimate upward: maybe thirty or thirty-two.

Cyrus glanced down at the way he was dressed. She was *Vogue;* he was gym rat: a pair of sweat-stained running shorts and a T-shirt with more holes than cotton. Anyway, she was the most beautiful woman he had ever seen.

Then she ruined it.

"You're not Cyrus Trigg, are you?"

Her expression, as her eyes traveled up and down his five-foot-seven-inch frame, said she was somehow disappointed.

"Guilty as charged," he replied. "I go by Russ."

She climbed the steps slowly, as if trying to make up her mind about something.

7

"You're a bodyguard?"

The way she said it would have made Kevin Costner die of shame.

"Personal security specialist."

The woman stared at her soft green pumps and then up at his face. Her eyes matched the shoes. "May I come in? I have a proposition for you."

Cyrus opened the front door and stood back as she walked into his apartment with her head tucked between her shoulders, and he wondered what she had expected, a scene from *Animal House*?

"You have a maid?"

The center of his living room was dominated by a huge Persian rug topped with a black leather sofa, a gray cord recliner and an off-brand nineteen-inch color TV set. On either side of the front windows were hanging plants and a pair of five-foot stereo speakers. To the right was a small kitchen with pots and pans hung in geometric rows from hooks in the wall, and to the left, across the room, was the door to the bedroom and bath.

The woman walked over and looked at her reflection in the top of the stove.

Cyrus went to the refrigerator and took out two cans of soda.

"Diet Coke okay?"

"Fine."

While he played the gracious host, she waltzed slowly around the living room, running her fingers over the books and tennis trophies that lined the homemade shelves on the wall and peering at the faded photographs of a short kid with light brown hair and aquamarine eyes. On another shelf was a more recent picture of Cyrus wearing a short white robe and black sash. On the top shelf were more trophies, this time topped with little gold statues holding pistols in impossibly steady hands.

Cyrus stepped into the bedroom and a moment later the deep sensual moan of Kenny G's sax filtered out of the speakers. He came out and leaned against the door. "What can I do for you?"

The woman said, "You some kind of super Republican?"

He smiled dubiously. "What do you mean?"

"Karate, tennis, marksmanship? Unless you're the Bionic Man, you have to be rich to be able to afford all this stuff."

"You know what they say about short guys, classic over-achievers."

She picked up the photo of Cyrus in his karate outfit. "Are you dangerous?"

She didn't wear much makeup: a touch of color on the cheeks, a pale lipstick that subdued her hair and eyes. Yet Cyrus thought her most attractive cosmetic was the natural sprinkling of cinnamon-colored freckles across her nose. They fascinated him.

"Dangerous?" he replied. "No, just careful, Miss . . ."

Instead of an answer he got a card pressed into his hand.

Kyna Rand
International Diamond Buyers, Ltd.

"So, Miss Rand, what can I do for you?"

"I'm not sure you can do anything for me."

Cyrus took a warm-up jacket from the coat closet behind the front door and slipped it on, and then let his hand rest on the front doorknob. "Well, when you're sure . . ."

"No," Kyna replied quickly. "What I meant to say was— I don't really know if I need a bodyguard."

Was this where he was supposed to say, *With a body like that?* But her attitude was beginning to get on his nerves so he just stared and watched her squirm.

"I have this trip coming up—diamonds. Did I mention that I deliver diamonds?" Cyrus shook his head. "Anyway, I have to leave in a couple of days and will be gone about two weeks and . . ."

Her voice trailed off.

Gary L. Holleman

"What are we talking about here?" Cyrus asked. "Dollar-wise?"

"Oh, retail . . . between twelve and fifteen million."

He let out a long, low whistle. "You always carry that much?"

"Anonymity has always been our best protection. Armored cars and guns just draw attention."

"So what changed?"

Kyna stared at him long enough for Cyrus to realize he wasn't going to get the truth. A spark of something dark stirred behind her eyes and then the shades came down and the attitude returned.

"Nothing's changed. It's just a large shipment and my boss suggested I get some help."

"Why me? Why not one of the bonded agencies?"

Shuffling through her purse, Kyna finally came out with a crumpled envelope. "Like I said, anonymity is our best protection. We've used the big agencies in the past and gotten burned."

"How did you hear about me? I'm not in the yellow pages."

"Julie Del Mar is my roommate."

Cyrus mentally repeated the name, but couldn't put a face with it.

"She's a model. You and another man provided security for a show she was in down at the convention center."

Cyrus remembered then. "Tall black woman? Face like Cleopatra? Beautiful eyes? Braids?"

Kyna nodded. "Hard to forget Julie."

"But I couldn't have said more than two words to her."

"It wasn't what you said. She mentioned that you were very . . . discreet."

"Oh?"

"Something about one of the girls' boyfriends?"

Cyrus remembered the incident; one of the model's friends was drunk enough to make a stink and had managed to sneak backstage. The pageant's organizer wanted to call the cops,

10

but Cyrus had taken the guy by the arm, none too gently, and walked him around out back till he sobered up enough to listen to reason.

"Right."

"You mind?" Kyna pointed to the couch and then took a seat before he had a chance to reply. She set the empty glass on the end table and folded her hands protectively around the envelope in her lap. "Tell me about yourself."

I don't need this shit, he thought. But his eyes strayed to the envelope. "You mean like how many notches do I have in my gun? Or how many bad guys have I beat up?"

The blood crept up her neck.

"Maybe I've made a mistake," she said, rising to her feet.

Cyrus thought about the stack of past-due bills sitting on the desk in his bedroom and drained his glass. "Hold on. I guess I'm not much on oral résumés." He got a towel from the closet in the hall and dried his face. "I was an MP, first in Okinawa and then in Berlin . . ."

"MP? You mean like a soldier?"

The way she said it was like he cleaned stalls with his bare hands.

"You got it."

"Oh."

"Nowadays I mostly do personal security work, sometimes like with your friend I do conventions and shows. I know some guys down at the sheriff's department that send jobs my way. If things are real slow, I bartend."

He didn't bother to mention that "bartend" meant bounce, or that once in a while he collected money for . . . friends.

Kyna eyed his body under the bulky warm-up jacket. He was short, but his shoulders were wide and he had big hands. His face was tanned from working outdoors, but unlined, almost boyish. He had calm eyes and heavily muscled runner's legs. More important, if what Julie had told her was accurate, he had the one qualification that was absolutely indispensable: he worked cheap. Kyna could ill afford to throw away a lot

of her own money on what was probably going to turn out to
be a misunderstanding.

"Have you ever, you know . . . lost anyone?" she asked,
and then laughed.

"Lost? You mean had anyone shot? Killed? No way. Worst
thing ever happened was one guy got drunk and threw up all
over his dinner jacket." He eyed Kyna for a moment. "You
have some reason to expect trouble on this trip?"

"No, no."

She said it too quickly, then abruptly held out the envelope
like it was a note from the principal. Cyrus took it and
thumbed through the bills.

"Cash?" he said, his eyebrows arching under his hair.

"My boss only deals in cash."

He counted silently.

"Naturally we'll pay all of your expenses."

It wasn't as much as he'd have liked—it must have showed.

"And," she added quickly, "a bonus if . . . when we get
back."

He let that slide. "When did you want to leave?"

"I'm on a very tight schedule. We must leave tomorrow
and we must be finished by the thirty-first."

"Halloween?" he muttered.

She looked surprised. "Why, yes. Halloween."

The Bahamas Air DC-10 touched down at Miami International Airport in the middle of a driving rainstorm. Ten
minutes later the Dark Man strolled down the telescoping
boarding corridor with an ancient leather suitcase in one hand
and an ornate walking stick in the other. At the end of the
tunnel he looked around until he spotted two black men in
pin-striped suits waiting at the check-in desk. One of the men
was tall—though not as tall as the Dark Man—and wore a
short, neatly trimmed goatee. The other man looked like a
bowling ball with legs: short, bald and muscular.

The Dark Man strode past them without a word, forcing the

two men to run to catch up before he reached the customs area.

"You have located him?" The Dark Man's guttural Garifuna dialect was as rough as a smoker's cough.

"Yes."

"It is far?"

"No. Key Biscayne. About twenty minutes in this weather."

"You will take me to a hotel," the Dark Man said. "We will visit him tonight."

"What of the weather?"

"I will ride to him on the back of the storm."

Kyna drove with quick, sure movements of her hands and feet, running through the gears without so much as a glance at the Miata's tachometer, darting between dinosaur-sized semis and blowing past mud-splattered pickups with baseball bats—their handles wrapped with electrical tape—hanging in window-mounted gun racks. She was on her way back to Germantown, to the apartment that she shared with super-model Julie Del Mar, and trying to figure out why she had done what she'd just done: hire a total stranger to go with her to deliver the diamonds.

"It's all your fault, Bryan," she muttered as she slammed on the brakes to keep from rear-ending another pickup truck with Mississippi tags.

"Learn to drive on pavement, you redneck!" she screamed as she accelerated around the truck.

The white-haired man behind the wheel waved and smiled.

"Shit!" she muttered, feeling guilty for taking her frustrations out on some poor old dirt farmer. "Damn you, Bryan."

After calling in the middle of the night and giving her extremely detailed instructions for a totally unexpected, totally harebrained delivery trip, Bryan Douglas, Kyna's boss and on-again-off-again lover for the past two years, had promptly vanished from the face of the earth.

And now Kyna was spooked. She knew there was no one

Gary L. Holleman

to blame but herself, for Bryan had always been as thoughtful as Attila the Hun. Only this time she knew something was terribly wrong; it had been in his voice—even on a telephone all the way from London. He'd been excited and he'd been too smooth. He'd said "honest" twice, and called her "love" three times—a sure sign he was lying through his teeth.

It was probably just another woman, Kyna mused. She wasn't crazy enough to think a man with Bryan's looks and money was always going to be faithful, but still . . . where the devil was he? And why all the rush about this trip? She hadn't been scheduled to make any more deliveries until after the first of the year and yet he'd practically made her swear in blood that she'd go and be done by the thirty-first. What was so special about Halloween?

The Dark Man stood comfortably in the eye of the storm. As the rainwater ran down over the scabrous tattoos on his face, his eyes—bleak and unseeing—were fixed on a renovated art deco house in the middle of a palm tree clearing. Neither the rain nor the wind that buffeted his face, nor the lightning that ripped the night like the claws of a beast could intrude upon the memories that flashed like grade-school slides across the screen of his mind.

It was inconceivable, of course, that anyone would be insane enough to steal anything from him—much less the talisman. It was the most sacred thing he possessed.

In and of itself, the talisman was just a rather odd-looking strand of stones and shells, scarabs and fossils, all topped off with a two-thousand-year-old death's head bead from Tanzania. But Macumba, the Butcher of West Africa and a genius of evil, through years of torture and bloody sacrifice had instilled the necklace with the ability to magnify the essence of the wearer. To paraphrase the pasty-faced devils in the white collars: dark from darkness, true evil from the essence of evil. As long as the Dark Man had the Butcher's Broom in his possession, he was invulnerable. But even he had to sleep.

And to sleep wearing the talisman was to invite the spirits of his dead enemies into his dreams. And now it was missing.

After tearing his hut apart looking for the necklace, the Dark Man had gone looking for his son, Tomas, to ask the boy about the talisman, and had found him sprawled on the dirt floor in his hut—his handsome young face half submerged in a pool of blood. When the Dark Man turned the boy over, he had seen it all: the chalky-gray skin, the wide blood-engorged eyes, the puckered hole, like a third eye, in the middle of his son's forehead.

And the talisman was gone.

It was clear that Tomas had taken the Butcher's Broom and that someone had killed him for it.

The Dark Man was old—older than he looked, and he looked like he could have held the rudder for Noah. Tomas had been his only child—a late gift from the Loa. His fifth wife, an eighteen-year-old woman from the nearby island of Guanaja, had been the vessel, but the child had been his. And as often happens in these cases, the Dark Man had fallen under the boy's spell and had been too soft. He had tried to get across the idea that human beings are fleshy sacks of conflicting wants and needs, emotions and impulses. And that this dichotomy of purpose makes them weak, vulnerable to every petty dictator or religious fad. True strength, the Dark Man had preached, came from purity, and the one true icon of purity in an otherwise diluted universe was evil.

As much as the Dark Man had tried to explain, Tomas had never understood this. His instruction in the arts of Shango and Obeah had barely begun when the boy had started running off to town.

"Ha! Town," the Dark Man muttered under his breath.

Coxen Hole, the capital of the island of Roatan, was a dirt street full of wooden shacks built by the descendants of pirates and disease-ridden whores.

"Yes, a hole."

Staring at his son's ashen face, the Dark Man had reached down and stuck his finger into the hole in the boy's skull,

15

working it around until the bullet squirted out into his palm—
a half-inch piece of misshapen lead covered with blood and
gray matter. He held the slug up to the light, turning it this
way and that—the way one might look at a black widow in a
glass jar.

Yes, he thought, the boy had been a dupe, but a willing
dupe.

Then the dark giant had opened his robe and removed a
World War II vintage combat knife from the sheath at his
back. As he mumbled the familiar words of the blood oath—
calling upon Baron Samedi and all the Guédé—promising
them the lives of his son's murderers in return for their support—he drew the blade down across his body from left nipple
to lower right side. The skin parted like the petals of a red
hibiscus, drenching the old scars and tribal tattoos on his belly
and allowing his blood to mingle with that of his dead son's.
The Dark Man clenched his jaws and refused to make a
sound—his pain was his gift to the dark lords. Then he repeated the ritual on the other side, skillfully carving a scarlet
X into his chest.

The vow complete, all he had to do was find the fool who
had the Butcher's Broom and the man would die—painfully,
to be sure—and his soul would suffer an eternity of agony.
Stepping to the door, the Dark Man stared up into the cobalt
sky. He didn't need a watch or a calendar to tell him that a
clock had started ticking. All Hallows' Eve was only weeks
away. And without the talisman . . .

As he examined the sky, a large bat flew low across the
tops of the trees. The creature's red eyes glinted hungrily in
the light from the dying sun. The Dark Man had known then,
yes he had known . . . the spirits were watching.

No amount of time or icy rain would ever cool the fury that
burned in the Dark Man's breast. He had followed the talisman
from Roatan to the Monkey River on the mainland of Belize.
From the jungle to Mexico City. From Mexico City to Nassau.
And now, finally, to Miami. The Dark Man's eyes—eyes one

might expect to find in a spider or some deadly cold-blooded reptile that slithered through the world on its belly—refocused on the house's low rambling silhouette. Each time the lightning flashed, the house momentarily blinked into view, blatantly pink against the background of greenish palm trees. The lights inside had gone out more than an hour ago, but the Dark Man was nothing if not patient. The men with him were cold and wet, but they were also intelligent enough not to grumble. In hopes of keeping dry, they had retreated into the sea grape trees that fringed the beach but the water ran right off the large saucer-shaped leaves and only added to their misery.

At long last the Dark Man snapped his fingers once and the men hurried to his side.

"Now."

As soon as his aides had unfurled a blanket over the sand, the Dark Man knelt and spread the tools of his trade around him: a black three-legged bowl made of fire-hardened clay, leather and human skin pouches, two horsehide rattles and a small obsidian statue of Legba—in voodoo lore, the youngest son of the creator. From the leather pouch he poured a black-and-green granular substance into the bowl, then quickly fired a match and tossed it in. The powder ignited with a muted pop that sent a foul-smelling ball of smoke rolling up into the storm. As he shook the rattles, the Dark Man hummed a melody that had originated in the Olduvai Gorge region of Tanzania back when Mount Kilimanjaro was a small bump on the horizon and men were still dragging their knuckles in the parched, red dirt as they walked.

The storm responded to this chilling refrain with wind that lashed the trees and lightning that came so fast and furiously that it changed the night into day. As the howl of the wind increased in pitch, the Dark Man began to chant, spitting out strings of incomprehensible incantations like phlegm. Behind him, the men covered their ears and bent over to take the brunt of the storm on their backs. Just when it seemed that the earth must surely implode under the weight of the storm's fury, a massive bolt of lightning struck the power pole at the end of the street and every light on the island winked out.

"That takes care of the alarm system and the phones," the goateed man said to his companion over the roar of the wind.

The trio paused to watch the windows for any sign of activity. After five minutes, they went around to the back of the house and examined the door. The goateed man stepped up, wedged a crowbar between the door and the jamb and pushed. The wood around the jamb splintered and the door swung open into the house's shadowy kitchen.

The Dark Man stooped just inside the threshold and used powder from his pouch to draw an intricate fetish on the linoleum. Then he stood and held a pinch of the powder high overhead. As he recited a brief incantation, he turned slowly and cast a bit of it in three different directions around the kitchen.

"Come."

As silent as a lewd thought, the trio passed through the dining room and entered the living room, passing along the way a large pit bull sleeping under the dining room table. The animal did not stir. The Dark Man led the way unerringly through the cavernous house, while his coadjutors struggled to keep up without bumping into the furniture. As they entered the hallway, the bald man tripped over a second dog—a large German shepherd bitch. The dog whined and tucked her tail between her legs in her sleep, but did not move. At the end of the corridor was a massive set of double doors. The man with the goatee tried the knob and shook his head.

"Stand back," the Dark Man hissed.

The corridor was too dark for the men to see, but they could hear the Dark Man's rhythmic droning and smell the pungent aroma of his powdery concoction. When the chanting stopped, the doors swung open by themselves and the intruders tiptoed into a large bedroom suite full of shadows and heavy Mediterranean furniture. The air smelled of cigars and flowery perfume. Against the far wall was a giant-screen television set, a VCR and a stereo. In the middle of the floor was an oversized bed on a raised dais; in the middle of the bed, two people, a man and a woman, were snoring.

The Dark Man took up a position at the foot of the bed with his men flanking him on either side. From under his shirt he took an amulet fashioned of wood, feathers and bone—a poor imitation of his precious talisman—and pointed it at the man, softly singing in the harsh tongue of his people. When the man on the bed began to stir, the Dark Man took another pinch of powder and blew it over the bed. The sleeping man immediately started to twist and moan like a man in the grip of a terrifying nightmare. The Dark Man continued to sing, his voice rising and falling in perfect tempo with the rain hammering against the windowpanes. Finally, the man threw off the bed covers and sat up, his feet swinging unerringly down into the slippers positioned beside the bed. At first his eyes were fat with sleep, but they quickly opened wide and grew round when he saw the dark shapes hovering around the bed.

In his youth the man had been powerful, but the years of soft living had turned much of his muscle to fat. The flesh of his arms sagged like rolls of Polish sausage. Above his lip was the traditional down-turned *bandido* moustache and above that, the tiny mean eyes of a wharf rat, now shining saucers of terror.

"Good evening, Mr. Morales," the Dark Man said.

Morales's mouth worked up and down, but nothing came out and sweat popped out of the man's forehead like condensation on an ice-cold can of beer.

The Dark Man glanced at his men. "Help Mr. Morales."

The goateed man took hold of one of Morales's arms, the bald-headed man the other, and they jerked him to his feet and quickly peeled his silk pajamas off. In the bed, the woman continued to snore peacefully.

The Dark Man's assistants then dragged Morales over in front of the television set and lowered him onto his back, chuckling to themselves as the man's hairy belly sagged to either side like a water balloon. Morales's eyes were frantic, bouncing from face to face, but the rest of his body was as stiff as the Dark Man's long-lamented son.

The Dark Man stood with his feet straddling Morales's head and peered down as if he were contemplating the man's soul. From his vantage point on the carpet, Pablo Morales was beginning to realize that life as he had known it was over. Yet the man was still too much of a weasel not to look for a way out. He tried to speak, but again nothing came out.

Turning to his assistants, the Dark Man said, "Leave us. And close the door."

The men glanced at each other, but did as instructed.

The Dark Man shook his head sadly. When he spoke, the reasonableness of his tone was more unnerving than a scream. "You may speak now, Pablo. Please tell me about the talisman."

Now that he knew he could speak, Morales was afraid to. After a moment of silence the Dark Man asked again, this time in English. When Morales didn't reply the second time, the Dark Man kicked the man sharply behind the right ear with the toe of his sandal.

"Pablo, I suggest you listen to me as if your life depended on it. If you do not answer me, I am going to kill your dogs— just so that you will understand that I am a serious person. If you still remain mute, I will kill your daughter, and then your wife, and then . . . I will kill you. After you are dead, I will rip you open like the pig that you are and squeeze the information I seek from your entrails. So you see, you *will* tell me what I want to know. The only question is . . . how much pain do you want to endure beforehand?"

The Dark Man waited patiently, his head cocked to one side, but Morales kept his mouth shut and just shivered.

The Dark Man went to the door, opened it and said to the man with the goatee, "Bring the dog."

Paula Inkarha dropped the cup of herbal tea she had been drinking and grabbed her head. It didn't help. The images exploded like strings of tenpenny firecrackers on her stunned optic nerves. Her bedroom was gone. In its place was a room she had never seen before—a bedroom, yes, but large, opulent and full of shadowy strangers.

Paula stood so still that the beating of her heart felt like one of the earthquakes that periodically rattled the windows of her San Francisco shop. She saw three men, two standing and one lying naked on his back in the middle of a plush carpet.

"Open your eyes, Pablo," the man with the goatee whispered.

The fat man on the floor shook his head.

"Come on. Don't be like thaaaat—open up."

The fat man's lids opened and it was as if he were staring straight up into Paula's soul. Everything about the man seemed paralyzed and yet his eyes were bouncing around the room like Ping-Pong balls. Paula realized that she was seeing everything through the eyes of a fourth man—a being of incredible occult power. Horrified by what she sensed in the man's mind, she squeezed her consciousness into a tiny little ball, but loosed a psychic hint for the man to move his eyes around the room.

The bedroom was lavish—*Architectural Digest* lavish—with Goyas in gilt frames and chandeliers that looked like spaceships. Only now, in addition to the Greco-Roman discus thrower standing coiled on a pedestal in the alcove next to the fireplace, someone had nailed a German shepherd's head to the floor between the fat man's thighs, its open mouth and lolling tongue mere inches from his shriveled penis.

As Paula's host swept the room with his eyes, she noticed more bizarre decorative touches: bloody animal parts, clumps of fur, a dog's front leg resting like a paintbrush in a bowl of half-congealed blood and a wall smeared with obscene symbols and pictures—the excess blood had run down the stucco and soaked into the carpet.

"Would you care to answer my questions now?"

The voice inside Paula's head was harsh, like a man gargling glass, and ice cold—no emotion, no humanity.

"Señor," the fat man sobbed, "I do not know what you mean."

21

The man with the goatee shoved a little girl into the room and stood at her back with his hands resting lightly on her frail shoulders. The girl was not fully awake yet and she was rubbing the sleep out of her eyes with tiny balled fists.

The fat man cried, "*¡Madre Dios!* Not my Sally, no!"

"Papa?"

"Please, señor. Please. I will do anything."

A spark of something malevolent ignited deep inside her host's mind. To Paula, it felt like an explosion of foul-smelling swamp gas. "Excellent. Where is it?"

Tears and mucus were clotted in the man's moustache. He tried to lick the snot away as he replied, "Señor, I swear to you on my daughter's life . . . I do not know. I was contacted by a man over the phone. He knew me, or at least knew of me, and had heard I might be willing to . . . broker your—"

A black hand seemed to come out of nowhere to grasp the fat man's throat, the bony fingers digging into the spongy flesh until the man's eyes bulged out like bloodshot grapes and his tongue flopped in his mouth like a dead leech. The hand remained until the man's face turned the color of an eggplant and then relaxed and withdrew. The fat man gulped air until his color returned to normal.

"How do you contact this man?"

"I don't. He calls me. If I do anything for him, he leaves the cash in a locker at the bus station or the airport and leaves the key at a prearranged spot. I get the key, drop off the merchandise, pick up the cash and split. Sometimes it works the other way around—I pick up a package and return cash."

"What is in the package, drugs?"

"Diamonds. Once in a while emeralds. Emeralds are big down here with the—"

The hand lashed out, crushing the man's nose and splattering blood all over his face.

"I am not interested in your marketing report! You expect me to believe that you never saw this man? That you never waited at the bus station to see what he looked like?"

"Of course I did. I had my men watch the drop, but somehow he always knew. Once they staked out the bus station for twenty-four hours, but no one came. Finally I pulled them away and when I sent them back an hour later, the cash was there and the package was gone.''

''So you cannot help me, is that correct?''

A knife appeared at the little girl's throat. The blade was long and thin, a lewd exclamation mark beneath the child's pale ear.

''Wait, wait!'' the fat man screamed. ''You . . . you swear you will not hurt my wife and child?''

''Of course. You have my word.''

Paula tried not to think, not to breathe, but she couldn't help herself.

Don't trust him!

''Once . . . one time the drop was delayed and a woman called . . . here on my home phone.''

''A woman? So?''

''I have that service on my private telephone—the one that displays the number of the caller. I traced the number.''

''And?''

''It was a private telephone in Memphis, Tennessee.''

''Ahhhh!''

Suddenly Paula felt as if her soul had fallen into a psychic cesspool. Sensing the rolling tide of blood and death that was coming, she recoiled in horror and slingshot her mind back to her own body. When she came to she was on the floor, staring up at her utilitarian furniture as if it had just beamed down from a spaceship. She was stunned, sickened. In all of her years dealing in the occult, Paula had never come in contact with a mind so totally vile.

Climbing to her feet, Paula saw her long gown was stained with tea and her foot was bleeding where she had stepped on the broken cup. She went to the mirror over her dresser and brushed the locks of her silky black hair out of her eyes.

''Shit!''

Her eyes were smoldering red embers—a sure sign that her vision had been real and not a hallucination—and her normally smooth café au lait complexion was sallow and grainy.

Leaving a trail of bloody footprints on the polished hardwood floors, Paula limped down the narrow staircase, past the shelves filled with fetishes and potions, to the table in the rear of her shop—a room that also doubled as her kitchen. She began shuffling a worn deck of tarot cards. Her hands were shaking, but she dared not stop once she had begun—that could completely foul up the reading. After dealing the cards faceup on the table in a formation known as the Celtic Cross Spread, she closed her eyes and ran the tips of her fingers over the warm pasteboard. The cards were old, an heirloom from a great-grandmother once burned in the cracker part of Louisiana for witchcraft, and they were her only friends. Except this night the cards felt odd, foreign. They seemed to burn her fingertips like acid.

Paula gritted her teeth and concentrated harder, pulling images like splinters out of her mind. Finally, when she was ready, she opened her eyes and examined the cards.

The central card was the image of a winged devil crossed over the lovers reversed.

The devil could only be the dark host from her vision. But the lovers? That couldn't be her. It must mean that she was going to come in contact with someone—a couple—and they would be in great danger from the dark host.

The top card showed a man struggling with ten tall poles—the 10 of Wands—indicating a man who takes on the burdens of others. The bottom card was the Tower, from which Paula received an impression of vast blackness like the inside of a dark cathedral.

The intermediate cards showed the usual mix of danger, opportunity and love, but the outcome card was the most feared of all—the smiling skeleton of death reversed.

Death? Death for whom? The lovers? Or the Devil?

Paula picked up the last card and stared at the skeletal figure's grin. She closed her eyes and kneaded the card carefully between her sensitive fingers. She saw the image of a mountain, cold and stark under an ashen moon. And trees, their bare arms forming hairline cracks in the fabric of the night. Surrounding everything was an aura of power the likes of which she had never felt.

Replacing the card, Paula got up and went to the calendar on the wall over the sink. On the top of the calendar was a picture of a woman in a peaked hat, riding on a broom in front of a yellow moon. Perched like a hood ornament on the front of the broom handle was a black cat. Over the witch's face, she had pasted a carefully cut-out photo of her own face in profile—Paula's idea of a little joke.

Paula ran her fingers over the numbers on the bottom: 15 . . . 16 . . . 17 . . . Down and down until she reached the number 31.

"Halloween? Why am I not surprised?"

She picked up a black crayon and circled the thirty-first.

Chapter Two

Downtown Memphis had all the charm and fading glory of an aging and forgotten Southern belle. For years America's cleanest city, her wide avenues were now laced with decades of ground-in grime. Her cotton exchanges and department stores had become wig salons and pawnshops. Her promise— like the belle's virginity—had been raped and abandoned by white flight, turning her sidewalks and alleyways into cardboard abodes for the helpless—homeless people who suffered under the combined weight of apathy, mental illness and hopelessness. Not the kind of place one would normally expect to find a cheery, red Miata.

Kyna left the car at the curb with the motor running and the alarm set and practically ran into the bus station. She hated the place, full as it was of winos and creeps. But Bryan insisted it was the best place to store the shipment. As she scurried across to the lockers, she whispered his words like a litany to keep from thinking about what could happen to her.

"Don't keep it at home, it's the first place the cops would look. Don't keep it at the airport. The DEA has more cameras at the airport than there are in Hollywood. Don't use banks. Don't use post offices . . ."

And on and on. Like Mr. Oxford Graduate had ever been any closer to a real cop than watching *Lovejoy* on the BBC.

Sidestepping a puddle of chunky yellow vomit, Kyna walked to the last row of lockers, where she paused, staring at the man snoring in the corner, at his oozing sores and sand-paper stubble. In spite of herself Kyna wondered if he could really be a cop and was only made up to look like the world's most disgusting bum.

"Ugh!"

Finally she decided that if the guy were a cop, he deserved to make a good bust and opened the top locker and pulled down a stainless steel attaché case. After checking to make sure the clasps were still locked, she walked as calmly as she could back out of the depot.

Once safely locked inside the car, she sat behind the wheel for a few moments to let her heartbeat return to normal and then drove down Park Avenue—paying strict attention to the speed laws. At Audubon Park, she stopped in the shade of a huge oak tree to check the contents of the case. Inside she found a hundred plastic bags of loose diamonds and a package about the size of a brick wrapped in plain brown paper.

This must be the package Bryan had mentioned when he called, she thought. He'd also told her in no uncertain terms not to open it.

Kyna picked the package up and shook it.

"Hmmmm."

She stared at the package for all of ten seconds and then began tearing at the paper with her nails.

"Serves you right for disappearing, you prick."

Inside the paper was a box taped and tied with white string.

"Jesus!"

It cost two of her brand-new nails, but at last she lifted the lid and peeked inside.

"Oh wow!"

It was a necklace—sort of.

Kyna held the thing up to the light. It was the oddest piece of jewelry she had ever seen: a mishmash of seventeen semi-precious stones, rocks and crystals, spaced widely apart on a strip of what looked like rawhide, but felt rough and scaly like snakeskin. At one end was a hunk of black rock tied to a weird-looking head-shaped bead that had two red dots like eyes.

Kyna recognized a few of the stones: turquoise, which was her favorite, a clear quartz crystal, an opal, an amethyst and a lapis lazuli. One triangular piece appeared to be an arrowhead.

"Oh Bryan," she whispered, mentally taking back all the nasty things she had been thinking. He knew how much she liked Indian jewelry.

The necklace looked incredibly old and smelled slightly rancid, but she slipped it over her head and tucked it away under her blouse—it felt warm and strangely oily next to her skin.

Glancing at her watch, Kyna started the engine and pulled back onto Park Avenue. It was time to pick up her bodyguard and head to the airport. As she passed the entrance to the Brooks Museum of Art, she noticed a yellow bus unloading a group of schoolgirls in plaid skirts and white blouses.

All those shining faces, she thought. All those naive hopes and dreams. Kyna could almost hear Sister Mary Agnes's voice.

Your body is the temple of the Holy Spirit. If you don't respect it, who will?

"Not Bryan," Kyna muttered. "That's for damned sure."

Boys are only interested in one thing . . . and it's not your minds.

"Ditto."

All at once Kyna felt flushed. Beads of sweat rolled down her back and she could feel the hair lying like clammy fingers on her neck.

"What the devil's going on?"

Kyna turned the air conditioner up as far as it would go and unbuttoned her pin-striped jacket. When she glanced up into the rearview mirror, she suddenly screamed and slammed on the brakes, skidding the car sideways into the parking lot of a strip mall.

A woman driving a minivan full of snot-nosed kids honked and gave Kyna the finger, but Kyna ignored the woman and turned quickly to look behind her seat.

"Move it, lady!" a man yelled from the window of his station wagon.

Kyna pulled over into the corner of the lot, turned halfway around and looked behind the seat again. Either she had lost her mind or just a moment before she had seen a nun peering at her in the mirror. Black penguin suit, bib, the whole nine yards. It hadn't been anyone she'd recognized—a woman with ice-blue eyes and creamy skin, but she'd been right behind the seat, staring over Kyna's shoulder.

Kyna laughed and pawed through the console, hoping to find one of the cigarettes she'd given up.

"You got all that from a split-second glance in a mirror?" She chuckled.

But the nun's face was indelibly etched on her mind's eye and Kyna wondered if thirty was too young to be going through the change. Hands shaking, she upended her purse and came up with a badly crumpled cigarette with about five strands of stale tobacco left in it.

"Last one, I swear."

The cigarette didn't help. Kyna rolled the window down, leaned back and blew a cloud of smoke into the air. Her head was buzzing like she had a dozen angry bees trapped between her ears.

Nights growing up in New York had sounded like that. From her parents' twentieth-floor apartment in Queens, the sound of traffic on the BQE had sounded just like the buzzing of bees—angry bees. God, she could still see the place: tiny, the closet in the room she'd shared with her cousin had been barely big enough to hold two plaid school uniforms and a winter coat. The apartment always smelled of cabbage and cats and the stale, somehow milky odor of the old couple two floors down. In the summer the place was like an oven and you could smell the garbage and diesel fumes from the buses. In the winter it was a meat locker and she remembered hearing her father, when he was sober enough to notice, banging on the radiator with a wrench and screaming at the top of his lungs, "Send up the heat, you son of a bitch!"

Gary L. Holleman

Then, after high school, there had been the endless succession of dead-end jobs: the phone company, Macy's, assistant for a vet who spent more time trying to get his hand up her dress than to get pills down cats' throats. Later, she'd waited tables and tended bar, cleaning ashtrays and glasses and dreaming of seeing the world—any world, just as long as it wasn't New York.

It had taken her twenty-eight years to find Bryan Douglas, but the moment he'd walked into the bar she'd known he was her ticket out. Tall, good-looking, dressed like he'd just walked off the set of *Lifestyles of the Rich and Famous*. He had a soft, round face that looked like it needed a shave maybe once a week and dark brown hair with just the right touch of gray at the temples. His eyes were blue and at times cold, and his nails were meticulously kept and freshly manicured. It wasn't until much later that Kyna heard Bryan threaten to shoot a manicurist if he got so much as a hangnail.

But before that, she'd done it all: parties, yachts, drugs. Until the cruelty and banality of the creeps in Bryan's circle of sycophants began to feel like worms burrowing their way slowly into her brain. The first time she had shared these feelings with him was the first time he broke her arm.

The memory of that cast floated like a cloud in front of her eyes, rough and white with Bryan's friends' stringy signatures all over it like bird droppings.

He'd been sorry.

Glancing at the silver-and-turquoise bracelet on her wrist, Kyna remembered how sorry he'd been—and how sweet. She looked at the other bracelet and at the rings on her fingers. Her medals. She thought of them as her medals—like purple hearts. Besides, had it really been any worse than what her old man used to do? Certainly not bad enough to make her leave. Where would she go? Back to New York?

It was all mental masturbation anyway. Bryan wasn't about to let her leave—she knew too much. Customers, routes, amounts, dates, even the names of some of his contract burglars. More than enough to keep an army of prosecutors busy into the next millennium. No, she could never leave.

Why not?

Kyna's eyes popped open. "What?"

She looked over her shoulder again and then at her watch. "Shit fire!"

Throwing the car in gear, Kyna floored the accelerator and left a trail of rubber all the way down the street.

You fell asleep! You idiot!

But if that were true, why was she so frightened?

She worked through the gears, shot through a red light just ahead of a Cadillac's bumper and threw the car into a turn onto Ridgeway. She got caught by the traffic light at the intersection of Ridgeway and Winchester Road and sat drumming her fingers on the steering wheel and staring at a sign in the window of a gun shop across the street. *Cyrus likes guns,* she thought.

On a whim, she turned into the parking lot when the light turned green and went into the store.

Cyrus had to bounce up and down on the suitcase to close the zipper. He had never packed for such an extensive trip and, as a result, had packed nearly everything he owned.

The front door slammed. "Hello!"

Won't you come in, he thought. "Back here!"

Kyna waltzed into the bedroom and tossed a paper bag at him. Cyrus caught it but lost his seat on the suitcase.

"Love those catlike reflexes." She laughed.

His face flamed as he pulled a leather shoulder holster out of the bag. "What's this?"

"A present," she replied. "You don't have one, do you?"

The fact was, he did. But the gift was so unexpected, given the picture he had formed of her, that he lied. "No."

"Try it on. The guy at the gun shop said it's one of the quick-release types."

The contraption wasn't as simple as it looked. Cyrus slipped it around his shoulders, shrugged and twisted at the waist a couple of times and then took it off. After adjusting the straps by removing and replacing a couple of pins, he went into the closet and returned with a 9mm semiautomatic pistol. He shoved the gun in and out of the holster a few times, then fastened it in place with the retaining snap.

"I get the right thing?" Kyna asked.

"Yep."

"We'll pack it in the camera case and check it."

Cyrus's face settled into a thoughtful frown. "Won't it show up on the X-ray gizmo?"

Kyna went into the living room and returned a moment later with the metal attaché case and a fancy black metal camera case. "Stuff it in here next to the camera. I'll lock it and send it through with the bags. They hardly ever check domestic luggage."

"Why don't I just lay my permit on them?"

"It's a hassle. This way saves time. If anything happens you can always show it to them then."

"What's in the briefcase?" Cyrus asked. The metal case looked awfully heavy to him.

"About twelve million dollars. Come on. It's time to go."

At eight-fifty that evening a connecting Delta flight from Atlanta landed at Memphis International Airport. Among the last passengers to deplane were three black men wearing business suits that had been made on Oxford Street in London. The first man was short, muscular and bald. The second was taller, with short bushy hair, a wide flaring nose and a neat goatee. However, it was the last man who turned heads in the terminal. He was bald, with a hawklike face covered with tattoos and a body that was so tall and thin that he would have had to gain twenty pounds to be considered anorexic. Where his companions sported silk ties and heavy, gold Swiss and German watches, the Dark Man wore a band of colorful beads around his neck and a tarnished Timex old enough to be used in a TV testimonial on his right wrist. The trio went directly outside and walked up to the first taxicab they saw.

The goateed man leaned through the open passenger window and held out a piece of paper to the driver. "Do you know this address?"

The cabbie glanced at the note and nodded. "Sho, brother. Hop yo asses in."

The bald man tossed a battered leather suitcase into the trunk and ran around to hold the passenger door for the Dark Man. The goateed man climbed in the back next to his master and then the bald man took a seat in the front beside the driver.

The cab pulled away from the terminal and followed the signs to Interstate 240 East. As the driver casually maneuvered through the light evening traffic, the Dark Man's mind was racing. Time was running out and all he had gotten out of the man in Miami was a lot of talk about diamonds and the telephone number of some woman in Memphis. Now he had the address to go with the number, but he still silently cursed his son for a fool and wished that he dared perform the ceremony to cast the boy's soul into everlasting darkness. But he couldn't. Without the smokescreen of this vendetta to avenge the boy's murder, the Dark Man's companions might start asking the wrong questions—like why he was really searching for this woman. And that wouldn't do. The Dark Man glanced at his two companions. No, that wouldn't do at all.

Of its own volition, his hand strayed to his neck and his fingers played over the outline of the stones hidden underneath his shirt. They were fakes, as was the necklace, but good fakes. The same types of stones in the same order. The Dark Man had even made a sacrifice to the dark lords to instill the necklace with power. Of course, it was nowhere near as powerful as the original—a kitchen match to a raging forest fire. But it would fool the casual eye and that included his protégé with the goatee and his fat, bald-headed friend.

The Dark Man glanced through the window at the rain-slick streets. He saw the reflection of his own dark face and felt like smashing his fist through the glass. It was all so frustrating! With the Butcher's Broom in his possession, the workings of time and space had been as clear to him as his reflection. Now he was reduced to running around the globe like a blind

Gypsy! And as long as the damned thieves kept the necklace close, he would be unable get a clear fix on them. He was probably wasting his time chasing after this woman, but it was the only lead he had. He had to have something! Something of theirs to focus on . . .

During the Dark Man's reverie, the cabbie had been studying him in the rearview mirror. The driver took in the cut of his passengers' suits, the jewelry on the wrist of the bald man beside him, and remembered their strange accents. "Say, brothers, you interested in meeting some fine young ladies?"

When no one said anything, the driver tried a new tact. "How 'bout some primo grass, or a little blow?"

"What makes you think we would be interested in drugs?" the Dark Man asked. His tone of voice was neutral, but his eyes had taken on a spark of interest.

"Don't get yo panties in a twist. I just noticed you was from out of town. Just came off the flight from Miami, did you?"

The bald man glanced over the back of the seat at his leader. He saw the way the skin around the Dark Man's eyes and mouth had tightened and noted how his leader's eyes bore into the back of the driver's head.

The Dark Man replied, "Maybe you *could* be of service to us. Would you pull over for a moment?"

"Sho."

Several cars slammed on their brakes and blew their horns as the boxy yellow cab abruptly swerved to the side of the interstate. The cabbie saluted his fellow drivers with his middle finger and eased the gearshift into park and then turned to face the backseat.

"Now, I can make you a really fine deal on—"

The Dark Man had unbuttoned his shirt and was holding out a strange-looking necklace.

"What's that, bro, a badge? You ain't the man, are you?"

While the driver was frantically trying to recall his lawyer's telephone number, the Dark Man recited a string of alien phrases under his breath. In a moment, the cabbie heard a gurgling noise coming from the seat beside him and turned.

"Good God Almighty!"

The man dove for the .38 special he kept under the front seat, but before his fingers could close over the butt of the gun, a huge paw slammed into the back of his head, driving his nose hard into the steering wheel. The cartilage shattered with a sickening crack, and minute constellations of stars exploded inside his head.

In a way it was a blessing. For as his throat was being ripped out by the set of exceedingly long and sharp fangs, the cabbie was too stunned to feel a thing.

Cyrus sipped the complimentary rum and coke and rubbed the callus on the heel of his right hand back and forth across the armrest. Every so often, he cut his eyes over at Kyna sleeping curled up in the seat beside him. She was a strange bird, he thought. A shitty personality, but beautiful . . . and weird! Boy, even asleep, she kept her legs folded protectively around the briefcase under her seat. Twelve million bucks was twelve million bucks, but man, she should learn to lighten up. When they checked in at the airport, Kyna had showed the inspectors a letter stating that she was only a courier for the IDB and that she did not have the combination to the briefcase. She allowed the security people to X-ray the case to their heart's content, but insisted that she didn't have the combination. The way the airport security guards clustered around the tiny viewing screen, they must have had visions of major drug busts dancing in their heads. But after three passes through the machine—from three different angles—all that showed up were little packages of gemstones. Finally the guards had been satisfied and let Kyna and Cyrus go on their way. The odd thing was, Cyrus had seen Kyna open the case in his apartment. Not once, but half a dozen times.

What was she really up to? he mused.

They had been in the air for a little over an hour and a half and Cyrus hoped they would be starting their descent into Denver soon. Airline seats—even first-class, jumbo-jet seats—

were as comfortable as wooden church pews after a while.

Pity, he thought as he settled down in the seat and closed his eyes. *She really is a looker.*

Kyna cracked one eye and watched until Cyrus's breathing became regular. She knew he had been looking at her, studying her. Men were always looking. She had been mentally kicking herself for the last hour. What had she been thinking of? Twelve mill in hot rocks and a stranger dogging her every step? Bryan was going to go ballistic. What would she do if Cyrus got suspicious? She'd have to call Bryan—if she could find the prick—and ask him to take care of it.

Pity, she thought. *Russ has the personality of a rock, but he is kind of cute.*

The air in Kyna's bathroom was thick with the fetor of butchery and bayberry. The cabinets, the sink, even her tastefully framed *New Yorker* cover reprints hanging on the walls, were splattered with blood. The white tile floor was a mosaic of red hand- and footprints and melted wax from dozens of thick black candles. In the bathtub, the cabdriver's body floated half submerged in a pool of his own blood. The flesh of the man's throat and his chest had been torn out by some incredible force. The Dark Man was leaning over the sink washing his face and watching water the color and consistency of tomato soup corkscrew down the drain. His bald-headed assistant was using the shower in the other bathroom.

"I found these in that brush over there." The goateed man held out a knot of auburn hair.

The Dark Man nodded his approval. "Excellent! As soon as you finish harvesting the driver's organs and blood we will hold the ceremony."

"Is it really possible that this redheaded woman is responsible for Tomas's death?"

Probing, the Dark Man thought. *He is always probing.*

"Unlikely. But she can lead me to the one who is."

"Then we follow her?"

The Dark Man read the unspoken question in the goateed man's eyes.

"First, I will offer the cabdriver's soul to Baron Samedi and the Guédé. Then . . . I may send something else."

Chapter Three

October 15, 12:10 A.M.

Cyrus stood next to the luggage at the curb outside the baggage claim area of Stapleton International Airport. Twenty minutes later, just as he was about to pass out from the exhaust fumes, a silver Lincoln Town Car squealed to the curb and sounded the horn. Kyna sat behind the wheel while he loaded the bags into the trunk and then followed the Avis courtesy map to Golden and exited I-70 at the first motel sign she saw. As soon as she checked in, they drove around to the back and Cyrus climbed out and stretched. It was too dark to make out more than a vague outline of the mountains around Golden, but he could feel and taste their presence in the cool of the night air. After the oppressive humidity of Memphis, it was like walking into an air-conditioned theater.

Kyna opened the trunk and then started for their room. "Well? You coming?"

Cyrus looked at the pile of suitcases and mumbled, "Yow'ser mass'er."

Kyna had booked only one room—for security reasons, she claimed—but it had two queen-sized beds, a hanging chain lamp over a round table and a TV set bolted to a built-in dresser. Above the beds were two faux oil paintings of mountains—what else? And a gold shag carpet with dark wear marks running from the door to the bathroom.

Kyna dumped the camera case on the chair beside the table, slid the attaché case under the bed closest to the bathroom and then set about preparing for bed. She slipped off her suit jacket, pulled the tail of her blouse outside her skirt and ran her fingers through her hair. Cyrus felt like an invisible man in a Fellini film.

"You don't smoke, do you?" she asked.

Ah! She speaks. "Nope."

Kyna sighed and began unbuttoning her blouse. "Neither do I."

She picked up her overnight case, walked into the bathroom and closed the door; a moment later Cyrus heard the lock turn.

"No, that's okay," he muttered. "You go ahead."

With nothing better to do, Cyrus got the gun and holster from the camera case and a box of cartridges from his suitcase and began feeding bullets into the clip. After checking the slide, he slapped the clip home, replaced the gun in the holster and draped it over the back of the chair next to his bed.

"Now what?" he muttered.

Removing his shirt, Cyrus dropped down between the beds and did a fast twenty push-ups. He didn't know Kyna was out of the bathroom until he heard the TV come on.

She was standing in the door in a knee-length T-shirt that proclaimed, "Life's a Bitch and then you Marry One" and punching the buttons on the remote. The bathroom light was behind her, drawing the outline of her body against the cotton.

"Uh . . ." he started to say.

"Shhhh!"

On the TV, a disembodied voice was explaining a series of grisly video images.

"This is the scene at the Key Biscayne home of reputed gangland figure Pablo Morales. The bodies of Morales, his wife and seven-year-old daughter were found by friends this afternoon."

In the background, men in blue windbreakers with an alphabet soup of initials across the backs were running around like ants: taking samples, directing forensic photographers and generally just being in charge. The news cameras swarmed the front of the house as two morgue attendants carried a small black vinyl bag out of the front door. Right behind the first pair, two more attendants wheeled a stretcher with a much larger body bag.

"Reports from inside the house indicate that the Moraleses were tortured before being killed, leading local authorities to fear the resumption of the perennial gang wars."

Cyrus was only half paying attention to the TV. He was trying to figure out if Kyna knew what the light was doing and if it was some kind of come-on.

Back on the TV, a third set of attendants wheeled a grossly misshapen body bag past the inexorable live eye of the television camera. Cyrus thought the bag looked like it had been stuffed full of modeling clay.

"Makes me glad I live in Memphis," he said. "Nothing like that ever happens there."

"Shush!"

"This was filmed just minutes ago from inside the house," the reporter said.

The camera zoomed in on a section of linoleum floor with a white, chalky looking curlicue drawn in some kind of grainy powder. The lens brushed over a bloody sheet and then cut to an interior wall and the most chilling example of demonic art Cyrus had seen outside a New York City subway station.

Crescents, stars, what looked like the portrait of a grinning chicken and alien words—like EKG graffiti—scribbled in globs of what appeared to be thick maroon paint.

"I'm surprised that the cops would let—" Cyrus started to say.

Kyna was so pale that her freckles stood out like red polka dots on a white bow tie. Cyrus jumped to his feet, took the remote from her and switched off the TV set.

"What's the matter?"

She looked at him like she'd never seen him before. "Nothing. I detest violence."

She walked slowly to the door and slipped the chain on and then climbed into bed. " 'Night."

" 'Night."

Cyrus went into the bathroom, closed the door and took a

long hot shower. When he came out the room was dark. He felt his way over to his bed, then stripped down to his briefs and climbed under the covers.

"You're good at what you do, right?" Kyna's voice sounded very small.

Good at tossing drunks, he thought. *Good at tracing skips. Damned good shot at anything under fifty yards.*

"Yeah. You can count on me."

Kyna lay awake for a long time, trembling like a frightened doe each time some car's headlights swept over the ceiling tiles. It had finally happened—Bryan had hung her out to dry. It was the only thing that made any sense. First he vanished and now Morales had been murdered. The bastard had hung her out to dry. So much for love! Fuck love! she fumed, so much for loyalty. She glanced over at Cyrus's sleeping form and whispered, "Count on me. That'll be the day."

October 16

Kyna navigated the Lincoln through the construction maze outside Salt Lake City with judicious applications of anti-lock brakes and invectives. Cyrus had been in the midst of a dream about lacy black garter belts until he suddenly found himself testing the limits of the car's shoulder restraint system. He leaned forward and patted the head of the plastic Jesus that some farsighted Avis employee had thoughtfully left on the dashboard.

"Sorry," Kyna said. "That fucking flagman back there is as blind as a syphilitic bat."

Her tone made it clear that she was anything but sorry and Cyrus wondered what was wrong with her. Her eyes were red and swollen and all morning she had been as pleasant as a grizzly bear trying to pass a kidney stone. He rubbed the sleep from his eyes and noticed they were weaving in and out of a corridor of orange construction barrels, their safety lanterns blinking like tiny runway lights. Kyna had evidently turned off onto I-15 sometime during his nap and she asked him to keep watch for the exit to their motel. A few minutes later she said, "I've got a delivery tonight."

"Okay."

"Downtown. At one of the malls across from the Mormon Temple. You ever seen it?"

"The Temple? Nope."

"It's pretty impressive."

"You trying to get rid of me already?" Cyrus chuckled.

"I'll be right across the street. I just thought it would be more fun than listening to some old geezer bitching about the quality of my stones."

He wondered why all of a sudden she was being so nice. "You won't need me?"

"I don't think so. I've done business with this guy before. He's okay."

"All right. Hanging out with the Mormons might be fun."

They found their exit, checked into the motel and showered. At five o'clock they dined on rare roast beef and homemade bread at a place in the downtown area that had once belonged to Brigham Young, a man famous to the non-Mormon world for being San Francisco Forty-Niners quarterback Steve Young's great-great-great grand-something. After the meal, they stood in front of the high-rise building that housed one of the major downtown shopping malls. Across the street, giant spotlights highlighted the high gothic spires of the Salt Lake City Temple of the Church of Jesus Christ of Latter Day Saints; the Mormons to everyone else. The structure would have been impressive anywhere, but situated as it was in the middle of Temple Square with its sister buildings, which included the world-famous Mormon Tabernacle, it was truly awe inspiring.

Cyrus watched until Kyna disappeared into the mall, the briefcase still clutched firmly in her right hand, and then he crossed the street. It was a bit after six P.M., yet scores of people were still milling about inside the walled square. He noted the crowd was predominantly white and well dressed. The women seemed to favor long flower-print dresses, while the men preferred business suits or slacks and plaid shirts from Lands' End or L.L. Bean.

"Welcome to yuppie heaven," he muttered.

Feeling distinctly underdressed in his jeans and polo shirt, and intimidated by all the fresh-scrubbed faces, he abruptly changed course and recrossed the street.

The mall was packed. Men and women and kids—lots of kids. All loaded down with shopping bags and stuffed Barneys. All smiling; all clean; without a doubt, all Republican. Cyrus felt like the grubby Alice who had just fallen through the mirror into Limbaughland. He cast his eyes down and wondered why he felt so bitter. After a moment he looked up and suddenly realized he didn't have a clue where Kyna's appointment was supposed to be. He went to the mall directory to check the listing of jewelry stores.

The mall had four levels and two jewelry stores, one on the fourth floor and one on the third. According to the "You Are Here" arrow, he was on the second floor and he noticed that there was a food court in the basement and that they had a cookie store.

That settled it.

He took the escalator to the bottom level and followed his nose to the red-and-white-striped shrine of Debbie Fields. He bought three hockey-puck-sized chocolate chip cookies and a medium diet drink and carried them around the white brick wall that separated the dining area from the food vendors. He looked for an empty table and saw Kyna sitting across from a handsome man with swarthy skin and a long ponytail. They were sitting with their heads close together the way people do when trying to keep from being overheard, and Cyrus felt a totally unexpected pang of jealousy.

Some old geezer.

When Kyna saw Cyrus, she appeared momentarily disconcerted, but quickly smiled and waved him over.

"Russ, this is Georges."

The man stood and Cyrus shook his hand.

"Join us, señor," Georges said.

43

Gary L. Holleman

Cyrus pulled a chair over from a neighboring table and quietly munched one of his cookies while Kyna wrapped up her business. As he chewed, he gave Georges the once-over.

The man was a sharp dresser: pleated silk slacks, a hand-woven silk blazer and a conservative blue-and-red club tie. Georges was polite enough and smiled a lot—and he made Cyrus feel like a slob. Before Cyrus knew it, Kyna and Georges stood and shook hands. Cyrus stood too, nodding and smiling and eyeing the diamond earring in Georges's left ear.

I should have studied gems instead of guns.

After Georges had disappeared up the escalator, Kyna and Cyrus reclaimed their seats. Kyna picked up her coffee cup and Cyrus offered her the last cookie.

"Thanks." She broke off half of the cookie and popped it into her mouth.

They finished their drinks and strolled around the mall for a few minutes, stopping at the bookstore and wandering through a huge department store.

"I have to meet someone here tomorrow evening," Kyna said on the way to the car.

"Georges?" It popped out before Cyrus could stop himself.

Kyna kept walking, but peered closely at his face. "You're not jealous, are you?"

"Don't be ridiculous," Cyrus sputtered. "I was just concerned. The guy looks shifty to me. He could be hiding anything in that ponytail of his."

Kyna stopped walking and started laughing. "Georges is gay."

"Oh. Right. I knew that."

"How?"

"A good bodyguard picks up on things."

"Personal security specialist."

"Yeah, right."

Her teasing tone made him squirm until she relented and started walking again. "Since we're going to have to hang around town another day, I wondered if you wanted to do something tomorrow morning?"

44

Cyrus thought for a minute. "I don't know. What is there to do?"

"Well, there's a national park not far from here. I hear it's full of old dinosaur bones. I'd kind of like to see it, if you don't mind."

"Sounds safe enough."

They were nearing the exit.

"Stick close," Kyna said.

Cyrus noticed for the first time that she was carrying a large paper tote bag in the hand opposite the briefcase.

"Always," he replied.

"What did you think about the Temple?" Kyna asked as they stepped out onto the sidewalk. The wind had picked up and a quarter moon hung like a half-closed eye above the juniper trees to the east. Fall was in the air, crisp with a foretaste of snow.

"Nice architecture."

"You came back awfully fast."

"I don't like crowds."

As they walked back to the car, Kyna turned the collar of her jacket up. The chill wind seemed to have sent everyone scurrying for home and hearth and their footsteps echoed like blows from a rock climber's hammer down the canyon of man-made mountains.

"What *do* you like?" she asked.

"Oh, working with my hands—building things. Target shooting. Karate."

Kyna adjusted the back of her collar. The necklace seemed to be rubbing her the wrong way. "How did you get into that stuff?"

He was quiet so long that she finally said, "So don't tell me."

"No, it's just . . ." Cyrus took a deep breath. He never confided anything personal to any of his clients—until now. "My mom and dad were killed by muggers."

"And?"

"After it happened I went kind of crazy for a couple of

45

years. That's when I took up target shooting and karate. I went to see *Death Wish* twenty-seven times. After a while karate seemed too tame, so I went into jujitsu, the full-contact stuff. I had grand ideas of becoming the next Chuck Norris. But then I got my bell rung in a tournament. Shortly after that, I started taking classes at U of M and now I take out my frustrations in the gym or on the shooting range.''

I sure can pick 'em! Kyna thought. *Charles Bronson or Chuck Norris—oh boy! He's sure no Bryan . . .*

Then again, Cyrus was there and Bryan . . . Who the hell knew where Bryan was? Kyna cut her eyes to Cyrus's boyish face, watching the way his eyes moved, always alert, his fingers always moving like they were tingling from lack of circulation. He wasn't really *bad*-looking—if you liked the type. He was just so . . . rough.

When they reached the Lincoln, Cyrus stood on the sidewalk, looking both ways while Kyna put the case and the bag of cash in the trunk. And since she was tired of thinking about Bryan and damned tired of the necklace rubbing her neck, she took it off and tossed it into the trunk too.

''Good riddance!''

''Wait!'' the Dark Man snapped. ''I see her.''

He had been pacing the floor in his hotel suite, rubbing the strands of auburn hair between his fingers and silently cursing the inadequacy of his new amulet.

The goateed man and his bald companion quickly sat up in their chairs.

''Where?'' the goateed man asked.

''Ah! Damnation!'' the Dark Man hissed.

The goateed man glanced at his bald friend but knew better than to comment.

''She's gone.''

''I . . . I don't understand,'' the goateed man said. ''How could she just—''

The Dark man unleashed his icy glare on his apprentice. *''You dare—''*

Throwing his hands up to protect his face, the goateed man fell to his knees. "Forgive me, master."

The Dark Man's fingernails dug into his palms until blood flowed, but the pain helped him get himself under control. He reminded himself that he needed the goateed man. At least for now.

"She is far away, but distance will not save her for long. Come," he said to the bald man, "we must prepare you for the spirit ceremony."

October 17

When Cyrus returned from his morning run Kyna was already up and dressed and waiting at the door with a steaming cup of coffee in her hand.

"Listen, I got a call from my customer. The meeting has been moved up. Have some breakfast, take a shower and I'll meet you back here in about two hours."

"You think it's a good idea to go alone?"

She glanced at her watch and replied, "Just this once. It's an unscheduled stop so it shouldn't be a problem."

Cyrus nodded and went to the shower.

Kyna sat behind the wheel and waited for the engine to warm up. She felt bad about lying to Cyrus—the meeting had always been scheduled for that morning, but she couldn't let him go with her. The guy she was supposed to meet was so geeky he might just as well have "fence" written in neon letters across his forehead. He really wasn't so bad—Cyrus, not the geek. It was just that she was so down on men. They were all a bunch of macho assholes who believe a woman's life is run by a combination of her biological clock and PMS. Thinking about men started her thinking about Bryan. Kyna threw the Lincoln into gear and floored the accelerator. As the car leapt backward, she caught a glimpse of something big and shaggy in the side mirror and slammed on the brakes.

"Shit!"

Figuring she had just turned somebody's pet collie into

Gary L. Holleman

roadkill, she shoved the gearshift back into park then climbed
out and walked around the car. On the back bumper was some
blood and a few wiry gray hairs, but the parking lot was deserted.

"This is too cute," Cyrus remarked. "Every street is named
after a different dinosaur."

"I think you missed the turn." Kyna flipped back a few
pages in the auto club map booklet.

"Yeah, I think you're right."

Cyrus stopped at a service station to ask directions to the
national park, which, as it turned out, straddled the Colorado-
Utah border. And then he turned around and took US-40 back
into Utah and found the turnoff just outside Vernal. After driving for another half hour they reached the park.

"Okay," Kyna exclaimed as she climbed out of the car,
"let's act like tourists."

They strolled through the building that the National Parks
Service had erected over a partially excavated fossil site and
Kyna took photographs of a bunch of dusty dinosaur bones
still half submerged in the side of a red dirt hill. One or two
of the fossils looked big enough to have been King Kong's
femurs. Kyna took a close-up of a set of fossilized footprints
from a two-legged lizard that had been compost long before
Homo erectus ever got his first campfire going. In all, the tour
took about an hour.

"What now?" Cyrus asked.

Kyna examined the Park Service map they had picked up
in the building. "There's a nature trail about five miles down
the road. According to the map, there are some Indian ruins
and petroglyphs."

Cyrus had often admired the turquoise and silver on her
wrists and asked, "You're really into Indian stuff, aren't
you?"

The look she gave him could freeze air. "So?"

"Jesus! Lighten up, will you? You don't have to be a bitch
every day."

48

Kyna stopped in the middle of the parking lot and stared at her feet. After a few seconds she looked up and said, "Look, I'm sorry. I've been under a lot of pressure."

"I figured something was eating you. You want to talk about it?" He gave her a lopsided grin. "Bodyguards are almost as good as bartenders at listening to people's problems."

She stared at him long enough that he thought she might actually open up. But then Kyna shook her head and smiled. "It's nothing. Just work."

Boy, Cyrus thought, *she's got more walls than Fort Knox.*

"Are we dressed for this nature trail?" he asked.

"Sure." She looked down at her candy-striped shorts and sneakers—then at his high-top street boots and cutoffs. "Jeans and those boot thingies are fine. It's not like we're climbing the Matterhorn, or anything."

Five miles down the highway, they turned off onto a gravel road that took them to an unpaved parking lot. They pulled up in the shade of a cottonwood tree, in the center of an arid depression between low hills of red, tightly packed dirt and plates of shale rock. Kyna jumped out and ran to the sign that marked the trailhead while Cyrus was still fumbling with his boot laces.

"I don't think we're going to have time to do this," he said when he caught up to her. "It's almost six."

Kyna finished reading the sign and examined her watch. "Come on, please! I want to see the petroglyphs. The trail is only a little over two miles. We should be able to do that in less than an hour."

Cyrus took a long look at the sun resting two fingers above the hills to the west. Then he glanced at the parking lot. Other than the Lincoln, there was only a battered red pickup truck. "Okay, but I'm not lugging this cannon."

He went back to the car and locked the pistol and his jacket in the trunk.

"Ready?" Kyna asked.

"I guess so."

He trailed Kyna down a dusty creek bed between hills dotted with wind-sculpted mesquite and sagebrush. Every step, clusters of dry rabbitbrush scraped their legs.

"This is really beautiful," Kyna said.

Cyrus was watching the fluid way she moved, the way her calves tightened as she took a step and at how her shorts tightened across her behind. "Yeah. It's not bad."

"You should get out more. See the wonders of nature."

Cyrus was beginning to feel like a pervert so he tore his eyes away from Kyna and looked around. She was right—it was beautiful. And quiet. The muted colors soothed the eye and even the wind seemed to work to their advantage, blowing at their backs and keeping the bugs away.

They went over and around withered brush—a harsh testimony to the scarcity of rainfall—and finally down into a small valley. The footing was tricky and they had to concentrate to keep from turning their ankles on the loose stones. About twenty minutes into the hike Kyna suddenly stopped and whispered, "Shush! Look."

On the far ridge, a female mule deer was grazing on the smelly leaves of a rabbitbrush plant.

"Wow," Cyrus whispered. "And it doesn't even have a collar."

All at once, the deer's head popped up and it stood so still that the hill behind it looked like *it* was moving.

"You think she heard us?" Kyna whispered.

The deer spun around and, with her black-tipped tail tucked tightly against her behind, bounded over the ridge and out of sight.

"What do you suppose spooked her?" Cyrus asked.

At that instant, the sun slipped below the hills to the west and the sky quickly went from daffodil to iris. With the sun's departure, the evening breeze turned mean and ran like wildfire through the dry wash.

"Maybe we better head back," Cyrus suggested. "I hear it gets cold awfully fast in these hills after dark."

Kyna sighed, but then nodded and they began to retrace their steps up the path, their feet kicking up tiny nuclear clouds of dust as they stomped over their old footprints.

They had gone almost three-quarters of the way back to the parking lot when Cyrus caught a glimpse of mottled-gray fur as it passed between two boulders on the other side of the creek bed. He paused, hoping to see another deer or maybe a gray fox. Instead, the head of a large gray wolf appeared around the rock.

When the wolf saw Cyrus staring at it, it bared a set of yellowed fangs and crept out from behind the rock—moving slowly and deliberately toward Cyrus and Kyna with its head slung low between bony shoulders.

"Holy shit!" Cyrus mumbled.

Kyna had not seen the wolf, but she stopped and turned around when she noticed that Cyrus had stopped.

"Is that a wolf?" Her smile was as excited as a schoolgirl's.

"Yes," Cyrus whispered. "Now shut up and don't move."

The smile vanished. "What's the matter?"

Maybe it was the tricky light or maybe just his imagination, but the animal was limping and looked like it had white flecks of foam around its muzzle. Cyrus did a slow, crablike shuffle over to Kyna and whispered, "Don't freak out, but that wolf may be rabid."

Her mouth flew open.

"No!" he hissed. "Don't say anything—don't do anything! Just listen! We are going to walk very slowly toward the parking lot. You are not going to run unless I tell you to run. And if I tell you to run, then run like your ass is on fire. Got it?"

Kyna gulped, but her head went up and down.

"Okay. Now, I'm going to keep an eye on our friend and you're going to pick your feet up and try not to disturb anything. Go real slow and keep listening to me. Ready?"

She nodded again.

"Go."

Kyna moved like she was trudging across the surface of the moon, picking up one foot at a time and bringing it down in slow motion.

Cyrus allowed himself a grim smile. "We may have to go

51

a little faster than that or brer wolf is going to die of old age before we make it back to the car."

The path was going to take them through a thick stand of sagebrush. Cyrus didn't like the idea of walking blind so he tapped Kyna on the shoulder and motioned her back down into the creek bed. As he stared down behind her, he noticed a gnarled tree branch sticking up out of the soft dirt. The branch was about five feet long and a quarter inch in diameter and looked like it had been used by some other hiker as a walking stick. The branch's size and shape reminded him of the broom handle that he used to push when he worked for the neighborhood butcher, and for some odd reason one of his mother's favorite Bible passages flitted through his head—
"thy rod and thy staff they comfort me."

Cyrus grabbed the stick and used it to steady himself as he climbed down the crumbling embankment. A few minutes later they rounded the bend and lost sight of the wolf.

"Let's pick it up," Cyrus whispered.

"I don't see it anymore."

"That doesn't mean he can't see us."

Every couple of feet Cyrus took a peek back over his shoulder. He was no Marlin Perkins, but rabid or not, he didn't think the wolf was acting right. When they reached the mouth of the wash, Cyrus glanced back once more. As he did, his ankle turned on a stone that had been polished smooth by aeons of snow wash and he fell, dropping the walking stick as he threw out his hands to catch himself.

Kyna turned around and gave him a look.

"You just going to lie there all day?" she asked with a grin.

Cyrus rolled his eyes to Heaven, pushed himself up on his knees and dusted his hands off on his cutoffs.

"Look out!"

The wolf seemed to come out of nowhere. It slammed into Cyrus's back and knocked him flat down on his face again. When Cyrus rolled over, the wolf was standing over him, a huge paw on either side of his head. At first, the animal only stared—its fat red tongue sliding in and out over teeth that looked from Cyrus's point of view like railroad spikes. Its eyes were pale yellow and flecked with particles of the purest gold—yet at the same time their scrutiny was somehow dispassionate and strangely human.

Without moving anything but his lips, Cyrus said, "Kyna, go get help."

The wolf growled and lowered its fangs to Cyrus's throat. The creature's breath was hot and smelled as sour as stale wine. Saliva from its tongue dripped into Cyrus's face and ran down his cheek.

"Kyna!" Cyrus said with more emphasis.

The wolf flicked its eyes up to locate Kyna. She was moving away—not exactly running, but not strolling along whistling with her hands in her pockets either. The creature returned its gaze to Cyrus and curled its lips back in what Cyrus could almost swear was a grin. Just as he turned his head to escape the animal's foul breath, Kyna broke into a run. Distracted, the wolf gave Cyrus a hasty nip on the side of the neck and then took off after her at a gallop, heavily favoring its right front leg as it ran.

The pain of the wolf's bite spread like caustic acid through Cyrus's neck and shoulder. He slapped one hand over the wound and reached out with the other hand for some kind of weapon. As luck would have it, the other hand landed on the walking stick.

"Oh God!" Kyna screamed.

Spurred by her cry, Cyrus gritted his teeth and crawled to his feet. The fall had snapped the last ten inches off the end of the stick, but he didn't have time to look for anything better. The wolf had Kyna backed up against a tree and was down on its belly creeping slowly, almost playfully toward her. Five feet from Kyna, the creature stopped and crouched, growling and wagging its mangy tail.

Cyrus gripped the makeshift spear tightly with both hands, raised it above his head, then took two lightning-quick strides and drove the point down between the wolf's shoulder blades.

The animal screeched like a child in agony and sprang straight up into the air, twisting and snapping slavering jaws at the shaft embedded in its back. It landed hard, but got right up again and began hobbling toward Kyna. Less than three feet from her, the wolf convulsed once, like it was trying to cough up a lung, and fell over on its side.

Cyrus was too stunned to do anything but stare as the wolf vomited its lifeblood out in a crimson pool on the ground. In moments the animal's labored breathing became erratic and its eyes began to film over. It raised its head, looked up into Cyrus's face, bared its fangs and then died.

Kyna ran up to Cyrus and gently fingered the wound in his neck.

"Did you see that?" he said.

"Come on. Lets get you to a doctor."

"That was the darnedest thing I ever saw."

"You don't look so good," Kyna said. "Let's get going before you go into shock."

They reached the trailhead in time to see a man in an olive-green ranger's uniform insert a key into the door of the red pickup truck.

Kyna screamed, *"Help us!"* but they were too far away.

Cyrus was starting to believe Kyna was right—he *was* going into shock. His head felt like it was lighter than air and the pain in his neck was subsiding; even the ankle he'd twisted when he fell was feeling better. He collapsed against the side of a dusty boulder and said, "I think I'll just take a little rest. Go get him."

Kyna ran across the road waving her arms over her head like she was trying to flag down a train. The ranger saw her and pulled his green Mountie hat out of the truck, then ran to meet her. Cyrus could see Kyna's hands flying around and pointing at him. Finally the man nodded and they came back to Cyrus at a trot.

"The lady says you were attacked by a wolf," the ranger said. He gently pulled the bloody collar away from Cyrus's neck. The ranger was a big man, with a big ruddy face, but he had a surprisingly gentle touch.

"A big bad wolf." Cyrus giggled. "With shaggy gray fur and gigantic teeth."

Kyna looked at Cyrus oddly.

"Lot of blood," the ranger observed. "But not much of a wound. Really just a few scratches, and they look about three weeks old."

Kyna pushed the man out of the way and ran her fingers over Cyrus's neck. "This is weird. Just a minute ago he was bleeding like crazy. Look at his shirt! All that blood didn't come from those tiny scratches."

The ranger shrugged. "Beats me. Maybe it came from the wolf. Where is it?"

The trio followed the trail of footprints back around the bend, but when they cleared the turn, Kyna stopped. "Where did it go?"

"I don't see anything." The ranger gave Cyrus a sideways glance. "This isn't some kind of prank, is it? It's been a long day and I'm in no mood for any tomfoolery."

"I swear," Kyna said. "The body was right here . . . somewhere."

The ranger removed his hat and ran a handkerchief over his forehead and up through his thinning salt-and-pepper hair. "I've gotta tell you, we haven't seen a gray wolf in these parts for a number of years. Coyote. A fox or three, sure. But wolves? Unlikely."

"Here!" Kyna called. "Over here."

She pointed to a drying pool of brownish blood with the remains of Cyrus's walking stick lying next to it.

"What do you call that?" she asked triumphantly. "Tomato soup?"

The ranger mopped his head again. "Well, I'll put out a call. A wounded animal's dangerous. You two better run over to the hospital in Vernal and have those scratches looked at. Mister, if we can't find the carcass, you may have to take the rabies shots."

Cyrus touched his neck. He could barely find a scab. He

was so relieved that he wasn't about to die that he was positively giddy.

"Let me have a look," Kyna said.

She pulled the collar away and ran her fingers over the skin. Then she turned his head and checked the other side. "That hurt?"

"Nope."

"This is freaky. It isn't even red anymore."

The ranger took a look. "Darnedest thing I ever saw."

"Well," Cyrus remarked dryly. "I sure as heck didn't bite myself."

The Dark Man sat cross-legged on the floor of his hotel room, staring at a squat wax effigy. He suddenly blinked several times, scowled and cut his eyes to the bald man stretched out unconscious on a blanket next to the statue. The bald man was lying facedown, nude, and was bleeding heavily from a jagged quarter-inch hole in his back.

The thin man with the goatee looked over the Dark Man's shoulder as the witch doctor used his magic to close the wound. In a moment, the bald man groaned, flexed his fingers and rolled over onto his side.

"What happened?" the Dark Man demanded.

The bald man dropped his eyes. "There was a man with her. He attacked me from behind."

"This man, what did he look like?"

"Short, muscular, brown hair."

"And how did this happen?"

"I . . . I don't know." The bald man winced as he massaged his shoulder. "He was very fast, but I knocked him to the ground. I hit him hard enough to knock him unconscious."

"Why did you not just kill him?"

"I would have, but the woman was getting away and there was another man nearby; I could smell him. I planned to finish the short man when I was through with the woman."

"Finish him?" The Dark Man's face contorted in alarm. "You did not bite him?"

The bald man hesitated just long enough to send the Dark Man's blood pressure soaring and then shook his head. "No. I just knocked him down and then went after the woman."

The Dark Man peered into the bald man's eyes. "You are sure you did not bite the man?"

The bald man averted his eyes. "I couldn't have. It happened too fast. I couldn't have."

"And what happened to your shoulder?"

The bald man stopped flexing the arm and looked shamefaced. "I tried to take her outside her motel, but she hit me with the car."

Throwing up his hands, the Dark Man went to the window and peered out. "You attacked her in broad daylight, on a busy street?"

"The street was not so busy."

The Dark Man shook his head and allowed the man with the goatee to drape the cape of brilliant-colored feathers over his shoulders. Then he said to the bald man, "Get up!"

The man moved to his knees and rolled his neck around on his shoulders as he tested the stiffness of the healing wound. Then he stood up and faced his master.

"You were wilding," the Dark Man snapped. "You let the animal take control."

The bald man hung his head in reply.

The Dark Man's bony hand moved with the speed of an adder, striking the bald-headed man in the solar plexus with the flat of his palm and dropping the man back to his knees.

"I could just as easily have killed you with that blow. You disobey me again and you will wish I had. You understand what I am saying? If you will not serve me in one capacity, you *will* serve me in another."

The bald man fell at his master's feet and wept like a lost child.

Paula had just sat down at the dining table when her eyes suddenly rolled back in her head and her body went completely limp. After a few seconds, her head began to move slowly back and forth and her lips peeled back from her teeth in a grimace of almost unendurable horror.

"The teeth!"

Her cry was like the wail of a lost soul, then suddenly her eyes flew open and she leapt from the chair.

"The fiend! He has loosed the loup-garou!"

Chapter Four

October 18

The penthouse sat atop a thirty-story high-rise on High Holburn in London, between Oxford Street and the British Library. The dwelling was divided into two parts. The public part was pure London: all dark paneling and antiques, glass displays of raw, uncut diamonds and framed originals by Chagall and Picasso. In the exact center of the structure, behind a maze of sliding wall panels, was the private part: floor-to-ceiling bookcases containing the works of Albertus Magnus and Aleister Crowley, bulbous lamps with human-skin shades from Auschwitz and Bergen-Belsen, mummified skeletons wrapped in rotting cotton shrouds from Peru and the Yucatán, ceremonial masks and voodoo dolls from Benin (formerly Dahomey) on the Dark Continent.

In the middle of the secret room was a huge table and in the middle of the table was a soot-streaked cauldron. To the left of the cauldron was a black candle, to the right, a red candle, and to the rear, a white candle. Around the outside of the pot was a circle of dried elder blossoms, marjoram, rue and mint. Inside the cauldron were equal portions of oil of cloves, frankincense, lavender, jasmine and the blood from a newborn foal. Beside the table, Bryan Douglas stood flipping through the pages of an ancient copy of the *Grimoire of Honorius*—a book reputed to contain coded instructions on how to contact the most malevolent inhabitants of the supernatural world. Bryan was of average height and above-average looks with watery blue eyes and a baby face that at the moment was the color of a beet. He slammed his fist down on the table like a child in the midst of a colossal tantrum.

"Goddamn it, Conrad, it's not supposed to be this hard!"

Conrad, Bryan's chauffeur/bodyguard, was as big and intelligent as a commercial refrigerator. He had a high forehead, thin dishwater-blond hair and tiny brown eyes that were always either bored or confused. He always dressed in black. Always.

During his ten years with Bryan, Conrad had seen it all—the orgies, the séances, the black sabbats where Bryan and his pack of weekend sociopaths from London's beau monde turned stray cats and kidnapped French poodles into sashimi. It wasn't the first time Conrad had seen his employer in a snit when one of his cockamamy spells went haywire and Conrad wasn't impressed.

"Oh! Here it is."

Bryan placed his hands, palms down, over the cauldron. He bent down over the yellowed pages and read, "Power of the rising moon, conceal me both midnight and noon."

Bryan turned to face the south.

"Power of the blazing sun, protect me from the evil one."

He turned to face the west.

"Power of the dark of night, be my shield, my armor tight."

Finally Bryan turned and faced north, bowed and recited, "Full moon in the blackest sky, protect me from the evil eye. Foul spirits rebound from my cloak of dark, I fear not your dagger, nor your foul heart. My powers prevail, I am set free. Begone! You have no power over me."

Bryan reread the passage to make sure he had said it correctly, then looked up at Conrad and beamed. "There! That should hold it until tomorrow night."

"That's great, boss. Hold what?"

The frown that split Bryan's face made him look slightly demented. "Hello! Don't you pay attention to anything I tell you?"

Conrad rolled his eyes. "Sure."

"The Butcher's Broom! Remember?"

"The necklace, right?"

"The talisman!"

"Yeah, right. The talisman."

"The talisman that belonged to Macumba, the Butcher of Cotonou?" Bryan held out his hands, palms up. "The talisman he brought to Haiti in 1789 and used to create an occult empire? The talisman that acts as a magnifying glass, enhancing a thousandfold the psychic power of the wearer?"

"Oh . . . *that* Butcher's Broom."

"The one that spick stole for me?" Conrad nodded. "You remember me telling you about that Hungan on Roatan?"

"That's the witch doctor?" Conrad asked, just to piss his boss off.

Bryan sighed hard enough to blow out a forest fire. "Correct."

"The guy that everybody in your club is about to pee their pants over?"

"Coven, goddamn it, Conrad. It's a coven!"

"Sorry."

"With that talisman the man is one of the most powerful sorcerers on the planet. Without it, he is vulnerable. As long as I keep the psychic shield I just constructed in place, he won't even know I exist."

"That's good. So you got nothing to worry about."

Bryan glanced at the cauldron. "Well . . . except Morales went a little overboard."

"Which means?"

"He killed the man's son."

"Oops."

"I didn't tell him to," Bryan added quickly. "I paid the spick a damned fortune. He should have been able to buy the kid off. . . ."

"Shit happens."

"Succinctly put."

"So that's why you're so spooked."

"Spooked?" Bryan's face went red again. "I'm not

61

spooked. Just cautious. It seems Mr. Morales and his family have had a little accident. . . ."

"Ah! But what I don't get is why Kyna has the necklace. Why haven't we picked it up already?"

Bryan grinned. "That's the genius of my plan. This witch doctor is supposed to be some kind of superpsychic bad ass . . ."

Conrad loved it when Bryan tried to talk funky. With his British accent he sounded like Richard Burton doing Sly Stone.

"What if he has a way of keeping tabs on the necklace?" Bryan's grin slipped. "What if it gives off emanations?"

"Then I guess you'd be in big trouble."

"*We* would be in big trouble. That's why I had Morales pass it to Kyna; that's why I sent her off on this trip . . ."

"Yeah?"

"If anything happens to her, we'll know this witch doctor character can track the thing. If not, I can safely pick it up and use it to control the powers of the universe."

Conrad shook his head and grinned. "Gotta hand it to you, boss. You're one sneaky son of a bitch. But I thought Kyna was too smart to go for something like this. How did you talk her into it?"

Grinning wider, Bryan said, "Who said I told her?"

"That's cold. So how will you know if this bogeyman zaps her?"

"If what he did to Morales is any indication, it'll be all over the evening news."

"And if he just makes her disappear?"

Walking back to the table, Bryan pointed to a black clay bowl half full of clear water. In the bottom was a mound of black sand and an oddly shaped crystal. "I have other ways of keeping tabs on Ms. Rand."

Conrad walked over to the table and peered down into the bowl. "So what's she doing right now?"

Bryan frowned again. "It's not like turning on the telly. It's not that simple."

"Which means you don't know."

Not for the first time Bryan wondered why he kept Conrad around. The man was loyal enough, but his familiar attitude and manners . . .

"Look," Bryan snapped, "you see that crystal?" Conrad nodded. "As long as I know exactly where she is, I can align that crystal to her life energy. As long as the crystal is clear, she's okay. If it turns black . . ."

"We head for Tibet?"

"Exactly."

"So how long? I mean, how long before you know it's safe?"

Bryan tapped his finger on the pages of the book on the table. "It's all right here. If this witch doctor has killed half as many people as reported, then all we have to do is lay low till All Hallows' Eve and the spirits of his victims will take care of him for us."

"All Hallows' Eve? When's that?"

"Halloween, Conrad. Halloween. It can't come too soon."

Cyrus rolled out of bed well before sunup. He dressed quietly and slipped out of the motel room without waking Kyna. After a quick stop at the front desk to ask directions to the closest park or playground, he set off two blocks north to an elementary school in the middle of a large open field. As soon as he was loose, he began his morning run, pounding along in the fringe of grass between the sidewalk and curb to save his knees. It was a glorious morning. The sun was out, the sky was high and blue and in the distance, hazy white clouds sat atop the Wasatch mountains like meringue frosting. Pop-up sprinklers sent rotating arcs of water high over the field, cooling the air and covering the grass with liquid diamonds and rainbows. As he ran, Cyrus thought about his brush with the wolf the day before, and about the hours he had spent at the hospital in Vernal.

At first the ER nurse had refused to believe their story. Then, after the doctor had talked to the ranger on the telephone and given Cyrus a thorough examination, the man had admitted that he had no explanation for Cyrus's injuries . . . or lack thereof. The hospital staff had taken X rays, drawn about a gallon of blood, and as a last resort the doctor had offered to start Cyrus on the rabies vaccine. But by that time the man's heart really wasn't in it.

"If you want to be on the safe side, Mr. Trigg, I'll start you on the injections. But to be honest, they're very painful, and I really don't believe you need them."

Since Cyrus was terrified of sharp objects anyway, he had decided to skip the shots and the doctor promised to call if anything turned up in his blood work.

Cyrus stopped after one lap around the field and glanced at the timer on his digital wristwatch.

"Jeez!"

He took another look at the field. It appeared to be about a mile around, but he'd done the lap in under five minutes—and at a very leisurely pace. Cyrus started around again. He figured either the field was smaller than it looked, or running in the mountains had just cut his time by nearly a third.

Kyna was still asleep when Cyrus returned to the room. Early on he had figured out that she was not what you'd call a morning person. He took a shower, then went to the coffee shop and brought back breakfast. After he plied her with hot coffee, biscuits and jam, she stretched like a cat and looked up at him appraisingly.

"You make a pretty good butler."

"All part of the service."

Kyna polished off the coffee, then sat on the side of the bed rubbing her eyes. Cyrus watched her in the mirror as he shaved.

"You didn't sleep very well," he said.

"I know. You didn't either."

"I didn't? Did I keep you up?"

"Not really. I was having strange dreams, but nothing compared to yours. It sounded like you were running a marathon, and you kept muttering, 'The mountain, the mountain.' What mountain?''

Cyrus blinked slowly several times. He did vaguely remember something about a mountain, about an icy wind and a big yellow moon. But the details were fuzzy.

"I don't know. You know how dreams are. What about you?"

She stretched again. "I don't remember much. Something about a nun trying to get me to do something. Probably my homework."

Cyrus noted the way the T-shirt pulled tight across her breasts.

"Shit!"

"What's the matter?" she asked.

Cyrus held a damp facecloth to his neck to staunch the blood. "Some bodyguard. I almost cut my own throat."

"Should have been watching what you were doing."

He felt his face flush but didn't reply.

Later, as he was taking the last suitcase out to the car, the telephone rang.

"Mr. Trigg? It's Dr. Barton," the voice on the phone said. "I hope I didn't call too early, but you said you were leaving today."

"No, it's okay, Doc. We were just about to hit the road."

"Good. How are you feeling?"

"Fine. I beat my best time on my morning run by over twelve minutes."

"Great. The reason I called is to talk to you about the results of your blood tests."

Cyrus felt a tickle of alarm in his stomach.

"It's nothing to worry about, really," the doctor said, correctly interpreting Cyrus's silence. "But something strange did show up." Barton waited for a response and, receiving none, plunged on. "The lab found a foreign organism in your blood."

"Foreign organism? What exactly does that mean?"

"It's not rabies, but . . . well, to tell you the truth, they can't identify it. It doesn't appear to be dangerous or anything. But the thing is . . . Mr. Trigg, we were wondering if you had been out of the country recently?"

Cyrus thought, *Oh shit! Kyna has.* *Great!*

He reached out and closed the door. "No I haven't, but my, uh, employer travels a lot. Listen, Doctor, be straight with me, okay. This thing, you know, it's not AIDS or anything contagious?"

"No, no, it's nothing remotely like that. It acts like some sort of symbiotic parasite. It's just . . . strange. Can you come back in? I want to repeat the tests. It's just possible that some form of contamination got into the test tubes, hard as we try to prevent that sort of thing."

Cyrus breathed a mental sigh of relief. *Doctors!*

"Sorry, Doc. No can do. We're already out the door."

"Well"—the doctor sounded relieved—"I guess if you're feeling all right . . . Just be careful. If you begin to feel anything strange: loss of appetite, nausea, fever, anything like that, go to a hospital at once. You have my number here if they need to call."

"No worries. If my appetite were any better, they'd have to airlift food into Salt Lake."

They rang off and Cyrus hurriedly checked the room.

That Kyna!

He pitied the poor maid who had to come in behind them. Wet towels were piled on every flat surface and her bed looked like it had exploded. Cyrus shrugged and carried the last suitcase out to the waiting Lincoln.

"What kept you?" Kyna asked.

"Had to take a leak."

As soon as he said it, Cyrus wondered why he had lied.

The next stop on Kyna's itinerary was Kalispell, Montana. When Cyrus said he never pictured Montana as being a hot spot for diamonds, she replied, "You'd have to ask Bryan. Far as I know, they use 'em to decorate their saddles."

Kyna could have taken the expressways and main highways,

but she found herself sticking to the narrow back roads that twisted through the rugged high country like worms. Part of the reason was that Cyrus had told her he had never been out West before, and to her surprise she found that she liked showing him the countryside. Another part, the part that she didn't understand, was that she had this terrible feeling they were being followed. Cops? The FBI? She wasn't sure. To combat this growing sense of unease, she found herself opening up to Cyrus, and even more surprising, he opened up to her. She was amazed to discover that he was charming and smart and he had a real odd-ball sense of humor. She drove well out of their way to give them more time to talk, passing through Jackson Hole, Wyoming, and then turning up toward Yellowstone National Park. But as the afternoon wore on, and the shadows of the mountains grew long, she pressed down on the accelerator, flying through the western part of Yellowstone at warp factor ten. In fact, they were going so fast that Cyrus kept having to ask, "Were those buffalo? Were those elk? Was that a geyser or a giant lying on his back taking a whiz?"

After eighteen hours on the road, they stopped at a steak house for a quick bite to eat. It was one of those faux Western places where the waiters and waitresses wore cowboy boots, jeans and plaid shirts with white piping on the pockets. Every window had a set of long horns mounted above it and the restroom doors read: HEIFERS and BULLS.

A waiter named Buckaroo Bob led them to a table next to a window overlooking the highway and winked at Cyrus when he lit the candle in the center of the table. Kyna had a salad and a cup of soup from the chuck wagon salad bar and Cyrus ordered a T-bone—rare. After Bob took the steak back twice for being overcooked, he rolled a flaming grill up to the table and said to Cyrus, "Say when."

Bob dropped a sixteen-ounce slab of meat on the grill and the moment it hit and started to sizzle, Cyrus said, "Turn it."

Bob looked at Cyrus the way most people look at Branch Davidians, but he did as instructed. Again, the moment the meat began to cook, Cyrus said, "When!"

Shaking his head, the waiter went back to get the rest of Cyrus's dinner and Kyna said, "I've heard of rare, but really, Russ, that thing's going to get up and run the minute you try to cut it."

"I've been feeling a bit run down," he lied. "I heard rare meat is good for anemia."

To change the subject, Cyrus regaled Kyna with one of his bodyguard stories.

"I once took the daughter of an actor shopping."

"Anyone I might have heard of?" she asked.

The candle flame did magical things to her eyes.

"Probably. He was in a movie with Kurt Russell."

"Come on, who was it?"

Smiling a little secret half-smile, Cyrus shook his head. "Sorry. Anyway, she said she needed a new fall coat and wanted me to take her to the mall. She bought a forty-thousand-dollar mink coat and asked me to shoot the salesman when he wouldn't give her a monogrammed garment bag to carry it in."

"No!"

"I don't think she was serious."

Kyna broke up. "Come on!"

"Honest. Women are a mystery to me. When I think they're serious, they're kidding, and when I think they're kidding, they turn out to be as serious as a tax audit."

She knew he was flirting and she knew what he wanted her to say. "Big, strong boy like you, you must have lots of girls willing to teach you what a woman means."

"Not all that many." He grinned. "The day of the romantic is past."

"And you're a romantic?"

"Alas, a dinosaur. 'Tis why I felt such kinship with those old bones back at the park. One day some fresh-faced young couple will stand over my grave and read the sign 'Homo romanticus; species extinct—killed by women's lib.' "

"Oh ho, a chauvinist on top of everything else. I should have known."

"No," Cyrus replied, suddenly serious. "I have nothing in common with Nicolas Chauvin. He had a cause, a belief."

Kyna detected a sadness in his eyes, a vulnerability that took her by surprise. "And you have none?"

He couldn't answer. For it had suddenly dawned upon him that in a roomful of people and cigarette smoke and greasy food, he could smell the faint scent of musk coming from Kyna's skin. And underneath the din of rattling dishes, laughter and squealing children, he could hear the slow, steady beat, beat, beat of her heart. His eyes were riveted to his plate as he cut a large slice of steak and shoveled it into his mouth, chewing slowly, feeling the rush as the bloody juices trickled down his throat.

He glanced out the window.

The moon was just coming up over the mountains and its light spilled over the valley and trees like pale, green milk. A montage of irrational impulses swirled inside his head like leaves in a wind tunnel: *can't breathe! Got to get out! Got to run. GOT TO RUN!*

Kyna mistook his silence for shyness, but it wasn't that—he was afraid.

Oh my God! he thought. *That doctor was wrong. There's something terribly wrong with me!*

But the odd part was, he felt wonderful; he felt like he could climb a mountain, or run a marathon, or . . . make love to a beautiful woman.

Kyna watched his face closely, mentally comparing him with Bryan. Cyrus wasn't as polished as Bryan, he didn't dress as well, and he was so young—she figured he couldn't be more than twenty-five. But she sensed something solid about Cyrus, something that she had never seen in Bryan. She felt she could trust him. And in Kyna's experience, trust was harder to come by than gold.

Her eyes followed the curve of his jaw as he chewed, the hair on his arm as it disappeared under the rolled-up cuff of his shirt. She noted the way his eyes crinkled in pleasure as he swallowed.

69

Christ! she thought. *Get a grip. You're not sixteen anymore.*

But in spite of her good intentions, Kyna felt a ball of fire ignite low in her belly and her heart started to beat faster.

Cyrus's head came up and his eyes bore into hers with an intensity that was frightening. She swallowed hard and almost choked on a piece of lettuce.

Good God! she thought in amazement. *Did he read my mind? Or hear my heartbeat?*

But that was crazy—wasn't it?

They finished eating in silence and then checked into a very elegant Best Western Inn on the outskirts of Kalispell. While Cyrus was unloading the bags, Kyna collapsed onto the bed, threw her arms out wide and faked a loud snore.

"How come you aren't dead?" she asked. "I feel like I could crawl into a cave with one of those bears we passed and sleep till next spring."

He considered the question seriously. Why wasn't he tired? He'd run five miles that morning, traveled over tortuous highways for eighteen hours, and yet he felt like a caged animal. All he wanted to do was get outdoors and run.

"I don't know," he shrugged. "I'm just not."

"Well," Kyna said on her way into the bathroom, "I'm going to take a bath and go to bed. We're going to be back on the road early and I need my beauty sleep."

"I guess I'll do another five miles," he said to the bathroom door.

Cyrus found a pair of only slightly smelly black sweatpants and a navy turtleneck in his duffel bag and then dug his high-tops out of the Lincoln's trunk. To avoid being turned into road pizza by some passing farmer, he stuck to the high grass at the side of the highway until he found a gravel road that trailed off into the forest. As he ran, he kept his gaze fixed on the distant mountains and put his mind in neutral. The night air was cold, his breath came out in great white puffs, yet it filled his lungs like nitrous oxide, and except for the monotonous pounding of his feet, it was blissfully quiet. His sneakers had become magic carpets that allowed him to glide over the road, and only every now and then they picked up a small stone and hurled it off into the night. Overhead, the creamy-yellow moon filled the world with cardboard cutouts of massive fir trees and butterscotch meadows. Being a city boy, Cyrus had never imagined a place of such serenity and beauty. Time seemed to be trapped in a web of dancing moonbeams and before he knew it he had reached the foot of the mountains where the debris from aeons of erosion had erected a massive colluvium city.

He slowed to a walk and then, without breaking stride, began leaping from boulder to boulder like an intoxicated mountain goat. Seventy feet above the meadow he reached a plateau and sat cross-legged on the icy rock and stared at the lights of Kalispell twinkling like fireflies eight miles away. He felt good. Warm, but not sweaty. He was barely panting and already looking forward to the run back. But first, he decided to take a break and just listen to the night.

Turning away from town, he lay back on a bed of dried lichens and let his eyes follow the slope of the mountain up to where the moon crowned the tree line and the oxygen-starved stumps of ancient trees looked like an army of deformed trolls. It was so beautiful that it filled him with emotions and urges he had no name for.

"Just look at that moon," he whispered.

He stared at the softly glowing orb, trying to make out the individual craters and mountains that the universe's plastic surgeon had molded into the kindly humanoid face that mankind had been staring at since it climbed out of the primal soup. As he stared, the moon seemed to grow until it filled the sky. Cyrus felt a quickening in his blood, a warm rush, a pounding in his ears.

Do I have a fever? he wondered.

But it seemed unimportant.

Deep in the forest, a wolf howled. A long, low, soul-wrenching cry to which his throat longed to respond.

I must be nuts. A lunatic? How appropriate.

Better start back, he told himself.

71

But the moon was so beautiful.
Just a few more minutes.

He dreamed. It was the most wonderful dream he had ever dreamed—the wettest of wet dreams.

He was running through the woods, leaping over fallen trees and scaling boulders and chatter marks like they were pebbles. The ground rose to meet his feet, pushing them along as if he were riding through the forest on a supersonic tread-mill. The wind sang to his ears. Near the summit of a strange mountain, the forest gave way to short stubby trees and a garden of small boulders under a series of wavelike nappes. He slowed, finally pausing at the edge of a clearing.

In the half-light, a silver shadow slipped into the shelter of a split-faced rock—a shadow that moved like raindrops flowing over wet leaves. The wind carried a scent: warm, musky, clean. He felt a cauldron of conflicting emotions: the desire to keep running—just running and running—yet he wanted to investigate the sexy smells too.

The shadow shot across the ground between boulders like an arrow made of ice. And suddenly she was standing in front of him. Her coat was sleek, silver and shaggy. Her eyes were obsidian chips, her ears twin peaks of curiosity. She took several more steps toward him and paused, her nose wrinkling as she took in his odor.

Other than the excited trembling that he couldn't control, Cyrus didn't move. He was afraid, and yet thrilled. Like watching a horror movie where he wanted to close his eyes but didn't want to miss anything.

The bitch closed the distance between them, whining softly and wagging her bushy tail. As she came she kept glancing back over her shoulder, back to a shadowy cleft in the rock face. Sensing her unease, he raised his nose to the wind. A cold wind came from the cave, dank and musty. It was a dangerous wind—a death wind—and Cyrus snorted hard to clean his palate. She came close and touched his face with her nose. Her nose was so cold that it branded his skin like fire, and all at once he knew her. Knew her like he had known her all of his life. He saw her as a gangling wolf pup, all skinny legs and floppy ears. Piddling every time she heard an unfamiliar noise. He knew her scent, an aroma that filled his head like helium. And he felt the stirring of molten lust in his belly.

Cyrus reached out to caress her muzzle, but instead of a hand with five fingers, he had a hairy brown paw.

Kyna woke in a sweat and for a moment she couldn't remember where she was. The room was as dark as a tomb with only the glowing red numbers from the alarm clock between the beds to tell her which way was up. It was three A.M. and she'd just had another of those dreams of a dark presence dogging her through a world of nightmare shadows. As with most dreams, Kyna had never seen the man's face, but she knew it had been hideous.

She sat up on the edge of the bed for a moment, staring in the dark at Cyrus's bed. She had never felt so frightened and alone. More than anything she wanted to be held, but what was she supposed to do? Climb into bed with him? A total stranger? What on earth would he think?

Scratch that, she thought. She knew exactly what he'd think. The question was: Did she care?

Strangely enough, she did.

"Well," Kyna whispered to his shadowy bed, "you wanted to know about women? Lesson one: Sometimes we just need to be held."

She reached out to touch his face and found an empty pillow.

"Russ? Russ?"

She turned on the lamp.

His bed was still made up.

"You son of a bitch," she hissed.

Kyna shot off the bed and went to check the door—it was locked. Still, the bastard was getting paid to take care of her and here he was out chasing after a case of the clap, and here she was . . .

She collapsed onto her bed and began beating the pillow with her fist and sobbing big, fat tears.

"Damn you! Damn you to hell."

She cried until she was gasping for breath and then went into the bathroom and washed her face. Looking at herself in the mirror only made her start crying again. She couldn't decide whom she hated more: Bryan for setting her up, Cyrus for going off and leaving her or just men in general for being such inconsiderate assholes.

Ten minutes later she washed her face again, all the while glaring at her reflection in the mirror. "Not a tear! Not a fucking tear."

Kyna hated weepy women and hated herself all the more for acting like one. After drying her face, she climbed back into bed and stared at the clock—it was almost four o'clock.

What to do when he came back? That's what she had to decide. Firing him would only make things harder for her. She could lock him out, but then he'd know how really pissed she was. No! Better to try and go back to sleep and then act like she hadn't even noticed that he was gone. Then, when they got back to Memphis, she'd pay the bastard off with the sharp point of her size-seven pump right between his legs.

Smiling, Kyna fell asleep five minutes later.

Chapter Five

October 19

Cyrus woke to the dark lavender pre-light of dawn. He sat up on the tabletop rock and looked down at Kalispell, covered now under a hazy blanket of wood smoke corkscrewing up from a thousand chimneys.

A dream, he thought sadly. *Just a dream.*

When he slipped back into the room, Kyna's bed was empty and he could hear the sound of water running in the shower. He quickly undressed, wadded up the dark clothing and stuffed them into his bag. He sniffed himself.

Not too bad, considering, he thought.

The water in the bathroom stopped and he heard the plastic shower curtain slide back—Kyna was humming softly. From the bedroom he could smell her—sweet with soap and pungent with shampoo. He sat on the bed with just a towel around his hips, his body as taut as a guitar string.

She came into the bedroom with her arms up, weaving a towel around her wet hair. When she saw him, she stopped, so startled that for a moment she forgot she was naked.

"Oh! You're back. You certainly were up early."

His eyes were drawn to her breasts. They sagged only slightly, as if their weight was partially immune to the laws of gravity. The nipples were brown and sat in the middle of large round areolas like melted chocolate kisses.

She sensed the tension in his body. "What's wrong?"

Then she glanced down and realized why he was staring

and dropped her arms to cover herself. "Gosh, I'm so embar—"

He rose and walked over to her, all the while thinking, *This isn't me. I could never do this.*

"What?"

The hunger in his eyes sent a shiver to her core, but she didn't flinch or try to back away. His hand came up—slowly, like he was afraid of his own strength—and lightly brushed her lips.

"I—"

"It's all right," she whispered.

Cyrus swept her up into his arms and carried her to the bed.

Next stop: Calgary, Alberta, Canada.

Kyna took the scenic route to give Cyrus a chance to see Glacier National Park. They entered the park through a wondrous valley stepped with heavy fog and wound around a glacial lake that was as deep as the Sears Tower is tall. Kyna stopped several times to take pictures of the lake and a pair of grizzly bears raiding the garbage cans along the side of the road. They escaped the park and the fog by taking the tortuous Going-to-the-Sun Highway up and over the mountains. During the trip, Cyrus was unusually quiet. But that was okay, because Kyna couldn't seem to shut up.

"I don't know what got into you this morning. If it was your run, I hope you get up and run every morning. Matter of fact, if you want to get out and run along beside the car right now, it's fine by me."

She winked at him and smiled. It was a big happy smile. The first he had seen from her since the wolf attack.

Cyrus gazed out the window and let her enthusiasm wash over him like spring sunshine. Since their almost violent bout of lovemaking, he had felt listless and melancholy. Making love with Kyna had been like trying to hold on to an Olympic gymnast on speed. For her, sex was food and he was the banquet. It had been wonderful, warm and at times funny. Still

. . . that morning he felt as if something significant had been missing.

He glanced down into the valley and let his eye follow a silver ribbon of water as it snaked between dun-colored mountains, their tops dusted with powdery patches of white. At that altitude, winter came early. By September the aspens were already as much gold as green and the Rocky Mountain dwarf maples looked like they were on fire. By mid-October, their limbs were bare, bleak, dead.

After surviving a cursory customs inspection at the border, they crossed into Canada at Waterton Park and ate lunch at the park cafeteria. Later, they drove past seemingly endless fields of grain surrounding Calgary—a city of over half a million secure in the belief that all the real cowboys left in the world resided there.

Kyna had reservations at the posh Canadian Pacific Hotel that stood like a twenty-story exclamation mark next to Calgary's airport. While she was at the front desk going through the check-in ritual, Cyrus strolled through the stadium-sized lobby. It was an impressive place. Half of the floor space was taken up by a heated swimming pool and the other half by a steamy jungle of potted plants and trees. This sweltering combination gave the lobby all the homey ambience of a South American rain forest. The center of the building was enclosed under a huge circular dome and ringed by floors that appeared to extend all the way to the mesosphere. Four bullet-shaped express elevators were located strategically around the lobby, ready to whisk weary travelers up to their waiting rooms. As Cyrus watched, one of these modern marvels blasted off, and he figured anyone unwise enough to stay in the penthouse would get a nosebleed before they reached their room.

Kyna finished at the desk and set out like Henry Stanley to track down her Dr. Livingstone. Ten minutes later she found him loitering in the palms behind the hot tubs, watching two coeds from Wisconsin soak off their jet lag.

"Pervert!" Kyna said, and marched off toward the elevator.

"No. You don't understand," Cyrus insisted as he hurried

to catch up. "I was just looking at the palm trees. Have you ever seen any like them before?"

"Palm trees, my ass . . . And speaking of which"—she pointed at her derriere—"this is the body you're supposed to be keeping an eye on, remember?"

After dumping the bags in the room, they had an early dinner by the pool and then Kyna drove into town.

Downtown Calgary turned out to be a confusion of Western-wear shops and international banks. As a result, the streets teemed with men wearing pin-striped suits and ten-gallon hats, and secretaries in sequined dresses with rawhide trim and reptile-skin boots. In the local restaurant row, neon-lighted Chinese take-out joints clashed with rustic hamburger cafes where they served a side of beef on a bun that made the Big Mac look like a finger sandwich.

By the time Kyna found a parking spot near the fairgrounds, the sun was on its way to bed and the temperature was in the teens. Cyrus checked to make sure the 9mm was loaded and snug inside the shoulder holster before donning the brown leather jacket he'd unpacked.

"What do you think?" he asked, flipping the coat collar up. "Spenser or Hawk?"

Kyna slipped into a fur-trimmed doeskin jacket with the ever-present briefcase clutched in her right hand. "Mickey Rooney?"

"Aw, please. No short jokes."

Kyna locked the car. "Come on, Kareem."

She led him through a mostly residential neighborhood, passing a few gas stations and mom-and-pop groceries before crossing the street and entering the Calgary Fairgrounds.

"Not very busy," Cyrus remarked. "Everyone must be eating dinner."

Because of the hour, only the main gate remained open. After forking over twelve dollars to a semicomatose attendant, they walked past several large exhibition buildings, the giant rodeo stadium where the city held its annual stampede, and across a bridge over an anemic gray river. On the other side of the bridge, Kyna stopped to lace up her boot and to get her bearings from a map plaque next to a mock Sioux tepee.

The more Cyrus saw of the fairgrounds, the less he liked the place. It was too big, too dirty, too deserted. Most of the buildings were dark, the crowds having retreated to the warmth and safety of their homes and fires. The streetlights were just beginning to come on and the wind roamed like a wild animal through the midways, converting the street trash into tumbleweeds.

"Damn, it's cold," Cyrus muttered. "Where the devil are we going, anyway?"

"That pavilion over there." Kyna pointed to a three-story, prefab, aluminum building about a quarter of a mile away.

"This place reminds me of a scene from *Death Wish*. All we need are a few ten-dollar bills hanging out of our pockets."

"Don't be such a baby," she said not unkindly. "I do this all the time and nothing ever happens."

No sooner were the words out of her mouth than two cowboy types came sauntering around the side of a pronto pup stand. Both men had cigarettes dangling from their mouths and both were dressed in out-of-date cowboy chic: faded jeans that hugged their thin frames like blue skin, long-sleeved plaid shirts and wide leather belts with large silver-and-turquoise buckles.

"Keep walking," Cyrus whispered.

The cowboys were walking slowly, blowing smoke and laughing. They could have been exactly what they appeared to be: two friends having a smoke together after work. There was nothing in their behavior to indicate that they were even aware that anyone else was around. And that's what made Cyrus suspicious. For unless a man was gay or dead, he couldn't help but notice Kyna.

Something deep inside Cyrus's mind clicked. All at once his body started to tingle. The smell of the sour sweat oozing from the men's pores reached his nose and made his eyes water. To his suddenly supersensitive ears, their footsteps thundered like giant redwood trees crashing to earth. He noticed two telltale tube-shaped bulges in their front pockets and instinctively moved between Kyna and the strangers. She deftly shifted the briefcase to her left hand. As they strolled past, the men nodded politely to Kyna and then a split second later, Cyrus heard the scrape of leather soles followed by the stereophonic clatter of clasp knife blades unfolding.

Cyrus pivoted.

The men were already in motion, their arms extended and their knives carving the air where Cyrus's kidneys had just been. To Cyrus, everything after that seemed to happen in slow motion, and yet by the time Kyna turned around, both men were on the ground—one out cold and the other one probing the brand-new gap in his front teeth with the tip of a bloody tongue.

"You motherfucker!" the cowboy rasped through his ruined enamel. "You kicked my fucking teeth out!"

The man lunged for the knife lying beside his knee.

Cyrus applied the toe of his boot to the bone behind the man's left ear. The man rolled over several times and went to sleep.

Cyrus grabbed Kyna's arm. "Let's get out of here."

"Christ!" she mumbled.

Cyrus sat in a very uncomfortable patio chair under a gaily striped umbrella, sipping a diet soda while two tables away, Kyna and her customer haggled like a couple of Italian fishwives. This time, Cyrus thought, at least the man *looked* like a jeweler. None of this yuppie ponytail and gold chains stuff for this guy—he had on an Armani suit, his hands and fingernails were long and well manicured, *and* he had a real haircut.

Four tables away, at an identical patio table, another man was sipping a Coke and watching the transaction. This guy was older than Cyrus, and beefier. But he had the same bulge under his right arm that Cyrus had, and his eyes never left the man in the suit.

Unsure of the proper bodyguard etiquette, Cyrus wondered

if he was supposed to go over and introduce himself. Maybe compare pistols? No, he decided. They'd probably get into that old mine's-bigger-than-yours thing. Besides, the other guy looked like a pro. What if he asked Cyrus about his experiences as a bodyguard? What could Cyrus say? *I threw three drunks out of a bar last week?* How 'bout, *Just tonight, I beat up two starving cowboys?*

At the proper moment, Kyna's customer waved the other man over. The bodyguard abandoned his drink and started toward Kyna's table with a fat, legal-sized manila envelope in his right hand.

Cyrus never moved. Something about the way the bodyguard moved, relaxed and unconcerned. And the way he . . . smelled? . . . told Cyrus the man was all right. The fact that he could smell the guy all the way across the room was a little disconcerting, but when Cyrus thought about it, he realized that he could smell Kyna's perfume and her customer's sugary cologne as well.

What's the matter with me? he wondered. *Nerves from the encounter with the cowboys—or something else?*

It had always taken Cyrus a while to unwind after any type of confrontation, so he hoped that what he was feeling was just adrenaline withdrawal.

The bodyguard gave the envelope to the man in the suit, who in turn handed it to Kyna. She checked the contents and then removed three bags of gems from the briefcase and pushed them across the table. The man nodded once, scooped the bags up and then stood. Kyna shook the man's hand one last time and then came over to Cyrus.

"Ready?" she asked, tucking the envelope inside her coat.

Cyrus peeked out through the window in the pavilion door. It was as dark as pitch. "Ready."

When they reached the pronto pup stand, as Cyrus had expected, the cowboys were long gone. If it hadn't been for the spots of frozen blood spattered on the concrete, he might have convinced himself that he had imagined the whole thing.

With the trouble behind them and her delivery complete,

Kyna relaxed. In spite of the wind she seemed to be in a very good mood, laughing and joking—hanging onto Cyrus's arm one moment and then waving her hands around in flights of fancy as she told him funny stories about her customers. But as they approached the stampede stadium, Cyrus found that he was only half listening. Something back in one of the cavernous tunnels that led down into the arena had caught his attention. Something that smelled . . . bad.

At first he thought that it was the cowboys letting their lust for revenge override their common sense. But as he got closer to the stadium, he decided that it wasn't the cowboys' smell, or their sound. And it most definitely didn't *feel* like anything Cyrus had ever run into before.

"Are you listening to me?" Kyna snapped.

Cyrus stopped and held up his hand for quiet.

"What?" She stopped and threw out her hip. "Here I am, freezing my tush off and you want to stop and chat?"

"We've got a problem."

Kyna inched closer. "What is it? Those two men?"

"No. It's . . . something else. I'm not sure. I want you to go back to the pavilion and call the police."

Kyna shook her head vehemently. "No way. I go where you go. You come with me."

But he couldn't. Whatever was out there was challenging him in a way that had nothing to do with machismo. He didn't like it, didn't understand it, but something inside his body wouldn't let him ignore it.

"Do as I tell you, and take this with you." He pulled the automatic from the holster. "You know how to use it?" He pulled back the slide and fed a round into the chamber.

"Yes," she replied. "But won't you need it?"

"Not for this. Now go on, make the call."

Even in the meager light Kyna could tell from Cyrus's expression that there was no room for argument. She took the automatic, checked the load and then, without another word, took off at a brisk walk back the way they had come.

Cyrus kept an eye on her until she was safely out of sight,

then turned and faced the shadowy stadium.

"Okay, my friend. Let's dance."

Facing an unknown opponent in the dark should have put Cyrus on edge. Yet for some strange reason he found that he was more angry than scared. He approached the stadium cautiously, one foot following the other as easily and surely as an alley cat walking a fence. Strange new sensations were filling his head. The thing was out there moving around in the shadows—he could hear it. A few more yards and he could smell it too, rank and foul—the stench of an open grave. And not a new grave either.

When he was ten feet from the tunnel entrance the thing came shuffling slowly out into the watery light from the street-lamps across the main highway. It was the size and shape of a man, but it didn't move much like a man. Its steps were slow and arduous. The sound its shoes made as they scraped over the concrete was like the sound of a giant sheet of canvas ripping. Then Cyrus saw the thing's eyes. They were round and red, like two molten balls of flame.

Cyrus calmly removed his jacket and the empty shoulder holster and dropped them on the ground. Then he unlaced and kicked out of his boots, pulled the turtleneck over his head and stood in his jeans and stocking feet. The thing stopped. It appeared confused—what was this crazy man doing?

Cyrus wondered the same thing.

He waited with his right foot in front of his left and his knees flexed, no longer cold, not scared. He told himself he was ready.

The man thing came on, step—drag—stop! Step—scrape! Until it was almost on top of him. And then it stopped again like a toy robot with a dead battery and stood horribly still.

It was dead all right. Had been for some time by the looks of it. The face that had once been human had gone gray and knobs of pearly-white bone protruded through the backs of its hands. It was dressed in a dark suit that had patches of green-ish mold growing on the sleeves, and black wing tips caked with fresh cemetery mud. Up to this point the thing's movements had been so clumsy that Cyrus figured it was safe to take a closer look. He did. And the thing's arm shot out and knocked him flat on his back.

"Okay, fine," Cyrus said as he scrambled away and bounced to his feet. "If you're dead, I don't have to worry about hurting you, now do I?"

Taking two quick steps, Cyrus spun on his left heel and kicked the thing square in the face—it was like kicking a brick wall. He danced back out of reach, bouncing lightly on the balls of his feet.

The blow had flattened what was left of the creature's very prominent nose, but otherwise it was standing as before and evidently no worse off. Undaunted, Cyrus decided if he couldn't knock the thing down, he'd go for its wheels and try to cripple it. He faked a punch at the head then dropped down on his heel and tried to sweep the thing's ankles with his right leg. That worked as well as trying to cut down a full-grown tree with a rubber axe. And this time, before he could spin away, the thing grabbed him by the throat and lifted him off the ground.

Still unruffled, Cyrus tried to kick his way free, and when that didn't work he tried slamming his cupped palms into the thing's ears.

The right ear came off in his hand.

"Shit!"

Disgusted, he dropped the leathery piece of flesh like it was a dead slug and tried shoving his thumbs into the creature's dry eye sockets. It countered by clamping down on Cyrus's throat and squeezing until his windpipe felt like a drinking straw. With his wind cut off, Cyrus pulled out all the stops. He tried every trick his sensei had ever taught him: flailing away at the thing's neck with the hard edge of his hands and finally jamming his thumbs into the arteries on the side of the thing's neck.

It didn't take him long to realize that a dead man wasn't likely to pass out from lack of blood to the brain.

In desperation he brought his knees up, put his feet flat against the creature's chest and then shoved with all of his might. The dead man's chest caved in like a rotten gourd, trapping Cyrus's right foot behind a tangle of shattered ribs.

At this point, Cyrus realized things were not going well. Black spots were going off like flashbulbs in front of his eyes and his hands felt like they weighed fifty pounds apiece. As his struggles diminished, the dead fingers dug deeper and deeper into the soft flesh of his throat. He couldn't breathe—he couldn't swallow—and he couldn't break the thing's steel-like grip on his throat.

Cyrus must have passed out, for the next thing he knew he was down on one knee on the asphalt. He had no idea how he got there, but when he glanced down, he saw one of the creature's hands was still wrapped around his throat. Cyrus jerked the hand loose and threw it behind him. For the moment, he remained as he was. He ignored the dead thing standing in front of him and he forgot about Kyna. He forgot who he was and why he was there. All memory, all pain, all fear were blotted out by an all-consuming rage that coursed through his body in great orgasmic waves.

Around him, the night exploded with ghostly green light. The overflow of this mysterious energy rushed into his body, energizing each individual cell and driving it mad. He could see everything: the darkest corners, the night birds staring down from the rooftops. Even the dried-up pores in the dead man's face stood out like the craters of the moon.

And it wasn't only Cyrus's vision that was affected. He began to taste the bite of the chilled night wind, and hear the heartbeats of children sleeping in their beds in the houses across the street. Even his own blood on the creature's fingernails smelled as rich and pungent as orange blossoms. As this strange power continued to pour into him, energizing his body like a living voltaic cell, the bones in his back and arms creaked and popped like a giant cracking his knuckles and he began to grow. His calves and thighs ballooned with cords of new muscle and his mouth felt as if it were suddenly too full of teeth.

But the best, the absolutely most wonderful part of this strange metamorphosis was the lust. Cyrus had never felt such desire, such an intense need to rend and destroy. He sprang to his feet and literally flung himself on the creature—ripping and tearing into the dead flesh like a living chain saw. A shriveled arm went this way, a desiccated leg that. Cyrus plunged his arms up to his elbows in the thing's chest and ripped its rotted lungs to pieces. Finally, leaping high into the air, he slammed his foot into the thing's face—and this time the creature's head disintegrated.

The torso stood balanced on its remaining leg for about another five seconds and then tipped over on its back, landing on the asphalt with a hollow thud. Cyrus came down on all fours and waited. When the creature did not stir after two minutes, he crawled over to it and sniffed. Bad move. Whatever had animated the corpse was gone and the thing was decomposing faster than before.

He backed up a few feet, snorted and then took a deep breath and let it out slowly. The moment he started to relax, he seemed to shrink and every joint in his body began to burn as if it were on fire. Unlike the first time, the agony seemed to go on for hours, the burning, the spasms. Like being stretched on a rack in reverse.

When Cyrus opened his eyes he was lying on his side. The ground was cold and as soon as he was able, he pushed himself into a sitting position and looked around. The thing was not only still dead, but looked like a jigsaw puzzle. It took Cyrus a few moments to climb to his feet. The legs of his jeans were hanging down in tatters and his socks were little more than strips of white cotton—perfect for surgical dressings but useless for anything else.

"What happened?" He turned in a slow circle. "What the fuck happened?"

* * *

The wildest part of Tennessee's Wolf River winds past an old maplewood shack in the backwoods near Somerville. Here, tall live oaks grew close together and their overlapping limbs formed caches of rain that drip down on the lower leaves like tears. The ground was still soggy from the spring floods and back in the underbrush, water moccasins were as thick as night crawlers. It was the kind of rustic little hideaway that Jack the Ripper or Hannibal Lecter would have adored, for the closest house was more than nine miles away and no amount of screaming could ever disturb the bullfrogs and catfish.

Inside the cabin, the Dark Man stood tall in the midst of his magical trappings. His hands were around the bald-headed man's throat as the man's feet scissored helplessly in the air a good foot above the floor.

"You told me he was not bitten!" the Dark Man howled. "You said there was no time." He shook his hapless servant until spittle flew. "Do you have any idea of what you've done? Do you?"

The bald-headed man croaked in reply.

"I'll tell you what you've done, you miserable slug, you misbegotten piece of pig dung. You bit him while you were in the spirit form and let him live!" The Dark Man squeezed until the bald man's eyes bulged. "With one careless snap of your jaws, you created a beast five times—ten times—yes, maybe even a hundred times as powerful as you were. If that man ever realizes what he has become, and he has the time to explore his powers, *we* will become the hunted and he will be on our trail like all the hounds of hell."

The Dark Man relaxed his grip and the bald man fell painfully to the floor.

"Leave me. Go out into the swamp with the rest of the vermin and stay there until I summon you."

The bald man crawled like a whipped dog out into the sticky night. The thin man with the goatee stepped to his master's side.

"What must we do?"

"Do? We must kill them before the man's powers accrue.

If we fail . . . the consequences are too terrible to contemplate.''

Cyrus rushed back to the pavilion and peeked through the glass in the door. Kyna was sitting at the table closest to the exit with her arms folded protectively over her chest and the tip of the gun barrel sticking out from under her coat. He opened the door and motioned for her to come.

"My god!" Her eyes grew round when she stepped outside. "What happened to your clothes?"

Cyrus had put everything back on, but his jeans looked like they had been caught in a lawn mower. "A big dog."

"Must have been Cujo's cousin."

"Did you call the police?"

"Uh, no. The phones don't work."

"Okay then, let's get out of here."

She handed Cyrus the gun and he replaced it in the holster. "Ready?"

Taking her arm, he hustled her to the car, making sure to give the rodeo stadium a wide berth. On the drive back to the hotel, the reality of what had happened to him at the stadium came crashing home. Cyrus hardly said a word the rest of the evening and later, as he lay in bed listening to Kyna's soft snoring, his mind tried to sort through the whole improbable nightmare.

I fought with a dead man!

And at the time it had seemed the most natural thing in the world.

"Okay, fine." His whisper was lost in the dark. "I'll pretend I'm Scarlett O'Hara and think about that tomorrow."

So what happened to me? People just don't suddenly turn into the Incredible Hulk.

"Adrenaline." He nodded. "Pure and simple. I was scared shitless."

Right! Six months ago you couldn't last two rounds with Jimmy Quong and all of a sudden you can rip a dead man apart like he's made out of tissue paper?

88

Thinking about it only made his head hurt. He eased out of bed and pulled on a soiled turtleneck, a pair of clean cord jeans and his trusty sneakers. After a breathtaking elevator ride down to the lobby, Cyrus strode quickly out into the subarctic darkness. He walked down the sidewalk until he reached the fence around the airport perimeter. Then, seeing no one around, he climbed the fence and began jogging through the field of tall brown grass that surrounded the runways. After about three miles, he came to a low hill overlooking the south end of the north-south runway. Here the grass was shorter but no less dead. He lay down, crushing the grass into the outline of his body, and cupped his hands behind his head. The moon hovered like a cold chrysanthemum atop the air traffic control tower to his left. As he stared up at the softly glowing satellite, he let his organic data banks run free. He was so deep into his thoughts that he didn't realize he was mouthing the words to one of his favorite songs: "I see a bad moon rising. I see trouble on the way."

Chapter Six

October 20

A little after seven the next morning Kyna and Cyrus took Canadian Highway One west out of Calgary. Once safely outside the city's womb of concrete and steel, they re-entered Canada's bread basket, rolling across rich fields lying dormant under a blanket of light mist. It was late October, after all—since the time of the Druids, the season of the harvest when the earth gave up her bounty to the reaper's blade. The time when Samhain, the lord of the dead, prepared to call forth hosts of evil spirits to avenge those who had wronged them in life. The Romans called this time the Festival of Pomona, the goddess of the fruits and trees. The early Christians called it the eve of the feast of Hallowmas, or All Hallows' Eve. Later it became known as Halloween.

Traffic on the highway was sporadic, but they were slowed by the occasional migrating tractor or school bus. By nine o'clock the mist had burned off and the purple and white Canadian Rockies could be seen in the near distance, jutting up into the sky like the breastplates of an entire chorus of Wagnerian sopranos. After an infusion of cholesterol at a Burger King on the main highway, Kyna went to the trunk to get a heavier jacket. While rummaging through the suitcases she found Bryan's necklace. Holding it up, she was struck anew at the way the two little red stones on the end seemed to glow like the eyes of a cat.

"Damn!"

Cyrus had stopped to talk to one of the locals and his laugh carried to her over the sounds of the diesel engines and horns of the passing cars. His laugh, as quick and fleeting as lightning, sounded as young as he looked.

"Double damn!"

Guilt makes people do strange things. Torn by her sense of loyalty to Bryan and her budding feelings for Cyrus, she fastened the necklace around her neck and tucked it away under her blouse.

"There! Now leave me alone."

Back on the highway, Kyna informed Cyrus that she wanted to make a brief stopover at the international shopping and ski resort at Banff. On the way, she took a detour through an animal preserve on the outskirts of the town, blowing a whole roll of film on a herd of lethargic buffalo and a few mangy elk. Afterward, she drove into town and found a parking place two blocks from the main shopping district.

The morning that had started out so gloomy had turned into a glorious day. The sun was hot, yet not so hot as to chase the autumn chill from the air. The streets were packed with a veritable United Nations of shoppers: Germans, Japanese, Spaniards, French nuns and of course the ubiquitous ugly Americans.

Cyrus took Kyna to lunch at a "New York" style diner just off the main avenue and listened patiently as she babbled about her photographic coup at the buffalo farm. While he wolfed down a real old-fashioned hamburger—lots of grease, tons of cholesterol and very rare—Kyna, who Cyrus now believed consumed more green things than any herbivore on the planet, had the house salad with ranch dressing on the side.

"Yuck!" Kyna muttered when she saw the bloody juice dripping from his burger. "You think maybe they should run the match under that thing a few more times?"

He cast a wary eye at her lettuce. "You should talk. You don't eat, you graze."

During lunch Kyna reached across the table and took Cyrus's hand and asked if he minded doing a little souvenir hunting.

"Souvenirs?" he said, secretly pleased that she wanted to hold hands. "Sure. Sounds like fun."

It wasn't.

Kyna went through stores the way General Sherman went through Atlanta. Cyrus ran along behind her with his arms loaded down with clothing, cosmetics, enough film for an African photo safari and a fur hat that would have made Davy Crockett turn green with envy. In one store Kyna found a lavender lamb's wool sweater that she wanted to buy for her roommate and bullied the poor Pakistani shopkeeper into dropping the price forty Canadian dollars. Cyrus was amazed—she had seemed so normal.

They stopped in a small park at the end of the main street and joined a crowd of gray panthers oohing and ahing over a herd of elk calmly munching the grass.

"You should have waited," Cyrus said with a grin. "You could have had lunch with them."

An old man at the elk-in casually mentioned that moose and beaver were sometimes seen along the golf course on the other side of the river.

"Moose?" Kyna exclaimed, her eyes glowing hot with the fires of photo fever. "Really?"

On the way back to the car she grabbed Cyrus's shoulder and said, "Wait here," and then ducked into a T-shirt shop. She came out five minutes later holding out a hooded sweatshirt with a cartoon beaver in a Mountie hat on the front. "I got this for you."

"Great," Cyrus replied with a grin that was more of a grimace.

Kyna dumped her loot in the backseat of the Lincoln, then drove across the river and around to the far side of the lush Banff Springs Golf Course. In addition to the usual acres of manicured greens and fairways, they skirted a small mountain, nearly ran over a family of bighorn sheep and finally pulled over in a patch of high brown grass on the west bank of the Bow River.

Kyna opened the door and jumped out. "Stay here. Moose are very shy."

"Oh? And when did you become an expert on moose?"

She snapped a telephoto lens onto the front of her Minolta.

"I'm not," she replied with great dignity. "But if I were a moose, and I wanted to take a bath, I'm sure I'd want my privacy."

"Does the word 'paparazzi' mean anything to you?"

Kyna stalked off through the grass, working the focusing ring on the lens. Ignoring her instructions, Cyrus got out and leaned across the hood of the car. He shook his head and laughed as he listened to Kyna crashing through the brush; she had as much chance of seeing a moose as he had of being elected president of the National Organization of Women. Just as he lost sight of her, he heard voices behind him and looked over his shoulder.

Two strangers were coming across the golf course toward him. Their faces were partially concealed behind long scraggly beards and their clothes were covered with road dust. They walked close together with stiff, nervous strides. Unaccountably, watching the men approach made the hairs on the back of Cyrus's neck stand to attention. He put a smile on his face and went to meet them before they crossed the road.

"Hey, man," one of the strangers called out. "You American?"

Cyrus kept the smile in place, but held his breath to keep from being overwhelmed by the cloud of cannabis smoke that surrounded the men.

"Yes."

The men exchanged glances. The taller man—the spokesman—had nice features but cold eyes, and he couldn't seem to stand still. Cyrus noted that he kept one hand deep in the pocket of his filthy hiking shorts.

"We were wondering if, you know, you had any spare change?"

After giving it some thought, Cyrus decided it had to be tough being flat broke in somebody else's country. He fished a twenty-dollar bill out of his wallet and offered it to the men. The tall man's hand came out of his pocket and he offered Cyrus the point of a switchblade.

"While you have that wallet out, man, why don't you just give us the rest?"

At that point, Kyna came stumbling out of the bushes. She saw Cyrus talking to the two strangers and called out, "I'm ready when you are!"

The shorter of the two men peered around Cyrus.

"Hey, take a look at the cunt."

The phony smile dropped from Cyrus's face. "Come on, fellas. I don't need this shit."

The man with the knife jabbed at Cyrus's chest. "Get smart with me, man, and you'll get a lot more 'n shit."

The partner said, "While you two are busy, I think I'll go talk to the lady."

Before Shorty could take the first step toward the car, Cyrus moved in front of him so fast that for a second he appeared to be in two places at once.

"You don't want to do that, friend."

Shorty blinked twice and fell back. The other man looked from his friend to Cyrus and then quickly moved the knife to cover Cyrus again—but he didn't seem quite as sure of himself.

"Forget the bitch!" the taller man snapped. He waved the knife in the general direction of Cyrus's face and said, "Give me the wallet or I'll fix it so the cunt never looks at you again."

After a sleepless night and an afternoon following Kyna around like a Zulu gun bearer, Cyrus's earlier happy mood was taking a definite nosedive. He started to get angry, and as he did, he started noticing things that he'd missed before. Things like the angry caterwauling of a flock of jays up in the trees, the sounds of cloven hooves moving deep in the underbrush and a slightly gamey odor that for some odd reason made him think of rabbits dozing in their underground condos.

This is one hell of a time to start daydreaming, Cyrus thought.

He tried to concentrate, but the crotch of his jeans was binding him in a bad spot and the sleeves of his polo shirt seemed to be too full of arms.

"Don't fuck with me, man!" the man with the knife hissed. "Give me the goddamned money."

Then, all at once, the tall man and his companion began to glow like they were made of kryptonite.

"I have a better idea." Cyrus's voice came out way too deep. "Why don't you and your friend haul your scraggly asses back where you came from before I take that knife and shove it so far up your ass it'll take an entire platoon of forest rangers to find it?"

The tall man's eyes almost popped out of his head. The knife dropped from his hand, and with his compatriot at his heels, he slowly backed away. When the two men reached the first green, they turned around and did a pretty fair imitation of Carl Lewis all the way across the golf course.

Cyrus watched them go and chuckled silently to himself. *First time I ever had that kind of effect on anyone.*

A wave of mild muscle spasms swept through his body and left him feeling nauseous and a little shaky. Again, he attributed them to nerves from the confrontation.

"Maybe you'd better consider a new line of work, Cyrus me boy."

He took a deep breath and let it out slowly as he followed the fading sounds of panicky feet. In a matter of seconds the sounds were gone and he turned and recrossed the road.

Kyna was still snapping away at every bird and squirrel that would stand still long enough.

"Shoot!" she said. "You scared that little ground squirrel."

"Sorry."

"What did those two young men want?"

"Oh, just a kind word."

* * *

The goateed man lay naked in the middle of the cabin floor. His body was covered with ancient runes drawn in white, red and yellow acrylic paints and accented with a variety of exotic bird feathers. The rest of the cabin had been converted into a kind of voodoo fun house. Following his master's detailed instructions, the goateed man had slapped coat after coat of cheap white paint over everything and then scrawled ancient boustrophedonic phrases around all the doors and windows. For the writing he'd used animal blood instead of ink. The Dark Man had then added several crude depictions of Legba and the stovepipe-hat-wearing Baron Samedi—the chief of the Guédé, or death spirits. After removing the rusted kitchen stove and all of the cabinets, they had erected wooden shelves and filled them with glass jars and statues. The jars contained all manner of organic parts and pieces: bat livers, lizard skins, snake fangs, dragon's blood, High John the Conqueror powder, compelling powders, roots and potions. A large mayonnaise jar on the bottom shelf held almost a quart of human blood . . . its neighbor contained three human hearts.

The statues resembled the mummies of little black leprechauns that had died in agony. They had been carved from a mixture of boiled tree roots, lye soap, ashes from burned and crushed bones, human and animal blood, wax and hair from the various poor unfortunates who had crossed the Dark Man's path over the years. The statues were his version of notches on a gun.

"You know what you are supposed to do?" the Dark Man asked for the fourth time.

The goateed man looked up at his master's face and stifled an imprudent remark. "Yes."

"Say it to me again."

"The woman and man will be in the city tomorrow. I am to wait for them and then find some way to give the woman the box."

"And?"

"And then return to my body."

"Correct."

"But . . ."

The Dark Man rolled his eyes to the roof. "But, what?"

"I am sorry, Master. But why do I not just kill the woman?"

The Dark Man felt like screaming. If the woman died at the wrong time and in the wrong way the dark lords would be cheated and he could lose the Butcher's Broom forever. But of course he couldn't tell the moron that. Instead he replied, "Your hold on the body you inhabit will be tenuous at best— you will certainly be no match for the white man."

"But what if she will not accept the box? Can I give it to the man?"

"No! No! No! How many times must I tell you? You must place the box in the woman's hands!"

The goateed man tensed as he waited for the blow that never came.

The Dark Man took a deep breath and let it out through his nose. "Do you have any *other* asinine questions?"

"How . . . how long do I have?"

"I can maintain your essence in the host body for forty-eight hours."

"You . . . you said you only got a glimpse of where she will be. . . ."

"Don't make the mistake of asking me to explain myself!"

"Of course not. I only wondered, if I cannot find her and give her the box, what then?"

"I will bring you back. *But!* If you do not pass her the box, you may wish that I had not. Now, prepare yourself!"

Kyna and Cyrus departed Banff around three in the afternoon, following the highway north while keeping their eyes peeled for the turnoff to Vancouver. They raced the setting sun all the way and it was well after dark when they arrived at their hotel. Most of the downtown area had already closed for the night and they were forced to settle for cold corned beef sandwiches and warm diet sodas at a murky, wood-paneled pub in the basement of the hotel. Most of the other patrons were too busy sloshing down room-temperature stout and playing darts or billiards to pay much attention to a pair of weary American tourists, but later, when Kyna got up to go to the ladies' room, Cyrus caught one or two of the solitary drinkers giving her veiled but approving looks. Cyrus downed a second diet soda and then led Kyna up to the room.

While he was busy surfing through the TV channels, Kyna went into the bathroom, took off all of her clothes and stood at the sink brushing her teeth while she waited for the tub to fill. She casually glanced up at the mirror and her heart almost stopped. The face staring back from the glass belonged to some horrible-looking old hag with a face that was a mass of wrinkles, a head full of dried-out, hennaed hair, bags under her eyes and loose flaps of skin dangling down from her chin like the neck of a turkey.

Slamming her eyes shut, Kyna swayed drunkenly as she slowly reached out with one hand to wipe the condensation from the glass—the other hand instinctively went to her throat, grasping the necklace with all of her might.

"Please!" she hissed.

A faint voice spoke to her through her fingers. "What is it you fear?"

She was shaking so badly and she knew she was hallucinating, but she couldn't repress the thing that frightened her most.

"Please, I don't want to get old."

A wave of icy cold passed through her body and when she opened her eyes she almost laughed out loud.

She was back. The face in the mirror *did* look haggard and there *were* dark circles around the eyes, but it was her face and she felt like kissing the glass.

"Thank you!"

Yet even as relief washed over her, she felt a mild tingling sensation in the hand gripping the necklace. The tingling spread like hot soup up her arm and into her chest, filling her body with a strange sensual warmth. She threw back her head and closed her eyes.

"Ahhhhh!"

The warmth spread through her stomach and down between her legs. She sucked in a lungful of air and cupped her free hand over her pubic mound and pressed—hard.

"Oh God!"

She was on fire. Her breasts and nipples were so sensitive that the air in the bathroom felt like sandpaper and her legs quivered like a two-day-old filly's. This time, when she opened her eyes, the bags under her eyes had disappeared and her face was as smooth as fine silk.

It's an illusion, she thought, running her fingers over her lips and down her chin. *Or the lighting. It has to be.*

But the burning in her loins was no illusion. She was as randy as a she-goat. After a quick bath, she dabbed her favorite cologne behind her ears, at the back of her neck and both knees, the bend of both arms, and then worked a few drops into her navel and pubic hair.

You never know!

She slipped into the bedroom and paused to let her eyes adjust to the dark. All of the earlier guilt she had felt over jumping into the sack with a kid while her boyfriend was missing had vanished. She heard Cyrus's soft snoring and thought, *Boy, are you in for a surprise.*

Even as she tiptoed across the room, Kyna knew she wasn't acting like herself. When she saw him stretched out across the bed with his arms thrown across his eyes she wanted to rip his shorts off and devour him. Instead, she reached out to touch him, but the necklace somehow got tangled in her hair. She hastily removed it and put it in the night table drawer.

"Russ?" She shook his arm gently. "Russ?"

Cyrus peeked over the crook of his arm and his eyes almost popped out of his head.

"Surprise!"

They made love like two trains colliding. Cyrus's ardor was real but perfunctory and he wondered if the city's tall buildings and dirty streets were somehow inhibiting him. Even inside the hotel room with the drapes drawn, he could feel the cloying presence of civilization clinging to his body like old sweat. When they were spent, Kyna kissed him warmly.

"That was wonderful," she purred. Then she rolled over.

But Cyrus tossed and turned until the leaden weight of exhaustion forced his eyes shut.

The forest filled him. The fragrance of living sap, bark, leaves, and the sweet scent of pine needles—the grating sounds the wind wrought as the boughs of the trees rubbed sensuously against one another. What incredible sights his eyes beheld: the leaves—tiny acrobats somersaulting over the littered forest floor. Rodents—large and small, furry and sleek—darting this way and that in panic at his approach. And the forest—his world—painted pale gold by an ice-thin sliver of moon.

He was in no hurry, but not without a destination . . . the clearing above the tree line. At last he broke out of the brush and there she was—the silver bitch. She was resting on her haunches on top of a flat boulder, sitting as still as a statue as Cyrus snaked through the maze of rubble. He leapt from round rock to flat rock, vaulted small boulders and large, until he was at her side. She turned then, and allowed him to drink the richness of her musk and the sweetness of her breath. He could taste her last meal on the air between them: muskrat— bloody and lean. His nose touched hers—ice to ice, fire to fire. He whined deep in his chest and she answered with a playful nip to the hair of his cheek.

Suddenly the bitch sprang to her feet and presented him with her backside, swishing her bushy tail provocatively in his face. The scent of her glands poured boiling lava into his lower body and brought his member to painful erection. He mounted her from behind, plunging deep into her molten interior and held on with forelegs and shiny teeth, pumping faster and faster. The she-wolf twisted and fought. She almost but not quite pulled away, turning to bite him gently on the face one second and to bathe his neck with her tongue the next. The heat between them built—churning in his loins until it pushed him to the pinnacle. Cyrus raised his head and howled his joy to the night. And then he . . . woke up.

Kyna was sitting on the side of his bed. She had apparently been shaking him and for some time, and for a moment he wanted to slap her for bringing him back.

''That must have been *some* dream.'' There was laughter in her voice.

Cyrus blinked away sleep enough to realize that she was stroking him under the sheet. Smiling now, he threw off the covers and pulled her roughly to him. They kissed slowly, so as to make sure that everything fit just right, and after only a few seconds her lips parted and admitted the exploratory tip of his tongue. His hand traveled up the swell of her hip, gliding lightly over the waves of her ribs to close over her left breast. Her breath caught in her throat and her nipple burrowed into his palm like a friendly mole. When she straddled his waist, he discovered that she was sopping wet and he slipped into her like a fist into a tight, fur-lined glove.

Careful, he thought, *this one's special.*

Kyna braced her hands on his shoulders and rode him, her breasts swaying in his face like overfilled balloons, the nipples thrusting out enough to put his eyes at risk. This time the heat that built in his belly was real. He wrapped his arms around her and pulled her so tightly against him that their hearts—separated by only two micro-thin slabs of flesh—seemed to flow together into one hot throbbing organ. As his lust built, his body began to expand. His arms bulged until they threatened to crush the life out of her. He couldn't control it. But Kyna was locked in her own frenzy of passion: eyes screwed shut, mouth open—panting. And she seemed unaware that anything had changed.

Just when it seemed certain that his lust was going to destroy her, Cyrus exploded in a flood of white-hot semen and he buried his teeth in her shoulder to stifle the howl.

''What's up, Doc?'' Conrad asked.

He had just entered the penthouse's inner sanctum and noted

the latest sour expression on his employer's face.

Bryan didn't look up from the crystal in the bowl. "I don't know."

Peering over Bryan's shoulder, Conrad saw that the crystal, which before had been as clear as ice, was a pale shade of pink, and as he looked on, it turned bright red.

"Why'd it do that?" the bodyguard asked.

"Kyna's up to something."

"Where is she?"

"Vancouver."

"She in trouble?"

Opening one of his musty books, Bryan began madly turning pages. He found the one he wanted and read, moving his finger and lips in unison.

"Shit! This is no help. Clear means she's okay. Black means she's dead. But what the fuck does red mean?"

Kyna sighed. "I wish I hadn't given up smoking."

"I'm . . . sorry I was so rough," Cyrus whispered in her ear.

She ran the pads of her fingers over the two deep, round indentations in her shoulder.

"Did I break the skin?" he asked.

"No. I'm okay."

She turned on her side, facing him, and draped her arm across his chest. "Tell me about the dream."

Cyrus listened to their hearts beating in syncopation. "I can't remember."

She twirled her fingers in the thick hair of his chest. "Can I tell you something?" When he nodded, she continued. "I liked it." She saw his expression and hurried on. "Don't get me wrong, I don't like being slapped around. I got enough of that when I was a kid. It's just . . . you were so . . . I don't know how to describe it. To make you crazy like that . . . It made me feel so sexy, so incredibly hot."

He ran his fingers through her hair and then gently pulled her head down on his chest. A few minutes later she was snoring.

What am I supposed to tell her? he asked himself. *That I'm turned on by animals? That people should start locking up their collies when I come to visit? That they're going to hang my picture in veterinarians' offices?*

A few minutes later Cyrus followed Kyna into sleep. Exhaustion sealed his eyes and ears so that he neither heard the stealthy tread in the hallway nor saw the shadow that blocked the light under their door.

Chapter Seven

October 21

The next morning Kyna and Cyrus joined a line of about four dozen cars waiting to take the auto ferry across the Strait of Georgia to Nanaimo—a flyspeck on the map of Vancouver Island that provided little more than a landing place for the boats. The weather was gray, the wind cold and damp, and exhaust fumes swirled out of tailpipes like breaths of a herd of mechanical beasts. Cyrus had expected the ferry to be something like the old-fashioned paddle wheelers that plied the Mississippi between St. Louis and New Orleans. Instead, this gigantic multilevel floating garage chugged up to the pier like some prehistoric whale and disgorged a mob of engine-racing, horn-honking fanatics. In addition to cars, the ferry had been constructed to haul both tractor-trailers and vans and contained an onboard restaurant for the locals, and gift shops and promenade decks for the tourists.

On the trip across, they passed through a maze of rocky islets, many of which were no larger than grave markers. Some supported a scattering of skinny fir trees and a few were just large enough to provide platforms for multimillion-dollar homes where the inhabitants used motorized racing boats instead of cars to run out to the 7-Eleven. Halfway across, they encountered a pod of orcas playing tag in the icy-green waters of the strait. Kyna ran back to the car for her camera and snapped two rolls of black-and-white triangular fins so tall that the tops folded over like nightcaps.

"This is wonderful." She laughed. "Aren't they magnificent?"

The orcas endured the finger-pointing and flashbulbs with the bored indifference of priests listening to grade-school confessions and finally submerged just before the ferry touched land. Long before the boat was secure, the passengers were in their cars—engines fired up, motors revving and bloodless, white-knuckled hands gripping padded steering wheels. As soon as the gate went up, the entire complement shot down the ramp and raced up the road to Victoria in a kind of moving traffic jam. Kyna promptly got into the spirit of the chase. Using her driving skills and the Lincoln's bulk and larger engine, she was able to intimidate her smaller Japanese- and English-made competition and made it to the provincial capital in record time.

Victoria was a small slice of Old London transplanted to the New World. The city's winding streets were lined with old chipped-brick buildings and staid English restaurants where you could still get steak and kidney pie with a mug of Guinness stout. The center of commercial activity was the harbor, a beautiful crescent-shaped area overflowing with flower gardens and wrought-iron fences. In the middle of the crescent was the Provincial Capitol Building and the ivy-covered Empress Hotel, and right down in front was the multinational yacht club.

Kyna found a place to park in the public lot down at the water's edge. She unlocked the trunk and held up her raincoat in one hand and her cardigan in the other. "What do you think?"

The skies were clearing, but the air was cool enough to raise goose bumps. Up the hill, the sidewalks and awnings were shedding water from an early shower, but that only made the place more magical when the sun broke through and turned the gardens into fields of glitter.

"The sweater," Cyrus replied.

Kyna's meeting was set for right after lunch so they killed the meantime combing the streets and narrow alleyways in hot pursuit of a sale or a photo opportunity. After a quick bite at a glitzy "American" hamburger place, Cyrus accompanied Kyna to the harbor and waited at the end of the gangplank of a seventy-foot motor yacht while she swapped the stones for cash.

Kyna bounced back down the gangplank with a shopping bag in her left hand to balance the briefcase in her right and they went to the car to make the deposit. The Lincoln's trunk was filling up fast. Cyrus had never asked Kyna how much cash was in there, but from the looks of it, there was enough to keep a body living comfortably for a lot of years.

With the cash locked safely in the rolling vault, Kyna turned to Cyrus. "We still have two hours to kill before we can board the ferry to the States."

"So what now?" he asked.

"Oh, I don't know."

They went back for more shopping.

At four-thirty Cyrus was standing in front of a mirror in one of Victoria's finer haberdasheries, giving a critical eye to a cashmere sports jacket that he knew he could never afford and listening to Kyna's unsolicited opinion. He happened to glance up at the clock on the wall.

"Jesus!" Cyrus turned to the tailor. "What time does the ferry leave?"

The man—a very distinguished older gentleman with a white moustache—looked down his long patrician nose and replied in a voice that left no doubt to anyone within earshot that he thought Cyrus was an idiot, "Why, five o'clock, of course."

They raced down the cobblestone slope to the parking lot. As they approached the Lincoln from one end of the lot, an old man with a burlap bag draped over his shoulder was pushing a rusty shopping cart toward them from the other end.

"Isn't that the old geezer that was hanging around the hotel lobby this morning?" Cyrus panted.

Kyna was fumbling in her bag for the car keys. "I don't know, maybe."

The old man stopped at every car, placed a yellow sheet of paper under the windshield wiper and then started off again. Two cars away from the Lincoln, the shopping cart turned over on a loose cobblestone and pulled the old man down on top of it. The stack of handbills spilled out of the cart and the wind sent them skittering across the lot.

Kyna tossed her latest shopping bag into the Lincoln's trunk and ran over to help. With Cyrus on one side, she managed to get the old man up on his feet and right his cart.

She touched Cyrus's arm and whispered, "Oh, Russ, his things."

Cyrus took a long look at the old man's stained clothing, palsied hands and scab-covered face and decided that the old guy was probably no threat to anyone but himself.

"Okay." He rushed off to collect the circulars.

Kyna had to use both hands to lift the burlap sack into the cart.

"Thank you, lassie," the man said.

"No problem." Kyna smiled but was really watching Cyrus chase after the papers.

"No, no, kindness like yours is all too rare in the world today. Please . . . let me repay you."

He pulled a polished mahogany box about ten inches square out of the burlap sack. The top of the box was covered with strange gold letters and it fastened with a fancy brass swing clasp. He held the box out. "Here!"

"What's this?" Kyna asked, her eyes sparkling with delight.

"A pretty present for a pretty lady."

She accepted the box, startled by its weight and the way her fingers tingled when she touched it. But when she tried to open it, she found the clasp was stiff with age and at first refused to budge. She tried wedging her thumbnail underneath the clasp . . .

"Ow!"

"Hurt yourself?"

The nail had snapped and the sharp edge of the clasp had

sliced into the tender skin of the nail bed. She was busy sucking her thumb and didn't notice the way her blood disappeared almost spongelike into the ancient metal of the clasp.

"No. I'm okay."

She finally managed to slide the hook to the side and lifted the lid. Inside, resting on a form-fitting green velvet pad were four perfectly round white globes about two inches in diameter.

"What are they?" she asked quizzically. "Golf balls?"

Kyna looked up at the old man's face and wished she hadn't. His teeth were black with decay and his right eye was ringed with a hard yellow crust. The good eye was focused on her with an intensity that was disconcerting.

"I don't rightly know what they are, lassie, I found 'em. But I know they're good luck. Just look at 'em. See how they glow. And they're warm too. Feel."

Kyna put a finger on the closest globe, but quickly drew it back. The globe *was* warm, but it gave a little when she touched it and the moment her finger came in contact with it, the necklace had started to burn like a ring of embers.

"Ow!"

As soon as she removed her finger and slammed the lid, the pain went away.

"What's the matter?" The old man took another step closer and the smell of his unwashed body nearly made her nauseous.

"Nothing," she replied, taking a step back. "They are nice, but I can't accept them. They must be worth a lot of money. Just look at the workmanship on the box."

"They are just play pretties, lass. If they was worth anything, why would the owner have tossed 'em in the garbage?"

"No, really . . ."

"Here, darlin', make an old man happy. Keep it. It'll bring you luck, you'll see."

Kyna didn't know how to say no without hurting his feelings. Laughing and shaking her head, she dug a twenty-dollar bill out of her pocket and tried to give it to him.

"No," the old guy insisted. "My reward is seeing your happy face."

Kyna reached out and slipped the bill into the pocket of his stained trench coat. "I will," she whispered, "if you will."

He glanced over her shoulder and saw Cyrus trotting back across the lot with the stack of water-stained handbills. "All right."

Kyna really didn't want the box, but she waited until the old guy was busy thanking Cyrus, then opened the trunk and tossed it into the back next to the spare tire. By the time Cyrus slipped into the front seat, Kyna had the motor idling and was staring at the clock on the dashboard.

"We're never going to make it," she said, and floored the accelerator.

"That old bugger is crazy as a shit-house rat," Cyrus gasped as he held up one of the handbills. The paper was blank.

The Lincoln rolled onto the ferry just as the tender was lowering the gate. As soon as Kyna shut off the engine she grabbed Cyrus's hand and dragged him up to the observation deck, where they sipped hot chocolate and watched out the window as the boat passed through the Strait of Juan de Fuca. Just before the ferry docked at Port Angeles, thick rain clouds rolled down from the Olympic mountains and sapped all the color from the sea, leaving it as gray and lifeless as flawed steel. At the same time the wind brought the aroma of brine and wet earth to mix with the greasy diesel smell from the ferry's engines.

The Lincoln was the last car to disembark. Undaunted, Kyna suggested they drive over to the Pacific coast, then backtrack up the east side of Puget Sound to Seattle. She said the drive was scenic, lots of wild creatures. She said it would be romantic—the rocky coast, the tall trees, the blue ocean.

They got lost and by the time they reached the coast it was dark. All Cyrus got to see of the rugged Washington coast was a blur of midnight-green conifers under a pall of low-hanging clouds. The only wildlife he saw was a fat porcupine that ran in front of their headlights and almost sent them into a ditch. When they pulled up in front of their motel room outside of Seattle, it was after midnight. The Lincoln was covered with mud and they were too exhausted and dirty even to think about food.

"All I want is a hot shower," Kyna said, "a pair of clean underwear and to sleep for a week."

But when Cyrus opened the trunk to dig out their clean clothing he discovered that everything they owned had been worn at least once and then stuffed into two large plastic garbage bags. Soon after checking in, he hauled the garbage bags into the room, upended them in the middle of the floor and began separating the whites from the colors. While he was busy playing maid, Kyna dropped the overnight bags next to the bed and went back to the car for her pillow and the novel she had been reading. When she pulled the pillow out of the trunk, she saw the wooden box and decided to show it to Cyrus—maybe he could figure out what the strange spheres were. Unfortunately, right after she returned to the room they got into one of those arguments that people have when they're tired and have been on the road too long. It started when Cyrus offered to take their laundry down to the Laundromat in the motel's basement so that Kyna could stay in the room and rest. He was trying to be gallant, but Kyna decided his grand gesture was really a veiled criticism of her housekeeping abilities.

She said he was anal retentive.

He said she was being childish.

In the end, they both trooped down to the basement. Kyna crammed her dirty clothes, whites and colors both, into one washing machine; Cyrus shoved his whites into a second and his colors into a third, and they sat on a pair of pink tulip-shaped chairs that were physically close, but emotionally as far apart as the Bosnians and the Serbs while their clothes sloshed round and round.

It was a few minutes before two by the time Kyna got her

hot shower and climbed into bed. Cyrus followed a few minutes later and they lay in the same bed without speaking, their backs to each other but not touching, like the two rails of a railroad track.

The mahogany box was on top of the dresser, forgotten.

He was floating like a cloud—that's what tipped him off that it was another dream. He felt warm and safe and kind of curious, because it was so different from the dreams he had been having lately. There was no mysterious mountain, no ghostly moon, no feeling of freedom. Only a dark tunnel with a light no bigger than a candle flame at the end. And he was moving through the tunnel—not walking—sort of gliding along effortlessly.

Then, just like that, he was standing in a room he had never seen before. In the center of the room was the silhouette of a woman, hovering above the floor with her legs folded up like a Hindu holy man. Cyrus knew it was a woman by the shape of her shadow, for her body was surrounded by a halo of blinding white light from the lone candle on the table behind her. He waited patiently for her to speak, but all he heard was the rushing of the wind coming from the tunnel at his back. Holding out her hand, the woman beckoned him forward. He stood his ground and waited.

The woman beckoned again, and even though Cyrus felt no threat in her gestures, he did receive an overwhelming sense of urgency.

"What do you want?"

His words took the form of bats that flew from his lips up into the dark. Behind him, the whistle of the wind slowly diminished, coming in pulses like wind blowing through the open doors of passing boxcars. The pulses became a babble of voices—high-pitched, repeating a single sound.

"What?"

Finally, the woman's voice seemed to explode inside his head: "Wake up!"

Cyrus opened his eyes.

The motel room was too bright.

At first he thought that he had forgotten to turn off the lights, and he started to get out of bed. But then he realized that the light wasn't coming from the lamps. It was that strange greenish night vision that he had been experiencing the last few days.

So what brought it on? he asked himself. And why did the woman in the dream want him to wake up?

He didn't move a muscle.

He didn't need to.

He could feel each and every molecule in the room as if he were attached to it by some kind of giant invisible web. Kyna was still asleep—he could feel the even beating of her heart and hear the soft whisper of her breath rushing in and out of her mouth. He could even hear the scurrying sound of cock-roaches under the bathroom sink.

But there was something else too.

A delicate puff of air brushed his face. Something was mov-ing in the room. Something that from its smell was so vile and unnatural that it made the hairs on the back of his neck stand up as stiff as the bristles in a toothbrush.

Cyrus forced himself to remain calm—any impetuous move might provoke an attack. He let his eyes roam the room. Everything appeared normal. He could see each piece of fur-niture, each shadowy nook with such absolute clarity—and yet he was missing it.

"Damn!" His exclamation of frustration was little more than a whisper. "Where the fu—"

A shadow flickered across the bathroom mirror.

Cyrus turned his head ever so slightly.

The shadow was no longer there.

Whatever it was, it cast an awfully big shadow. Yet it didn't seem to make very much noise.

The bed moved!

Not a lot, just enough to set Cyrus's heart racing. He glanced over at Kyna and for once was thankful that she slept like a corpse. When the bed shook the second time, he eased

112

his hand over her mouth and waited patiently until she opened her eyes. The moment Cyrus saw the expression on her face, he knew two things: a) she was still mad at him. And b) she had completely misunderstood why his hand was over her mouth.

Her eyes narrowed into slits and she began to struggle.

"Shush!" he hissed.

She tried to bite him and he pressed down until her eyes crossed. Then he leaned down and put his lips right next to her ear and whispered, "Something's in the room."

Her eyes popped open wide.

"Crawl under the covers and don't come out until I tell you—understand?"

Clearly terrified, Kyna kept her mouth shut and replied with an abbreviated nod.

The girl's got guts! You gotta give her that.

He waited until she was safely underneath the quilt, then crouched on the bed and scanned the room.

The bed bucked—once—like something really big had crawled under the mattress and was now trying to stand up. Kyna let out a muted squeal and he reached over and patted her leg through the covers.

"Shush!" he whispered. "It's okay."

He could hear them now—a sneaky, creepy rasping as they scooted over the carpet. It sounded like the things were all around him—over near the bathroom, under the bed—but even with his super-duper night vision he couldn't see a fucking thing and he began to panic.

Then the pain hit and his body felt like it was being crushed by a giant hand. Wave after wave of muscle spasms rolled down his neck, into his back and all the way down to the soles of his feet. In that eternity of agony Cyrus couldn't move—couldn't talk—couldn't breathe. He clenched his teeth until they threatened to crack and closed his eyes until, in a moment, the spasms began to subside. As the pain passed, his senses were assailed from a new direction—an ancient stench that evoked one of the most terrifying memories from his childhood: the visit he'd made with his mother to the reptile house at the Memphis Zoo.

"Shit!" he whispered. "Snakes!"

As a child he had been repelled and yet fascinated by the way the place had smelled—hot and rank—and at the way the reptiles had slithered over and around each other, their oily black tongues darting in and out of tiny slit mouths. He remembered that the snakes' skins had looked wet and slimy and that their eyes had been black with a depth that had no end.

Then his mother had said, "Oh look, Russ! They're going to feed one." And the keeper had dumped a small gray mouse into the sidewinder's cage.

The mouse had just sat there twitching its whiskers as the snake slithered across the cage. It had been over quickly after that. The snake's strike was faster than an eight-year-old's eyes could follow. The mouse leapt straight up into the air, landed on its side and lay there—panting—as the snake slowly swallowed it. The last things Cyrus remembered seeing were the rodent's tiny round eyes. They seemed to be staring right at him—pleading.

The bed bounced hard enough to make the springs squeak and Cyrus experienced a grinding explosion of pain in his hands and arms. It was no longer possible for him to ignore the changes that were taking place in his body. He brought his right hand up and was not surprised to see the skin had turned almost black and that fine brown hairs were sprouting on the back. Nor was he much amazed by the claws popping out of the tips of his fingers. Other, more subtle changes were taking place as well. In addition to the night vision and the enhanced sense of smell, his hearing had become so sensitive that he could almost hear the moonbeams as they passed through the windowpanes and crashed into the floor. And even less apparent, but more important, his fear of the unseen creatures was slowly being replaced by a mindless red tide of rage. When his stack of clean clothing in the corner toppled over,

114

the dam of human restraint that was holding back the tide broke.

"Fuck this!"

He sprang off the bed like he had been shot out of a catapult, landing in the center of the room and dropping down on all fours. The second he hit the carpet, a creature slithered out from behind the chair, raised up on its tail and hissed. He had been partly right. The creature was reptilian—it was definitely reptilian. It had a lizard's wide diapsid skull and a long tapered snout full of teeth that any self-respecting shark would have killed for. It was the thing's lower body that resembled a snake, long and slender, covered with chitinous ambulating scutes that moved it over the carpet with surprising agility. Just to make things more confusing, up front it had a pair of stubby arms sticking out of its chest with three-fingered hands tipped with wicked-looking hooked claws.

Cyrus should have been terrified, but he was amazed. "What the fuck are you supposed to be?"

The creature flicked its tongue and hissed like a faulty tire valve.

His eyes widened. *Wow! Nice set of fangs.*

The thing didn't seem to see Cyrus. It had stopped in the middle of the floor, curled its tail around its body and was rotating its thick neck slowly from side to side as if searching for him. It hissed again, and this time it received an answering hiss from the creature under the bed.

The snazard—for that was what Cyrus had unconsciously christened the thing—uncoiled and started crawling toward the bed. The instant Cyrus moved to block it, the thing turned on him, baring its fangs and clawing the air in front of Cyrus's face.

Instinctively, Cyrus fell into an offensive posture: one leg in front of the other, knees flexed, the remaining strips of his briefs tightly wedged up between the cheeks of his buttocks. He took a gliding step and kicked the thing right square in the snout . . . and got raked across the chest by the creature's claws for his trouble.

115

Cyrus began retreating toward the bathroom, hoping to draw the reptile with him.

That was one of my best moves, he grumbled to himself. *You should be flat on your ass.*

The creature followed him cautiously, slithering almost silently over the cheap carpet and constantly testing the air with its tongue. Cyrus's chest was relatively free of hair and was leaking blood from four deep gashes. He wondered if the creature was attracted by the smell.

The snazard hissed again and Cyrus waved a hand in front of his face. "Phew!"

Cyrus was so involved with the reptile in front of him that he momentarily forgot about the one under the bed and glanced around only when he heard Kyna squeal.

The second creature had started dragging itself up the footboard of the bed.

The change went into high gear. Cyrus's face felt as if it were suddenly being ripped apart. He grabbed his head and tried to hold it together with his hands as his lower jaw shifted down and out to create a platform for dozens of razor-sharp teeth. His shoulders thickened and spread, his body stretched and expanded as if his skeleton were made of rubber.

Then, it was the creature's turn to give ground . . . only it didn't move fast enough. Cyrus vaulted onto the snazard's back and dug his claws into the creature's eyes. The reptile let out a massive blast of foul-smelling air and started to sway like a runaway fire hose. Cyrus let go, hit the ground, rolled and sprang again all in one motion—this time landing on the thing's chest. He tried to sink his teeth into its throat, but the creature's armorlike scales were too tough for even Cyrus's needle-sharp fangs.

"Russ! Is that you?"

At the sound of Kyna's voice, the reptile went crazy, slashing at Cyrus's back and shoulders with its claws. But Cyrus's body was protected by a thick coat of silky fur, and out of frustration the creature tried to spit venom in his eyes.

"Russ?" The unmistakable sound of panic was creeping

into Kyna's voice, which came from under the blanket she had pulled over her head.

One look at the second monster and Cyrus knew he didn't have time to play around. The reptile was already up over the foot of the bed and was sniffing like a bloodhound at Kyna's blanket-covered feet. He dodged the first reptile's venom, released his hold, dropped to the floor and rolled to the bed. Behind him, the first snazard kept right on hissing like a broken radiator and blindly waving its arms in the air.

He sprang to his feet and wrapped one arm around contestant number two's snout and yanked like he was cranking a lawn mower. The snazard's neck snapped with a crack like lake ice breaking and it went limp.

Since Kyna was no longer in immediate danger, Cyrus figured he could afford to take a second, catch his breath and try to find a weak spot in the remaining creature. From three feet away, he saw an indentation about the size of his thumb at the top of the reptile's spine. He moved a step closer for a better look. The scales at the base of the skull didn't appear to be as thick and the ridge of protective bone looked more supple.

What the hell, Cyrus thought.

He slammed the heel of his hand right at the apex of the thing's spine and its head imploded like a soft-boiled egg. With the last creature's demise, Cyrus's anger drained away like the afterbirth of a nightmare. He felt empty. The killing rage was like the memory of a toothache that had happened to someone else. When he looked up, he discovered that he was standing in front of the mirror over the alcove washbasin and he was numbed by what he saw staring back at him.

"Russ? Can I come out now?"

Good God! he thought, *Kyna is going to freak.*

He had to keep her from seeing him, but he didn't know if he could form words.

"Kyna, stay there."

It came out sounding like, "Ina a air," but she stayed put.

Great, he thought, *on top of everything else, I sound like*

Gary L. Holleman

Gilligan from the frigging Island of Dr. Moreau.

Cyrus tiptoed into the bathroom and managed to shut the door before the pain of reversion crumpled his knees. He slid down into the corner with his back against the sink and crammed his hands into his mouth to stifle the screams as his muscles and tendons reformed. When the pain had passed, he slowly climbed to his feet and faced the mirror.

He was back to normal—more or less. Across his chest were three fading red scratches—all that remained of the massive gashes the reptile's claws had left in his skin.

"Oh, God . . . what's happening to me?"

But Kyna was waiting so he shelved his angst and went back into the bedroom to make sure she was okay.

Without his night vision he could no longer see the reptiles and that made him very uncomfortable. Even without a supernose he could still smell them, but that didn't prevent his bare foot from coming down in a cooling puddle of scales, teeth and slime.

"Ugh!" He shivered. "Gross." He wiped his foot on the carpet and said, "Kyna, you can come out now."

She brought the blanket down as far as the bridge of her nose. "What happened? Where are those men you were fighting with?"

"Take a look." Cyrus pointed to the wet spots on the carpet.

"I don't get it. What is that stuff?"

"Let me ask you a question. Have you pissed anybody off lately?"

The Dark Man sat Indian fashion on his blanket on the floor of the cabin, staring sightlessly down into the shallow clay saucer. Inside the saucer, on an island of two-tone sand surrounded by clear water, stood the tiny wax doll with the strands of autumn-red hair glued to its misshapen head. The thin man with the goatee sat in a frayed wicker rocking chair at his master's side.

After what seemed like hours, the Dark Man sucked in a

lungful of air and blinked several times like a myopic bat and looked around.

"They were successful?" the goateed man asked.

The Dark Man rose, stretched and shook his head. "Two were damaged before they hatched and the two that did emerge were no match for the loup-garou."

"You do not sound surprised."

"The Guédé were merely a test. If they had been successful, that would have been incredibly good luck. But I needed to know how powerful the man has become."

"And?"

"He is still confused. I do not believe he has accepted the reality of what he has become and it weakens him."

"Then why do you not use all your powers to destroy them before the man's powers grow?"

The Dark Man's eyes bored into his apprentice. "That would not have been necessary if that hairless imbecile had not infected the white man with his bite. Now, at such a distance, it will be difficult to marshal the necessary powers. And as long as the man lives, I cannot reach the woman. We may have to face them directly."

"You mean in person? How will we know where they are?"

"I have an idea."

After giving his assistant a list of ingredients to gather from the swamp around the cabin, the Dark Man took a seat in the chair and slowly rocked back and forth. He was perturbed, but he dared not let the goateed man see it. During his trance, as his mind had struggled to maintain contact with the ancient reptiles, he had felt the presence of others around him in the ether. His surprise had been such that at the critical moment in the battle with the white man he had been distracted.

The Dark Man got up and went to the window. His skinny assistant was down on his knees beside a log. Around him, the moonlight transformed the bog into a surreal canvas of black mud and black trees, hung with stringy black mosses. Giant spiderwebs of spun moonbeams draped like lace curtains above quicksilver pools of mosquito-infested water. The night throbbed with the croaking of frogs and echoed with the whisper of predatory wings. It was a bad night to be a fly or a furry rodent.

Who could it have been? the Dark Man wondered. Surely not that goateed idiot digging like a dog with his bare hands in the mushy ground. No, one entity had been much too strong, its aura alive with ebony. It had been cautious, slipping in and out of the psychic plane like one of those little swamp mice.

And that's what was so disturbing. The fact that the entity had been so circumspect, so painfully careful, indicated that it was aware of the power it faced. And yet it chose to challenge him anyway—to challenge *him!*

Turning from the window, the Dark Man began to pace slowly around his self-made chamber of horrors.

The second entity had been even more puzzling. Its power had been weak and seemed to come from far away. And yet it hovered around the redheaded woman like a noxious vapor.

Why all the interest in this damned woman? the Dark Man fumed.

"To hell with it," he muttered.

Neither entity could do him any real harm. They were just flies in the ointment—two more tiny irritants in a world suddenly full of tiny irritants.

He returned to the rocking chair and settled his lanky frame onto the wicker. His inflamed joints screamed in protest, but he ignored them the way he ignored all of the little aches and pains he had suffered since the talisman had been stolen. For the first time in decades he felt his age, and he cursed his son as he had cursed him every day since his betrayal. Time had become a cancer that was rapidly ravaging his body.

He glanced up at the bottles and jars lining the shelves on the walls. All those hearts. All those souls that had died in torment.

All Hallows' Eve was just over a week away. Time was running out.

Chapter Eight

October 22

"I'm not cleaning up that mess," Kyna said.

By morning, all that remained of the snazards were a couple of greenish spots that smelled like the East River in July. Every time Kyna looked at the carpet, she turned a little green herself. They had spent the rest of the night in the bathroom—Cyrus on the floor in the corner and Kyna in the tub on a nest of blankets.

"Okay, okay!" Cyrus said as he opened the door. "Don't get your panty hose in a twist." He didn't have the stomach to clean the mess up either.

He went down the hall, grabbed the first woman he came across who was wearing an apron—an elderly Spanish lady in sensible shoes—and gave her thirty dollars to clean the carpet. After slipping the money into her pocket, the woman stared at the mass of buzzing flies crawling on the green goo and gave him a look.

"Uh, my girlfriend had some bad pea soup."

"Señorita very sick, yes?"

Kyna had deliveries scheduled for the next two days so they couldn't leave Seattle, but after the midnight encounter with the lizard people Cyrus insisted they move to another motel. While they were throwing their things in the suitcases, he came across the mahogany box.

"What's this?"

Kyna told him about the old man.

Cyrus raised the lid. "Jesus!"

The remains of four eggs were scattered across the velvet pad. Two were just empty shells, their leathery skins split down the middle, but the remaining pair had shattered and their contents had splattered all over the inside of the box.

"Must have happened when I tossed it in the trunk." Kyna shrugged.

"I don't get it," Cyrus said. "Why would he do it?"

"Maybe he didn't know what they were," she replied, staring at the dried embryos. "Hell, I don't even know what they were."

Cyrus glanced at her face—still pale as paste from the ordeal—and said, "Maybe. But what was he doing hanging around the hotel yesterday morning?"

"You can't be sure it was the same old man," Kyna insisted. "He was so covered with grunge it was hard to be sure he was even human."

That gave Cyrus pause.

Kyna's first appointment was before lunch, which left them little time for discussion, and in a way Cyrus was glad. Kyna swore that she didn't know why all these bizarre things were happening to them and he was afraid to push it. Why? He didn't have any idea what to do about them anyway, and being hopelessly male he wasn't about to admit it. But mainly he needed time to come to grips with his own little secret before they started baring their souls. Besides, if he had turned into what he was afraid he'd turned into, how was he supposed to tell Kyna that they were going to have to forgo plans for any future moonlight strolls?

Before leaving the motel, Cyrus strapped on the automatic. He had made a vow never to take the gun off again except to shower, and *maybe* when he and Kyna were making love. To vary his Sam Spade disguise he put on a dark green turtleneck under the holster and a denim jacket over it. Kyna looked like the Avon lady: an abstract print dress over a smocked torso, dark hose, heels and the briefcase. This time her meet was on the patio of one of Seattle's harbor-side nouveau-yuppie salad-

and-granola houses, leaving Cyrus to wonder once again what all the cloak and dagger was about.

"Don't you diamond types ever meet in a, you know, a jewelry store? Or is that too bourgeois?"

Kyna shook her head. "Not if I can help it. Surest way to get ripped off is to go hanging around jewelry stores carrying a briefcase."

She drove around until she found a parking spot under the interstate. Then, after a short walk, Cyrus took up a position next to a creosote dock piling where he could keep an eye on the swap. The gemologist du jour was a beefy young man wearing a bow tie and a pair of glasses with lenses that looked like they came out of the Hubble telescope. After the exchange, Kyna made her deposit in the Lincoln's trunk and they had lunch at a bagel place on the other side of the expressway. Later, they took a stroll through the shops and exhibits along the harbor to talk. It was time for Cyrus to find out what was going on. If for no other reason than to protect Kyna.

"What's going on, Kyna?"

"I'm as freaked by all this as you are." She stopped to peer in the window of a sourdough bakery. "It was all I could do to stop shaking long enough to make the exchange."

Cyrus stopped and turned in a circle, staring at all the faux nautical shops and stores as if they had suddenly appeared out of thin air. Just past the end of the pier, a Russian tanker cut through the gray-black water of Elliott Bay as silently as the grim reaper's scythe. Sea gulls, their white feathers ruffling like kittens' fur in the breeze, sat atop the pilings as if placed there by the Seattle Board of Tourism. Aside from the gaily painted restaurants and bars, the street was lined with memento mills and stores hawking trendy brass trinkets and Korean-made yachting caps.

It was too much. Too much junk, too many smells, too much color. All that sunlight without the softening effect of clouds created shadows in the alleys and overhangs that were sharp enough to cut flesh. The sky was so blue that it hurt

Cyrus's eyes. He couldn't help wondering why the world was suddenly so vivid. So vibrant. He should have been frightened by all that was going on. Or at the very least depressed. Yet he felt disgustingly chipper and it irritated him.

"What do you think's going on?" Kyna asked.

"I feel like someone or something is breathing down our necks. I can almost smell them."

"What an odd thing to say."

"Yeah, well . . ."

"Like who?"

"Babe, if I knew that, I'd know I wasn't just being paranoid. That's the worst part. Wondering if I'm crazy or if stuff like this happens out West every day. I keep thinking the government or the chamber of commerce or . . . I don't know, maybe the CIA is keeping it a secret from the rest of the world. It's like somebody, some . . . power is pissed at us. But I've never been out this way before, and as far as I know, I haven't done anything to get anybody mad enough to send these things after us."

"Things? What things?"

"The things last night. That wolf."

"The wolf? Come on! Now you *are* being paranoid. That was just bad luck."

"Maybe. But the other night too. Outside the pavilion in Calgary."

"Those muggers? You think somebody sent them?"

"Somebody sent something." Cyrus took a deep breath and let it out a little at a time. "Kyna, I didn't exactly tell you everything that happened after I sent you back to call the cops."

He spent the next ten minutes giving her the edited version of his confrontation with the zombie. Her expression started out somewhere between curiosity and concern, but quickly changed to skepticism when he got to the part about the dead man with his moldy suit and unnatural strength. It took fifteen minutes of fast talking, but by the time he finished, Kyna wasn't laughing anymore.

"I don't know what to say, Russ. I mean, it's all too fantastic. How did you ever get away from something like that?"

She would have to ask that, he thought.

"Mostly luck. Listen," he added quickly to change the subject, "maybe we should think about cutting the trip short."

"No way." Kyna laughed bitterly. "My boss would kill me."

"Oh, come on. No job is worth all this."

"No, Russ. You don't understand."

"So explain it to me."

Kyna made a sharp turn onto one of the piers that jutted out between the rows of stores. At the far rail, she rested her chin on her folded arms and fell into the depths of some private memory that was so painful she had to approach it cautiously—the way one would approach a loaded gun. Cyrus stood nearby in the shadow of a totem pole that looked to have been carved by the dreaded generic Indian tribe. As he waited for Kyna to find her way back, he glanced at the soda cans, milk cartons, seaweed and dead fish floating on top of the water and wondered if Indians had ever been as free with their garbage.

When Kyna began to speak, her words came out in a rush, like water too long held in check by a dam. She opened the floodgates.

"What you don't understand is that my father is in a nursing home and my younger sister is in college in Virginia. If I go home, I'll lose my job and I don't know what we'd do."

She was sobbing and trying to blot her nose with her sleeve. Cyrus put his arm around her shoulders.

Okay, he thought. *So what else can possibly go wrong?*

On the way to their new motel Kyna suddenly whipped into the parking lot of a 7-Eleven and slammed on the brakes.

"I'm damned tired of being scared and depressed," she declared. "And I'm double damned tired of looking at you in nothing but jeans."

Cyrus glanced down at his clothing. "I . . . I . . ."

"Well, *I* only know one cure for what ails me."

They spent the remainder of the afternoon touring the city and hitting the shopping malls.

"What are your sizes?" she asked as they walked into a huge mall on the outskirts of Bellevue.

"We don't have to do this now."

Kyna took his hand and led him into the first men's store they came to. "Don't give me a load of crap, Russ. Just tell me your sizes."

Glancing at the salesman looking on with amusement, Cyrus replied, "Sixteen and a half, thirty-five shirt. Thirty, twenty-eight slacks."

"Shoe size? Jacket?"

"I don't need—"

She gave him a look.

"Nine and a half. Forty-four regular."

"Fine. Now go to the bookstore or the food court and wait for me."

Two hours later, Kyna found him sitting at a table in the food court, sipping a diet soda and looking as if he had just lost his dog. After depositing her shopping bags in the empty chairs, she unwrapped and held up the things she had bought: a crewneck sweater with a brown-and-beige totemic pattern and three pairs of pleated linen slacks—black, blue and a light brown and black weave. Then from another bag: a long-sleeve Navajo shirt; a green, brown and black mock-turtleneck Colombian-print pullover; two more oxford dress shirts; a new tie and a pair of brown Italian penny loafers.

Cyrus opened the shoe box and picked up one of the shoes. "I'll never be able to pay you back for all this."

"Don't worry about it. I'm putting in an expense voucher for everything. Now shut up and look at these." She held out a Seattle Seahawks baseball cap in one hand and a box with a new pair of Nike running shoes in the other. "The cap's mine," Kyna said. "But those smelly old running shoes of yours had to go. I've seen cheap retreads with more rubber on the bottom."

They repacked everything, ordered pizza from one of the food court vendors, and then Kyna said she wanted to take a nap and asked Cyrus to drive her back to the hotel.

"Don't be mad, Russ. I just need some time to myself. Why don't you take in a ball game or something? I'll be okay in a couple of hours."

"I'm not crazy about leaving you alone," he replied.

"I'll be fine. I'll put a chair in front of the door."

As soon as they returned to the room, Cyrus unzipped the top inside compartment of his suitcase and extracted a small leather gun case.

"Here." He held out a nickel-plated automatic. "It's a three-eighty. Small, but it'll stop anything that can be stopped with a bullet."

A few minutes later Cyrus strolled up to the front desk with his running clothes tucked under his arm and asked directions to the nearest park or ball field. He followed the clerk's hand-drawn map to Jefferson Park Golf Course near the Beacon Hill reservoir. It was nearly five-thirty when he arrived. To the west, the bottom half of a blood-red sun was sandwiched between masses of charcoal-gray clouds and the steel-gray ocean, and the wind whistling in the car window was as cold and clammy as a three-day-old corpse. He stopped at the end of the parking lot and by the time he had changed into his running outfit the last car was just heading out to the nineteenth hole. He got out to look around and get his bearings. The wind made him decide to keep his warm-up jacket on, and after everything that had happened, he decided to keep the shoulder holster on too.

"This has got to be a first."

After locking the Lincoln, he took a few moments to stretch his legs, squatting and then—one at a time—pulling his feet up tight into his buttocks. When he was good and loose, Cyrus started around the reservoir, taking his time and letting the sweat come when it was good and ready. The gun slowed him a bit. He had to keep his left elbow tucked in to protect his ribs, but after one lap—about six tenths of a mile—he was used to it and took off around the golf course.

On the far side of the links, he slowed to a trot to admire the way the setting sun turned the modern glass-and-steel skyscrapers that surrounded the course into pillars of fire. He made four more laps around the course and then glanced at his watch; it was six forty-five and the fairways were completely deserted. He paused beside a stand of trees at the edge of a small water hazard to catch his breath. A red-breasted robin up in the branches of the nearest tree took time away from her busy schedule to sing a welcome: "Cheer-up, cheerily, cheer-up, cheerily."

Giving the little bird a salute, Cyrus said, "Thanks for the advice."

After a quick look around, he stepped back into the shadows of the trees. It was cold. He shook his arms and shoulders and rolled his head around his neck, whispering as he did so to his little feathered friend, "Okay. Lets see if I can do this when something isn't trying to have me for lunch."

First Cyrus tried to clear his mind—not an easy task when you're freezing to death and a bird is chirping in your ear. Then he thought about Calgary and tried to remember what had been going through his head when the zombie started choking him. He had no trouble recalling the touch of the creature's cold dead fingers or its soulless red eyes. He even remembered being scared, but that's all it was—a memory. He wanted to re-create the same mind-numbing terror and it just wouldn't come.

Then he tried to recollect every detail of the attack in the motel room—the snazards' foul stench and the slimy feel of their skin. But after five minutes of intense concentration, all he got was a headache.

"Hard to rerun being scared."

The robin had no opinion.

Things weren't working out the way he'd hoped so he decided to try a new tack.

After undressing and stacking his clothing in a neat pile, Cyrus took a seat at the base of the robin's tree and made himself as comfortable as possible on the damp grass. He leaned back against the tree and tried to picture that ghostly, beautiful mountain and the silver bitch.

The robin peered down from her perch, incensed that some crazy, naked human was apparently taking a nap on her doorstep. She hopped to a lower limb and watched the man's odd, angular face relax. In a moment he smiled dreamily and whispered two words: "The moon!"

However, Cyrus wasn't really asleep. If anything, he was more aware than he'd ever been in his life. Since his encounter with the wolf in the desert, a new set of glands had developed at the top of his adrenal gland. These new glands—genetic precursors from a race of humanoid beings that had succumbed to the cataclysmic environmental upheavals of the first ice age—were flooding his system with a hormone that was both ancient and magical. The hormone accelerated his heart and pumped new blood and sinew into his arms and legs. It caused new "super" skin cells to form at a rate of millions per second and it altered his nervous system, sharpening his senses while increasing his tolerance for pain.

He felt the changes—both external and internal—but he didn't fight or try to control them. Before he knew it, his head was in the trees and he was standing eyeball to eyeball with his little red-bellied friend.

Startled by the sudden appearance of such a hairy monster, the robin hopped to the end of the branch and took flight without so much as a by-your-leave.

Don't go away mad, Cyrus thought.

His upward growth stopped almost as fast as it started, but his chest and shoulders continued to expand, filling out like oil spreading across the surface of a pond. He found that when he relaxed, the transformation wasn't nearly as bad—no worse than falling down a short flight of steps. True, his bones popped like bundles of dry twigs and his skin felt like it was two sizes too small and his jaw felt as if he had swallowed a pound of tenpenny nails. But it was merely uncomfortable, not painful.

Gary L. Holleman

As usual, the aftermath of the change was wonderful. The dusk had been beaten back by the strange spectral glow of his night vision. He could see both the striations and veins in the leaves that fluttered around his head and the tiny red berries on a holly bush on the far side of the golf course. He was standing upright on two legs, but would have been just as happy down on four. His hands still resembled hands, with five distinct fingers, but they were thick and he had developed heavy pads like hard calluses on his palms. His feet were both thinner and stronger than his hands. He stretched out a foreleg, flexed, and claws slid out—shiny and sharp—like they were controlled by hydraulic pistons.

Christ, he thought with no small amount of pride, *I could hurt myself with these things.*

The fur that covered Cyrus's body was the same color as his hair, but much thicker and as soft as down. The fur also kept him warm in the wind and didn't itch the way he had expected it would. Curious as to what his face looked like, he dropped down on all fours and crept to the edge of the water hazard. It was late, so he wasn't that worried about being seen. Besides, he figured that if anyone did see him, they would probably think he was a stray German shepherd.

The face in the greenish water had long, pointed ears topped with tufts of white hair, a long tapered snout and a round, black nose. Cyrus opened his mouth.

Wow—he whistled silently to himself—*what a set of choppers.*

The rear teeth—the ones that in humans were normally flat and used for grinding—were conical and slanted toward the back of his throat like the teeth of a shark. The teeth in front were as round and sharp as ice picks. And of course there were the fangs: four ivory-yellow daggers, each about four inches long.

Thirsty, Cyrus sniffed the water and instantly wished he hadn't. His brain was flooded with a collage of olfactory images: urine from a female French poodle, the oily-electrical smell of golf carts, decomposing leaves and grass, old beer cans and a Heinz-57 blend of dog shit. The remaining pictures flashed across his mind like strobe images on the walls of an LA discotheque.

He sneezed the aromavisions away.

A few yards down the asphalt-paved golf-cart track, the bushes parted and an old man poked his head out. From the looks of the geezer's clothing, he must have crawled all the way from New England on his hands and knees. Cyrus aimed his nose radar at the old man and discovered that the guy was either a wino or he used muscatel as an after-shave.

The man saw Cyrus and grinned. "Nice doggie."

Deep in the most primitive part of Cyrus's brain, something dark and incredibly savage stirred. Saliva flooded his mouth and his eyes zeroed in on the pulsating vein that ran down the side of the old derelict's neck. Underneath that week-old stubble, below the accumulated dirt, sweat and vomit, Cyrus smelled rich, red meat and hot blood. The claws on his hands and feet silently eased out of their fleshy sheaths.

I didn't do that, Cyrus's mind protested.

He experienced a sinking sensation in the pit of his stomach akin to stepping on the brake of a speeding car and having the pedal go flat to the floor. He clamped his jaws tightly together, but a growl that started as a burning ball of blood-lust down deep in his gut rose through his chest and escaped past his fangs.

The old man's face fell.

"Aw, come on now. Don't be like that." He patted the patch of grass at his knee. "Here, boy."

The inside of Cyrus's head was a kaleidoscope of insane urges and half-formed thoughts, cravings on a nonverbal level that he felt but didn't understand: *Cull the herd! He's old and sick—take him!*

Cyrus had no way of knowing that his conscious mind was fighting it out with the wolf's primitive id.

"Come on, puppy. Don't be afraid of old Ben."

The old man began crawling toward Cyrus, the odor of tenderloin rolling before him like a perfumed mist.

* * *

"What's the matter with you?" Kyna asked. "You look like you saw a ghost."

Cyrus had just returned from his run. His face was drawn and his eyes were sunk so far back in his head that he could easily be mistaken for a Somali refugee. "I'm okay. Are you feeling any better?"

"Come on, Russ. Don't jerk me around."

"It's nothing. I almost had a wreck in the car, is all. On top of everything else that's happened . . . I guess it shook me up a little."

She gave him a skeptical look but didn't push it. "Fine. Can we go to bed? I made some calls and moved the rest of the deliveries to tomorrow night so we can sleep late in the morning and leave for San Francisco the next day."

"How's that going to sit with your boss?"

"Screw him."

Cyrus nodded and went into the bathroom. He slipped out of the jacket and holster and then removed the sweatshirt and shook the grass and dried leaves from the inside. He glanced at his gaunt features in the mirror and shook his head.

"Shit!"

October 23

Kyna and Cyrus left the motel at five after six the next evening. They had spent a quiet day around the hotel's indoor pool and were hoping to make the last two deliveries and get out of Seattle without further incident. They met the first customer at a small deli across from the Kingdome, where Kyna handed over the packets of gemstones while Cyrus munched on a tuna bagel. For the last delivery, they drove back to the harbor and rode an elevator to the penthouse of a high-rise overlooking the yacht club.

"Stick close," Kyna whispered as she rang the doorbell. "This guy's a creep."

On the surface, the man who opened the door seemed okay.

He greeted Kyna warmly and he dressed well. But of late Cyrus's senses had become attuned to the obscure traits in people. The usual external characteristics a bodyguard had to contend with: facial expressions, hairstyles, a favorite cologne, even certain mannerisms and ways of speaking, had always been a snap for him. Now other things, things like moods and nervous habits—things which before the change he probably would have passed off as bad vibes—these things now registered on his subconscious much like a struggling fish registers on a shark's lateral-line system. When Cyrus shook their host's hand, he felt a subtle change in the man's pulse and noted the tightening around his eyes. Underneath the man's welcoming smile, Cyrus could almost taste the nervous sweat that coated his skin like old cooking grease on the walls of a Bronx tenement.

Taken together, these involuntary reactions told Cyrus that their host wasn't quite as happy about him being there as he would have them believe. No big deal. The part that bothered Cyrus was that he was doing his best to hide it from them under a veneer of phony Mediterranean charm.

The man made a big show of leading Cyrus to the balcony and offering him the use of the refreshment cart. Yet his eyes never left Kyna and the way he kept looking at her—like she was spread-eagled, naked and bound on a bed—only added to Cyrus's unease. And for the umpteenth time, Cyrus found himself wondering about Kyna's clientele.

To keep from saying or doing anything that might embarrass Kyna, Cyrus roamed the balcony and pretended to watch the lights of the ferries and freighters as they moved about over the velvety-black water of the harbor. He had been leaning on the rail for about fifteen minutes when his ears picked up the change in Kyna's voice. He tuned in.

"This isn't the agreed amount, Mr. Dessotti."

The man's reply was as slick as olive oil on iceberg lettuce. "*Ms.* Rand, this merchandise is—how shall I put it?—questionable at best. Until I see how it moves, how can I possibly make a fair determination of its value?"

"That's between you and my boss. My orders are to make the delivery and pick up the prearranged payment. Otherwise the stones stay with me."

Cyrus strolled with feigned indifference to the sliding glass door. He kept his eyes on the water and his back to the door, but he kept his ears trained on the conversation. The smell of tension in the air was as strong as the odor of burning leaves.

"Look, Ms. Rand . . . Kyna, why not just leave the shipment with me. After I make the sale, I'll send London the payment."

"No can do," Kyna replied tersely.

Cyrus turned around, stretched and strolled back into the living room. He smiled and nodded to Dessotti as he walked to the rolling bar cart and took a can of diet soda from the ice bucket. When he looked up, Dessotti was staring at him.

"Your friend seems a little nervous," Dessotti said.

Kyna glanced at Cyrus and gave him a reassuring smile. "Not nervous. Just, shall we say, cautious. Look," she said, getting to her feet. "I'll be leaving in the morning. You call London and work things out with my boss. If he says it's okay for me to leave the shipment, fine. He can call me and I'll meet you. For now, I'll have to take it with me."

The bedroom door opened and two men stepped into the living room. One man had dressed right out of the Spiegel catalog: loose gray slacks and a black cashmere polo shirt. The other man seemed to prefer the NRA catalog. He had on brushed jeans, a plaid shirt and an M-16 rifle.

When Kyna saw the men, she paled. "You don't want to do this, Mr. Dessotti."

Dessotti got up out of the chair, walked around the table and ran a finger down the side of Kyna's arm. His touch raised goose bumps all the way to her toes.

"I don't know, *Ms.* Rand. Maybe we can work out a new and more . . . friendly arrangement."

Cyrus stepped away from the beverage cart and the barrel of the M-16 moved to cover him. The man in the black shirt pulled a snub-nosed .38 from the back of his waistband and walked up to Cyrus. Without a word, he backhanded Cyrus across the face with the revolver and then quickly reached under Cyrus's jacket and removed the automatic from the holster.

Kyna made a grab for the briefcase and Dessotti slapped her across the face hard enough to spin her around. Her knees buckled and as she fell, her head smashed into the edge of the table.

In that fraction of a second when Dessotti's gunman was distracted by Kyna's fall, Cyrus moved. He seized Black Shirt's hand—twisted—and the wrist snapped like a green stick. The gun dropped to the floor and Cyrus kicked the man square in the face. Black Shirt's eyes rolled back and he crumpled to the carpet.

The M-16 barked three times. Two of the bullets flew harmlessly through the open door but the last one cut a deep crease in Cyrus's shoulder. He lunged headfirst over the long Southwestern-style sofa, landed on his shoulders and rolled. Halfway through the somersault, his body began to change, and by the time he came to his feet, his clothes were rags and he no long resembled anything human.

The gunman took one look at the snarling, wolflike creature, then one look at the M-16 and turned to run. Cyrus grabbed the man's head like he was palming a basketball, twisted, and his neck popped like a dry carrot snapping in two.

The first guy was dragging his body across the floor toward the pistol. Cyrus cleared the distance between them in one massive leap and snatched the man up like a G.I. Joe doll.

"Please!" Black Shirt cried. "Please. I—"

Another time Cyrus might have let him go—not this time. He wasn't in a forgiving mood. There was blood on the man's arm and blood on his face—the very air in the penthouse reeked of blood and that destroyed any chance the man might have had. Cyrus tore a massive chunk of flesh from the side of the gunman's neck with his teeth and then raised him high overhead and heaved him through the open balcony door and over the railing. The man was still screaming when he smashed through the windshield of a two-seater Mercedes thirty-five stories below.

Cyrus swallowed, then whipped around and sniffed the air. *Who's missing?*

The bedroom door slammed.

He trampolined off the couch cushions, flew over Kyna's unconscious body and followed the pheromonelike trail of fear to the bedroom door. He used his claws to scratch on the smooth wood.

"*Stay the fuck away from me!*" Dessotti screamed through the door.

Open up, Cyrus thought, or I'll huff and I'll puff . . .

He smashed through the bedroom door like it was made out of straw. Dessotti had squeezed his body down between the bed and the wall and was simultaneously working the charging handle on the jammed M-16 and issuing frantic calls for help to Mary, Joseph and Jesus. Cyrus rose to his full height, a little over seven feet, bared his fangs and snarled.

"Stay away!" Dessotti moaned. "I'll kill you . . . kill you. *Kill you!*"

He raised the rifle over his head like a club and charged. Cyrus let him come, then slapped the M-16 away with one arm, grabbed Dessotti by the shoulders and lifted him off the floor. Dessotti continued to kick Cyrus in the chest and scream: "*Kill you!*" over and over again. The man's eyes were as empty and devoid of humanity as the deepest darkest jungle. A tiny voice in the back of Cyrus's brain asked, Am I really any better? But the wolf wasn't interested in philosophical musings, and at least for the moment, the wolf was in charge.

Cyrus shoved Dessotti's head back and ripped into the man's throat with his fangs, gnawing through tendons and veins and stringy red meat and relishing the rush of hot blood that was as tangy and sweet as vermouth. Dessotti's mouth flew open, but nothing came out except gurgling sounds. Cyrus ignored the man's struggles and continued to gorge himself, drinking deeper and deeper until he had drained every last drop of blood from Dessotti's body.

Naked, cold, his clothing in tatters and covered with the blood of three different men, Cyrus crouched trembling in the corner of the bedroom until his body returned to normal. Even the shoulder holster Kyna had given him and his faithful pair of old sneakers looked like a bomb had gone off inside them. As soon as the pain of reversion stopped, he went into the living room, lifted Kyna off the floor—cradling her in his arms as if she were made of cobwebs—and eased her down on the couch. He listened to make sure she was breathing normally; then he went into Dessotti's bathroom and took a quick shower, using the remains of his favorite shirt to scrub the blood from his face and chest. After toweling off, he searched through Dessotti's closet. The man had had more clothes than the Prince of Wales.

Cyrus selected a pair of designer jeans that he had to roll up to keep from tripping over, and a short-sleeve crewneck shirt with purple-and-gold stripes. He found underwear and socks in the chest of drawers, but the shoes under the bed were two sizes too large. He tiptoed back into the living room and borrowed the dead gunman's black sneakers. They were a half-size too large, but under the circumstances that was good enough. He had just finished tying the shoes when the far-off wail of a police siren came through the window. Quickly gathering up the remains of his clothing, he stuffed them into a paper sack and then scooped some water from the ice bucket and went to see if he could rouse Kyna.

"What!" she sputtered, coming slowly back to her senses.

"Are you all right?" he asked.

Her eyes looked like Wily Coyote's after one of his Acme gizmos backfired, and she had a nasty-looking purple lump behind her ear, but she nodded that yes, she was okay.

"Right," he said. "We gotta get out of here."

She glanced around the apartment. "Where's Dessotti?"

"He had an accident."

137

"What about the other two?"

"They had accidents too."

Kyna's eyes landed on a pair of too-pale bare feet sticking out past the edge of the couch. "Oh!"

The siren was getting closer.

"Come on, Kyna." Cyrus pulled her gently but firmly to her feet.

Her eyebrows were stuck in the up position. "Why on earth are you wearing that tacky shirt? What happened to your clothes?"

Cyrus slipped his automatic into the waistband of Dessotti's jeans, picked up her briefcase and tucked it under his arm. Then he picked up the paper sack containing his old clothing with the same hand and pushed Kyna toward the door with the other.

"You can do a fashion critique later. Right now I think we better leave before the police arrive."

"Police? Who called the police?"

"Probably the doorman."

Kyna paused long enough to grab Dessotti's briefcase before she hurried out the door.

When they got to the car, Kyna was still woozy so Cyrus drove back to the motel. While she was at the front desk checking out, he threw their suitcases into the Lincoln. Then they fled Seattle. It was late and there was little traffic, but he drove below the speed limit and kept one eye glued to the rearview mirror. To the west, the moon had just found a gap in the clouds and its light tipped the turbid, black Pacific waters with creamy-yellow caps of foam. To the east were the mountains under a crown of angry black clouds that sent waves of icy wind down through the coastal firs to coat the car's windshield with layers of airborne salt.

Once they passed Portland, they switched places. Cyrus needed time to think, so he scooted down in the front seat and pretended to sleep. His mind kept straying to the moon, and every time its steely eye peeked through a gap in the trees his skin tingled.

"Look at that moon," Cyrus whispered. They were the first words he had uttered in over an hour.

Kyna glanced over. "You seem awfully preoccupied with the moon lately."

He fell back into his thoughts.

A little after three in the morning, Kyna exited I-5 at the California border, and a short time later they entered the outskirts of Crescent City.

"This place is really jumping," Kyna muttered, anxious to hear even the sound of her own voice.

Crescent City was a tourist way point and fishing village with more mom-and-pop motels and Burger King restaurants than permanent residents. The city's claim to fame was U.S. Highway 101, the Redwood Highway. A two-lane blacktop road that snaked down from the Oregon border, passing through the coastal redwood forests along the Northern California coast. After driving through what passed for the downtown business district, Kyna followed the big curve in 101 that turned south toward San Francisco—a little over 350 miles to the south. They had just started past the town's motel row when Kyna suddenly pulled over at a small roadside park and announced that she was too exhausted to go on. Cyrus nodded and suggested they pick one of the inns across the highway and catch a few hours' sleep.

To Cyrus went the thankless task of shaking the innkeeper out of bed, and after weathering the old woman's indignation, he deposited their overnight bags in a frumpy second-floor room on the back side of building two, the side that faced the forest. Kyna made a beeline for the bathroom and ten minutes later marched across the room and climbed into bed.

" 'Night." She was asleep before her head hit the pillow.

Cyrus stepped over the wet towels to take his turn in the shower stall, a medieval contraption so narrow that he had to step out, turn around and step back in to rinse the last traces of dried blood from his back. When finished, he wrapped a towel around his waist and—wet hair and all—walked out on the balcony and leaned stiff arms on the wrought-iron railing.

Gary L. Holleman

The night was cool and ethereal. Wisps of fog drifted across the highway like wraiths and the forest was a living presence only a few dozen yards across the parking lot, a dark evergreen barrier as much keeping humankind out as holding the creatures of the wood in. The wind from the trees offered up a smorgasbord of tantalizing fragrances: the slick odor of impending rain—thick enough to wring out of the air with his hands; the spicy-damp aroma of wet sequoias seasoned with a touch of ancient mosses; the cool, dry taste of decomposing wood. His ears detected the terrified scuffling of feet followed by the urgent beating of wings as an owl swooped down from its lofty perch. He felt the impact of the predator's talons and then inhaled the rich red soup that was a mouse's blood.

"How did I live before this?" he asked the trees.

The trees understood. Their answer was the mournful cry of a wolf deep in their murky heart. Cyrus's throat ached to respond and his muscles began to ripple, but he fought the change. It wasn't the right time. He was terrified by what had happened in Dessotti's penthouse and was twice as confused by his lack of remorse. But that haunting call came again and his resistance melted away like candle wax. The towel dropped from his waist and in a matter of seconds he was over the rail and streaking across the parking lot. By the time he entered the redwoods, he was fully changed, a sleek brown shadow flowing over brush and downed trees like a rushing stream.

Chapter Nine

October 24

Sunrise was only minutes away when the shaggy shadow stepped out of the mist at the edge of the forest. Cyrus stopped on top of a fallen tree and sat comfortably on his haunches, his pink tongue lolling slowly in and out as he scanned the parking lot and buildings as if they were the artifacts of some alien civilization. As he sat there, wondering why humans chose to stay in such odd concrete caves, he was torn between remaining in his new world—the world of the wild—and returning to the world he had come from—the incredibly sterile world of man.

Why go back? a part of Cyrus insisted. *They stink. They're stupid. They can't run, or smell. And they're so incredibly blind to everything!*

As far as Cyrus could tell, the only drawback to being a wolf was not having anyone to share his adventures with.

But naturally he had to go back. He owed it to Kyna. Kyna of the pale skin, the auburn hair and the laughing green eyes. She didn't stink. He could smell her sleeping body all the way across the parking lot, all musty and ripe with night sweat. She could be a bitch at times, but she could be amazingly tender and sweet too. Besides, someone really was after her and he couldn't just leave her high and dry.

He sighed—a strangely human sound coming from a wolf—then turned and cast one final wistful glance at the unsullied green. Then he relaxed and willed his body to reform.

A few minutes later, Cyrus—naked and shivering—tiptoed

141

out of the trees and made a dash for the stairs at the end of the balcony. With his hands cupped protectively over his genitals, he took the steps two at a time, ran to the door to his room and twisted the knob.

Locked!

"Shit!"

The towel was still where he'd left it so he grabbed it and held it over his groin with one hand while rapping softly on the door with the other. He waited a moment, then rapped again.

The curtain over the window beside the door moved and a second later the door opened. Kyna stood in the opening wearing nothing but a pair of panties, a million goose bumps and an amused expression. She took a long look at her lover— nude, grass and leaves in his hair—and said, "I can't wait to hear this."

Cyrus stepped out of the shower, toweled off and put on a pair of cord jeans, a cashmere sweater and his new running shoes. He wadded up the clothing he had taken from Dessotti's penthouse, then ran as fast as he could downstairs and shoved the bundle all the way to the bottom of the Dumpster in the parking lot.

It was a perfect example of the type of dreary Northern California morning that had earned for the inhabitants of the area the adjective "rugged." The sun was up there—somewhere—but the only way anyone could tell for sure was by double-checking the clock. Rain was coming down in glassy sheets from layers of thick, low-hanging clouds while pedestrians scurried about stooped over like Quasimodo as the wind off the ocean burned their faces raw. The thermometer on the wall of the motel office made a valiant effort to climb out of the miserable range but failed to reach thirty-six degrees.

"Dress warmly," Cyrus said when he returned to the room. "Somebody forgot to tell these people about the greenhouse effect."

"Doesn't seem to bother you."

His clothes were wet, but his face and hands were flushed and he made no effort to dry off.

"I come from pioneer stock."

"Oh? Family came over on the Mayflower?"

"That's the Pilgrims. The blood of Dan'l Boone and Davy Crockett runs in these veins."

Kyna chuckled and shook her head. "More like the blood of a used-car salesman." He looked aghast. "Seriously, don't you want to change?"

Cyrus glanced at her in alarm, but then he realized what she meant and said, "Oh! You mean my clothes?"

"Of course, silly. What else?"

What else indeed? he thought. "No, I'm okay."

"This weather really doesn't bother you?"

He tossed his shaving kit in his overnight bag. "Not so much anymore."

After a breakfast of French toast, sausage and hash browns, Cyrus had to endure a hundred miles of teasing as they followed the highway down the California coast.

"This morning you go out after ice in nothing but a towel and lock yourself out. Yesterday, you managed to let a couple of bozos rip your clothes off. Russ, is there any chance that you're a closet streaker?"

A few hours' rest seemed to have restored Kyna to her usual sarcastic and feisty self. She had put on a tiny bit of lip gloss and attacked her hair with a hairbrush until it sparkled like fire on ice. The cold air had brought the color back to her cheeks and a single look from those gorgeous green eyes was enough to steal his breath away. Oddly enough, he felt pretty chipper himself. After his nocturnal romp in the woods he had expected to be exhausted—sleepy at least—but he couldn't recall ever feeling better. It was an anomaly that he decided to enjoy while it lasted and ponder over later.

On the way south they talked about tennis, shopping and movies—the ones they liked and the ones they didn't. Anything to keep from talking about what had happened at the penthouse the day before. Yet in spite of their best efforts to sweep the subject under a rug of frivolous chatter, the memory of three dead men was lodged like a lump of undigested food in the forefront of their minds.

Before many miles had passed, the Lincoln outran the rain, and the deep green of the forest gave way to the washed-out browns of dry brush and water-starved trees. Stunted grasses grew in great sagging clumps along the sides of the road and on the other side of the highway, giant black boulders jutted out of the cobalt-blue sea like the crenellated towers of abandoned crusader fortresses.

"How can everything be so dry," Cyrus asked, "with all that water right across the road?"

"One of the quirks of nature," Kyna replied. "Nature can be funny, huh?"

He stared out the window, watching as a black-and-white gull plucked an eyeball from the desiccated carcass of a harbor seal and flew away with the prize dangling from its beak.

"Yeah. A real scream."

At noon they stopped for lunch at a combination health food restaurant and art gallery in Mill Valley. The owners had spent a bundle to make the place look like an old-time general store. The walls were decorated with rusty license plates and sketches by the local artist wannabes. Green plants hung from the exposed ceiling beams, and the tables were packed with the beautiful people grazing on their daily ration of bean sprouts.

While Kyna went to visit the ladies' room, Cyrus placed their orders at the cash register and found an empty table under the threat of hanging asparagus ferns. A few minutes later Kyna came to the table with a Seattle newspaper in her hand; she looked scared.

"Russ," she whispered, "what . . . uh, what exactly happened at Dessotti's?"

He studied her face, trying to read what was going on behind her eyes. "Like I told you, he had an accident."

"Look, we both know the man was slime." Kyna's eyes darted over the crowd. "He was going to rip me off and undoubtedly would have killed us. What you did was self-defense. But exactly what did happen?"

She said it so easily, Cyrus thought: self-defense. As if he had performed some unsavory yet necessary public service—garbage collection, for example. Or perhaps pest control. Yet in his whole life he had never killed so much as a rabbit before. Somehow it bothered him that Kyna was taking it the way she was.

Yet if he were truly honest with himself, he'd have to admit that in spite of all this mental masturbation about Kyna's reaction, he personally felt nothing for the three dead thugs. Not remorse. Not guilt. Not even nausea. He had been trying to convince himself it was just shock, but he was beginning to fear that the physiological changes wrought by the wolf's bite had also permanently thrown the scales of his psyche out of whack.

"Why do you ask?" he asked.

Kyna put the paper on the table and turned it around so he could read the small box in the lower right-hand corner of the front page.

LOCAL BUSINESSMAN FOUND MURDERED
ENTREPRENEUR ROMAN DESSOTTI TORN APART IN PENTHOUSE

"The article says his head was almost torn from his body. And . . . and that he was all chewed up." Kyna looked a trifle green.

Cyrus pretended to read the report to give himself time to come up with a plausible explanation. He finally looked up. "He must have had a dog or something."

It sounded lame even to him.

"A dog?" Kyna snorted. "What? Like Benji? Like Lassie?"

"No. Like a German shepherd or one of those pit bulls that are always chewing people up. It's in the papers all the time."

Kyna cocked her head to one side and looked at him pretty

145

much as Pandora's father must have looked at her.

"What?" Cyrus grunted in an angry whisper. "You think I ate him? I admit I've been a little hungry lately—"

"A little?" Kyna broke in. "You can't be referring to those blood burgers you've been shoving down?"

"So I like rare hamburgers," he hissed. "Big fucking deal. If the paper said the guy had been chopped up with a Veg-O-Matic, you think I'd accuse you of having him for dinner just because you like salads?"

Kyna laughed in spite of her self.

"But, Russ. You've got to admit, you've been acting so weird lately. We haven't even . . ." Her voice dropped to a whisper. "We haven't even made love in days."

Blood rushed into Cyrus's face as he hurriedly looked around to see if anyone had overheard her remark. Then he caught himself and shook his head and silently laughed at himself.

Bad enough if people think you're a cannibal, but Heaven help you if anyone thinks you're a lousy lay.

"Kyna honey, this whole trip has just been one long roller-coaster ride through Fantasyland. First, you got your attack by the disappearing wolf and your muggers—both living and dead. Then you got those lizard things trying to get revenge for twenty generations of American Tourister luggage and la-dies' pumps. And you think this newspaper story is bizarre?"

Kyna seemed to be thinking it over.

"Okay, so maybe you're right," she admitted after a while. "But I'm warning you . . . if I find you running around with-out your clothes one more time"—she reached across and took his hand—"I'm slapping a chastity belt on you for the duration of the trip."

It was ten minutes to five in the afternoon when they passed the Sausalito exit and started across the Golden Gate Bridge. On their left, across the bay, was the city—San Francisco—spread out like a multilayered wedding cake with the elon-gated pyramid of the Transamerica building for a topper.

Somewhere behind the steel-gray wall of fog on their right was the Pacific Ocean. And, seeming to be the referee between the two, was the bridge under a blazing hot afternoon sun.

Over the last fifty miles Kyna and Cyrus had fallen into a comfortable silence—an experience that she found decidedly odd.

What is so different about Cyrus? Kyna mused. *He's so self-contained, so comfortable with who he is. Bryan used to be that way. He used to be fun. He used to care about people. Boy, how he's changed. Now all he seems to worry about is who he's going to impress with his money, his diamonds or his cars.*

She wondered if it was meeting Cyrus or this bizarre trip that had suddenly made her see everything so clearly.

Underneath all the glitz Bryan's just an empty shell. The manners, the phony charm, they're just a suit he struts around in to impress himself. He doesn't really care about me or those so-called friends of his, or even the money.

How could she have been so blind?

During her ruminations, Kyna had been unconsciously fingering the necklace through her blouse. She glanced up at the rearview mirror and was amazed how the tiny lines at the corners of her eyes seemed to have just vanished, how her skin seemed to have lost the pallor that the years had slapped on it like coats of cheap paint.

Maybe Bryan hasn't changed, she thought. *Maybe I have.*

She cut her eyes to Cyrus. He was watching the city approach with the same rapt expression that Lancelot must have worn the first time he saw Camelot: eyes bright, a tiny half-smirk on his boyish face.

Wouldn't that be something if I really have changed?

On the far side of the bridge, the Lincoln shot the narrow gap between toll booths and then roared down Lombard Street, following the signs to Fisherman's Wharf. After depositing their bags and the exhausted automobile at a hotel a few blocks from the Wharf, they set out on foot to sightsee.

The sidewalks were packed with a mixed bag of tourists in

shorts and sweatshirts, mimes in white face and tails and street people, doing their own sad imitation of Atlas by carrying their whole worlds on their backs. The air was tempered by the bay and reeked of iced fish and crab boil. Steam leaked like camp fire smoke from sidewalk stands where fresh calamari, shrimp (both fried and boiled), red snapper, blue and king crabs and lobster could be had for a few dollars. Cyrus was gingerly poking at a squid with two fingers when Kyna grabbed his arm and pulled him over to a stand that sold fried sourdough bread dripping with honey and cinnamon. Afterward, he let her talk him into taking the tour boat over to Alcatraz Island.

Cyrus hated the prison from the moment he stepped foot inside the entrance. The walls were filthy and dank and seemed to vibrate with the accumulated misery of untold thousands of men. When the park guide led the group down into the blocks, all the steel and masonry closed around him like a fist and the inhumanly small cells brought a rash of cold sweat to his neck. Halfway through the tour, Cyrus excused himself and practically ran back to the boat landing. He sat on the dock and let the bay air purge his nostrils of the stench of confinement. By the time the shuttle docked at Fisherman's Wharf he was back in control.

"You have a problem with tight places?" Kyna asked.

"Not that I was aware of."

She let it drop and he suspected that it was the sight of all those tiny cages that had precipitated the attack. The steel bars, everywhere the bars! The idea of being locked up like that— caged—made him want to throw up.

Kyna bought Cyrus a soft drink, then informed him that she had to make a delivery at five o'clock. "I want to get the deliveries out of the way so we can take some time and see the city."

They returned to the hotel to pick up the briefcase and Cyrus's gun. He checked the clip and the safety, then slipped the pistol into the waistband of his slacks and covered it with his navy jacket.

The way to Kyna's meeting followed a circuitous route up

and down steep hills, down narrow alleys and past scores of T-shirt shops and stalls selling a variety of totally useless tourist crap. Four blocks from the Wharf's main shopping avenues, she stopped in front of a plate-glass window. In the middle of the window was a huge painted diamond done in shades of blue surrounded by an array of gold and red zodiac signs. The stores on either side were vacant, their windows plastered with yellowed handbills and posters for meetings and concerts that had taken place years before. The street in front of the store was paved with a permanent layer of gritty black dust and the sidewalk under their feet had buckled from decades of San Andreas hiccups. The block was so dead that even the cockroaches had moved on to greener pastures.

Cyrus opened the door for Kyna and followed her into the shop.

At last, he thought, *an honest-to-God jewelry store.*

But it turned out to be a lot different from any other jewelry store he had ever visited. The walls were painted black and had been adorned with a variety of African artifacts: bulbous knobkerries, crossed assegai short fighting spears, ebony statuettes and handcrafted wooden drums covered with dried hides. The floors were spotless white tile, and despite being inexpensive, the merchandise was arranged in neat rows inside clean glass display cases. The main aisle was the domain of off-brand watches and rings and pendants mounted with semiprecious stones. The place was old and musty, and either the owner was burning some type of exotic incense to cover the building's creeping BO, or someone had been smoking hashish.

Kyna kept going down the aisle, but Cyrus lingered next to a display of digital diving watches where he could inspect the wares and still keep an eye on everything. When Kyna reached the counter at the back of the shop, she offered her hand to a stunning black woman with a round, pixieish face framed by long dreadlocks. The woman was wearing a rainbow-hued dashiki that swept the floor when she moved, sandals and a single half-moon earring in her left ear.

Kyna and the young woman spoke with their heads close together for a few moments, and then the woman made a sign with her hand for Kyna to wait and vanished through a beaded curtain at the back. Kyna turned and gave Cyrus a tired smile to assure him that everything was all right. The woman returned in a few minutes with a tall black man. Next to the woman's beauty, the man appeared incredibly ugly. He had a long equine face, flaring nostrils and cheekbones so sharp that they threatened to puncture the skin of his face. He was dressed all in white—white knit shirt, white tennis shorts, white sneakers—and he spoke with a heavy British accent. After shaking hands, Kyna motioned for Cyrus to follow, then preceded the man through the curtain into the back room. The woman smiled and nodded to Cyrus as she held the curtain open.

The back room had been converted into a combination workshop and kitchen. A grinding machine, lathe and several vises were mounted on a bench against the left wall, and a small icebox, a microwave and a hot plate sat atop a shelf attached to the opposite wall.

Kyna followed the man into a small glass-enclosed office at the very back of the room. The man glanced at Cyrus through the glass, then pointed Kyna to a seat in front of a wooden schoolteacher's desk.

Cyrus looked around for a place to sit. The only chairs were a pair of antique wire soda-fountain chairs next to a small round dining table in the center of the room. One chair was occupied by an old black man eating a bowl of couscous with a tin spoon and sipping from a bottle of Mexican beer.

"May I?" Cyrus asked, indicating the vacant chair.

The old man looked up. His eyes were vacant—dazed. The sclera was the color of old ivory with pupils the size of black marbles. On top, his hair was as thin and white as new cheesecloth, and above his lips was a silky-white moustache now caked with dried broth. Underneath the aroma of steamed vegetables, Cyrus detected the unmistakable odor of hemp.

"Of course," the old man replied.

"I'm Cyrus Trigg."

The old man slowly put the spoon in the bowl, wiped one hand on his pants leg and offered it across the table.

"Kazie Mabuto."

"Nice to meet you, Mr. Mabuto." Cyrus took the man's calloused hand. "You work here?"

At the touch of Cyrus's hand, the old man's eyes suddenly snapped into focus. He stared at Cyrus for about fifteen seconds and then dropped his hand and returned to the bowl, nodding his head slowly up and down like one of those dog statuettes in the rear window of an automobile.

"Do a little a this, a little that," Kazie Mabuto said. "Nowadays mostly I fix the watches and remount the rings."

The woman was standing in the doorway where she could watch the shop. "Papa, we couldn't run the place without you, and you know it."

The old man snorted and waved an impatient hand at his daughter.

The bell over the front door jingled and the woman disappeared. The old man chewed his stew slowly. Every few seconds he cut his eyes up to Cyrus's face.

"You from around here?"

Cyrus shook his head. "No. Memphis. How 'bout yourself?"

"Live here now, but I grew to be a young man in the Sudan, along the eastern Tibesti range. I'm Susu." Kazie waited to see if Cyrus would say anything and when he didn't, the old man continued. "You know anything about Africa?"

Letting slip a shy smile, Cyrus replied, "Only what I got from the *National Geographic* and Tarzan movies."

The old man kept nodding his head sagely. "You ever get down to the islands?"

"Islands? You mean like Hawaii?"

"The Caribbean. Haiti? Jamaica? How 'bout Roatan?"

It was Cyrus's turn to shake his head. "Nope. Never had the chance."

"New Orleans?"

151

"Yeah. I've been there a couple of times. The French Quarter, shopping at the River Walk."

Kazie kept right on eating. Cyrus sensed something was bothering the old man, but decided to wait him out. Kazie brought the beer bottle up to his lips, but never let his eyes stray from Cyrus. After draining the last swallow, the old man set the bottle on the table. "You know anything about magic?"

Cyrus's eyebrows shot up to his hairline. *The old guy's bombed,* he thought. *Humor him.* "Magic? I watched David Copperfield a couple of times. Does that count?"

Kazie made a rude noise with his lips. "TV magic? No, boy." He leaned back against the springy wire back of the chair. "I'm talking Congo magic. Magic black as a pusher's heart."

"Sorry. Why do you ask?"

"Let me see your hand," the old man said, holding out his own hand.

Cyrus hesitated.

"Come on, boy. I don't bite."

Cyrus couldn't say he cared much for the old man's choice of words, but he placed his hand—palm up—in the old man's.

Kazie brought his face down so close to Cyrus's hand that his nose almost touched. "Like I thought. Smooth as a baby's behind."

Cyrus jerked his hand back and his mouth dropped open in slack-jawed amazement. "I'll be damned. You're right! I never noticed that before.

"Wait a minute! I had my palm read once and it sure as shit had lines then." Cyrus stared at the hand. "This is too weird. How do you suppose something like this happened?"

Kazie got to his feet and went to the refrigerator. He came back to the table with two frosty bottles, set one down in front of Cyrus and took a long pull on the other. Then he reclaimed his chair and asked, "Anything unusual happen to you lately?"

"Unusual?" Cyrus did his best to appear cool.

"Don't dick around with me, boy. You get bitten by anything? Like maybe a wolf?"

Okay, don't lose it, Cyrus cautioned himself. *This old man knows something.*

Cyrus turned around to check on Kyna. She was still deep in negotiations with Mabuto Junior, her hands swooping through the air like canaries as she made her point. Cyrus turned back and lowered his voice.

"We were hiking in Utah. That's where it attacked us."

"A wolf?" Kazie asked. Cyrus nodded. "Was the woman bitten?" Kazie shifted his eyes to Kyna.

"No."

"How bad it get you?"

"Not too bad. A lot of blood, but it hardly left a scratch."

"You didn't think that strange? All that blood and no wound?"

"Well, yeah," Cyrus admitted. "Both the ranger and the doctor mentioned it."

Kazie nodded again. His know-it-all attitude was beginning to get on Cyrus's nerves.

"Been having any strange dreams? Maybe doing some strange things?"

"Look, Mr. Mabuto, why don't we skip the dance and get right to the meat of the matter? What's going on?"

Kazie smiled without a trace of humor. "Get to the meat? You a comedian, boy?"

When Cyrus first sat down he had been pretty sure the old man was stoned out of his mind. Now he wasn't so sure.

The office door opened and Kyna and Mabuto Junior came out.

Kazie glanced at Kyna and whispered to Cyrus, "Come back tonight by yo'self."

Cyrus thought it over. "It'll have to be late."

Kazie's smile would have put the Cheshire cat to shame.

"How 'bout midnight?"

* * *

153

After stopping at the motel to pick up the car, Cyrus drove Kyna to her last two meetings. The first was a drive-by at— of all places—a laundry in Chinatown, and the second was in a high-rise office building across from Macy's department store. After the last delivery, they walked down to Union Square, bypassing the legions of AIDS victims who lined the sidewalks like an honor guard of scarecrows, only these poor devils were brandishing signs for help instead of crossed swords. At the corner, while they waited for the light to change, Cyrus surreptitiously dropped a twenty-dollar bill into the basket of one particularly filthy young woman with purple spiked hair and rings through her nose. The girl gave him a smile that had a lot more empty spaces than enamel.

"You're such an easy mark," Kyna said as they crossed.

"Oh," he muttered, "you saw that?"

"You're so predictable. You know she's probably running to find her pusher as we speak?"

Cyrus glanced over his shoulder. "No, she's not. Besides, she doesn't look like she has the strength to stand up, much less run anywhere."

Kyna rolled her eyes. "I hear they've got this bridge for sale in Brooklyn . . . you interested?" He blushed and Kyna added, "I know you only wanted to help, but—"

Cyrus broke in. "I didn't do it for her. I did it for me."

Kyna detected the hard edge of pain in his voice and let the subject drop, but she made him take her hand and smiled inside when he lost the fight to keep from grinning.

After one circuit of the park—almost getting high on the marijuana cloud floating above the homeless men lounging on the grass—they crossed the street and entered FAO Schwarz. When they exited the toy store it was already dark. The city had been invaded by a cold creeping fog that seemed to eat right through their clothing to the marrow of their bones.

"Brrr!" Kyna grumbled. "I don't think I'll ever be warm again."

Cyrus looked up and down the street. "Where to?"

"I'm beat. Let's head back to the hotel."

"How 'bout a quick bite first?"

"I don't know . . ."

"Come on. It's San Francisco. You can't just have room service. Besides, I'm a growing boy."

Kyna laughed. "You're a bottomless pit."

He drove around Chinatown for twenty minutes before finding a parking place, but then they walked right into a restaurant on Stockton and got a table without having to wait. They split an order of cashew nut chicken and sweet-and-sour pork—Kyna picked out the cashews and chicken and gobbled down the vegetables—and then shared a pot of green tea. When the check came, Cyrus glanced at Kyna and tossed his fortune cookie, unopened, into the trash barrel on the way out of the restaurant.

Kyna drove back to the hotel and parked in the garage.

"You still beat?" Cyrus asked.

"No." She smiled.

They walked hand in hand down Columbus Avenue to Ghirardelli Square. It soon became obvious that Kyna was skating on the edge of exhaustion; her footsteps were slow, her eyes were rimmed with red and her smile—when it came—was perfunctory. Cyrus purchased a red woolen shawl in a shop on the second level that specialized in Irish goods, and draped it around her shoulders to help cut the chill. Later, while Kyna was looking in the window of an art gallery, Cyrus wandered into The Nature Company next door. He picked up a stuffed wolf from a display basket of fuzzy predators and stared into its marble eyes. The toy wolf reminded him of his midnight rendezvous with Kazie Mabuto and he glanced at his watch—it was almost ten. He would never quite be able to put his finger on the exact moment when his feelings for Kyna crossed the line between business and oh-so-personal, but the fact that they had made the meeting imperative. He was still staring at the stuffed canine when Kyna eased up behind him and slipped her arm through his.

"You look like you're a million miles away." She chuckled.

Gary L. Holleman

Her touch seemed to melt a little of the ice that had formed around his heart. "No place I'd rather be."

She squeezed his arm. "Good answer."

They stopped for a nightcap at T.G.I. Friday's and then walked with several other couples back up the hill to the hotel. Their room was spacious and had been recently renovated. The walls were overlaid with a rough-textured grass paper and decorated with pastel watercolors. The bed was firm and large. The moment Cyrus walked into the room, he removed his jacket, put the 9mm into the drawer in the bedside table and stretched.

"Boy, am I beat." He sighed.

Kyna pushed him back onto the bed.

"What's up?" He laughed. "I thought you were tired."

She was wearing a form-fitting gray turtleneck dress with a wide black leather belt and a pair of gold hoop earrings. The outfit looked good on her, but all evening it had sort of reminded Cyrus of the getup his second-grade schoolteacher used to wear. Taking a cassette tape from one of the dress's pockets, Kyna gave Cyrus a long sultry look and slipped the tape into the tapedeck/alarm clock on the night table. Then she pushed the play button and went to the foot of the bed.

"What's that? *Learning German the Easy Way?*"

It was The Trogs—*Wild Thing*.

She closed her eyes and began to move her hips, slowly at first—an emphatic bump followed by an exaggerated grind, each movement timed to coincide with alternating pulses of the music's strong bass beat. As the tempo increased, Kyna's hips revolved faster and faster. Her hands slid down the outside of her thighs, grasped the hem of her skirt and raised it—a few agonizing inches at a time—until her legs were exposed from toes to the tops of her sheer black stockings. The dress continued up past her waist, over her shoulders and then flew off out of sight.

As the blood began to invigorate a few of the more ticklish parts of Cyrus's anatomy, any resemblance Kyna may have exhibited to his second-grade teacher vanished. The woman

156

had been built like a fireplug and he just couldn't imagine Mrs. Kempster ever wearing a sexy black stretch bra or a pair of those tight black satin hipsters.

Kyna still had not uttered a word. She held his attention with quick glimpses of her nipples and by slowly sliding her hands under the waistband of her panties. She moved like a snake—fluid and loose—dancing to the charmer's flute. As she continued to gyrate, a fine sheen of musk formed on her body and ran down her belly and flanks like liquid diamonds.

At last the music stopped.

Kyna stood dead still in the middle of the room, opened her eyes and stared a challenge straight at Cyrus. By this time, he was in a semi-swoon of lust and hyperventilation. Aside from being positive that he had never been so aroused in his entire life, he was afraid that if he so much as took a breath, he'd explode. And she knew it. She gave him a tiny smile, turned her back—giving him a full view of her tight buttocks—unhooked her bra and let it slide—as slow as cold molasses—down her arms to the floor. Still bent over, she hooked her thumbs in the waistband of her panties and pushed them to the floor.

"Kyna!" he growled. His mouth felt like the floor of Death Valley.

She straightened and gave him a cool look over her shoulder. "Yes?"

The teasing, little-girl voice did little to quiet his blood.

"If you don't come over here right this minute, I'm going to come over there and rape you where you stand."

"Oh?" She batted her eyes. "All of a sudden you're interested in little ole me?"

Turning, she gave him the full frontal view of her lush hills and valleys. It was a truly awe-inspiring landscape.

"Kyna!"

She cupped her breasts, juggling them slightly as if she were evaluating the size and weight of a pair of ripe melons. "This what you want, lover?"

He made a dive for her, but she skipped lightly away and shook her head.

"Not so fast." She used her fingers to tease and pinch the nipples until they stood up straight and tall like good little soldiers. "You made me wait. All day today—all day yesterday. It won't hurt you."

"Aw, Kyna, don't be like that."

"You want me?"

The best he could do was nod.

"Down, boy."

"What?"

"Down. On all fours."

"Now wait just a minute . . ."

Kyna spread her legs and flicked her index finger in and out of the thick pubic hair.

Cyrus moaned, but he got on his hands and knees. "The things you do for a woman."

"Now, come here."

Oh well, he thought, *it's not like I haven't been down on all fours before.*

He crawled over to her and looked up, honing in on the red V between her thighs.

Kyna twined her fingers in his hair and pulled his head forward. "Next time, don't make me wait."

Kyna fell back on the pillow with a smile as wide as the Grand Canyon. Cyrus was lying flat on his back across the bed, panting.

"I thought you were tired," he said.

"Sometimes when I get this tired, I have trouble falling asleep." She turned her head and grinned. "It was you or a sleeping pill."

She got up and went into the bathroom. A few minutes later she came back and crawled under the covers.

"Good . . ." Cyrus started to say. She was snoring before he said, ". . . night."

"Sleeping pill . . . right."

While Kyna slept the sleep of the embalmed, Cyrus counted the holes in the ceiling tiles. He was sure she wasn't faking because her snoring was beginning to shake the bed. At eleven-twenty he slipped out from under the covers and pulled on a black turtleneck sweatshirt, a pair of navy cord jeans and the pair of black Nikes he had taken off Dessotti's gunman. Giving Kyna one last look, he tiptoed out of the room and locked the door behind him.

It was less than half an hour until midnight when he stepped out on the sidewalk in front of the hotel, and yet Columbus Avenue was teeming with people. On one corner, a group of men held a whispered conversation in the umbra of a pawn-shop awning while overhead the ocher glare of the high-intensity streetlamps cast the night in Halloween shadows. Across from the hotel, a pair of elderly streetwalkers took advantage of the stark visibility to strut their tarnished wares up and down the avenue. A two-tone squad car suddenly rounded the corner of Lombard and immediately transformed the animated street scene into a still life.

Cyrus walked briskly but calmly down to the corner and then turned in the direction of North Beach. He arrived at the jewelry store one minute before midnight. The place looked deserted.

Suckered by an old man. He mentally kicked himself. Feeling like a complete fool, Cyrus rapped softly on the re-cessed front door and was relieved when a light appeared in the back. A moment later he saw the snowy crown of Kazie Mabuto's head moving through the dark.

Chapter Ten

October 25

"On time, I see," Kazie said when he opened the door.

The old man re-bolted the door, then led Cyrus to the back room. The place smelled like an opium den and was as dark as a cave, with only the light from a candle in the middle of the table to cut the blackness.

"Want a beer?" Kazie asked.

Cyrus shook his head.

They sat and stared at each other over the burning comma of the candle's flame.

"What can you tell me?" Cyrus asked at last.

The old man chuckled. "About you? Or about the loup-garou?"

"The what?"

"You never heard that term?" Kazie asked with a disbelieving smirk. The flickering light deformed his face and made his expression sly and somehow sinister. "Man in your position, ignorance can be lethal."

"I may have heard it somewhere, but I don't recall."

"How about 'werewolf'?"

Cyrus stared into the old man's rheumy eye. "Yeah. That one I've heard."

"I bet."

Cyrus waited, but Kazie appeared to be in no hurry.

"I grew up in the wild part of the Sudan. Back then, my people didn't have much contact with the so-called modern world. We was so poor, we dreamed of making it into the

Third World. Our tribal leader and physician was our Hungan—witch doctor to you.''

Cyrus kept his thoughts to himself.

''The things I saw that man do, people in this country would lock me up for telling about today. Lock me up and throw away the key.''

Kazie took a long pull on the beer bottle; his Adam's apple bobbed up and down like a pile driver.

''If our Hungan liked you, that was fine. Your crops usually did okay and your family didn't get too very sick. 'Less of course there was a drought, and only Legba could do anything about that. But if he got down on you . . .'' More beer disappeared down the old man's gullet. ''People that crossed him died—died hard. In some very unpleasant ways. Some got ruptured organs: spleens, lungs, livers, kidneys. Ruptured kidneys is a bad way to go, let me tell you. I saw this man take a week to die and he never stopped screaming until they threw the dirt in his face.''

Kazie grinned then. His teeth sparkled like piano keys in the candlelight.

''The interesting part was, a week later I saw that same man. It was after sundown and I had been at our neighbor's helping birth a calf. I was walking back along the dirt track that went by the Hungan's hut when I saw the man. He was gray. Even in the twilight that man was gray as the mud mounds desert ants make. He was stacking wood beside the Hungan's hut. I snuck over behind this big old baobab tree for a better look and I nearly peed myself. Sure 'nuff, he was just as dead as when they put him down for his dirt nap, but his eyes . . . they kinda looked like red embers glowing way down deep in a fire pit.''

Cyrus's ears pricked up at the description of the dead man's red eyes. ''This man you're talking about,'' he said, ''after he died, was he unusually strong and fast?''

Kazie nodded. ''Fast? Fast enough to catch up the dry wind in his hands. And strong? He picked up a quarter cord a wood like it was a box of matches.''

Cyrus pulled on his bottom lip for a moment; then he said, "I'll take that beer now. If you don't mind?"

The old man got up and stretched. When he did, his eyes momentarily widened and he grabbed his back.

"You okay?" Cyrus asked.

Kazie nodded and went to the icebox. He returned with two bottles of beer and a leather drawstring pouch. After placing the bottles on the table, he shook some dried fibers from the pouch onto a piece of cigarette paper. Next he curled the paper, wet it like a stamp and stuck it in the corner of his mouth, where it dangled like the tail on the letter *Q*.

"Want one?" Kazie asked, pointing to the joint.

"No thanks."

Kazie lit the cigarette in the candle flame, threw back his head and blew a pungent cloud up toward the ceiling.

"Go on," Cyrus urged.

"Anyway, one day not long after that, the old chief in the next village died—natural causes, some said—and our Hungan offered to take over his duties. I guess you folks would call it a merger—he'd be the headman of both villages. 'Course, he'd also get control of the cattle and all the rest of the livestock from the other village—what there was of it. Now the new chief—the old chief's oldest boy—and just about everybody else for a hundred miles around knew about our Hungan, so the boy declined our Hungan's offer—politely. About a week later, the new chief's two-year-old boy was carried off by a wolf. A few days after that, the nephew of the new chief's wife was taken. Nobody ever found the bodies, only a few patches of blood and hair."

Cyrus took a sip of the beer, his eyes lost in the candle flame. "So maybe it was just a wolf. It was Africa, after all. Lions and tigers, and bears . . . oh my."

"Shows how much you know 'bout Africa, boy. That part of the Tibesti ain't got no wolves. Never had no wolves."

Cyrus mulled over Kazie's reply. "So maybe it was a lion, then."

Kazie chuckled. "I know where you coming from. Don't

blame you none either. But it don't do no good to sit there and argue with me. You gotta understand; every child in my country old enough to pee outside the hut knows animal tracks. Besides . . . I saw it.''

That quelled Cyrus's speculations.

"It was near twilight and I was down at the river fishing. The new chief's younger brother—boy name of Baku—he came down and put his pole in the water too. Me, I stayed on the other bank 'cause Baku and I never liked each other too good; different villages and all. Anyway, one minute Baku was sitting there fishin' nice as you please and the next, this thing had him in its mouth shaking him the way a terrier shakes a rat.''

"A wolf?"

"The kinda wolf that stands over seven feet tall on its hind legs.''

Cyrus bowed his head and ran his fingers through his hair. "Shit.''

"Ain't no shit, boy. I saw it.''

"No, no—you misunderstand. I believe you.''

The old man looked deep into Cyrus's eyes. "I bet you do.''

"So what happened? The werewolf?"

The old man got up for another trip to the icebox.

Where does he put it all? Cyrus wondered.

Kazie reclaimed the chair, speaking as he scooted up to the table. "Most folks would have given in to the Hungan right then, let him have what he wanted. But this new chief was a stubborn kid. He had gone to the university in Khartoum and didn't believe in the old ways. When his family started disappearing, instead of getting scared, he got pissed. He got a few of the men together—men who'd lost family or friends to the Hungan—and they went to the witchman's hut early one morning. They set fire to the hut and the Hungan came flying out—all seven feet of downright crazy-mad black wolf.''

"So the Hungan was the werewolf?"

"That he was."

"What did they do?"

"The villagers?"

Cyrus sighed. "Yes. The villagers."

"They cut his head off."

"Gross," Cyrus muttered. "Why'd they do it that way?"

"That's the way you do it. You got to remove the werewolf's head while it's a wolf." Kazie saw Cyrus's expression and hurried on. "Don't go giving me those looks, that's the way it works."

"So what happens if you cut off the head when it's a man?"

"Depends. Cut it off and later put it back on the body . . . little while later, he's good as new. But—and it's a big but—cut off the head while he's a man and keep the head away from the body . . . the body eventually dies, but head goes right on living. Forever!"

"You mean just the head? God, that's awful."

"That's what happened. First the mob wounded the Hungan with their spears and arrows. Pretty soon it had so many arrows sticking out of it, it looked like a porcupine and was howling and hopping around. The noise brought out the whole village and they surrounded the thing with torches to keep it from running away, and finally—when it was down—they came after it with knives. The Hungan tried to outsmart them by turning back into a man, but the young chief knew what he was doing and they cut off the head anyway. Then they burned the body and buried the head in the mountains where nobody could find it. Far as I know that man's head is still up there—alive. Buried in a dark hole for all eternity."

Cyrus shuddered uncontrollably. "That's horrible. Are you saying that a werewolf doesn't just die after a while like everything else?"

"Nope. They're immortal. Live forever. That's how I knew about you—your hand."

Cyrus looked at his palm and then at Kazie. "I don't get it."

"No life lines. No life lines 'cause your life has no end.

'Less of course you lose your head at the wrong time.''

"But I got hurt the other day. I was bleeding."

"Boy, I didn't say you was Superman. I said you couldn't be killed easy and that, unless somebody chops off your head, you won't die. Won't age none either."

Cyrus's mind was racing, too full of the implications to think straight. "What about all this crap about the full moon and silver bullets?"

Kazie threw back his head and roared. Cyrus frowned and took another sip of beer.

"You young 'uns today. If you see it on the TV it must be real."

"But the moon . . ."

"Oh you'll feel the pull of the moon, all right. All natural creatures do. It may even put you in a mood to go tearing through the woods. But it ain't got nothing to do with you changing."

Cyrus got up and began pacing the room. He felt like Alice after she had fallen through the mirror. "How did I get this way?"

"The wolf that bit you, what did it look like?"

"Like a wolf. Gray, shaggy. I thought it was rabid."

"How did you get away from it?"

"It turned on my girlfriend after it bit me. I picked up this broken tree limb that I had been using as a walking stick and stabbed it in the back."

"Then what happened?"

"We got help from a park ranger and went back to find the wolf. But it was gone."

Kazie nodded. "Any sign it could have crawled off?"

Cyrus shook his head. "Nope. No prints. Just a puddle of blood."

"Spirit wolf."

"Oh, good. It just keeps getting better and better. What the fuck is a spirit wolf?"

"You done pissed off the wrong fella, my friend. My guess is, a powerful Hungan, one that knows how to project the spirit of a manwolf. See here, this is how it works: The Hungan puts the man into a trance, then changes him into the form of a wolf and projects the wolf to where his enemy is. Since it's the essence of the wolf that's projected, the man appears as a regular wolf, but it is controlled by the mind of the man.''

"Was the man—the man in the trance—was he a were-wolf?''

"No. He was never more than a man changed to look like a wolf.''

"Why do that?''

Kazie sighed and rolled his eyes. "Don't ask me why a shaman does what he does. If I knew what he knew I'd be sittin' high somewheres playing with my juju beads and having zombies run my errands.''

"Then you're saying I was bitten by the ghost of a wolf?''

"No. It was real—horribly real. But it was a projection. After you wounded it, it reverted to disembodied energy and disappeared.''

Curiouser and curiouser, Cyrus thought. The next thing he asked himself was: *Can I actually swallow this crap?*

"So where does that leave me?'' Cyrus asked in a tired voice.

"I don't know. I'm not no werewolf. How do you turn into the thing anyway?''

Cyrus thought about it. "Different ways. I get scared. I get mad. Sometimes I think about this dream I have . . .'' He felt his face color and was glad the room was dark.

"That's another thing,'' Kazie added quickly. "A werewolf's dreams are sometimes prophetic.''

"Prophetic?''

"Not all dreams. And they're usually confusing or unclear. But some will foretell events in the future.''

"So I'm a man who can change into a wolf. I can only be killed by losing my head when I'm a wolf. I won't die and I won't age. Does that about cover it?''

"Mostly.''

"Okay, fine. But I'm curious about a couple of things. Why

did you bother telling me all this? And, if I'm this monster you describe, why aren't you scared?''

Kazie chuckled ruefully. ''Scared? What have I got to be scared of? Look at me. How old you think I am?''

Cyrus squinted. The old man's face was etched with wrinkles like erosion in a mud bank and his skin was as thin as onion paper.

''I don't know, seventy maybe?''

Kazie laughed. ''You're a good boy. I'm eighty-eight and I'm dying. I got the big C, in my lungs and my bones. Why you think I smoke this dope? You think I'm some old hippie? The therapy makes me sick and the dope helps.''

''I'm sorry. Isn't there anything that can be done?''

''We'll get to that. Tell me one more thing. You ever hurt anybody when you was a wolf?''

Cyrus shifted in the chair.

''Don't worry. I ain't no cop.''

''I never hurt anybody that wasn't trying to hurt me or Kyna. But it was close one time. I ran into this homeless man in a park in Seattle. It took everything I had not to . . . do something to him.''

Kazie nodded once more. ''You can't go feeling no guilt about that. The wolf always goes for the old and sick. Culls the herd. Why didn't you take him?''

''I don't know. It was hard not to. I guess I just couldn't do it.''

''So you was in control even when you were the wolf? You—I mean the man—was in charge?''

Cyrus shrugged and nodded. ''I guess so.''

''What's it like being the wolf? You hungry all the time?''

''Why, don't you know?'' Cyrus asked in exasperation.

''How many werewolves you think there are running around? You're the first I ever sat down with across a cold beer.''

Cyrus let slip a sad smile. ''Only difference I noticed is that I have this craving for rare meat. I don't think about hurting people much, just the opposite. I try to steer clear of men when

I change. Mostly I run in the forest.''

Kazie leaned forward and placed his elbows on the table. ''What's that like?''

''Running through the woods?'' The old man nodded. ''Mr. Mabuto, I can hardly describe it. It's the most wonderful feeling in the world. You see everything, smell, taste and hear everything. The wind speaks to you. The earth rises to meet your feet and the night embraces you as its own. Sometimes I don't want to come back.''

''Why do you?''

''Well . . . I'm responsible for Kyna. You've seen her. She's special.''

''Does she know?''

''No way. I'd lose her.''

''Okay. To answer your question: Why'd I tell you all this? I want something from you.''

Cyrus was on his guard then: His senses peaked and Kazie's body was suddenly outlined by that eerie green glow.

''Calm down, boy. All I want you to do is bite me.''

''Bite you? Are you nuts?''

''No. I'm dying. Dying slow and hard. Every day is pain and blood and runny shit. I go to that place they call a hospital and they zap me with X rays and shoot me full of poison. My hair is starting to go. I can't eat nothing but that soup shit.''

Cyrus was quiet, thinking. He looked at Kazie Mabuto and let his own form of X ray go out to the man. And he felt it. The cancer was chewing at the man's insides like slow acid with teeth. The smell of death in Kazie's lungs was like wet decay and the white-hot pain radiating from his skin was as plain as a Kirlian photograph.

''If I did bite you, what would you do?'' Cyrus asked.

''I'd go away. Maybe up north. Canada. Or east to Colorado. Get me a place in the mountains.''

''If you're sick, won't you be in danger if I change?''

''What have I got to lose? A few more weeks in that hospital? A few more days of pain? Either way, boy, you do me a favor.'' Kazie smiled then. It was the sad but hopeful smile of a little boy facing his priest. "'Sides. I don't think you're the type to eat a tough old man without no meat on his bones. If the man is good, he can control the wolf."

Cyrus stood and began pulling off his jacket and shirt.

"One more thing," Kazie said. "Who's after you?"

Cyrus stopped with his fingers on his belt buckle. "What do you mean?"

"Boy, you really gotta start listening. A Hungan set that wolf on you. It didn't just stroll out of nothing and you happened to be there. It was sent."

"I don't know any witch doctors. I'm a bodyguard."

Kazie got up and went to the workbench. He came back with a piece of paper and handed it to Cyrus.

"Put this in your pocket. It's the address of a woman that might be able to help. I talked to her this afternoon. Seems she was expecting you."

Cyrus looked at the address and then at the old man. "Who is she?"

"A mambo. A woman Hungan. She's not the most powerful I ever seen, but she's the best we got on this coast. She should be able to tell you something about the people dogging you."

Cyrus tucked the paper into his pocket. Then he removed his shoes and socks and stepped out of the jeans. He pushed his underwear to the floor, picked up his clothing and folded them neatly on the workbench. All the while, Kazie was watching like a hawk.

"I never thought about the clothes," the old man said. "You gotta take them off when you change, huh?"

"Unless you want them to end up as dust rags. Don't be scared, now."

Kazie shook his head. "Nothing you do gonna scare me."

Cyrus freed his mind and allowed his thoughts to drift back to the oddly-shaped mountain of his dreams, the cold moonlight, the woods, the she-wolf. The excited beating of his heart came as no surprise this time—it was welcome. His bones popped and his limbs stretched and the fur sprouted like grass. After a moment he looked down at Kazie from a new height.

Gary L. Holleman

The scent of the old man's sickness filled Cyrus's mouth with saliva. His claws popped out and he flexed his fingers. But he maintained control by shoving all the primitive urges deep into the far corners of his consciousness.

"You kinda pretty," Kazie said, and pushed himself out of the chair. The old man came around the table and stroked Cyrus's fur.

"Bless you, boy."

Cyrus spent the remainder of the night tossing and turning and trying to keep from waking Kyna. He was both relieved and frightened by what he had learned from Kazie Mabuto. Relieved—for now he had some idea what had happened to him, and as crazy as it may have sounded, he felt better for knowing. But he was frightened by the idea that some crazy witch doctor was dogging his heels. The questions of what it all meant, what he had become, what the future held, why a Hungan was after him, were just too big for him to tackle all at once. He pigeonholed the questions, and like Scarlett O'Hara, he decided to think about them tomorrow.

Some time later Cyrus noticed that the sheers over the windows had turned from white to pink and he glanced at the clock beside the bed and gave up all notions of trying to sleep. After a quick shower, he pulled on a pair of clean jeans and one of the Navaho prints that Kyna had given him and walked down to the sourdough bread stand at Fisherman's Wharf to pick up breakfast.

After breakfast, Kyna drove to Golden Gate Park. They made it through the park's maze of twisting roads and arrived in front of the Steinhart Aquarium half an hour before the place opened. Rather than sit in the parking lot with several busloads of screaming schoolchildren, Kyna suggested they take a stroll around the park.

With her trusty camera dangling like a leather lei around her neck, they explored the lush gardens, dodging arcs of water from the sprinklers, overzealous bumblebees and the occasional militant jogger.

170

"You only got two kinds of people out here," Kyna said as she sidestepped an oblivious runner. "The quick and the dead."

The park was vast and green, full of imported trees and flowers and green plants, all nourished by the city's temperate climate and an almost daily bath of fog. The sun had burned off most of the early morning haze, but the air was still loamy and tart and as sharp as a paper cut.

They returned just as the museum was opening and, opting to tour the aquarium first, they wandered the dark corridors, wading through throngs of scuffling and shouting children and their keepers. Cyrus stopped in front of the shark exhibit and watched closely as a snaggletoothed sand tiger lethargically circled the tank. On one trip around, the shark slowed and seemed to stare at Cyrus through the Plexiglas. The creature's eyes were as friendly as a trocar: black within black, like drops of ink in pools of oil. If Cyrus had been wearing one, he would have tipped his hat to his fellow predator.

When they'd had their fill of fresh- and saltwater aquaria, Cyrus trailed Kyna across a lobby filled with mechanical dinosaurs and entered the natural history museum. It was a wondrous place. Of particular interest to Cyrus were the full-size dioramic scenes from Africa and Asia. Especially the reenactment of four hairy humanoids frozen in the act of stabbing a snarling wolf with stone-tipped spears. The wolf's fangs were bared and the creature's glass eyes somehow conveyed real pain and rage.

"Not very pretty, is it?" Kyna asked.

"Gives new meaning to the word 'underdog.'"

"You feel sorry for the wolf?" she asked incredulously. "He's the predator. He probably attacked the men."

"I doubt it. No wolf is going to attack four men armed with spears," Cyrus replied. His eyes were fixed on the wolf's canines. They looked like sharpened pieces of blackboard chalk.

"After what happened to us, I'm surprised you feel that way," Kyna said with a sniff. "I certainly wouldn't hesitate to kill one if I had the chance." Cyrus's expression became so melancholy that Kyna laid a hand on his arm. "What is it?"

He laughed it off. "Nothing, really. I guess I just feel sorry for him. Dead, God only knows how many years. Stuffed and stuck in here for a bunch of snot-nosed rug rats to shoot paper wads at. I think he deserved better."

Kyna took a second to remove her Seattle Seahawks baseball cap and fluff her hair. She looked at him like he'd lost his mind, but let it pass.

Once they had completed the rounds of the exhibits, they walked outside, crossed in front of the band shell and entered the Japanese gardens. Kyna ordered tea and biscuits from a pale young Japanese girl in platform sandals, and then they returned to the car.

Cyrus said, "If we have time, I'd like to visit this shop Mr. Mabuto told me about."

Kyna unlocked the Lincoln and faced him across the roof. "Where?"

He fished the piece of paper from his pocket. "Eighteen-fifty San Carlos."

Kyna thought for a moment. "That's in the Mission District, isn't it?"

"Beats me."

"What's there?"

"This old black lady Kazie told me about."

"Kazie? You two got to be friends awfully fast."

"Yeah. You know how it is. After five minutes I felt like we were blood brothers."

"Is this it?" Kyna asked as they pulled up at the curb in front of 1850 San Carlos. "You came to get your fortune told?"

Cyrus smiled. The dingy glass window had a simple, hand-painted sign: TAROT.

"You bet. I want to make sure you're not gonna dump me and run off with some rich diamond merchant."

Stepping through the narrow doorway, they were momentarily blinded by the abrupt change from bright sunlight to gloom.

"Are they open?" Kyna whispered.

The shop was a shotgun structure with tall shelves lining the walls on both sides of a central aisle and a rectangular glass display case and cash register at the rear. The walls behind the display cases were hung with a regular "Night Gallery" of the most disturbing oil paintings and watercolors Cyrus had ever seen. As he preceded Kyna down the aisle toward the cash register, he stared at the macabre collection.

The first oil depicted a giant tree ringed by a group of white-clad natives kneeling in a circle of candlelight. Across from that painting was a reproduction of Bosch's *Adoration of the Magi,* and next to that was a particularly chilling portrait Cyrus recognized as Prince Vlad of Transylvania, a man famous for his strange ideas on how to make shish kebabs. Cyrus paused in front of a frame that contained nothing but molds of cloven hoofprints.

"I've been to some really nice places, Russ," Kyna whispered out of the side of her mouth. "But this isn't one of them."

He glanced through the glass to his left and saw a series of braided necklaces made from twigs, hemp and God only knew what else. The other case contained jars of powders, dried leaves and viscous-looking liquids. Down a little farther was a display of black statuettes—grotesque little things that looked like they had been carved by the insane and intended for the demented. There were squat dwarfs with enlarged penises and three bulging eyes, rail-thin golliwogs with flat heads and fangs and hunchbacks with huge arms and tiny shriveled legs.

Kyna stuck close to Cyrus all the way to the cash register, where he looked around for a hand bell. On the top shelf behind the register, a row of horned gargoyles looked down at them through slitted eyes.

"Must be anti-theft devices," Cyrus mumbled, nodding toward the gargoyles.

"And very good ones they are too."

The voice was deep and strangely melodious and seemed to have come out of thin air. Cyrus thought it sounded familiar.

He winked at Kyna and said, "Okay. I'm hooked. Where are you?"

The beaded curtain behind the register parted.

"How may I help you?"

Black, tall and regal, the woman was breathtaking. She had long hair that covered her shoulders like an obsidian stole and a body that any gymnast would have envied. Her clothing was simple and conservative: a teal-colored blouse over black stretch pants and black flats. The pocket of the blouse carried a crest embroidered in gold, red and black.

"Old woman!" Kyna hissed in Cyrus's ear, giving him the point of her elbow in the ribs.

Cyrus cleared his throat. "Paula Inkarha? Kazie Mabuto sent us."

"You are the one?"

"You are Paula Inkarha?" Cyrus repeated.

The woman's eyes were the color of robin's eggs. "Are you the one?"

"Look, Ms. Inkarha, Kazie sent me to talk to you," Cyrus said.

"Then you are the one. The Wicca welcomes you. Come into the back."

Paula disappeared through the beaded curtain and Cyrus motioned for Kyna to follow.

"She's a rip-off artist," Kyna whispered.

Cyrus lifted his eyebrows. "Oh? You can tell that after two minutes?"

"Good grief, Russ. It's obvious to anyone with eyes. Look at this place. It's right out of a Vincent Price movie. And that mysterious 'Are you the one?' What a load of manure."

Cyrus put his hands on Kyna's shoulders and gently steered her through the curtain.

The back room was lined with more shelves filled with more glass jars containing everything from shrunken heads to chickens' feet. Next to the door was a bench with a Mr. Coffee machine and a hot plate and in the center of the floor was a card table and four chairs. The only thing on the table was an oversized deck of cards. The woman pulled out two of the chairs and took a seat in the third.

Cyrus pushed Kyna to the first chair and stared at her until she sat down. Then he sat between the women, winching slightly at Kyna's catlike smile.

Paula returned a seemingly sincere smile to Kyna and then turned her attention to Cyrus. "May I see your hand?"

Cyrus was newly sensitive about his hands, but he let the woman take one. She turned the palm up and traced the skin with long red fingernails. Then she turned the hand over and examined the back.

At last! Paula thought. *The man in my visions.* She lifted her eyes to Cyrus's face. He radiated confusion and no small amount of fear, but his aura was pure. She glanced at Kyna.

That's more than I can say for her.

What is it about this woman? Paula wondered. Her aura was opaque. It was almost as if Kyna was shielding herself, but Paula sensed no psychic power in the woman. Caution seemed to be the most prudent course of action.

"I did not believe," Paula said. "It has been many years."

"What?" The question exploded from Kyna. "Believe what?"

Paula looked at Cyrus and asked a question with her eyes. He shook his head imperceptibly.

"Ms. Rand, Mr. Trigg has a very unusual palm. Look for yourself."

"Ms. Rand, huh? I suppose the spirits told you my name."

Paula grinned. "No. Mr. Mabuto told me when he called this morning."

"Oh."

"Kazie is . . . all right, then?" Cyrus asked.

Paula smiled and nodded. "Yes. We owe you a great deal."

Kyna took Cyrus's free hand and flipped it back and forth.

"Owe Russ? For what?" she asked as she carefully scrutinized his palm.

"Mr. Mabuto was ill and Mr. Trigg made a suggestion about a possible treatment."

Kyna released Cyrus's hand. "Okay, he has a smooth palm. So what?"

"It means Mr. Trigg is a very special person."

Kyna looked like she wasn't sure how to take that. "I know that, but how do you mean?"

"Mr. Trigg has great powers. Powers even he hasn't discovered yet. These powers will expose him to great terror and danger. But also to great joy."

"Powers? What kind of powers? What danger?"

"Babe, let's hear Ms. Inkarha out," Cyrus said gently. "Paula."

Cyrus nodded and smiled. Kyna looked like she had just bitten into a lemon. Paula poured her concentration into Cyrus's palm, constantly caressing the skin with the tips of her fingers. Several seconds passed before she said, "Shall we go to the cards?"

She picked up the deck of pasteboard tarot cards from the table, deftly shuffled them and then placed the deck facedown on the table in front of Cyrus. The backs were covered in dark green velvet with white hand-drawn runes.

"Cut the cards into four piles," Paula said.

"Do they have to be even?"

"Not necessarily. Do not look at the deck. Close your eyes and feel the cards."

Cyrus separated the cards into four relatively even piles. Starting with the left stack and going to her right, Paula turned over the top card from each stack. The images made no sense to Cyrus, but from the expression on the woman's face, the random pictures disturbed her. She raised her eyes.

"An incredibly powerful Hungan has beshrewed you."

Naturally, Paula already knew this, but she had to go slowly so as not to panic Cyrus. Nor did she trust the redhead.

"Beshrewed?" Kyna muttered, and then shrugged her apology to Cyrus and put a finger to her own lips.

"Invoked an evil spell," Paula explained. "Cursed."

"What did I do to him?" Cyrus asked.

"It isn't you he is after," Paula said, turning her mesmerizing blue eyes on Kyna. "It is her."

Chapter Eleven

Kyna exploded out of the chair.

"*Me!* What do you mean me?" she sputtered.

"You are the one the Hungan seeks," Paula replied. "And he is not about to stop. You are both in great danger."

Kyna turned to Cyrus. "Russ, this is a load of crap. Let's get out of here."

Unsure now what to think, Cyrus went to Kyna and wrapped his arms around her. "Calm down a minute. I need to hear what this lady has to say. It could be important to us."

Kyna shrugged out of his embrace. "You can't possibly believe any of this shit."

"Kyna, a lot of strange things have been happening. Or have you forgotten about the little Easter egg basket that old man gave you?"

"I haven't forgotten anything! But I can't believe you of all people would fall for such obvious carnival bullshit."

Cyrus latched on to one of Kyna's hands, unknowingly squeezing it so tightly that she winced.

"Ow!"

"Sorry." He loosened his grip. "But you have to listen to me! There's more going on here than you realize. I trust Kazie Mabuto and he trusts Paula. Will you please trust me?"

Kyna tried to pull free but Cyrus held on. When she couldn't get loose, she tried to annihilate him with her eyes. After a few moments, his calm gaze took the heat out of her anger and her shoulders slumped. Then he led her back to the chair and reclaimed his place at the table.

Paula studied Kyna's face, noting the flush on Kyna's

cheeks and the downcast eyes. "Ms. Rand, may I see your hand?"

Kyna clasped her hands together in her lap.

"Ms. Rand, I know what Kazie's son does for a living."

Kyna's head snapped up and her eyes became frantic.

Now it was Cyrus's turn to look confused. "Kazie's son? What has he got to do with anything?"

Paula's eyes went from Kyna to Cyrus and then back.

"I am going into the front for a few minutes," Paula said. "I think you two should talk. It is time for all secrets to be put aside. If you two are going to survive what's coming, you are going to have to work together and take care of each other. Trust! Trust is essential."

Paula got up without another word and vanished through the curtain.

A mixture of mascara and fat salty tears dripped onto the front of Kyna's white cotton blouse.

"Come on, babe," Cyrus crooned. "What's the matter?"

He got up and went to the coffee machine and came back with a handful of paper napkins.

"My mother always told me to keep a handkerchief handy, but I never listened."

She grabbed the napkins and buried her face in them, sobbing so hard that her shoulders shook like she had a fever.

"Honey, what is it?" Cyrus whispered.

Kyna looked up. Her nose was dripping and her eye shadow had run in streaks down her face so that she looked like some poor soggy jungle cat.

"I . . . I must look hor—hor—horrible!"

She broke into another fit of tears.

Cyrus was old enough to know there was a time for honesty and a time for diplomacy; this was *not* the time for honesty. He scooted his chair over beside her and draped his arm over her shoulder. "Don't be silly. You're beautiful. You're always beautiful to me."

She rested her head on his shoulder, nestling her wet face into his neck. "Oh, Russ. You're going to hate me," she mumbled. "You're going to leave and never speak to me again."

Cyrus stroked her hair and ran his hand down the back of her neck, feeling the muscle there corded like piano wire. "That's silly."

"No. You don't understand. I . . . I've lied to you about everything! About my job, my family . . . everything!"

She broke down again. Between sobs Kyna said, "It started out so simple. Bryan asked me to run a few special discount diamonds to some friends of his in New York. I knew they were stolen—any idiot would have known they were stolen. But he paid me five thousand dollars and I had to go to New York anyway."

By this time Kyna was sitting with her head down, staring at the floor between her feet.

"Before I knew it, I was running hot diamonds to Miami, Caracas, Brussels, everywhere the IDB did business—even South Africa, and God only knows why they needed more diamonds down there. After a few months Bryan took me off regular deliveries and I worked exclusively as his mule. At first, I was so paranoid about getting ripped off that I wouldn't meet anybody face-to-face, especially his special customers like"—she glanced toward the door and lowered her voice—"like Dessotti.

"After a while, I got tired of all the cloak-and-dagger bullshit and thought, What the hell? But there are still one or two sleezoids I won't go near under any circumstances. With those guys I set up drops."

"Didn't you ever want to quit?"

Kyna's tears were all spent and now her voice sounded like a computer animation. "Yes . . . Well, no. Aw hell, I wish I could say yes, that I was appalled at the whole thing. But the truth is, the money was too good. I was pulling down over a hundred and fifty grand a year."

Cyrus was quiet for a moment, thinking. Were his hands so clean? Was he so pure? There had been times in his life when a hundred and fifty large would have looked like a million.

What would he have done if someone had waved that kind of money in his face?

"I wouldn't blame you if you left and never spoke to me again," she said.

"I don't get it," he replied. "If you're so miserable, why don't you just leave?"

Her eyes were two red circles. "You mean like turn in my two weeks' notice? Are things really that simple in your world?"

Touché, he thought.

"Anyway, Bryan was more than my boss." Kyna stared until she saw the hurt pass like a shadow over his eyes. "And like most men, he liked to show off how clever he is. I sat in on meetings. I know most, if not all, of his buyers. I know which banks he launders his money through. You know what he'd do if I tried to quit? He'd sit there in his favorite bergère chair, wearing his red silk smoking jacket, and turn to Conrad—that's the ape he tells everyone is his chauffeur. He'd say, 'Conrad, break Kyna's arm.' And Conrad would do it—just like that."

She snapped her fingers.

"Then, after my arm was in a nice, neat cast, he'd take me out and buy me a new mink coat and tell me how sorry he was that I made him hurt me. No, I don't think I'll be quitting anytime soon."

Kyna's voice was so low it was like the dead speaking through a spirit medium.

The rage that welled up in Cyrus dropped a red veil over his eyes. His body tried to change, but he fought it—it hurt like hell, but he fought it.

"Why didn't you tell me?" he whispered.

She barked out a bitter laugh. "Why should I have told you? No offense, Russ, but when we started you were the hired help."

He tried not to flinch. "Why *did* you hire me?"

"A few days before we met, Bryan called in the middle of the night. He said he had a series of deliveries for me to make.

He was very specific—cities, days, customers—and that I had to be finished by the thirty-first.''

"Why the thirty-first?"

"Beats the hell out of me. All I know is that it was all very hush-hush and that he was very excited, almost manic. And then he dropped out of sight. I called his penthouse in London. I called his ski lodge. I called a few of his friends. *Nada*! I got this real bad feeling, so I asked around and Julie told me about you.''

"What did she say, 'I know this sap who will fall for anything anyone tells him'?"

Kyna grabbed his hand. "Come on. I was scared. You remember that story on the news that first night in Denver? The one about the man and his family that were murdered in Miami?"

Cyrus remembered; he nodded.

"That man was one of Bryan's biggest customers. One of the ones I was afraid to meet face-to-face. He moved stones in south Florida and throughout most of the Caribbean. When I saw what happened to him, I thought maybe the Mafia was moving in. It would be just like that prick Bryan to hang me out and not warn me. I didn't know . . . I didn't expect . . .''

"Expect what?" he asked, truly puzzled.

"She's trying to say she's in love with you, dummy," Paula said.

Cyrus looked over Kyna's shoulder and saw Paula leaning against the door frame.

"You knew about this?" Cyrus asked the woman. "Kazie knew about this?"

Paula shrugged. "Kazie knows Abner is a slug. But what was he supposed to do? The man's his son and Kazie was old and sick. The cancer treatments were costing a fortune and Abner was paying for them with the money he made on the diamonds.''

"Christ!"

Paula motioned for Cyrus to follow her into the front of the store.

He patted Kyna's knee. "Take it easy. I'll be right back."

"You believe her?" Paula asked when Cyrus joined her at the register.

"Which part?"

The woman gave him a crooked smile. "Let me have her cut the cards and we'll know for sure."

Cyrus peeked into the back room. Kyna was still in the chair, but now with her head back and her eyes closed.

"No," he said at last. "It wouldn't make any difference. I think I love her."

"Love?"

He turned his gaze on the beautiful witch. "You've heard of love, I take it?"

"Heard of it? I sell it in small black bottles to fools who think their lives are over if they can't possess Alice or Clarence or whoever their heartthrob of the moment is. I may not know what love is, my friend, but I know what pain is. Pain is what you will feel when she starts to grow old and you don't. Pain will be watching her die a day at a time. If you love her, spare her that . . . cut her loose."

"I can't."

"How do you know she loves you?"

"I don't."

Paula snorted. "Men! Man or wolf, you're all the same. I tell you, there's a lot more going on here than she's telling you."

"Like what?"

Paula frowned and then pursed her lips. "I'm not sure. I can't get a reading on her. It's like she's surrounded by a psychic fog."

"A what?"

"A damping field. Has she ever said anything about dabbling in the occult? Attending sabbats? Does she carry any good luck charms or odd-looking dolls?"

"No. Nor sleep with black cats nor fly about on a broom."

"In your position, I don't think I would be making fun."

"My position? What's wrong with my position? All I have

to worry about is keeping clear of razor blades and the dog-catcher when the moon is full.''

Grinning, Paula said, ''Kazie was right about you. I'm going to try and help. Come on.''

Cyrus followed the woman into the back. She leaned against the table facing Kyna and said, ''Your boyfriend has something to tell you.''

Kyna looked up and then over at Cyrus. She was shivering and her eyes looked haunted.

''It'll keep,'' Cyrus said.

''No, it won't!'' Paula snapped. ''Tell her!''

Taking Kyna's hands, he drew a deep breath and spoke softly. ''I don't care what you've done in the past. That's all over with now. We'll go back to Memphis. I'll take care of you.''

She stared at him for several seconds, then jerked her hands away and slapped him sharply across the face. ''Wake up, you idiot!'' she screamed. ''We wouldn't last twenty minutes.''

Cyrus's expression didn't change. ''We'll send your boss his money and then just disappear. We'll do whatever it takes.''

''How? It takes money to disappear. I've spent almost everything I had on this trip.'' She saw the look on his face. ''You're so gullible. He's not paying your expenses, I am. It's obvious that asshole no longer cares what happens to me so long as he gets his money.'' Kyna shook her head like she was talking to a slow child. ''Russ, the last thing he told me was that he'd meet me in Albuquerque to collect his money. Seven million dollars. You hear me? Seven . . . million . . . dollars! I've already collected almost five million. What makes you think he's just going to let me walk away knowing the things I know? If I try to, he'll kill us both on the spot. If we run, he'll hunt us down like dogs. This bogeyman or whatever it is Paula is talking about is nothing compared to Bryan.''

Cyrus looked up at Paula.

The witch arched her eyebrows and shook her head. ''You are mistaken, Ms. Rand. You may find this hard to believe right now, but this man—this witch doctor that is stalking you—is ten times more lethal than any hoodlum. This man controls powers that can not only torture your body, but can cast your soul into everlasting darkness.''

''I don't believe I have a soul anymore,'' Kyna whispered.

Cyrus sat back on his heels, deep in thought.

''I believe Cyrus has something else to tell you,'' Paula said.

''What?'' Cyrus muttered with a frown. ''You think this is a good time?''

''There will never be a good time.''

Cyrus racked his brain for a way to sugarcoat what he was about to say. He glanced at Paula. The witch was watching him with an amused half-smile on her face.

''I've got a confession to make too,'' Cyrus started, his voice little above a whisper. ''Something that may make you think better of your boss.''

''Ha!''

''Kyna, do you believe in the supernatural?'' Cyrus asked, trying to ease into it.

''After all the crap we've been through?''

''Well, yeah.''

''Are we talking angels here? Or Casper the friendly ghost?''

''How 'bout vampires and demons and . . . werewolves.''

''Don't be ridiculous. And what has that got to do with what we're talking about?''

''But you know what a werewolf is? You've seen the movies?''

''Yes, Russ.'' She sighed. ''*American Werewolf in London, The Wolf Man.* Is this going somewhere?''

''Do you remember how they became werewolves?''

''Of course. Everybody knows that. They were bitten . . .''

''Go on,'' Paula said.

Kyna's hand went to Cyrus's neck. ''Are you trying to tell me . . . Aw, come on, Russ. You can't be serious. You're as much a werewolf as, as . . . as Abner Mabuto's old white-haired father.''

Cyrus turned around and exchanged amused looks with Paula.

Kyna pounded her fist on the card table. ''Don't you dare make fun of me!''

He took Kyna's face in his hands and looked deeply into her eyes for a moment, then leaned forward and brushed his lips across her mouth, softly, the way a butterfly might land on a flower. When he pulled back she seemed to relax a little.

''Why did you do that?'' she whispered.

''It might be the last time you ever let me kiss you and I wanted to remember how you taste.''

Cyrus straightened up and walked around to the other side of the table. He looked at Paula and shrugged.

''You sure you want to be here?'' he asked the witch.

Paula laughed. ''I wouldn't miss this for the world.''

''Is she going to be all right?'' Cyrus asked.

Kyna was lying on the floor with her head resting in his lap.

''Yeah,'' Paula replied. ''She'll be fine. Get up from there now and go on.''

''Okay.'' Cyrus eased Kyna's head down on a folded towel and hurried out of the room.

Paula looked down at the other woman's face. Just standing so close to Kyna made Paula's head spin. She was tempted to search her, hoping to find whatever it was that was causing the disturbance, but that would be a breach of Cyrus's trust, and in spite of herself, Paula liked the man.

Kyna opened her eyes. When she could speak, she asked, ''What happened?''

''You fainted,'' Paula replied.

Kyna sat up and looked around the room. ''Where's Russ?''

''He's outside. He told me to come get him if you still wanted to see him.''

"It wasn't a dream, then? I mean, it really happened? He . . ."

Paula nodded. "It was real. He is what he is."

Paula took Kyna's hand and helped her to her feet and got her to one of the chairs. Then she went to the sink and came back with a handful of wet paper towels. "Here, wipe your face."

"Cyrus is a werewolf," Kyna said more to herself than to Paula. "Cyrus can change into a wolf. A large, shaggy wolf with teeth the size of steak knives." She took a deep breath and let it out slowly. "This isn't happening."

"Kyna, listen," Paula said. "The world of the supernatural is my stock and trade. My mother was born to the Wicca, and her mother before her. It is a world as wonderful as any you are familiar with. It has laws that exist parallel to, and work in conjunction with, the natural laws you know about. Like in your world, there are good people and bad, good spirits and bad."

"Glenda the good witch," Kyna muttered. She looked down at Paula's feet. "Where are your ruby slippers?"

Paula smiled and nodded. "Good! You're feeling better. Seriously, Russ isn't a freak and he isn't a monster. He is still the man you fell in love with, if you really love him."

Kyna gave Paula a sour look.

"He just has . . . powers," Paula continued. "Skills, if you will. Like a surgeon or a professional athlete."

"I fell in love with a hairy Michael Jordan, is that what you're trying to tell me?"

"Not exactly."

"Will he hurt me?"

"Never! His mind and will are incredibly strong. The Hungan that caused this made a big mistake with Cyrus. I believe Cyrus's conversion was an accident, but he was an unusual individual to start with and his new status has magnified those powers. Kyna, even Cyrus doesn't know what he is capable of."

"What do you mean?"

"I'm not sure. It's in his aura and something I got from his hand and his cards. Something I have never encountered before."

"His aura? Come on, Paula. That sounds so sixties: peace, love, what's your sign, all that."

"I have never seen an aura like his," Paula said, as if Kyna hadn't interrupted. "It is both green and black, both angry and kind. The combination confuses me."

"But he wouldn't hurt me? I mean, even if he were hungry or mad?"

Paula smiled. She couldn't help it. "No, not even if he were starving. I have never seen a werewolf before, but my mother told me many stories about them. Did you know that a past president of the United States was one?" Kyna looked at her in disbelief. "They are as rare as black holes, but they do exist. They have existed since the dawn of time."

"Monsters do exist, then?"

"They aren't monsters. They are merely men who happen to be able to change their physical appearance. If the man is evil, then what he becomes will be evil too. If the man is good, the form he takes makes no difference. The spirit of the man controls the spirit of the beast."

"What should I do?"

"Do you love him?"

Kyna nodded.

"Truly love him?" Paula asked again.

"Yes. I guess this doesn't change anything—not really. It'll just take some getting used to." Kyna smiled for the first time. "At least he's housebroken."

"He is very close," Paula said. "His minions reach out even as we speak."

Paula, Kyna and Cyrus were sitting around the card table once more. Paula had watched as Kyna cut the tarot cards into four stacks, and then she turned over the top card from each pile. She had already examined Kyna's palm. Now the witch's forehead was creased with concentration. After a moment, she turned over the second card in each pile, this time going from left to right.

"This man . . . This is the most powerful Hungan I have ever encountered." Paula turned over another card—a huge man with the wings of a bat, pointed ears and horns. "He uses powers I would never dream—" Paula saw Kyna's expression and added, "I'm sorry, but this is giving me the creeps."

"What on earth could give a witch the creeps?" Cyrus joked.

Paula's voice grew cold to add emphasis to her words. "This man barters the blood and suffering of his victims to the dark forces for power. He has cast the spirit of the wolf and reanimated the dead and forced them to do his bidding. He has contacted members of the spirit world that others would never have the nerve to arouse."

Paula's head bent forward until her chin almost touched her chest and closed her eyes.

"He has many weapons at his disposal. When he walks as a man, he casts the shadow of Baron Samedi, and the rest of the Guédé ride his shoulders."

"Why, Paula?" Cyrus whispered urgently. "Why is he after Kyna?"

Paula cocked an ear to one side as if she was listening to voices hailing her from a long way off. "I see a boy lying on a dirt floor. His spirit is tainted and weak. His face is colored by debauchery from wallowing in the pleasures of the flesh. I see a dark form standing over the body. I feel awesome fury. I see—"

All at once Paula's eyes flew open wide and spittle flew from her lips as she tried to form words that would not come. As the blood drained from the witch's face, her skin turned the pasty-gray color of wet modeling clay and her lungs labored to pull in air.

"Paula!" Cyrus shouted. "Paula, what is it?"

He jumped up, pulled the witch from her chair and shook her.

"Paula, snap out of it!"

Gary L. Holleman

High up in the corner of the room next to the skylight, a fat, silvery-black spider sat in the middle of its dusty web. For some time the arachnid's cold, multifaceted eyes had been focused with interest on the human activity below, and just before Paula suffered her seizure, the spider had abruptly folded its legs and rolled itself up into a tight ball. In its own way, the spider experienced a brief moment of agony when the skin of its bloated belly split like a rotten melon right down the middle. Out of this jagged fissure came a tiny puff of foul-smelling green vapor. The vapor hovered over the web, swirling and twisting around itself, growing thicker and thicker like congealing blood, and expanding until it blotted out the sun's rays coming through the skylight.

When the light dimmed, Cyrus glanced up.

The cloud had grown to the size of a beach ball and was slowly drifting down from the ceiling. Cyrus was completely taken aback but had the presence of mind to connect the cloud's sudden appearance with Paula's mysterious seizure.

"Get out of here!" he snapped to Kyna.

"Not without you."

He grabbed Paula by the shoulders and tried to steer her toward the exit, but it was as if the woman's feet were embedded in quicksand.

"Go on!" he shouted at Kyna.

Kyna pressed her lips together and shook her head.

The cloud had grown and was filled with strange flickering lights. As the sphere continued to expand it abruptly changed color and shape, becoming more oval—its surface darkening and roughing into irregular peaks and valleys. In spite of himself, Cyrus became caught up in the almost hypnotic pyrotechnic display. He stopped trying to move Paula and just stared, a bemused half-smile tugging at the corners of his mouth.

Then . . . it dawned upon him what the sphere was becoming.

It was a head—a human head—but the face was straight out of one of Rod Serling's nightmares: hollow cheeks, a nose as thin and hooked as a vulture's beak and a host of exotic tattoos that covered the ebony skin like ancient graffiti on the walls of a soot-streaked cave.

Before Cyrus could give warning, the head's glacial eyes popped open and blinked several times. Then the head grinned. "Greetings, little sister."

Paula coughed until it sounded like her lungs were tearing loose, and then she began gulping air. Cyrus steadied the witch as she recovered enough to make a series of signs in the air with two sharply pointed fingers. The face flickered briefly like a TV set during an electrical storm, but the image remained.

"Now, is that any way to greet a colleague?" the Dark Man asked. "I see you are not alone. I recognize Ms. Rand, so I presume this must be Mr. Trigg?"

When no one spoke, the head continued. "Little sister, it is impolite to meddle in the affairs of others. Especially in the affairs of one powerful enough to cause you harm."

The Dark Man's eyes were round and black like two holes in the fabric of night. They wandered over the room aimlessly and never seemed to settle on anything. Cyrus wanted to ask Paula if such a thing could actually see them, but he took his cue from her and remained both silent and very, very still.

"Perhaps you doubt me?" The visage's grin spread wider. "A demonstration, then?"

The bell over the front door jingled and a moment later the sound of footsteps approached the back room.

"Paula!"

"Oh, no!" Paula hissed.

The curtain parted and a smiling man in a postal worker's uniform strolled into the room, his heavy mailbag causing him to roll from side to side as he walked like a sailor on the deck of a swaying ship.

"Paula, you've gotta sign for—"

When the man saw Paula and the others standing frozen in the middle of the room, his shy smile of greeting turned into a look of concern.

"What's—"

A bolt of blinding green light shot out of the Dark Man's empty eye sockets and struck the unsuspecting postman square in the face. The man's mailbag dropped to the floor and he staggered back into the door frame. In seconds, his skin began to turn gray and he started clawing at his throat with his fingernails.

"Do not move," Paula warned Cyrus. "There is nothing we can do for him now."

"It isn't nice to whisper." The head giggled.

The postman's eyes filled with blood and blood started leaking from his ears and nose. When he opened his mouth to plead for help, more blood bubbled out. He made a sound like a cat strangling and put his hands over his ears as if trying to block out some horrible sound that only he could hear. A moment later his eyes popped like a fish that had been brought up from deep water too fast and green goo spewed all over the walls and floor. Then he collapsed.

Cyrus cut his eyes to Kyna. Her face was as white as a sheet, but she was still on her feet. Paula looked like she was angry enough to chew nails, but she held her tongue.

"Well," the Dark Man said in a miffed tone of voice, "if you're not going to talk to me, I'll just have to talk to you. I have been looking for Ms. Rand for quite some time. I have some very personal questions I'd like to ask her, so, Ms. Rand, if you'd ask your friends to step outside for a moment . . ."

Kyna looked at Paula and raised an eyebrow. Paula answered with a minute shake of her head.

"Come now! What can that possibly hurt? Just ask your friends to step outside, tell me what I want to know and I will leave all of you in peace."

The offer hung in the air with the disembodied head.

The Dark Man laughed. "I sense that for some odd reason you do not trust me."

Kyna's body was quivering like a leaf in a strong wind.

"Come now! What kind of woman would rather see her friends die than answer a simple question?"

Without a word of warning, Kyna picked up Paula's teacup

from the bench and hurled it straight at the looming image, screaming, "Go to hell, you rotten son of a bitch!"

The Dark Man turned. "Ah! There you are."

"Oh shit! Oh shit! Something's happening!" Bryan sputtered.

Conrad ran over to the table and gazed down into the bowl. The crystal was vibrating like a tuning fork and had turned an ugly shade of purple.

"What is it?" the big man gasped. "Is she dead? What's going on?"

"Goddamn it, you have eyes. The damned crystal is almost black. Use your head."

"But does that mean—"

"Don't ask so many stupid questions," Bryan snapped. "Just watch!"

Chapter Twelve

With no time to change, Cyrus did the only thing he could think of that might save Kyna. He took a couple of quick steps and sprang straight up into the floating head's face.

The huge black head screamed, "Stop!"

Kyna and Paula had just enough time to relish the look of astonishment on the Dark Man's face before the image imploded in a flash of brilliant green light. The air cracked like lightning, and a blast of foul-smelling wind hurled Cyrus across the room. He crashed into the Mr. Coffee machine, rolled off the counter and landed with a thud on the floor.

For several seconds the room was completely silent, but stank of ozone and open graves. Paula finally came to her senses and ran over to Cyrus. "What in the name of Hermes Trismegistus did you think you were doing?"

He sat up, rolled his head around and pressed one hand into the small of his back. "Well, I can't actually say I thought about it. I knew I didn't have time to change, and besides, my wardrobe bills are killing me."

Paula laughed with delight and shook her head.

Kyna had collapsed into one of the chairs and was hanging her head between her knees. Cyrus climbed to his feet and began patting his chest, looking for a wound.

"That was an incredibly brave and stupid thing to do," Paula said. Then she added, "But that energy beam couldn't really have hurt you. The only thing you have to worry about is a sword or the like."

"Now you tell me." Cyrus sighed. Then he turned serious.

''So that's what we're up against, huh? A floating head like in *The Wizard of Oz?*''

''I've never seen anything quite like *that* before. I'm sorry. He must have felt my presence and followed my thoughts back here,'' Paula said, looking down on the postman's shriveled remains. ''I will have to take precautions.''

Paula took a seat at the table and stared at her deck of cards. ''I don't get it,'' she whispered.

''Get what?'' he asked, gently kneading Kyna's shoulders.

''Why he couldn't see us.''

''I wondered about that too. But hey, what do I know about floating heads?''

''He saw me easily enough,'' Kyna muttered.

''Not until you moved. It was almost as if . . .''

''Did you see what he did?'' Kyna asked. ''What he did to that poor man? It was like he was swatting a fly.''

''What should we do?'' Cyrus asked.

The witch considered the question for a moment as she absentmindedly twirled a strand of ebony hair around her finger. ''Well, this man obviously knows who and what you are. I'm afraid that means there is no place for you to hide. I have certain charms I can give you, but to be honest, I don't think they will be very effective against something like him.''

''Quit trying to cheer us up,'' Cyrus muttered, ''and just tell us what we need to do.''

''Not much you can do. I don't need to tell you it will be suicide to underestimate him. You have no idea of the kind of power it took to communicate with us like that.'' Paula glanced at the body on the floor. ''Not to mention what he did to poor Ed.''

''Can he be killed?'' Kyna demanded. ''Can something like him die?''

Paula nodded. ''Oh, he's mortal all right. He's not a demon or even a werewolf.''

''How do you know?'' Cyrus asked.

''The same way I knew about you: his aura.'' Paula noted the sour expression on Kyna's face. ''Okay, energy emanations, if you prefer. They were green. You saw that your-selves.''

"So?" Cyrus asked, deeply fascinated.

"What you think of as the natural world is full of colorful indications. Red dirt means that the earth is rich in iron. Green water means the ocean is full of suspended food particles and that means the fishing will be good. A yellow splotch on a green leaf means the plant is ill.

"In the occult world, black is a good color. It is the shade of the cool spirit. Green, on the other hand, is evil. It is the color of purification, of rot. A green aura with white radiating around the edges like we just saw indicates evil power. But it is power of human origin. If the green had been tinged with scarlet, that would have meant that the Hungan was supernatural."

"Supernatural?" Cyrus repeated. "Right. So this un-supernatural witch doctor can be killed?"

"The trick will be getting close enough to use your powers to defeat his. But with the kind of magic he wields that will not be easy. He will be able to see you coming and you will not see him. We know he has werewolves to assist him; other more unpleasant things too, most likely.

"The one thing that puzzles me most is why he has waited this long to strike." Paula stared at Kyna for several seconds, her eyes taking on a freakish red glow. "What is it he's after?"

Kyna shrugged. "How the hell am I supposed to know? This whole thing started when my boss sent me on this trip."

"This boss of yours, is he involved with the supernatural?"

"Bryan?" Kyna snorted. "The man can't even dress himself."

"Well, this sorcerer is after you for something—something to do with a member of his family. I got that much before he closed me out."

"This whole thing started with diamonds," Cyrus said, thinking more or less out loud. "Maybe Kyna's boss cheated him on some kind of diamond deal?"

Paula shook her head. "Neither money nor jewels means anything to this man. He feeds off blood and misery the way carrion worms feed off dead flesh."

"Nice simile," Cyrus muttered. "So how do we get to him?"

Paula paced the room like a mad scientist—hands behind her back, her face set with lines of concentration. Each time she approached the door to the shop, she paused to stare at the postman's corpse.

The body was degenerating at an amazing rate. The skin of the face had peeled away in layers like the skin on an onion, exposing grayish patches of underlying bone. The arms and legs had shriveled up like those of a dead fly, and judging from the stench, the internal organs had already started to liquefy. The man had died with his mouth open and his tongue was sticking out black and swollen like an overripe banana.

Unnoticed by Paula as she racked her brain trying to come up with a plan was the small, silvery-black spider perched at the back of the postman's tongue. Each time she approached the body, the spider scurried deeper into the man's throat. Every time she moved away, the spider crawled out again.

"You're going to have to let him come to you," Paula said. "He *will* come because whatever it is he wants, Kyna has. But now he must kill you too, Russ. You have become too powerful and he is smart enough to know you would never let Kyna's murder go unavenged."

"That's a comfort," Kyna declared bitterly. She stared at her reflection in the mirror of her compact as she tried to repair the damage the tears had wrought, but her hands were shaking so badly she finally gave up. "I'll be as dead as George Washington's butler, but it's okay 'cause Russ will avenge me. Oh yeah, I feel much better."

Paula ignored Kyna's grousing. "My advice is to continue your trip. He'll make his move somewhere along the way."

"I don't know," Cyrus replied. "I'm leaning toward burying those fucking diamonds, shipping Kyna's boss his money and going home. Let this witchman come at us on my turf."

Gary L. Holleman

"Outstanding idea, Russ," Kyna said. "Then we get to fight off this bogeyman and all of Bryan's goons at the same time. The people waiting to kill us will have to line up and take a number."

"Okay," Cyrus conceded, "dumb idea. We'll stay on the trip, but we dump the diamonds."

Kyna sighed. "Look, I know how you feel. But if we miss a delivery, telephones will start ringing in London and button men will start dropping out of the sky like paratroopers. We only have a couple more stops before Albuquerque. Let's just make the damned deliveries and then . . . Then you can turn into the wolfman and eat the prick a new asshole the second he sets foot in New Mexico."

Cyrus gave Paula an amused glance. She shrugged. He threw up his hands and said, "Sounds like a plan."

When Kyna went into the bathroom, Paula pulled Cyrus into the front of her shop.

"There's something I haven't told you," Paula whispered.

"Let me guess—it's about your bill?"

Her grin was lopsided, but without amusement. "Keep it up. You're going to need that sense of humor. It's about your coming here."

"About Kazie?"

"Kazie was just the means. I saw your coming days ago."

"Oh?"

"Don't give me that look, it's true. For the past several days I've been plagued by these recurring visions. The reason I'm telling you this is because of what else I saw."

"More good news." Cyrus ran his fingers through his hair.

"I saw a man and a woman—you and Kyna. You were in a huge cavern surrounded by blackness. I saw a mountain and moonlight. . . ."

"What did the mountain look like?"

"Oh, I don't know. I remember it had a kind of odd-shaped crest."

"I've been having dreams about a mountain like that."

"What about the cave?"

198

"No, nothing about any cave."

"I got such a strong feeling of . . . death."

"Death? Are we talking Kyna's death? My death? Who?"

"Just death. The whole cavern seemed to be charged with it. Like the air right before a big electrical storm. You know?"

"We're both seeing mountains, so what does it mean?"

"If I had to guess, I'd say something terrible is going to take place in this cavern on top of that mountain."

"Did you get a feel for when this something is going to take place?"

"A very specific feeling. All Hallows' Eve."

"Why then?"

"I don't know. But it was a very powerful feeling. . . ."

"From you, I consider that better than an eye-witness account."

"Then you must never relax," Paula said. "Never let down your guard—even for a second. He will know and that's when he will make his move."

"And stay away from caves on Halloween?"

Paula grinned. "And stay away from caves—most especially on Halloween."

"How will he come at us?" Cyrus asked.

"That depends. So far he's kept his distance. Why?—I don't have a clue. But I think not much longer. He seems to like using the undead, but I get the feeling that's just to keep you off balance. I think this is personal with him and when the time comes, he'll want to be up close and watch you die."

"You know, Paula, I bet you'd be a scream at a church social."

She did a little curtsy. "Why, thank you. At *my* church, I am."

"Well, if we live through this, I may just start going to church again myself."

"It's clear again," Conrad said. "What does that mean?"

Bryan stared at the crystal. "Shit!"

He began turning pages in his book. Nothing was turning

out the way it was supposed to—nothing! Finally he slammed the book closed and turned on Conrad.

"Why are you always hovering over my shoulder? Don't you have anything better to do?"

Conrad put his hands out to ward off his boss's anger. "Chill out, boss. If you don't know, just say so."

Pacing back and forth behind the table, Bryan cursed under his breath. He cursed the book he had purchased from a so-called "reputable" occult bookstore in Soho. He cursed the alcoholics and dopers in his coven. And he cursed Conrad for being such an idiot. They were all idiots. In fact, the only person in his entire life whom he had ever been able to rely on was Kyna.

Bryan shot Conrad a withering glare.

He should have sent Conrad to pick up the talisman and make the deliveries. But he could never have depended on the big ape to stick to the schedule.

"The damned book isn't clear," Bryan said. "But let me tell you one thing: In six more days I won't need that stupid book. I won't need the coven. I won't need anyone! Once I get my hands on that talisman, I'll be the most powerful sorcerer on the planet!"

Yeah, right, thought Conrad.

Paula surrounded the Lincoln with apotropaic charms to help conceal it from the Dark Man's probing eye, but after talking it over, everyone decided it might not be a bad idea for Kyna and Cyrus to keep moving. As soon as they left Paula's, they drove directly back to the motel and checked out. Kyna was too keyed up to sleep so she got behind the wheel and drove south out of the city, taking the scenic route toward San Jose before turning west toward Half Moon Bay and then south again. The beaches along the coast highway were narrow and dingy, dotted with tall brown grasses and low creeping vines. The sky was the color of slate and the wind was like a scalpel. It was a dreary landscape that even the occasional sailboard or Day-Glo wet suit couldn't mitigate.

Around five o'clock, Kyna turned off the highway at Monterey and followed the line of traffic to a public parking lot at the head of the city piers. They got out to stretch their legs and strolled down to take a look at the fishing fleet.

The skies were still dreary, but the effects were softened by the cries of sea gulls, the laughter of children and the hoarse bark of harbor seals. The air was pregnant with rain and the smells of fresh fish and cotton candy. Most of the tourists brave enough to take on the weather had fortified themselves with heavy sweaters or coats. A few of the ''old salts'' even sported calf-length yellow rain slickers, the kind that crossing guards and sea captains wear.

Cyrus dug Kyna's thick cardigan sweater out of the trunk for her, but he was comfortable in the light jacket he had on. The gun was lying in the bottom of the trunk next to the extra box of ammunition. He glanced around the lot. Mixed in with the tourists and artists were several scruffy-looking street people; a few were even pushing rusty shopping carts. None of them resembled the old man from Vancouver.

Cyrus muttered, ''Aw, to hell with it,'' and left the gun where it was. Constant suspicion was just too damned exhausting.

By mutual consent, conversation on the trip down from San Francisco had been taboo. Kyna had been lost in her thoughts and Cyrus hadn't wanted to intrude. But now, as they strolled past the forest of aluminum masts in the marina, Kyna looped her arm through Cyrus's and snuggled up tight against his body. When they came to the end of the pier, they leaned on the rail and listened to the wind in the sailboats' rigging—just two people on a wooden peninsula surrounded by a sea of trouble.

''I'm not scared of you,'' Kyna said, breaking her self-imposed silence.

Cyrus searched her upturned face for any hint of duplicity. Her cheeks had been rouged by the wind but her eyes were as clear and free of guile as the restless waves in the bay.

''I hope not,'' he replied. ''I would never hurt you.''

She cupped his head and pulled his lips down to hers. She tasted of brine and toothpaste.

"Hungry?" she asked.

"For you?"

"For food."

"Always."

They had lunch at a kind of seafood Kmart at the end of the next pier and made believe it served the finest cuisine in the world. Kyna ordered shrimp dipped in beer batter, coconut and almonds, and Cyrus had a New York strip steak—extra rare. Kyna even managed to make a joke out of that. Afterward they checked into a twelve-room motel and paid an exorbitant price for a gas fireplace and a picture window that overlooked Monterey Bay.

As soon as Cyrus finished unpacking his overnight bag, he grabbed his wallet, told Kyna he'd be right back and ran down to the local liquor store. A storm had blown up from the west and walking through the fog and rain was like trying to walk through a bunch of wet sheets flapping on a clothesline. The trees were heavy with water and the meager lights that lined the back streets did little to dispel the gloom. It was not a good night to be out roaming the byways alone. The memory of what happened in the back of Paula's shop kept replaying in his head–the insane look on the witch doctor's face, the look on the postman's face when the light beam struck him. Cyrus's home, his friends, his life, seemed like a story from a child's novel that he had read one time on another planet.

He returned to the room with a bottle of cabernet sauvignon. After he got the fire going, they sipped the wine from a pair of water glasses while sitting on the floor in front of the fireplace with a blanket draped over their shoulders like plains Indians. Before they knew it, the wine was half gone and they began to kiss. Slowly at first—lips, tongue . . . teeth—until their passion matched the intensity of the storm. Almost too late, Cyrus spread the blanket and then carefully undressed Kyna, drawing out the undoing of each button and clasp until she was writhing with need. They made love like two puppies on the floor, and the sweat generated by their passion sizzled across their bodies in the light from the fire. When they were done, they lay naked on top of the blanket—whispering and renewing the memory of each other's touch. They exchanged funny but painfully personal stories while drinking the last of the wine, and then it was Kyna's turn to tease Cyrus to arousal.

At the exact instant she lifted her leg to straddle Cyrus's hips, a fat black widow spider crawled out of a crack up in the corner of the room. The creature scurried across the ceiling to a spot directly above the lovers, affixed one end of its silken thread to the acoustical tile and lowered itself onto the decorative wooden beam that ran across the center of room. There, the spider squatted down on its belly and fixed its bleak eyes on Kyna's undulating form. As she approached climax, and threw her head back in ecstasy, the creature let out a nearly silent hiss and slowly extended and retracted its poisonous fangs.

For the Dark Man, it was like looking at the world through a fish-eye lens. The fire made the man's and woman's bodies look like puppets, dancing and jerking on the strings of their passion. The room looked enormously large, the bed appeared to be the size of a circus trampoline, and the beam on which the tiny arachnid crouched, a giant sequoia. When he spoke of what he saw, it was to his apprentice thousands of miles away.

"I can see them. They are at it again—the woman has the morals of an alley cat."

"Where are they?" the goateed man asked.

Even without looking, the Dark Man knew the woman was no longer wearing the talisman. The fact that he could see them at all attested to that. But it was near enough to make accurate spatial determination difficult.

"They are near the Pacific Ocean—I can smell it."

If the goateed man wondered why his master's reply was so vague, he was smart enough not to let on.

But it was the best the Dark Man could do. He had no way

of knowing if the cursed woman was aware of the power in her possession, but so far she had been very careful not to stray far enough from the talisman for him to make any substantive move against her. Oh, he could keep sending his zombies where he thought she was going to be. They might get lucky. But that was as likely as hitting a black hawk at midnight with a slingshot! The Dark Man was further restricted by the blood oath he had taken back in his son's hut. He had promised the woman's soul to the dark lords and so the manner of her death had to be very precise. And on top of all this, Halloween was less than a week away! His time was running out like blood from a slashed artery and the foul breath of the dead was hot on the back of his neck. Two nights before, the Dark Man had cut the eye from a stray dog and put it in the middle of a pentagram he had drawn on the floor of the cabin. Then he had taken his astragali, the knucklebones he had collected over the years from his victims, and thrown them into the pentagram. The eye had turned and stared directly at him and then exploded in a puff of black smoke.

The night before, he had taken the liver from a cat and buried it under a live oak just as the moon was rising. The moon had turned red.

Then tonight, just before entering the trance, he had seen a cloud in the shape of a wolf pass before the moon.

All were signs that the walls between the worlds of the living and the dead were crumbling—signs that the dead had not forgotten him. He had to keep this woman off balance, but how?

The Dark Man abruptly broke the psychic connection with the spider and slammed back into his body. As he sat up, the goateed man draped the feathered cloak around his master's bony shoulders.

"Pack our things," the Dark Man said. "We will be leaving soon."

Chapter Thirteen

October 26

The next morning the sky was still overcast, but the temperature was a little warmer. Cyrus woke feeling breathless from a nightmare he couldn't remember. Something about bony fingers crawling all over him. He was too tired to go out for his run so he placed an order for fruit and juice from room service and served Kyna breakfast in bed. Later, after he had checked out of the motel, Kyna said she wanted to stop at the bakery they had passed the night before near Cannery Row and pick up some fresh bagels. On his way back to the car with the bagels, he spotted a BICYCLES FOR RENT sign in the window of a sporting goods store. As he peered through the window at the rows of gleaming 10-speeds and mountain bikes, his rear end suddenly felt the weight of all the long hours sitting in the car.

"Let's rent a couple of bikes and go for a ride," he said to Kyna when he returned to the car.

"We shouldn't," she said with a sigh. "I have a delivery—"

"And if I remember correctly it isn't scheduled until mañana. Come on. Don't tell me you never played hooky before?"

"Do you think it's . . . safe?"

Cyrus held his arms out at his sides. "It's a nice day. I'm a nice guy. What could happen?"

Kyna frowned at his foolishness, but then gave him the nod.

They rented a pair of 21-speed mountain bikes. At the shop owner's suggestion, Cyrus took a helmet for Kyna, but refused to wear one himself. When she started giving him a hard time about it, he took her aside and whispered, "You fall off, you might dent the curb with that head of yours. The only thing I have to worry about is something incredibly long and sharp . . . like your tongue."

She stuck her tongue out and wiggled it and then grinned, zipped her camera into the fanny pack that she had brought along for just that purpose and they were off.

At first the going was slow. They had to weave around joggers and busloads of tourists that swarmed across the sidewalks and parking lots like hungry ants. In spite of this, they made the two miles from the sporting goods store to the entrance of the scenic Seventeen Mile Drive between Monterey and Carmel in just over seven minutes. Not long after they passed through the guard gate at the north end of the private drive, they entered a sparsely populated subdivision of environmentally correct wood-and-stone mansions tucked securely back among the tall cypresses. The road was a schizophrenic's dream, at first curving down toward, then up away from the ocean. For a while it was smooth and wide and then it was narrow and bumpy, and by the time they emerged from the trees atop a low hill at the edge of Pebble Beach Golf Course, their behinds felt like punching bags.

At the crest they took a break, standing astride the bikes and watching a trio of white-haired men in loud plaid slacks and white V-necked sweaters studiously lobbing golf balls at a tiny circle of grass like they were American soldiers mortaring the Nazi lines.

"Why do you suppose they dress like that?" Kyna asked.

"Beats me," Cyrus replied. "Maybe staring at golf balls all day dulls your fashion sense."

He took a sip from the plastic water bottle that came with the bike and then they coasted down the slope to the beach.

At the first turnout, Kyna rolled to a stop and leaned her bike up against the guardrail. "Come on."

She hopped nimbly across the oil-stained boulders to the edge of the water. There she knelt and took out her camera.

In addition to its movie-star residents, the Seventeen Mile Drive was famous for its sea mammals and birds. It was not at all unusual to spot sea otters and harbor seals, and sometimes the head and tusks of a fat elephant seal could be seen bobbing among the floating islands of kelp. On truly magical days, the barnacle-encrusted backs of migrating humpback whale pods passed within camera range of the shore. Unfortunately, this morning the surf was rough—pounding the rocks and kicking spray high into the air—and the tourists outnumbered the sea creatures ten to one. For her trouble, Kyna returned a few minutes later with water rings around the cuffs of her jeans and beads of saltwater glistening like diamond dust in her hair.

"Darn," she muttered. "Not even one otter."

Seeing how disappointed she was, Cyrus got down on one knee beside a shallow depression the ocean had carved out of the rocks. Rolling up his right sleeve, he plunged his arm into the frigid water.

"Look at this," he said.

"What are you doing?" Kyna laughed. "You're going to ruin your shirt."

He came up with a bright orange starfish that he had pried from the side of the tide pool. Turning the lethargic creature upside down, he pointed to the multitude of tiny tube feet on the underside, explaining to Kyna how the creature fed by extruding its stomach and digesting its dinner outside its body.

"Wait! Wait!" She removed the lens cap from the camera. "Hold it up—no, not like that! Tilt it a little . . . more."

Cyrus good-naturedly played second banana to Kyna's Margaret Bourke-White imitation, and after she had finished the roll of film, he carefully replaced the indignant echinoderm.

When he stood up, Kyna threw her arms around his neck.

"I don't care what everybody else says," she whispered as she ran her tongue around the outside of his ear. "I think you're wonderful."

They remounted their bicycles and pushed on toward Carmel. On the way, they passed a pair of scuba divers trudging backward into very heavy surf, and stopped once to take a picture of a gnarled cypress tree perched precariously at the end of a rocky promontory. As they were walking away from the cypress, Cyrus buttonholed an elderly Japanese man, handed him Kyna's camera and asked him to take their picture in front of the tree. Later, they lunched on tuna salad and bagels at a general store in Pebble Beach and then made the loop back to Monterey. After turning in the bikes, they returned to the Lincoln and took the freeway to Carmel.

"Get a load of this place," Cyrus said as they entered the village.

Carmel reminded him of a set from *Lifestyles of the Rich and Famous*. An artists' and writers' colony, the town was a symbiotic union of brooding wood and brick buildings from the late thirties and gleaming multilevel shopping malls all wedged together like delegates at a cultural diversity conference. The business district was well laid out and contained both trendy shops and gourmet restaurants with a tiny flower park thrown in for color. The streets and side alleys were a narrow battleground where station wagons with Ohio plates and dusty VW vans from Alabama engaged in mortal combat with the local Mercedeses and Ferraris over the few public parking spaces.

Kyna picked a motel in a quaint, quasi-colonial building a half block from the main street. The room was spotless—if not much larger than a shoe box—with a gas fireplace in one corner and a king-sized bed that took up nine-tenths of the floor space. The walls were papered in a tiny lavender wildflower print, and above the fireplace mantel was a reproduction of a group of men on horseback chasing a red fox over the moors.

As usual, the second their suitcases hit the floor, Cyrus announced that he was starving. While he was in the shower, Kyna searched the newspaper for a place to eat. Her eye skipped over the local headlines, MOTHER OF FOUR DROWNS OFF MONTEREY, and the sales, END OF SEASON SAVINGS ON RANCH MINKS, and tore out an advertisement from a small brasserie named after a famous writer of adventure novels. After a short stroll, they found the place sandwiched between an art dealer and a rug store at the end of one of Carmel's myriad dead-end alleys.

A man wearing a short apron showed them to a table next to a wall-mounted, nineteen-inch television set and recited the menu to them from memory. Kyna ordered a draft beer and a slice of pizza and Cyrus asked for a steak sandwich—rare—and a beer. Between bites, they watched part of a football game between the Giants and the Jets while over at the bar, three old-timers with red noses sang off-key IRA protest songs. The soft lights, the good food and even the melancholy singing did wonders for their mood and for the first time Cyrus noticed that the tiny lines around Kyna's eyes had disappeared. In fact, her whole appearance was a puzzle to him. In spite of all they had been through, she looked younger than she had when they started the trip.

After dessert, Cyrus paid the bill and they stepped outside.

It was the kind of night that made Carmel a magnet for lovers from all over the world: cool with a heavy fog that filtered down like wood smoke through the tangled tree limbs. It was kind of spooky too, in a Hitchcockian sort of way.

"What do you want to do now?" Cyrus asked as he helped Kyna into her jacket.

"Feel like taking a stroll?" she replied.

"Sure."

Ocean Avenue was one long display window and Kyna felt the need to stop and peer in every one.

"Look at that," she said, pointing to a bronze statue of a Navaho warrior spearing a buffalo.

It was okay, Cyrus supposed, but in his opinion most of the stuff in the windows was TUS—totally useless shit. He did, however, see a graphite tennis racquet in the window of a sporting goods shop that he wouldn't have minded having.

As they strolled along, admiring the clothes, the art, the rare books and jewelry, the slope of the street became increasingly steep as it approached the ocean. Before they knew it, the sidewalk ended and they were standing in a grove of wind-stunted trees at the edge of a dimly lighted parking lot. The Pacific Ocean—vast, angry, roiling and churning with invisible life—was waiting just on the other side of a wide river of sand.

Cyrus asked, ''Walk down to the beach?''

Kyna zipped her jacket all the way up, then nodded.

The moment they stepped out from under the canopy of trees, Cyrus stopped dead in his tracks and stared up at the sky. The moon had broken through the mist and its pale light felt like chilled silk caressing his skin. His hearing was suddenly so acute that the sound of the waves crashing on the beach was like the thunderous discharge of a hundred cannons.

''What is it, Russ?'' Kyna yelled to make herself heard over the surf.

He couldn't respond. His head was full of the sounds of wind and water, swaying grass and shifting sand. His nose feasted on the tangy odors of dead fish, cold-charred firewood and rotting seaweed, and the spice of salt and smoke, leaves and decomposing flesh lay bitter on his tongue. This deluge of sensory input had blotted out the rest of the world.

''*Russ!*''

The urge to break free from the prison of his clothing—to run, to howl—was an inferno raging in his blood. It took all of his willpower and every ounce of his concentration to fight that fire. He won . . . barely. For he was afraid to give in to that craving—to change, to run. If he did, he might just keep right on running until he reached the deep green woods of Montana. No more problems. No more Dark Man. No more Cyrus.

Kyna saved him. He used the memory of her taste and smell to overcome the call of the night. By taking her hand and bringing it to his lips, he made her his anchor. The hand was cold, but her blood was hot and oh so close below a thin layer of skin.

''Russ?''

This time he was able to cage the animal, to push it back—

back where he knew it would wait and watch for the next chance to break free.

"I'm okay," he said at last.

"The moon, huh?"

"I guess. It's the first time I've been out when it's full like this since . . ."

"Russ, what's it like?"

"The moon?"

"No. When you change."

He held on to Kyna's hand and led her to a massive drift tree lying half-buried in the sand just beyond the reach of the breakers. The tree's bark had been bleached by the sun and salt to the color of old bone, and over the years all of its limbs save one had gone for bonfires. Idle hands had whittled so many initials into its soft wood that it resembled a papyrus column from an ancient Egyptian temple.

Cyrus brushed a spot clear of bird droppings and sand and spread his handkerchief. They sat, hips touching, sharing their warmth as they watched golden moonbeams skip over the crests of the obsidian sea. Just when Kyna was sure Cyrus had forgotten her question, he began to speak.

"Kazie asked me that same question and I had a hard time answering him too. I know what I want to say, but I need new words to say it. I need a way to describe the taste of the ground under my feet. For the image the smell of a rabbit brings to my mind. For the way my body seems to absorb energy directly from the earth as I run."

Kyna watched his face as he spoke. It was the face of a religious convert, the face of a child on Christmas morning and the expression of a starving man at the Thanksgiving table all rolled into one.

"Do you know you're a wolf? I mean, do you remember you're a man when you're a wolf?"

He plucked a long piece of dune grass and ran it under his nose and then tasted it, chewing it like it was candy.

"I know. But it just doesn't seem important. Sometimes I feel like I'm in this wonderful sports car, driving at the speed

211

of light. Other times I become the night, insubstantial as a shadow, as quick as a thought. Most of the time the part of me that's Cyrus Trigg sits in the backseat because I'm afraid to let myself go. Afraid to really get in there and drive.''

He felt the weight of her eyes on his face.

''I remember reading about this experiment where a bunch of lab rats were put in a cage. They were given a choice between food pellets or a chemical that stimulated their pleasure centers just by pushing a button. Don't you know, those old rats kept right on nosing the button for that pleasure pill until they starved to death. I'm afraid it might happen to me like that. So wonderful that I couldn't stop.''

''If it's that good, why do you come back?''

He looked at her and smiled. It wasn't what you'd call a happy smile, so full as it was of melancholy.

''Come on, Kyna. You know why.''

She laughed. ''Don't go blaming it on me. Ever since the first one of you men bashed his honey over the head with a club, you've been blaming us women every time you wanted to do something but couldn't. You want to go running through the woods chasing your tail, be my guest.''

She felt his body stiffen and blurted out, ''Jesus H. Christ, I was only kidding.'' Then she noticed how still he was—like a Labrador retriever on point—and she whispered, ''What is it?''

Cyrus pushed himself off the tree and turned his back to the ocean, focusing his hearing on the tall weeds at the end of Ocean Avenue. Something was moving back there. Something that walked on heavy feet.

The wind was coming from the sea, so he couldn't smell anything yet, but he could see four shadowy figures moving against the background of light from the parking lot.

''Trouble?'' Kyna asked.

''I don't know yet,'' he replied. ''Maybe just kids out for a walk on the beach.''

But he could tell by the way the silhouettes moved that they weren't kids. They were slow, plodding. Like they were carrying a great weight on their backs. And—they were heading straight for Kyna and him.

"It's trouble. Here, hold these." Cyrus peeled off his leather jacket and tossed it to Kyna. Then he kicked off his shoes and began to unbuckle his belt. Spurred by the moonlight, his body had already started to change. His Jockey shorts didn't make it.

Dropping down on all fours, he raised his nose to the wind. Now that he had changed, he could smell them and wished he couldn't; the things smelled like the reception committee from the charnel house welcome wagon. It was obvious that these creatures were nothing like the thing he had faced in Calgary. They were slow and smelled like they would fall apart any second.

This won't take long, he thought.

He slipped into the dark like he was slipping into a favorite suit. As he closed the gap, he could sense waves of inhuman hunger coming from the creatures and reminded himself not to get cocky. They were still coming right at him, a point man and three others fanned out in a wedge to either side. His first impulse was to hit the creatures head-on, just blow right through them in a flurry of teeth and claws. But then a funny thing happened: The wolf's onboard attack computer took over. He abruptly increased his speed and changed direction, sweeping silently around to the right to come up on his opponents from behind. He penetrated the tall grass like a knife, weaving between the stalks instead of mowing them down, and making no more noise than the wind. The moment he cleared the brush, he saw his first target highlighted against the backdrop of pearly-white sand. The remains were human, but just barely. A man who looked to have been about sixty when he died stumbling through the sand in the suit he had been buried in.

No time for Marquis of Queensberry, Cyrus thought.

He smashed into the zombie's back at full speed and the creature literally exploded. Caked flesh and greenish teeth flew in every direction, and the skull, minus the lower jaw, hit the sand with a dull thud. Cyrus turned on the next creature, a middle-aged woman in a tattered silk dress with masses of damp stringy hair hanging down in her face like a dingy wedding veil. The zipper down the back of the woman's dress had ripped and rolls of yellowed skin bulged out like dumplings cooked in greasy fat.

Even as a wolf, Cyrus had a hard time attacking a woman. He tried to just knock her off her feet, but his paw went right through her back and came out her chest—and the woman kept right on walking.

Well, damn!

He forgot about being Mr. Nice Wolf and removed the woman's head with one quick snip of his jaws.

The surviving zombies seemed unaware that their numbers had been cut in half. They were still slogging through the sand with their decaying brains locked on Kyna like a pair of two-legged cruise missiles. Cyrus took a moment to rid his mouth of the taste of rotting flesh and to line up his next target. This one had been young when he died, no more than thirty. And from the way he was dressed, the man could have been a lawyer. Cyrus had no qualms about attacking a lawyer. He extended his claws and as he streaked past, he reached up and clipped the man's head from his shoulders as neatly as snipping a rose from a rosebush.

And then there was one.

However, just as Cyrus made ready to take out the last creature, a freak gust of wind from the sea brought a new smell to pique his sensitive nose. He stopped short and raised his lupine head to check on Kyna. She was still crouched on the other side of the tree, anxiously staring in his direction. Everything seemed okay, but . . .

Later Cyrus would conclude that his instincts had been dulled by his lust to destroy. But right then, he dismissed the smell as a dead seal or sea otter that had washed up on the beach and gave his attention to his last opponent—the walking corpse of an old man with skin so thin that it was almost transparent. As he approached, Cyrus felt a totally atypical

214

wave of pity sweep through him.

Poor old guy, he thought. *Somebody's husband. Probably somebody's grandfather. Now all that's left is a shriveled husk.*

He felt the cooling of his blood that heralded the metamorphosis back into human form and he quickly fanned the fires of his anger. He accomplished this by focusing not on the old man, but on the mind that had set those sad dead feet in motion—the mind that used the dead as pawns to enact its twisted revenge.

That's when Kyna screamed.

Paula was washing her hair over the sink in her bathroom when the psychic alarm bells started clanging inside her head. She jerked upright and stared into the mirror. Instead of a reflection of a woman with ropes of soapy lather running down into her eyes, she saw a dark, windswept beach, a full moon and two people huddled together near a dead-white tree. At first Paula recognized neither Kyna nor Cyrus, for the stark shadows created by the pale moonlight made their features as nebulous as smoke. Then, when she finally did recognize them, she couldn't see what had triggered the vision.

That's when she saw the four shadows stumbling through the high grass, animated by dozens of thin green strands of psychic energy that emerged from their bodies and disappeared up into the ether. To any but the initiated, these strands would have been invisible, but it didn't take a clairvoyant to know where the strands led—the Dark Man's foul aura was all over them like blowflies on rancid meat.

Remembering from the legends that werewolves were supposed to be abnormally receptive to psychic communication, Paula crammed her knuckles tight into her temples and tried to think a warning at Cyrus. But then she noticed that he was already alert to the danger and had started to undress. She glanced at Kyna and noticed something extremely odd. Growing out of the top of Kyna's head was a single lime-green strand of energy. A strand so fine and so pale that a spider's silk would have looked like a fire hose by comparison.

As the drama unfolded, Paula looked away from the beach—there was precious little she could do from so far away—and followed that peculiar strand up into the cosmos. She felt the passing miles as a stream of lukewarm water caressing her face. It was dark—total and unrelenting save for the pale green strand stretching on and on like the center stripe in a never-ending asphalt highway. After what could have been minutes or hours she saw a light and, remembering her encounter with the Hungan, slowed her approach. She found a host—a tiny speckled ladybug perched atop a human-skin lamp shade in the corner of a strange, windowless room, and she used the tiny insect's black, bulbous eyes to scan her surroundings.

In the center of the room was a table and beside it were two men staring down into a black clay bowl. One of the men was as tall and as wide as a piano case, dressed all in black with the same gaunt, expressionless face and bad skin as Lurch from *The Addams Family*. The other man was much smaller and dressed better. He had on a silk smoking jacket and house slippers and the expression of a petulant child.

Paula continued to inspect the room. She could feel more than see the amateurish charms of protection that surrounded the dwelling. They were so weak that they wouldn't have stopped a sideshow palm reader once she knew the place existed.

Who is this bozo? Paula wondered. She focused her attention on the men.

"Don't start!" the small man said. "Black means black. Until it turns black I guess that means she's not dead."

"I hope you don't mind me saying, boss. But that crystal thing is about as useful as tits on a boar."

"Well, I do mind! If you think you can do any better, there's the damned book." Then the small man chuckled. "Tits on a boar. Where did you hear that?"

"That cowboy bar down in Soho. The one that transvestite rodeo rider owns. He . . . she . . . whatever the hell it is keeps

216

asking for you.'' The big man switched into a lisping falsetto. ''Oh, Conrad, where's Bryan? He's sooooo cute. I'd just love to hog-tie that little rascal.''

Bryan! Paula stared at the small man. *That's Bryan? How could Kyna get hooked up with a wimp like that?*

Paula guided the ladybug to the top of the bookcase near the table where she could gaze down into the clay bowl. She saw the water, the crystal and the sand and suddenly everything started to fall into place. Bryan had constructed the protective charms—such as they were—to hide from the Dark Man, and he was using a vaticinating crystal to keep tabs on Kyna. That meant that whatever the Dark Man was after, this Bryan was behind it and he had staked Kyna out like a Judas goat to draw the sorcerer's wrath.

You treacherous little son of a bitch!

Paula wished she had found a serpent to use as a host— preferably one with long fangs and about a gallon of slow, painful poison. Save that, she had another idea.

She flew to the chandelier suspended from the ceiling in the middle of the room. From there she could see the weblike emanations of Bryan's protective shield. The strands shifted and twirled and sparked like the aurora borealis, only on a spectral plane unseen to all but the most sensitive. As primitive as the barrier was, Paula decided, it must have been constructed specifically for the Dark Man. That was why she had been able to spot it and follow it back without being detected.

Okay now, easy does it . . .

Using her mind like a scalpel, Paula carefully snipped one of the invisible threads and then retreated quickly back into her tiny host to see what happened.

Nothing happened.

The man's as perceptive as a mud fence!

Paula reached out again, snipped another strand, creating a minute hole in the web.

Once more she pulled back and watched—surely this time the man would notice.

The truth was, after checking the spell for several days in

a row, and finding nothing amiss, Bryan had become convinced of his invulnerability and had concentrated all of his attention on monitoring Kyna's life force via the crystal.

Two more strands, and I'm out of here, Paula decided. *One! Two! Adios, asshole!*

As Paula's mind raced back to rejoin her body, she noticed that the green thread was now the size of a coaxial cable and it was glowing like a neon sign.

As the echoes of Kyna's screams were drowned out by the roar of the waves, Cyrus flicked out a casual paw and crushed the old man's skull. Before the corpse hit the sand, Cyrus was a brown blur streaking through the night. In the few brief seconds it took him to sprint from the high grass to the tree, he finally grasped the diabolical ingenuity of the Dark Man's trap: The four rotting corpses had been a diversion—the main attack had come from the sea.

He covered the last half-dozen yards in one massive leap, landing in the soft sand on the ocean side of the tree and spinning around all in one motion. Kyna was sitting with her back pressed up against the tree trunk, screaming hysterically as she used her legs to try to fend off the waterlogged corpse of a woman in a tattered bathing suit. The woman's brief slumber in the cold sea had left her a mass of gray wrinkled flesh and torn tissue. Her left leg was little more than strips of masticated flesh and bone and there was a gaping hole in her right side where a passing shark's scissorlike teeth had taken out about a pound of flesh; a host of tiny white crabs could be seen feasting on mushy pieces of the woman's lung.

The hackles on the back of Cyrus's neck rose like rows of spikes. He growled deep in his throat and dug his claws into the sand. The woman's movements appeared sluggish, but there was nothing wrong with her hearing. She whirled around, bared green, scummy teeth and hissed like a snake as her washed-out, dead eyes suddenly blazed with malicious intelligence.

Cyrus faked right, then moved left, hoping for a quick kill, but for a corpse, the woman was deceptively quick. Before he even got close to anything vital she dug her nails into his side and held on as he tried to back away, dragging her mutilated legs through the sand like the tail of a crocodile. Startled by her strength and speed, he tried to shake her off and when that didn't work, he fell on his back and began rolling over and over. But the zombie was like some kind of noxious parasite. Not only did she not let go, she actually began dragging herself hand over hand up his back. When she reached his shoulders, the woman wrapped her arms around his neck and began gnawing like a mad beaver at the thick fur. When Cyrus realized that the woman was actually trying to bite his head off, he leapt high into the air, bucking and twisting like a wild mustang.

It was no use. The zombie was literally bursting with supernatural strength and fought back like a savage beast, ripping great clumps of hair from his neck with her teeth. Once more Cyrus rolled over on his back in hopes of crushing the woman under his weight, but this time she wiggled like a snake under his front leg and began inching up his chest. If he could just get one good shot at her head . . . But it seemed that nothing a mere werewolf could do was going to be able to keep those scummy teeth away from his throat.

As the woman pulled even with his face and stared down into his eyes, his nostrils were filled with the sour stench of watery death.

This is getting serious, he thought.

All at once she stopped clawing at him and a shadow seemed to pass behind her eyes. Her burning gaze changed and became cold and almost thoughtful.

"It is too bad it has to end this way, Mr. Trigg." The voice—even bubbling up through a flooded throat—was too deep and devoid of human emotion to be a woman's. It made Cyrus's blood turn to ice. "You have learned well and are a truly magnificent creature. Oh well . . ."

The fires of rage ignited anew in the woman's eyes and she redoubled her efforts to gnaw through the skin of his neck. In an act of final desperation, Cyrus managed to get a foreleg up under her chin, but the way she was going he knew that wasn't going to hold her for long. He cast one last longing look up at the moon as he felt her teeth dig into his flesh.

In the midst of his trance, the Dark Man's lips peeled back from his teeth in an anticipatory grin of triumph. He hadn't expected the ruse with the drowned woman to work, but now it appeared that it might actually succeed, and with the man Trigg out of the way, the redheaded woman would be child's play.

But at the crucial instant, just when he could feel the woman's teeth ripping into Trigg's neck, the sorcerer was distracted by a new presence—a dark outline hovering over him with a rope of blinding green psychic energy shooting out of the top of its head. Before he could react, the Dark Man felt an explosion of pain in the middle of the zombie's back and he immediately broke the psychic link he had used to control the zombie. His mind floated free in the ether, bobbing like a blade of kelp lolling lazily in calm waters. Frustrated and yet intrigued, the sorcerer took a moment to examine this new and totally unexpected development.

The energy band was green enough, but it displayed a noticeable lack of power and sophistication. The color spectrum was flawed by intermittent bursts of pale yellow, signifying a mind fraught with debauchery—which in and of itself wasn't bad, but in the Dark Man's experience indicated a weak resolve.

As Paula had earlier, he made the decision to follow the strand back to its source, and in no time he had located the secret room and selected a suitable host—a fat cockroach wallowing among the dust bunnies atop a display cabinet full of ancient tools of torture.

The two men in the room were strangers to him—one short and pasty-faced, the other big as an ox. But it didn't take the Dark Man long to locate the remnants of Bryan's psychic shield or to recognize that it had been prepared especially to keep him out.

Ah! the Dark Man thought. *I do not know you, my friend, but you obviously know me. How can this be?*

The Hungan had long suspected that the Rand woman was only a pawn for someone else. Could this be the one? He noted the clay bowl and the crystal and again, as Paula had earlier, he drew the proper conclusions.

I may not always know where the redhead is, but I bet you do. I'll just watch awhile and see what happens.

The roach settled down in the filth to drain the juices from a dead fly. Its eyes, shiny and black, never wavered from the two men beside the table.

Cyrus had just about run out of ideas when the zombie's body abruptly stiffened. Then the woman's mouth flew open, spilling a river of stinking black water into his face. She let out a horrible, grinding moan, pushed herself up with one arm and began clawing at her back with the other.

Cyrus quickly wormed his hind legs up under the woman's chest and kicked out with everything he had, and she went somersaulting head over heels across the beach, landing with a splash on her back in the surf. When he looked up, Kyna was standing over him with a broken tree branch in her hand and a face that looked as pale as porcelain in the moonlight.

"I . . . I . . ." was all she could manage to say.

After scrambling to his feet, Cyrus ran to the water's edge. The woman was rolling back and forth in the icy surge, a jagged hole in the middle of her back leaking bits of greenish flesh and maggots into the water.

"It was the only thing I could think of," Kyna said as she dropped the limb.

Cyrus waded out into the water and without further ado, slammed his paw down on the woman's head, splattering her skull like a rotten watermelon and showering himself with stinking bits of gray matter and bone. He stood over the body for a moment, panting as the tide slowly reclaimed the woman's body.

What a mess, he thought, wrinkling his nose and spitting.

He felt he should have been depressed or at the very least disgusted, but all he felt was an intense sense of euphoria. He was alive, he was victorious. He wanted to howl at the moon!

Instead, after a quick glance to make sure Kyna was all right, he swept the beach with his senses. Once he was sure it was safe, he gave Kyna's hand a lick and then turned and plunged into the cleansing waters of the ocean.

Chapter Fourteen

October 27, 12:10 A.M.

Cyrus and Kyna stood in the shower with their arms wrapped around each other as they let the hot water soak the chill from their bones. Afterward, they gave each other a good rubdown with the motel's plush towels and climbed into bed. Kyna pulled the down comforter up to her chin and said, "I thought you were supposed to be *my* bodyguard."

They wrestled around under the covers for a while, not really making love—for after what they had been through, neither of them could work up much enthusiasm for that—just fondling and holding. Reassuring each other that they were all right. Cyrus coaxed a smile from her by bouncing around the bed on all fours, whining and pretending to tuck his tail between his legs as he told her how frightened he'd been. They slept with their arms entwined until a stripe of bright sunlight fell across Kyna's eyes.

Over breakfast they decided to pack up and hit the road early, before some beachcomber stumbled across the remains of the previous night's festivities. The plan was for a leisurely drive down the coast to San Diego, maybe pausing in Big Sur and stopping for lunch in Santa Barbara, then heading east to pick up the freeway in hopes of speeding through the madness of Los Angeles.

As the Lincoln powered its way south, the scenery changed once more. After the crippling rains of the summer, Southern California was in the midst of a drought and both the inhabitants of the tiny towns they passed and the surrounding foli-

223

Gary L. Holleman

age were withered and brown. The coastal mountains had
sucked every last drop of moisture out of the atmosphere and
just taking an un–air-conditioned breath was a chore. Between
towns, the fields were as hard and gray as concrete, and
plagued with dust devils that sprouted without warning, then
disappeared into air that tasted like hot asphalt.

Kyna stopped to fill up at a service station outside Santa
Barbara before she slowly cruised through the town. The business district was quaint and clean, but it was almost noon and
the streets were deserted. Most of the shop owners had sur-
rendered to the torrid weather, hanging signs on their doors
stating that they would reopen after sundown. The heat was
having its way with the Lincoln too, pushing the needle on
the temperature gauge all the way over into the red zone.

"If I don't get something cold to drink soon," Kyna said,
"I'm going to melt."

She parked in front of a Mexican restaurant with an OPEN
sign and an air conditioner and let the car cool its heels while
they went inside in search of a cold beer. The cantina was
long and cool—all brightly-painted tile and dusky wood. The
bar was an island of tall bottles in the center of the floor,
surrounded by small tables and booths. The walls were decorated with the usual mix of bullfight posters, animal-shaped
papier-mâché piñatas and sombreros with wide scarves tied
around the crowns. A cheerfully toothsome Mexican waitress
took them to a booth and set two cold Dos Equis beers on the
table without waiting to be asked.

"You have deliveries in San Diego?" Cyrus asked Kyna as
he finger-painted in the condensation on the scarred tabletop.

"One. Just outside the city limits. And then it's on to Tucson." She looked up and added, "Listen, Russ, I've been
thinking. I better try to call Bryan about what happened in
Seattle. If he hears about it first he's going to start sending
people around to ask questions."

"Bryan," Cyrus repeated, working the name around in his
mouth to see how it felt. "Bryan Douglas. Hmm . . ."

Kyna took another sip of rapidly warming beer. "Maybe

224

we shouldn't be too hard on old Bryan.''

"Oh? And how, pray tell, did you come to that conclusion?''

"Think about it. I've been so worried about him that all this voodoo crap has just sort of rolled off my back.''

"And a very pretty back it is too.'' Cyrus chuckled.

Kyna snorted.

"Don't be a jerk,'' she said, taking the bottle to her lips.

"I'm not a jerk,'' he retorted, raising and lowering his eyebrows like Groucho Marx. "I'm a wolf.''

Kyna had to cup her hand over her mouth to keep from spraying beer all over the table. When she was able to speak she said, "You're incorrigible.''

Cyrus took her hand and gently massaged the fingers. "I wouldn't worry about Mr. Douglas anymore.''

Kyna attacked the LA traffic the same way she did everything else—head-on. It was just before four P.M. and the swarm on Interstate 5 was lethal. It seemed that behind the wheel of every car was either a Mario Andretti wannabe or an escaped yuppie mental patient. Cyrus was so rattled that after the third near collision he thought he was about to undergo the change. Kyna, on the other hand, whipped the Lincoln through the concrete canyons like she had been raised in California. She always knew just when to accelerate, just when to slam on the brakes and just when to salute the other drivers with her middle finger.

"That's what sunroofs are for,'' she insisted as she stuck her hand through the opening in response to the honking of a Porsche on her bumper.

When they reached the south LA suburbs Kyna flexed her fingers and asked, "Why so quiet? My driving take your breath away?''

"No. Just thinking.''

As soon as he said it, he knew that no woman could ever leave it at that. It was like waving catnip in the face of a cat.

"Thinking about what?''

Gary L. Holleman

"My mom and dad. How they died. What they'd think of me now."

"What do you mean what they'd think of you? What have you done?"

Cyrus laughed bitterly. "Nothing much. I murdered three men in Seattle. I beat the crap out of two men in Calgary and scared the shit out of two more in Banff. I don't much count the rest, they were dead already."

"That's a crock and you know it. Dessotti and his men, it was them or us. If you hadn't reacted we would both be history now."

"Not unless one of 'em had a fucking broadsword."

"Did you know that at the time?"

"Well . . . no. But it wouldn't have made any difference. They were scum. I could smell it on them like cheap aftershave."

"So you rid the world of three cockroaches. Somebody ought to give you a medal."

"Yeah, right." He sighed.

The traffic was thinning and Kyna relaxed a bit, slowing the Lincoln to just under eighty. "Come on, out with it. What's bothering you?"

"Old lessons die hard, I guess. In spite of everything that's happened, I wasn't raised by wolves. I was taught that all life is precious and that God will forgive almost anything. But taking another life . . . I just don't know."

"Would you be happier if we were dead?"

Cyrus hung his head. "Of course not. I could never let anything happen to you. It's just . . . I didn't realize how much the talks I used to have with my dad had gotten to me."

"What do you think? Because you turn into a wolf, you can't go to church or wherever it is you go?"

Cyrus couldn't help laughing. "Yes, I go to church. At least I used to."

"So what is it?"

"Okay. Since you asked. What's the first thing that everybody thinks of when the subject of werewolves and vampires comes up?''

"I don't know what you want me to say. Bats? Fangs? Silver bullets? What?''

"How about evil? You ever hear of a werewolf that was a Boy Scout or a vampire that didn't freak out at the first sign of a cross?''

"No. But how much of that stuff is true? A silver bullet can't hurt you, can it?''

"Kazie said not. I hope I don't have to find out.''

"So you're worried you're some kind of evil monster? Don't you remember what Paula said? You're no monster. Well,'' she said, running her hand up his thigh, "at least most of the time you're not a monster.''

He refused to be cheered up. "Sometimes I don't know what I am. I've been running around trying to keep all these feelings bottled up. At times I feel like I'm slipping away. I look at people differently; I don't like the way they smell or the way they move. I find myself hating the day and counting the minutes until the sun goes down. I guess I'm beginning to like being a wolf too much and it scares me. I'm worried that I might hurt somebody without meaning to. I'm worried that killing is becoming too easy.''

He looked over and saw the expression of concern on Kyna's face.

"That all you're worried about?'' she asked.

He decided to give her a break. "And I'm worried you'll take me home to meet your family and I'll lift my leg on the plastic plants.''

She chuckled and squeezed his thigh. "Not to worry. I'm an orphan. Saint Agnes of Baltimore is my family.''

"You never told me that. We're both orphans?''

"I guess. All that crap I told you about my family, I don't even have any aunts or uncles.''

"Yeah? Well, I've got a sister, but we don't get along. She lives in Utah. Got half a dozen kids.''

"Why didn't you say something? We could have visited her when we were there."

"She lives way down in St. George. Besides, we don't see eye to eye on anything. She thinks Clinton is the new JFK."

"You should call her."

"I'm afraid to. After what happened to that postman, I figure our friend the talking head isn't all that picky about who he murders. As far as I know, he might be able to hear us every time we make a phone call."

"Talk about a monster!"

"Yeah. You can bet Will Rogers never met that guy."

They were approaching the outskirts of San Diego, passing through a valley between charcoal-gray hills covered with yellow grass. Kyna made a brief stop at a strip mall next to the expressway and they were back on the road in five minutes.

"Say good-bye to the Pacific," Kyna said as she took the ramp that headed away from the ocean. "That's the last we'll see of it this trip."

A short time later they exited I-8 at a motel in La Mesa. Just before they went inside to get a room, Kyna said, "I just had a thought. If werewolves are real, does that mean that vampires are real too?"

Cyrus paused with one foot on the ground and the door alarm buzzing. "That's a comforting thought."

"And if vampires are real," she continued, "maybe Santa Claus is real too."

"Let's not get carried away here, shall we?"

"Hurry up. I want to get to the room so I can show you just what a goooood little girl I can be."

The moment they walked into the room, Kyna crammed the briefcase out of sight behind the television set and whirled around.

"Drop that luggage and get naked, pardner, afore I rip them clothes offa you."

Cyrus thought she was kidding, but he eased the camera case down on one of the generic motel chairs and let his suitcase drop. By the time he turned around, Kyna's blouse was

228

across the room, dangling from the hanging lamp chain over the vanity table, and she had jumped up on the bed, kicked her pumps into opposite corners of the room and hiked her skirt up to her waist. When she started unhooking her bra, Cyrus realized this was no joke. He quickly unbuckled his belt, but when he tried to shove his blue jeans down over his boots, he lost his balance and fell on the floor.

"Take the boots off first, dummy." Kyna's bra hit him between the eyes.

Shit! Cyrus thought as he tore at the boot laces. *I'm gonna have to cut these fucking pants off.*

One bounce on the bed and she was out of her skirt. Cyrus had managed to get one boot off and was pulling on the other as if his life savings were in his sock. When he got the other foot free, he looked up.

Kyna was still on the bed, nipples jutting, her hand slowly massaging the thick hair between her legs, and smiling like she was Sylvester the cat and he was Tweedy Bird. Looking him right in the eye, she slipped two fingers deep inside herself—once . . . twice . . . three times—and then popped them into her mouth, rolled her eyes and moaned.

"I warned you once before," Kyna purred. "Don't make me wait." Her hand was back, buried in her curly red thatch.

"Honey," Cyrus replied as he stepped out of his white briefs, "if I don't drop dead between here and the bed, you're never going to need those fingers again."

Later, Cyrus came out of the shower just as Kyna hung up the phone.

"Well?" he asked.

She shook her head. "Still no answer."

"Maybe something happened to him."

"Things like you mean only happen to little old ladies and school kids. Things never happen to people like Bryan."

Cyrus picked up the decorative jack-o'-lantern candle that the motel had left on the night table and put it back down next to the papier-mâché witch.

"Well, one way or another, this whole thing's going to be over in a few days."

"I wonder how it's going to turn out."

"Even Paula didn't know that, and knowing, if you get my drift, is her stock and trade."

"I don't think she liked me very much," said Kyna.

"She doesn't know you."

Chuckling, she replied, "You don't really know me either, other than in the biblical sense."

Cyrus took her in his arms and held her close. He inhaled the scent of her hair, felt the rhythmical thrumming of her heart and listened to the steady snap-crackle-and-pop of the blood platelets bumping against each other as they raced through her veins.

Blood! he mused. *It always comes down to blood. She is my blood. Blood will tell. Blood is thicker than water.*

"Russ, you're hurting me."

He relaxed his grip but refused to let her go. He felt such an intense sense of devotion, of attachment to Kyna that it bordered on mania. He didn't understand his feelings, only recognized them for what they were. He stared over her shoulder at the pumpkin and the witch.

A few more days! Just gotta hang in there a few more days!

October 28

The next morning, Kyna suggested to Cyrus that he dress for hot weather. Then, after stopping for scrambled eggs and hash browns at McDonald's, they got on I-8 and spent the first three hours driving straight into the blinding glare of the emerging sun. Cyrus had not slept well. Strange images had slipped in and out of his dreams all night long. He couldn't remember the details, but the bits and pieces he did remember were disturbing. The silver she-wolf had been in one dream. She was on the mountain, but unlike in the past, the forest had been cold and wet and that strangely shaped peak had been partially obscured under a cap of black clouds. The she-wolf had been afraid and Cyrus had come away with the feeling that he was what she had been afraid of. In his dream state he had been able to hear her thoughts and she was pleading with someone not to hurt her.

In another dream Cyrus had been trapped between a giant anaconda and something that walked upright like a man but looked like a giant rat with long yellow teeth. Every time he struck one of them, a small piece of himself had torn away until there was nothing left but his head and one arm. When he woke, Cyrus discovered that his body had tried to change and that his claws had ripped the sheets on his side of the bed to shreds. After that, he had been too paranoid to sleep next to Kyna and he had spent the remainder of the night curled up on the chair next to the air conditioner.

As the Lincoln rolled down the back side of the coastal mountain range, the terrain underwent another drastic change. Dried grasses and stubby trees gave way to flesh-colored boulders and clumps of sagebrush that resembled giant brown cotton balls and sand—lots of sand. Between the boulders, the green-striped leaves of Spanish bayonets thrust their needlelike points into the soft underbelly of the blue-white desert sky. And the air really started to cook. The previous day had seemed hot, but now the heat came off the highway in waves of distorted light that made Cyrus ill if he stared at the road too long. If they ran the air conditioner for more than forty-five minutes, the Lincoln's engine would start to overheat and they had to ride with the windows down until the engine cooled. As soon as they cut the air, the inside of the car became a convection oven and sweat collected under their arms and behind their knees and ran in prickly rivers down their bodies. Three hours of this and they were ready to scream. When he couldn't take it anymore, Cyrus stopped for gas and cold drinks at a Shell station in Gila Bend. Kyna took a sponge and a roll of paper towels from the trunk and headed for the ladies' room while he strolled around the front of the station to kick the kinks out of his legs and to make certain that the human pimple in greasy coveralls who worked at the station checked all the fluids in the car. Kyna came back ten minutes later looking wrinkled but relieved. Her arms were filled with diet sodas and Ding Dongs. She dumped her hoard on the floor in the front seat and tore into the cellophane wrappers with her teeth.

"Diet colas and Ding Dongs?" Cyrus muttered as he climbed back behind the wheel. "Am I the only one that finds this funny?"

"Don't want to get fat now, do we?" Kyna replied with a grin.

After eight brutal hours in the desert, surviving wind and sun and three radar traps, they arrived at their motel in Tucson. Kyna went directly to the room, threw off her clothes and jumped into the shower. She came out half an hour later in a pair of panties and a towel turban and stood in front of the air conditioner with her arms raised above her head.

"I've never been so hot in all my gall-darned life," she said as she turned slowly in front of the vents.

Cyrus had stripped to his Jockey shorts and lay across the bed to enjoy watching Kyna do her air conditioner dance. He laughed at her accent. "Well shucks, little lady. You call that hot? Sometimes it gets so danged hot out here that even the sidewinders wear sandals."

As soon as her body temperature dipped below the century mark, she came over to the bed.

"You through worshiping the BTU god?" He chuckled.

"I have to make the call," she replied.

The grin dropped from his face. "You want me to leave the room?"

"We have no more secrets."

Someone named Conrad picked up the phone in London and Kyna asked to speak to Bryan. When her boss came on the line, she tried to ask where he had been but wound up spending most of the time explaining what had happened in Seattle. She downplayed Cyrus's part by emphasizing Dessotti's attempt to steal the shipment, but Cyrus could hear the man screaming all the way across the room and he saw the bitter tears that she tried to hide streaming down her face.

Cyrus had never felt so helpless. He turned over on his stomach and clenched his jaws together to keep from screaming. A few minutes later she hung up and came over to the bed.

"He wants to talk to you when he gets to Albuquerque," she said. "You know what that means?"

Cyrus glued a smile to his face and rolled over. "He wants to shake my hand?"

"Hardly. It means that if we're lucky, he only wants to have you beaten to a pulp. You know what that bastard said? He said Dessotti was his biggest client on the West Coast and I should have just given him the fucking shipment. Right! Given it to him. He's a real bastard."

"What about when you mentioned Dessotti's plans for you?"

"He told me to quit acting like an ingénue."

"Ah, yes." Cyrus shook his head and smiled until he thought his face would crack. "The man is a real charmer. I can hardly wait to make his acquaintance."

"Forget it," she said.

"What?"

"I know that tone. Forget what you're thinking. Bryan is better connected than Ma Bell. You do anything to him and it'll be like shooting ourselves square between the eyes."

"The thought never entered my head."

Kyna stood in front of the fake Spanish mirror over the dresser and rubbed her eyes with her knuckles.

"Fuck him!" she said at last. "Let's do something fun."

"I thought you were hot."

"Not as hot as I'm gonna be if I just sit around here thinking about that asshole. I need to work off some steam."

They drove to a shopping mall across town where Kyna purchased new hiking boots for both of them; then they had dinner at a pizza restaurant in the Mexican section of Tucson. Throughout dinner, Kyna was moody, picking at the pepperoni slices on top of her pizza and responding to Cyrus's feeble attempts at humor with half-smiles and grunts.

"So what's on for tomorrow?" Cyrus asked when they returned to the Lincoln.

"I have one delivery and after that we can do whatever you want."

"Okay. You said something about hiking?"

"Yeah. Last time I was out here, I heard about this trail up Sabino Canyon. It's supposed to be pretty easy and ends up at a series of small waterfalls."

"Sounds good to me." Cyrus smiled. "Now, how 'bout we go back to the motel. You look about done in."

Kyna went to sleep that night with her head resting on his chest. Every time he tried to turn over, she tightened her grip and held on as if her very life depended on it.

"Can you fucking believe it?" Bryan said, aghast. "She went behind my back and hired a bodyguard."

Conrad shrugged. "So?"

"She didn't trust me and hired some bozo to go with her."

Giggling, Conrad said, "You blame her?"

Bryan frowned, then looked thoughtful. "According to the crystal, she had several near misses. Maybe this guy is the reason she got this far."

"Maybe you should thank him."

"Maybe I should offer him your job."

Conrad made a rude noise and waved the suggestion away with his hand. "Nobody else is gonna put up with those idiots in your club."

"Coven! Goddamn it, Conrad—"

"All right, all right. Chill out."

"Well, anyway," Bryan said, suddenly all smiles, "it looks like she's going to make it, so let's get packing." He looked at the calendar on the wall. "I wonder if it's too early to get in some skiing. That mountain outside Albuquerque is supposed to have pretty good slopes."

It was Conrad's turn to frown. "Aren't we supposed to wait until *after* Halloween?"

Bryan straightened his ascot in the hall mirror. "It looks like I may have overestimated this voodoo doctor. If he were any good, Kyna would be on a slab in the morgue by now."

Conrad slammed his palm down on the hall table. "Ow! Shit!"

Bryan turned and raised an eyebrow. "What the devil are you doing?"

Conrad held out his hand. The palm was red and blood was leaking from two tiny holes in his thumb. "A fucking cockroach. You ought to spray this place."

Looking from his bodyguard's hand to the table and then back, Bryan said, "Where is it?"

"The son of a bitch bit me and ran off."

Bryan chuckled and shook his head. "Maybe I really should consider hiring this Trigg chap. Come on, let's find our parkas."

The goateed man trailed his dark guru down the long concourse at Memphis International Airport. Even in his banker's suit, the Dark Man was a magnet for almost every eye. When the mismatched duo arrived at the gate, they took seats well away from the other passengers, selecting a pair of seats in a corner far from the plate-glass window and placing their leather carry-on bags in the seats on either side of them. The Dark Man folded his lanky frame into the uncomfortable seat and turned his gaze on the potpourri of humanity milling around the check-in desk. After a few moments of sifting through the faces he selected an overweight man in a white shirt with yellowed sweat rings under the arms. Fingering the faux amulet through a gap in his shirt, the witch doctor moved his lips as if saying a silent prayer. A moment later, the fat man gasped and began frantically tearing at the collar of his shirt. In seconds, his eyes were bulging out of his head and his face had turned as red as a carnival balloon. The fat man's fat wife jumped up and started pounding him on the back and his fat little boy began to cry. When the man's face reached just the right shade of purple, the Dark Man released the amulet and leaned back with a smile to listen as the couple shouted obscenities at each other. By the time the paramedics arrived, the man was breathing normally and the wife and child were sitting on the opposite side of the room.

The Dark Man's smile quickly turned brittle. It had been fun, but it wasn't enough. He hated them! Hated the man's pasty face—hated the man's fat sow of a wife and hated his fat, snot-nosed brat. They reminded the Dark Man of the hypocritical, black-robed priests of his island.

Easing his head back against the wall, the Dark Man closed his eyes. It wasn't often that he allowed himself to relax, for it seemed that every time he did, his mind drifted back to the dirty little village of his childhood.

Once upon a time the Dark Man lived in a round mud hut high up on the side of a seven-hundred-foot mountain. The hut overlooked the Carambola Botanical Garden and the bay where years later they would open the Institute of Marine Sciences and a scuba diving resort. Back then, Roatan had been a wonderful place. In the summertime the mating cries of the giant iguanas on the next mountain sang his family to sleep. The summer rains fell like warm goose down and the trees were heavily laden with fruit and wild orchids.

The Dark Man's father had been called Joseph. Of course Joseph wasn't the name he had been given at birth. After the family moved to Roatan from Africa by way of Belmopan on the mainland, the black robes had changed his name to Joseph because they could not pronounce his real name. And like his biblical namesake, Joseph was a tall man—a bean pole, raw-boned and ugly, strong, quick with a smile and a helping hand. A part-time Hungan and a full-time fisherman, Joseph had been able to cure the children of swamp fevers and bring home ten more pounds of pompano or snapper than any other man on the island.

The Dark Man's mother had been a rare beauty, tall and regal like most of her people, with long silky-black hair and smooth honey-colored skin that had somehow managed to escape the ravages of disease and malnutrition. In a rare display of irony that the Dark Man did not understand until years later, the priests had named her Mary.

That was not all that the English fathers had changed. They had forced the fisherman to enroll his shy son in their school where, in the guise of saving the boy's soul, they had tried to beat an appreciation of their foreign gods into him with long wooden rulers and heavy strands of rosary beads. Later, the priests started to come to the hut—two of them; they always traveled in pairs. Both men had grown fat off the work of the islanders, both had bad skin and bad breath, and both had hot eyes that never seemed to stray very far from Mary.

They had told Joseph they came out of concern for his son's soul. They said the boy was obstinate and rebellious. They said he refused to say his prayers or to give up his totems and charms. In truth, it wasn't souls they had been interested in.

One afternoon the fishing had been exceptionally good and the Dark Man and his father had come home early. They were lugging three large red snappers over their shoulders and wearing strings of red and yellow hibiscus flowers around their necks. Joseph dropped the stringer of fish outside for the boy to clean and then walked into the shadowy hut. Inside he had found the priests. One was watching while the other quivered in ecstasy over Mary's unconscious body.

At first the priests had tried to convince Joseph that Mary had seduced them. But they had a hard time explaining why her nose was broken and she was unconscious. When lies didn't work, the men gathered up their black robes, fell to their knees and begged, reminding Joseph of God's laws of compassion and forgiveness. Unfortunately for the fathers, Joseph's gods knew only one law.

One at a time, Joseph dragged the men outside by their heels and tied them to a tree. He took the long boning knife away from his son and used it to slit the two men open from navel to neck. When the English police arrived, they found the Dark Man's father calmly sitting by an open fire pit, roasting one of the priests' liver. They never found the other liver nor either of the men's hearts.

The English hanged Joseph—AKA Matzulas Kebahala—in the main square of Coxen Hole and threw Mary into jail as a prostitute. She died there of pneumonia three months later. The villagers spirited the boy off to the jungles on the mainland, where he had been apprenticed to the local Hungan.

The Dark Man watched the clock over the check-in desk as if it were his worst enemy. In a way it was. Each tiny movement of the second hand was like someone tearing a small slice out of his gut with a pair of ice tongs. His eyes wandered to the glass wall that looked out at the waiting plane.

They were still there.

Quickly averting his eyes, the Dark Man glanced at his apprentice to see if he had noticed them—the drooling ghosts with their contorted faces pressed against the window.

The goateed man was surreptitiously picking his nose and staring at a passing stewardess.

Naturally, the sorcerer recognized the disembodied spirits— he had personally sent each soul on its one-way trip to hell. There was Kempa—his was the red spirit with the gaping holes for eyes. He had been the headman of the Dark Man's adopted village on the mainland. Then there was Hemat, the schoolteacher who had tried to turn the villagers against him. His was the ghost dripping ectoplasmic gore from the stump of a headless neck. And then of course there was Begalla, the Dark Man's old mentor—the Hungan who had first set the Dark Man's feet on the thorny road to Baron Samedi and the Guédé. His giggling ghost had a raw hole where its heart used to beat.

And there were others. So many others that their ghosts were buzzing around the window like flies around an outhouse. Their psychic howls of glee echoed inside his head like the screams of demented inmates in the bowels of the deepest, darkest asylum. They knew their time was near, and without the Butcher's Broom to protect him, there was little the Dark Man could do to stop them.

"It will be a good time?" the man with the goatee asked.

238

Startled out of his brooding introspection, the Dark Man quickly put a clamp on his emotions. "Not ideal, but good enough. The moon will be past full and the stars are favorably aligned."

"Is that how you discovered where the woman will be? The stars?"

The Dark Man knew his protégé was dying to know how he'd learned of the Rand woman's whereabouts. He smiled enigmatically. "No."

"Will you take her alive?"

The Dark Man thought for a moment. "It would be nice, but it is not necessary."

"Then . . . why?"

"She has caused me much trouble."

"I do not understand," the goateed man said. "Your life force is low?"

The Dark Man's head turned slowly and, if possible, his countenance grew even more grim. "You dare question me?"

"Of course not, Master. I but worry about your health."

"Best you worry about your own!"

The Dark Man knew the temptations the goateed man endured. He remembered well the long nights sitting at Begalla's feet, watching with impatient eyes as the old man's palsied hands mixed the ingredients for his poison potions, feeling the ambition rising like bile in his throat. Nights when he learned that hate and envy were the catalytic fires that stirred the dark lords' black hearts, and that blood and pain were the currency that purchased their allegiance. That's why he had cut the old bastard's heart out and taken his powers for himself.

The Dark Man fingered the fake talisman and watched his assistant sweat.

A sleek blond woman in a light blue airline uniform came to the check-in desk and picked up the microphone.

"We are now boarding rows one through eight for Eastern's flight two-ten to Albuquerque."

Chapter Fifteen

October 29

By sunup Kyna had put her black mood behind her and was cracking wise like the Kyna of old. She even performed a slow striptease with the motel's postage-stamp-sized bath towel, and when Cyrus got all hot and bothered, she emptied a glass of tap water over his head.

They put on shorts, T-shirts, their new boots and—because Arizona mornings had a tendency to be cool—Kyna brought along her cardigan sweater and Cyrus carried his navy jacket. Kyna made a five-minute stop at a shopping mall in the middle of Tucson where Cyrus watched her trade six bags of quarter-carat sparklers for enough cash to make a reasonable-sized dent in the national debt. As soon as the money was safely locked in the trunk, they followed a gas station attendant's instructions past a subdivision of quarter-million-dollar homes to the parking lot in front of the Sabino Canyon visitors' center.

The trail started between two tall cacti at the far side of the lot and followed a series of low hills through juniper, yucca and enough rabbitbrush to provide Brer Rabbit's entire clan with affordable housing. Up on the sides of the hills, dozens of stately saguaro and old-man cacti stood guard like medieval knights wearing prickly suits of armor. The ground was both sandy and rocky, and had been baked to the consistency of pottery by the fiery desert sun. On the way up the canyon, they surprised a roadrunner feeding on a small snake and later caught a glimpse of a mule deer's striped behind as it disappeared over the ridge. The trail was rugged enough to make them glad they had new boots—for traversing rocky streams, and taking them over or around huge chunks of granite that had split off from the face of the canyon. Two and a half hours and four steep miles later they reached a rock shelf several dozen yards long perched between two craggy, brush-covered peaks. The shelf had been scoured flat by aeons of snowmelt and infrequent rainfall until it was as slick and shiny as a ballroom floor. At the back of the shelf where the walls of the canyon narrowed was a pool of greenish water that had been chiseled out of the bedrock by the last in a series of small but perfect waterfalls that stepped down from the high peaks. The overflow from the pool nourished a fringe of tall grasses and cottonwood trees and then spilled over the front edge of the shelf and dropped to the floor of the canyon.

It was past noon and the high sun had obliterated all traces of shade and turned the canyon into a kiln. The air was full of sunshine, pollen motes and hungry dragonflies that buzzed around Cyrus's head like a squadron of biplanes from the Red Baron's flying circus.

Kyna, who had been bitching about the heat all the way up the trail, took one look at the tranquil pool and began unbuttoning her sweat-encrusted shirt. "This is like a tiny Garden of Eden."

"You know," Cyrus said, glancing around, "there are probably other people running around out here."

"I don't care," she replied, skinning out of her shorts. "I'm hot. I'm dirty. I'm thirsty. And I'm getting in the water."

She stripped down to her panties, casually dropping her odd-looking necklace on top of the pile, and waded out to the middle of the pool. Once there, she lowered herself until the water ringed her neck, then leaned back and let the falling water massage the dust from her hair and the trail aches from her bones.

"Ahhh," she purred. "This is Heaven."

"It looks cold."

"It's not. It's just right."

"I bet there are things in there."

Kyna opened one eye. "Russ, I'm older and wiser than you. Let me assure you, a couple of minuscule mountain trout or tadpoles aren't going to kill me."

"You never know," he replied, scratching under his arms.

Kyna closed her eye and raised her arms to work the water into her hair. As she did, her breasts popped out and Cyrus could see she hadn't been totally honest about the water temperature. He watched her splash around for as long as he could stand it and then trotted over to the edge of the shelf and looked back down the trail. The canyon was still as brown, dry and hot as before, but there wasn't a soul in sight. In the distance, the suburbs of Tucson shimmered like a mirage under the unblinking eye of the sun. It was a view that would make a camel thirsty.

Cyrus raced back to the pool, sat on a rock and began untying the laces on his boots. As he removed each piece of clothing, he folded it the way his mother had taught him and stacked it one atop the other.

"Anal retentive!" Kyna chuckled.

"Yeah, yeah."

He walked over to place his clothing on top of a pile of stones left over from an old camp fire, and as he bent over, he heard a high-pitched whirring noise coming from the bushes beside the rocks. He glanced down and saw a six-foot diamondback rattlesnake coiled next to his foot. The reptile was obviously unhappy about nearly being stepped on, for it was shaking its ringed tail like a fist.

"Whoa!" Cyrus hollered, and jumped back.

"What's the matter?" Kyna called from the pool.

"Nothing."

Loath to intrude on the reptile's sunbathing, Cyrus walked clear to the other side of the shelf to find a nice shady spot for his clothes and was dumbfounded when a second rattlesnake slithered out of the grass at the base of a cottonwood tree. This rattler was brownish in color, but no less indignant.

"What's going on here?"

Again Cyrus backed away. But this time the crazy snake came after him, slipping and sliding in a series of drunken esses as it fought for traction on the slippery rock.

Now, Cyrus never claimed to be Marlin Perkins, but he couldn't remember ever hearing about a snake getting mad enough to chase after a full-grown man. He glanced to his left and saw the grass moving when there wasn't enough wind to blow out a match. Then he looked right and saw the blunt snout of a sidewinder worming its way out from under a boulder.

Kyna was still in the pool, only now she was singing at the top of her lungs: "This is serious business; sex and violence and rock and roll," while she continued to use the waterfall as a shower massage. And all the while, snakes of every race, creed and color were literally coming out of the woodwork. Brown ones, black ones, thin ones, fat ones—even a couple of babies no thicker than strands of spaghetti. Yet every one of them seemed to have gotten thirsty at the same instant.

"Uh, Kyna. I think you better come out now."

"Not just yet, oh mother of all mother hens."

In their hurry to get to the pool, the reptiles were treading all over each other and expressing their irritation at their neighbors by shaking their tails and hissing.

"Do you have an alarm on your watch?" Kyna called.

"Come out!"

She pushed the hair out of her eyes and stared at him. "What? I'm not—" Then she spotted the squirming mass of iridescent scales and her eyes grew huge. "What the hell *are* those things?"

Cyrus had backed up so far that his heels were getting wet and he no longer needed to shout. "I believe those are called snakes. And if I were you, I'd haul my ass out of there before they jump in and start doing the backstroke."

She had a little trouble running over the algae-covered rocks, but once she managed to extract herself from the pool, she slipped first her T-shirt and then the necklace over her head.

"Ow! Shit!"

"What's the matter?" Cyrus called in alarm. "Were you bitten?"

She glued herself to his back. "No. My necklace burned the back of my neck. I guess it got hot lying in the sun."

"Super."

"What are they doing?" she whispered in his ear.

"I think this means that our big-headed friend hasn't forgotten about us."

"Oh, Russ," Kyna said, doing a little dance at his back. "I hate snakes."

You think you hate snakes! he thought. "Then finish getting dressed and let's get the hell out of here."

The slick rock slowed the reptiles' advance, but through sheer mindless tenacity they managed to encircle the humans. Kyna wiggled into her shorts, then hopped first on one foot and then the other as she pulled on her boots. After hastily tying the laces, she clutched her sweater to her chest like a shield.

Cyrus turned and held out the stack of his clothing. "Hold on to these."

Her eyes dropped below his waist and she managed a wry smile. "What are you going to do? Wave your magic wand and scare them away?"

He gave her one of his looks, then turned back around and tried to clear his mind. This time dredging up fear wasn't a problem. He used the epinephrine rush to push the transformation, and when the change was complete he dropped down on all fours and rubbed his shaggy head against Kyna's leg. She jumped—too scared to understand what he was trying to do. He snorted and decided the main drawback to being an animal was the lack of communication skills.

With the reptiles only a few feet away, Cyrus shoved his head roughly between Kyna's knees and eased forward until she was perched precariously atop his shoulders. She squealed and dropped the stack of clothing, then grabbed a double fistful of his fur. He turned his head and gave her what he hoped was a reassuring look.

"Do you know what you're doing?" she asked.

Good question!

Taking two quick steps, Cyrus launched himself high into the air. As he sailed over the first row of snakes, two of the larger reptiles raised their heads and tried to sink their fangs into his exposed belly. But without being coiled, the serpents lacked the necessary thrust and flopped helplessly back to the rock.

Cyrus landed, and as he prepared to spring again, he felt a sharp sting in his right shoulder, followed by a burning sensation that spread all the way up his neck. Ignoring the pain, he made like a great hairy frog and vaulted to the edge of the shelf in a series of gigantic leaps. At the drop-off he paused and looked back.

"Jesus!" Kyna gasped. "Where did they go?"

The plateau was empty—not a serpent in sight.

But Cyrus wasn't about to take any chances. With Kyna's arms wrapped tightly around his neck, he went straight down the side of the canyon—hopping from pinnacle to peak, skipping like light over the massive boulders and dodging the cactus spines until, in a matter of seconds, they reached the safety of the ravine floor. He followed the path of winding water, splashing through the cold shallows one moment and running easily over water-polished stones the next, and in less time than it had taken them to cross the parking lot at the beginning of their trek, Cyrus reached the trailhead and stopped. Through the trees he could smell the stink of human beings milling around the parking lot.

Kyna released her grip on his neck and slid to the ground.

"Oh Russ! You're hurt."

She gingerly touched away the drops of blood around a pair of puncture wounds in his shoulder.

"Does it hurt?"

He sniffed the wound. The poison smelled bad, but the puncture marks were already closing. He shook his shaggy head and gave her a big, goofy wolf grin.

"What am I going to do with you?" she said, and rubbed his snout.

He ran his tongue across her hand and then took off back up the trail to recover his pants.

The instant the Dark Man was safely inside his suite in the hotel across from Albuquerque International Airport, he set about weaving protective charms around all the windows and doors. Between Paula Inkarha's nightly ectoplasmic visits and the vengeful spirits that were following him around like packs of wild dogs, the Dark Man refused even to close his eyes until his place of rest was totally secure.

Of course the Inkarha woman was no real threat. Later, after he had disposed of Ms. Rand and Mr. Trigg, and after he had banished the spirits back to the dark regions where they belonged, he would pay a personal visit to the meddlesome Ms. Inkarha.

"When will they arrive?" the goateed man asked.

"Tomorrow. We will finish them the next day."

"All Saints' Day?"

The Dark Man nodded.

"Then we can go home?"

The Dark Man gave his assistant one of his rare smiles. "Then we can go home."

When Cyrus returned to the Lincoln, he found Kyna sitting inside with the doors locked, the engine running and the air conditioner blowing full blast. She saw him through the window and hit the lock-release button. He couldn't read her expression.

"You okay?" he asked.

Her face was flushed and she had pulled her T-shirt up, exposing her midriff to the AC vent.

"How's your shoulder?"

He unbuttoned his shirt and showed her.

"Not even a mark," she mumbled.

"Nope."

"This is so *Twilight Zone*. You know how lucky you are?"

"Didn't feel lucky when it bit me."

"What was he doing back there?" she asked in a neutral tone of voice.

"Who? The floating head?"

"Yes."

"Toying with us, I think. Keeping us on edge."

"Why? Why would he do that?"

"Beats me. Maybe it's the way he gets off. Or maybe it's just his way of cracking his knuckles."

She smiled. "Well, it didn't work."

"What didn't?"

"It was wonderful. I loved it!" She began squirming on the seat and rubbing his thigh.

"I thought you hated snakes."

"I do, dummy. But the ride back down the canyon . . . It was the most exciting thing I've ever done. It was like riding the wind. Can we do it again? Please?"

Cyrus realized that if he lived to be a thousand—an event that Paula had assured him was a very real possibility—he would never ever understand women.

After a brief trip back to the motel to shower and change into clean clothes, Kyna drove them to a Mexican restaurant in Old Tucson. It was a nice place with unfinished wooden tables and candles and a staff that relied less on fake sombreros and hand-painted castanets than on fast service, iced beer and large portions of good food. Unfortunately Kyna was too keyed up to pay much attention to her dinner. She mechanically shoveled taco salad into her mouth and sat in stony silence until Cyrus gobbled down his beef chimichanga. Yet with all the rushing around, it was still after eleven o'clock by the time they returned to the Sabino Canyon parking lot.

Cyrus got out to make sure the ranger station was locked and when he returned to the car, Kyna was standing by the passenger door in her stocking feet.

"You sure you want to do this?" he asked. "You're going to ruin your clothes."

"No I'm not," she replied, unzipping and stepping out of her skirt.

Cyrus sighed. "What do you think you're doing?"

"Why are you whispering? There's nobody here." Kyna reached over and tugged on his belt. "Come on, get undressed."

"Look, Kyna. I'm just a country boy. I play a little tennis, take a little target practice . . ."

"A real wolf in sheep's clothing, huh?"

". . . I vote Republican and pay my taxes on time. I'm not sure I'm ready for this."

She dropped her blouse on the front seat, then stepped out of her stockings and unhooked her bra. "Then it's time you loosened up a little. Come on, Russ, I promise not to look."

He looked around one more time—praying for a ranger or a jogger. Even a lost Girl Scout would do. Then, with a sigh big enough to blow out a forest fire, he began unbuttoning his shirt.

Kyna wadded up her clothing, tossed them in the trunk and removed the blanket she had borrowed from the motel.

"What's that for?" he asked, sure he didn't really want to know.

"You'll see."

He stripped down to his underwear and socks. The desert night was cool and brought a rash of gooseflesh to his shoulders and arms. When he was completely nude, he folded his things, placed them in the trunk and stood in front of Kyna with his hands cupped over his groin.

"Well?" she said.

He rolled his eyes and tried to relax.

"Would you mind waiting in the car?" he asked.

"Why?" She saw he was getting an erection and giggled. "Oh!"

The whole thing looked stupid and hopeless until the top of the moon cleared the hills to the east and Cyrus felt the feathery touch of its light on his skin.

Count your blessings, he thought as the fur began to sprout, *at least she isn't wearing spurs.*

He moved through the night like a phantom. He was aware of, but not slowed by, Kyna's weight on his back while his feet—as quick and silent as the desert wind—flew over the sand as if they were strapped to rocket pods. Kyna had placed the motel blanket across his back and sat astride his shoulders, hanging on with fingers and knees and wearing a feral grin. They took the right fork of the river, the one that went away from the rattlesnake shelf, and followed the shallows up Bear Canyon toward Thimble Peak. To Kyna, the trip was little more than a blur of shadows and low-hanging branches, of wind in her hair and spray in her face. To Cyrus it was pure joy. Each sound was a symphony, every smell a bouquet. Every inch of ground, every tree, every rock stood out in bas-relief as his eyes pulled in and enhanced each stray moon-beam.

Up the steep sides of the canyon they went, forgoing the well-traveled hiking trails in favor of brush-choked creek beds and game paths. Jackrabbits and lizards bolted as they raced past. Horned owls took flight at the sight of the nude Diana—goddess of the hunt—riding on the back of the great hairy wolf.

Cyrus reached the summit of Thimble Peak a little before midnight and stopped to rest on a ledge that looked down the sharp vee of the canyon. Kyna climbed down and tiptoed gingerly around jagged rocks and piles of deer droppings.

"Wow!"

Cyrus sat on his haunches and let his tongue loll. He wasn't tired in the least. The wolf skin he slipped into now as easily as he donned a pair of designer jeans seemed to draw energy from the very air.

"That was incredible," Kyna said, stroking his muzzle.

He answered by licking her face. She grabbed the scruff of his cheeks and rubbed her small, upturned nose against his coal-black and icy-wet wolf nose.

"Wouldn't you like to change back?" she purred.

He didn't think so. After the freedom of being a wolf, changing back into a man was like crawling into a mummy suit. His own skin isolated him from the natural world, dulling his senses and giving his life as much zest as a shuffleboard tournament.

Kyna cupped her breasts and rubbed the tips against his nose.

All at once he remembered there *was* something to be said for being human.

The thin man with the goatee sat in an uncomfortable wooden chair in the corner of the room while his master slept fitfully on the bed. The Dark Man's eyes were open, his body twitching as he communed silently with the grisly gods that renewed his powers.

The goateed man's job was to maintain the charms of protection and to wake his master at the first sign of a breach. This should have taken all of his concentration, but he was as nervous as a cat and his mind kept wandering. The Dark Man was so confident about the upcoming confrontation with the woman and her friend. Yet how could that be? the goateed man mused. This Trigg was no longer a man, but a creature with powers that seemed to grow exponentially with the rising of each moon. The goateed man had no experience with such creatures, yet even as the Dark Man decried Trigg as an opponent, the goateed man suspected that his master was worried too.

What was such a creature capable of? True, the goateed man allowed, his master had experience and great powers. Plus, the Dark Man would be able to select the time and place of the confrontation. Still, with such a creature . . .

The goateed man got up from the chair as quietly as possible and tiptoed over to the dresser. He unzipped his master's travel kit and removed a small velvet pouch. Inside the pouch was a multifaceted crystal about the size of an ostrich's egg. Cradling the crystal protectively against his chest, the goateed man slipped into the bathroom and closed the door. At the sink, he pushed aside the coffeepot, cups and packets of instant coffee and ran less than a quarter of an inch of water into the plastic tray the motel had provided with the coffee service. He then carefully balanced the crystal on its blunt end in the water. Cushioned by the thin layer of fluid, the crystal began to hum and emit a soft greenish glow. The goateed man rested the tips of his fingers on the rough outer surface of the egg and stared into its murky depths until a swirling rainbow-colored cloud formed in its middle. Several possible futures began to unfold in front of his eyes. Most of the outcomes were as expected: total victory for his master—horrible death for the woman and man. But one scenario was . . . cloudy. No future was ever certain, but the crystal was normally an excellent barometer of outcomes. The goateed man tried to convince himself that the nebulous nature of this particular vision was proof of how unlikely it was. Still, he was now more agitated than before and the thought of waking his master crossed his mind. He dismissed the idea just as quickly. Awakened from his meditations, it was unlikely that the Dark Man would be in any mood to listen to his apprentice's faulty visions. Besides, the goateed man assured himself, six of the seven possible futures had been positive. Six out of seven! Those were excellent odds . . . Weren't they?

After replacing the crystal in the Dark Man's suitcase, the goateed man went to his own valise and unzipped the inside compartment. He pulled out an oil-soaked rag and unfolded it over his bed. Inside was the shiny black .50-caliber British Army revolver that his father had bequeathed him. The goateed man had kept it more as a keepsake than out of any need for protection, and as far as he knew, the gun had never been fired. He opened the cylinder and checked to make sure it had bullets. Then he tucked the gun safely inside his overcoat.

One never knew.

* * *

Kyna lay on her stomach on the blanket with her chin propped up on her hands. Cyrus was on the ground at her side, his body folded almost casually into the lotus position. As the night drew to a close, the air grew progressively cooler, but so far they were comfortable beneath a protective film of lust-spent sweat. From their vantage point on the peak, they could see the lights coming on in the houses down on the edge of Tucson.

"Wouldn't it be wonderful if we could just stay up here forever?" Kyna asked. "You could bring the game you caught back to our little cave and I could cook it over an open pit. Our children would have to sneak into Tucson to go to school, of course. But in the afternoons they could turn into little wolf puppies and hunt with their father."

"Kyna, I hope you don't mind me saying: You're the weirdest woman I ever met."

"Not at all. Russ, do you think we could have children?"

He looked at the back of her head as he considered the idea. In the pale light, her hair was the color of blood.

"You mean normal kids?" he asked. "Or kids like me?"

"Either."

"Gee, I don't know. I guess we'll have to ask Paula."

"Do you want children? I mean, maybe I'm taking a lot for granted."

In truth, he really hadn't thought about it.

"Let me ask *you* a question," he said to give himself time to think. "You really want to be stuck with a guy that goes through electric razors the way Pavarotti goes through pizzas?"

While she pondered the question, Cyrus's mind was in turmoil. Did he want to marry Kyna? Did he want to marry anyone, for that matter? He had major feelings for her. He'd told Paula it was love, but was it really? Would he know it if it were? He took a long look at the curve of Kyna's neck, the slope of her back and the tight mounds of her buttocks. Her skin was a combination of cream and silk and smelled of sandalwood and dust. How could any man—any werewolf, for that matter—not be in love with that body?

He shelved the question of love for a moment to ask himself a more hairy question: What about what Paula had asked him in her shop? What would he do if he married Kyna and then she aged and he didn't? Cyrus shivered—and not from the temperature of the air. He was almost as terrified of the pain of such a loss as he was of a sharp blade. Even after all these years, he still missed his parents—still cried on the anniversary of their deaths. What would it be like to lose a wife? Several wives? To see them wrinkle and gray before his eyes. To see them dry up like bouquets of pale flowers?

He scooted closer to Kyna.

When it came right down to it, it wasn't that hard a decision. As frightened as he was of losing her, he was even more afraid of being alone. Of years without end living a sterile emotionless existence; no warmth, no caring, no tenderness.

He stroked the back of her leg. "You didn't answer my question," he said. "Having second thoughts?"

"I was thinking, yes. But not having second thoughts. I was wondering, what would we do? Where would we go?"

"Babe, I don't want to bring you down, but aren't we getting a little ahead of ourselves? We have a date tomorrow or the next day with your friend Douglas and then another with Mr. Floating Head somewhere down the line. Maybe we better just take one day at a time."

Kyna turned to face him, copying his position with her feet tucked behind opposing knees. She reached out and took his face in her hands.

"We're going to survive this! Do you hear me? I love you and I've never told anyone that before and I will not lose you now."

Cyrus recognized the fear in her eyes. But he saw the truth there as well. "Okay. First Mr. Bryan, then Mr. Floating Head, and then I guess we go rustle up a justice of the peace."

Chapter Sixteen

October 30

At dawn, Cyrus drove back to the motel so they could shower and get into clean clothes. They had a seven-hour drive ahead, but neither of them felt much like sleeping. Breakfast was coffee and cold cereal at the motel coffee shop with a somnolent waitress leaning over their shoulders. Then they pulled out onto I-10 and headed east. Just across the New Mexico state line—at Lordsburg—they turned off the interstate onto Highway 90. They followed 90 until it turned into State 152 and then picked up Interstate 25 at Caballo. As on the trip to Tucson, the landscape was dry and desolate, but had been climbing steadily and if possible was even more rugged. The air was still very warm, but now had a thin taste that often accompanies high altitudes.

"God, what a place," Kyna muttered. "It's like the dark side of the moon."

"What do you mean?" Cyrus asked.

"Dirt, sand, sand, cactus, cactus, rocks. No life!"

"You're kidding, right? We just passed a hawk circling up over that last hill. There's some kind of big lizard sunning on top of that rock over there. And we passed at least two dozen mice sleeping in their burrows, just in the last quarter mile alone."

"And how, pray tell, do you know all this?" She saw his amused expression and said, "Never mind. You're spooky at times, did you know that?"

"How do you think I feel?"

"I don't know. How *do* you feel? I'm not talking about when you change, but even when you're not a wolf, you're different. Is this something you work at? Or what?"

"Well, I guess it's some kind of weird side effect of the change. It's like I was born blind—I was comfortable with it, I got used to it, liked it even. But now I'm slowly beginning to see. It isn't anything I asked for."

"Would you go back to the way you were if you could?"

Cyrus stared straight ahead. "No. I think I'd rather be dead."

They took turns driving and napping, but there was very little napping going on. Their conversation of the night before was still with them, a third passenger as real as the plastic Jesus on the dashboard. More than once, when she was supposed to be asleep, Cyrus felt Kyna's eyes on him. He could smell the anxiety in her sweat and almost hear the wheels turning in her head, but he didn't say anything. She'd work it out, he told himself. And when she wanted to talk, he'd be there. It was funny in a way. This trip, all the hours in the car, had brought them together in a way no airplane or train ever could. On a long drive people relaxed. After a while they opened up, let their true natures show. Cyrus turned his head and smiled. Maybe he *should* thank this guy Bryan when they met.

At one-thirty they rounded a curve and got their first glimpse of Albuquerque. The mood they were in, instead of a modern Southwestern city of chrome and glass, they saw an evil kingdom filled with deformed buildings and malignant trolls.

"I used to really like Albuquerque," Kyna said.

"Come on. It'll be okay. Have a little faith."

"I can't help it, Russ. I'm starting to feel like a condemned prisoner."

"What happened to 'We're going to survive this'?" he asked.

"That was last night. Today I see things . . . differently. I've been picking at the scabs on my soul and I'm afraid. The life

I've led, what else should I expect? I've always lived by the nickel-plated rule: Screw unto others before they screw unto you. Now, when I finally find something to live for, I figure God is bound to zap me.''

"Naw. Only the good die young."

"Then I should live to be a thousand."

Their motel in Albuquerque was a small family-run affair a little over a block from the Old Town section. The buildings were old and situated close enough to the Rio Grande that John Wayne could have stayed in one of the rooms while filming one of his numerous John Ford epics. The old man behind the desk gave them a dirty look when he noticed the missing wedding bands and Kyna squared around to give him a piece of her mind.

"Whoa, there, Hoss," Cyrus said as he gently took her arm and steered her outside to unload the car.

The room was tiny—tiny bathroom, tiny bed and tiny black-and-white TV. But there were starched sheets on the bed and the air conditioner in the wall could turn water in a glass into ice cubes in a matter of minutes. As soon as they unpacked, Kyna began mechanically separating the dirty laundry.

"I'll do it," Cyrus volunteered.

This time she didn't argue. She upended her laundry bag in the middle of the floor, then stripped down to her panties, stretched out on the bed and threw one arm across her eyes. She was snoring before Cyrus went out the door.

After everything had been washed and dried, Cyrus folded his shirts and jeans. Then he took an extra few minutes with her things, smoothing the wrinkles out of each piece with his hands. There was something so intimate about handling her lingerie. In his mind it bespoke a trust, a willingness to be vulnerable that made him feel strangely vulnerable himself. He glanced around to see if anyone was watching and then hurried back to the room to arrange her clothing in tidy piles beside her suitcase.

Kyna was still asleep, moaning like a child, so he removed his shirt and pulled a chair over next to the bed. While he watched her sleep, he tried to put all of his conflicting feelings in perspective. Naturally, he was afraid for her safety—he was responsible for her. He was her bodyguard.

And lover? a tiny voice reminded him.

And lover, he conceded.

There were so many things he wanted for her—for the two of them. But the main thing he wanted, he couldn't give her: time. Today, tomorrow at the latest, something terrible was going to happen. He knew it. He felt it in his gut like a giant rubber band winding around and around until either it broke or he did. Bryan Douglas—the Dark Man: two sides of the same coin. And the idea that anyone could think of hurting Kyna . . .

His claws dug into the arm of the chair.

Down, boy!

But was it really love? Could he take the chance? Did he have a choice?

Wow! he thought, *what a scary feeling!*

His head began to nod and he slowly slipped into a deep sleep.

Once again Cyrus found himself roaming the top of that oddly-shaped mountain. If anything, the peak was even more eerily beautiful than he remembered—cold and wild in the light of a blood-red moon. But he sensed danger all around him: in the air, in the trees—eyes that sought his death filled the forest like malevolent leaves. He pushed on—over boulders and through brush thick with the scent of wild blueberries. Thorns tore at his fur, but couldn't slow him. He was on a quest. He had to find . . . someone—to warn them. But he couldn't remember who. Fear was his only companion. It was the coppery taste of blood in his mouth and the pain in his lungs. It was the nagging voice of terror that drove him on. Terrified? Yes, but of what and for whom? He couldn't seem to remember that either.

At the edge of the trees, he paused to survey the rubble field. The wind carried the smell of rain and wet earth—it also carried the odor of fresh blood. He followed the scent around the rocks, keeping close to the ground. His instincts told him not to let his outline be caught against the light of the moon. He rounded a massive boulder and saw her: the silver bitch. She was lying on her side, her neck and shoulder a mass of bloody fur. He went to her and tried to lift her with his snout, but she only whined.

"Get up!" his mind screamed. "Get up! They're coming!"

The she-wolf's eyes were twin pools of agony. He could smell the sickly-sweet odor of death oozing out of her with each staccato beat of her heart. Behind him he heard movement in the trees at the edge of the forest and panic seized his heart. He couldn't think. He had to get away, but he couldn't just leave her.

The she-wolf whined and licked his nose and he blinked back almost human tears. He placed his fangs at her throat.

"I'm sorry," his mind said. "I'm so sorry."

The penthouse at the Albuquerque Hilton was the size of a small warehouse. It had been lavishly furnished in leathers and accented with Navaho rugs and kachina dolls. The three outer walls were made of clear Plexiglas. The east wall gave a view of Sandia Crest, the opposite wall overlooked Old Town.

When the buzzer sounded, Conrad put aside the local paper he had been reading and went to the door.

"Yeah?"

The man in the hall was black and thin as a rail and had a neatly trimmed goatee.

"Mr. Douglas?"

"Who wants him?"

"I have a message from Ms. Rand."

Conrad looked the man up and down. The stranger had on a dark three-piece suit, his shoes were polished, and he was wearing a watch that had to have cost a thousand bucks. But Conrad knew better than to take a chance.

"Up against the wall."

"I beg your pardon."

''Beg all you want, but turn around and put your hands on the wall.''

After patting the man down, Conrad stood back and held out his arm. ''After you.''

The goateed man stepped into the suite and surreptitiously scanned the living room. He couldn't believe his eyes. The place was clean! No spells, no protective charms—nothing! He stared at the huge man standing in front of him and wondered, *Are these people crazy? They're just asking for it.*

''Wait here,'' Conrad said. ''I'll get him.''

On the way up in the elevator, the goateed man had been terrified that he was going to forget the words of the spell to lower the protective shield around Douglas's room. Now he simply walked over and turned the lock and opened the door.

The Dark Man slipped soundlessly into the room. He quickly scanned the corners of the room and then looked at his assistant. The goateed man shrugged.

The sound of angry voices echoed down the penthouse hallway.

''She doesn't know I'm here, moron, so how could she send a messenger?''

Bryan swept into the room holding together the front of a black silk kimono with a red dragon embroidered across the back. He saw the goateed man first and snapped, ''Who the devil—''

Bryan saw a black giant in an outrageous feathered cloak standing next to the bar and skidded to a halt. ''Who . . .'' Then, as he realized who was standing in front of him, his mouth dropped open and the blood drained from his face. ''No!''

The Dark Man's grin more closely resembled the grimace of a skull. ''Oh, yes. Yes indeed.''

''Hey!'' Conrad shouted. ''Who let you in?''

A .45 automatic magically appeared in the bodyguard's fist, but the Dark Man performed a little magic of his own. He opened his palm and blew a cloud of dust over the big man's face and Conrad stopped dead in his tracks.

"Boss! I can't move," Conrad cried. "Help me!"

But Bryan couldn't help himself. With no place to run, he began frantically waving his hands in the air, belatedly trying to weave a charm to ward off what he knew was coming.

The Dark Man watched Bryan's ballet with an amused smile. The smile grew wider when a tiny ball of green energy formed in the air in front of Bryan's face.

"Leave now," Bryan panted as his arms continued to windmill. "And I'll let you live."

"Alas," replied the dark giant, "I am at your mercy. Do with me what you will."

"I'm not kidding around here!"

"I understand," the Dark Man replied reasonably. "But as you must know, you have something that belongs to me and I cannot leave without it. Besides, I have debts to pay . . . very specific debts. And my debtors are not the type to accept excuses."

The strain of maintaining the energy ball was making Bryan's arms tremble. His eyes darted to the door, but he understood now that there was no place on earth he could hide and his face began to crumble. "No. Please! I'll tell you where it is. Just go and leave me alone."

The Dark Man glanced at his assistant and the goateed man stepped out into the hall, returning a few moments later with the leather suitcase.

"Sorry," the Dark Man said.

"Take Conrad! He's big and strong."

"Boss? What are you saying?" the bodyguard exclaimed.

The goateed man removed a large rolled-felt pouch from the suitcase. He placed the pouch on the coffee table, untied the gold string that held it together and unrolled it. Inside the pouch, each in its own individual pocket, were twelve incredibly sharp cast-iron spikes—each twelve inches long and each with the likeness of a woman's deformed face carved into its handle.

Bryan took one look at the spikes and his eyes nearly popped out of his head. "NOOOooo!" he screamed, and hurled the ball of energy at the sorcerer.

The Dark Man stood his ground—still with that contemptuous half-smile on his face—and caught the streaking ball in his hand. The energy blossomed like a tiny green nuclear cloud and encased his body inside a cocoon of transparent green power.

Speechless, Bryan tried to run, but it was as if his lower body belonged to someone else. He could still move his arms and feel his feet. He could wiggle his toes even. But from the waist down he was as stiff as a board.

The goateed man giggled and wagged his finger. "Mustn't leave now. The fun's just about to start."

In the meantime, the energy field had condensed into a halo around the Dark Man's head and was seeping down into his arms like thick gobs of petroleum jelly. He spread his hands apart and laughed manically as the energy sparked back and forth between his fingers like bolts of ball lightning. With each pulse, the air crackled and soon the living room reeked of ozone.

"You thought I was helpless," said the Dark Man. "You thought you had emasculated me."

"No!" Bryan hissed. "I swear! I meant you no harm." He held out his hands, palms up. "I only needed the—"

"Silence!" the Dark Man ordered. "Be silent and observe what real power can do."

Closing his eyes, the Dark Man offered up a whispered prayer to Legba, the chief of his voodoo gods. As the ancient words dripped from his lips like drops of deadly poison, his body underwent a chilling metamorphosis. The skin of his face turned chalky white and his eyes rolled back and disappeared into his skull. A tall stovepipe hat suddenly materialized on top of his head and the feathered cloak changed into a dusty black tuxedo jacket. When the chant was done, two burning red balls of flame peered down at Bryan from the Dark Man's empty eye sockets.

The goateed man dropped to one knee and bowed his head.

"Hail to you, Baron Samedi. Ride your servant to do thy will."

The energy still danced between the sorcerer's hands. Only now the stream was thicker and had started to coil sensuously in and out of the man's wide-splayed fingers. In a moment, the Dark Man lowered his left hand and the energy began pouring from his fingers like wine from a bottle. The stream humped and squirmed like a living thing as it slithered across the carpet toward Conrad. The muscles in the bodyguard's neck stood out like mooring ropes as he strained to free himself from the Dark Man's magic, but it was useless. Had Conrad been ten times stronger—fifty times—it wouldn't have saved him, for it was death creeping inexorably across the floor and everything it touched turned black and gave off a foul-smelling smoke.

"Please, boss! Please make it stop!"

The stream touched the bottom of Conrad's shoe and he screamed like his soul was being ripped from his body.

The Dark Man made a motion with his right hand and the bodyguard's cries were cut off as effectively as if someone had pulled a wire out of a stereo speaker. The soles of Conrad's shoes began to bubble, and as the energy tentacle inched its way up under his right pants leg, the cuff began to smolder. The bodyguard's eyes opened so wide that it looked like they might fall out, roll down his cheeks and disappear into his mouth. In a matter of moments his body began to vibrate and bloody puss began to ooze from every pore. More blood leaked from the corners of his mouth and dribbled in frothy strings from his nose. The smell of ozone was quickly replaced by the overpowering stench of charred flesh.

Then Conrad began to shrink.

It was gradual at first—his chin slipped below his collar and his hands blackened and shriveled and vanished up into the sleeves of his shirt; his feet drew up into his trousers with a slow sucking sound like a shoe being pulled out of a mud bog. Finally the bodyguard's wide, pleading eyes disappeared into his shirt and the last Bryan saw of his longtime companion was the shiny bald spot on top of the big man's head.

As Conrad disappeared, clumps of viscous-looking gray matter could be seen traveling back through the energy tentacle and up into the Dark Man's hand. In a few minutes, the only thing that remained of the bodyguard was a suit of empty black clothing that collapsed like a pile of rags the second the tentacle was withdrawn.

"Ah!" the Dark Man sighed. "That was refreshing."

The tentacle raced back across the floor and vanished like a retractable vacuum cleaner cord up into the sorcerer's fingertips. The Dark Man seemed taller, more robust. His face had been recast into its normal dour physiognomy and the top hat and tuxedo jacket had disappeared. He shook himself like a wet dog, then looked at the goateed man and nodded toward Bryan. "Prepare him."

The goateed man laid out the sorcerer's bags of sand and used the various colored grains to draw a five-pointed star inside a circle on the carpet. When finished, he glanced at his master. The Dark Man nodded and the goateed man got to his feet, drew a short broadsword with a convex cutting edge and a sharp point from the suitcase and went over to Bryan.

"What are you doing?" Bryan cried, holding out his hands to ward off the inevitable. "No, please! Don't touch me!"

The goateed man sprinkled a pinch of the Dark Man's powder over the diamond merchant's head. Then he averted his eyes, and with as little fuss as possible, he used the falchion to cut Bryan's clothing away. As soon as Bryan was naked, the goateed man went back to the suitcase and returned with several tubes of acrylic paints and proceeded to cover Bryan's body with red, black and green runes.

While his assistant was busy preparing Bryan, the Dark Man laid the spikes out in a row on the floor. As he worked, he hummed an eerie tune that set Bryan's already chattering teeth on edge.

"Pl-pl-please . . . Don't hurt me."

The Dark Man stopped humming and looked up. His eyes were as cold as glacial ice. "You talk of hurt?" He walked over to Bryan, standing with his face so close that the tattoos on his cheeks stood out like earthen mounds. "What do you know of pain?" Shrugging off the cape, the sorcerer ripped open his shirt. "Look at these scars! Try to picture the blood. Try! Stretch your meager brain and try to imagine the pain. Here"—he took Bryan's limp right hand and ran it over his chest—"Feel? Those are all I have left of my son."

"I never told Morales to kill anybody," Bryan said, licking his lips with a leathery tongue. "I told him to buy the—"

The Dark Man reached out with one hand and squeezed Bryan's throat until the man's face turned purple. "I am not interested in your excuses! I am trying to tell you about pain."

The Dark Man abruptly released his hold and stepped back, smiling slyly into Bryan's terror-filled eyes.

"But of course you are right. Why should I *tell* you about pain when I can show you?"

The goateed man lowered Bryan down on his back in the center of the pentagram. The diamond merchant's body was shivering from the cold and from a fear that threatened to make him lose control of his bladder. The Dark Man moved his suitcase and the spikes over next to the circle and pulled up a chair.

"Now," he said, holding up the first spike, "I know you will appreciate this—being a collector of occult memorabilia as you are." On the handle of the spike was the image of a woman with long stringy hair and horrible round eyes that were too large for her face. "Have you ever heard of the goddess Erzulie? No? Well, she has a special fondness for human beings. She lives in a very cold place and every chance she gets she just loves to visit our nice warm world."

The Dark Man put the spike down and picked up a glass mason jar. Inside the jar was a human eyeball swarming with dozens of fat, white maggots.

"Aren't they cute? I grew them myself," he said, fluttering his eyes modestly. "See how they squirm. Look how plump they have grown.

"These little fellows are what you might call the goddess's

emissaries to our world. Erzulie finds respite from her frigid world by inhabiting—or as we say, riding—the maggots' tiny little bodies as they burrow into the flesh of the dead and warming herself as the body decomposes. It is but a brief respite at best, as I'm sure you can imagine.''

Placing the jar on the floor, the Dark Man picked the spike up again.

''Now, one of my ancestors—a man named Macumba . . . You've heard of him, I believe? Anyway, Macumba had great respect for Erzulie and thought how unfair it was that all she ever got was leftovers—I hope you don't object to my little joke. So Macumba created this very special set of knives.''

The Dark Man spun the spike slowly in front of Bryan's eyes.

''Now, I know what you're asking yourself: 'What makes these knives so special?' Let me show you.''

The Hungan turned Bryan's hand over so that the palm was lying faceup and drove the spike all the way through it into the floor. Bryan opened his mouth to scream, but discovered— as Conrad had a few minutes before—that his vocal cords were paralyzed.

The Dark Man waited a moment, patiently savoring every instant of Bryan's terror and pain, and then jerked the spike free.

''Look there. Go on, don't be like that. See, no hole. No blood.''

It was true. Even though Bryan's hand still felt like it was resting in a vat of pure sulfuric acid, there wasn't a mark on it.

''That's what makes them special.'' The dark giant chuckled gleefully as he tested the point of the spike with his finger. ''They hurt like the devil, but don't do any permanent damage.

''Ah, now I see you are confused. The knives—the maggots—the knives—the maggots. What has all this got to do with you? I'm glad you asked.''

The goateed man appeared at Bryan's side with a spike in each hand. At his master's signal, he drove the spikes through

Bryan's right hand and right foot. Then he repeated the procedure on Bryan's left side. Next he took a mallet from the bag and hammered a spike through both of Bryan's knees, both hips, both shoulders and finally, taking the last spike from the Dark Man, through both earlobes. When he was finished, Bryan was pinned to the floor as neatly as a laboratory rat on a dissecting tray.

The pain must have been incredible, for in spite of the Dark Man's paralyzing spell, Bryan could feel. His cheeks were twitching like they were on fire and tears were streaming down his face.

The Dark Man waved his hand in front of Bryan's eyes.

"Are you still with me? I'm going to release your vocal cords—just for a second. Now don't scream—think of the neighbors."

"Please!" Bryan hissed.

"Good. Now I have some good news and some not so good news. The good news is there is no permanent damage done and no matter what you may think, I'm not going to kill you." The Hungan smiled benignly and leaned down next to Bryan's ear. "There, doesn't that make you feel better?"

"No."

Chuckling, the Dark Man whispered, "And now for the bad news. In a very few minutes you are going to be begging me to kill you."

"Ple—"

The Dark Man waved his hand and Bryan's plea was cut off. He held out his hand and the goateed man placed the falchion in it. Then, dropping to his knees, the Dark Man held the point of the sword toward the ceiling for a moment, whispering a brief incantation in Creole, then turned the blade over and made a careful incision down the middle of Bryan's abdomen, starting just below the rib cage and ending just above the groin. Bryan's belly opened like a zipper, exposing masses of gleaming pinkish viscera and yards of convoluted gray intestines—but spilling not a single drop of blood. As a result of this brutal surgery, Bryan had cracked his two front teeth, and the veins in his head were standing out like big blue worms.

"See." The Dark Man beamed. "No blood, no mess. Can you imagine what this would cost you in one of your hospitals?" He put his hand on Bryan's large intestine and squeezed—Bryan's two front teeth shattered like crystal goblets in a Memorex commercial. "Just wanted to make sure I had your attention."

Picking up the mason jar, the Dark Man unscrewed the top and plucked a single bloated maggot off the eyeball. Holding it gently between two fingers, he leaned over Bryan's stomach and dropped the wormlike larva into the open wound.

"Let's just give him a minute, shall we."

He sat back on his heels and watched Bryan's face like a hawk. The diamond merchant's eyes grew wider and wider as he strained to see inside himself. When the veins in Bryan's eyes began to look like cracks in a pair of glass marbles, the Dark Man was satisfied that Bryan could feel every move the insect made and glanced at his assistant.

"Start packing. We are almost done here."

He waited until the goateed man left to carry the bag downstairs before he whispered, "Can you feel him? I know you can. This is one of my special little pets and he has exceptionally large . . . oh, for lack of a better word, let's just call them teeth. Oh my! I see he has started in on your liver already."

He watched another few seconds, then said, "It isn't too late, you know. I'll give you one chance to save yourself. I'll ask only once. Where can I find Ms. Rand?"

He waved his hand and waited.

By this time, Bryan's lips looked like parchment. His tongue darted out, but it wasn't much help. Finally he rasped, "The mountain. Sh-she always goes up to the top of the mountain."

The Dark Man turned his head and peered at the huge, pyramidal purple and black silhouette slumbering under a blanket of cotton-ball clouds in the distance. Turning back to Bryan,

Gary L. Holleman

he smiled and said, "Thank you."

Then he upended the mason jar over Bryan's stomach.

Kyna shook Cyrus awake. She was sitting on the side of the bed rubbing her eyes. "I'm hungry."

He smiled as if everything was wonderful, then jumped up before she noticed that his body was wringing wet in an ice-cold room.

Kyna put on his favorite dress—a clingy black shirtdress that stopped just above her knees, and a string of cultured pearls. She said it was going to be a special night and insisted he wear a pair of his new slacks and the sport coat she had purchased for him.

"Better bring a coat," he suggested. "I smell a change in the weather."

"Whatever."

Cyrus wasn't happy with the way Kyna was acting—she was much too calm. But she brought along a topcoat, so he was momentarily pacified.

Wistfully, Kyna asked to have Mexican food—again.

"I'm not complaining, you understand," he said. "But aren't you tired of Mexican food?"

"Maybe," she replied. "But it's a tradition. And sometimes traditions are the only things that last."

And again Cyrus felt a pang of concern at her fatalistic tone. But he did as she asked and found a cozy little place on the edge of Old Town where, with only the flame from a candle in a small lamp for light, they sipped margaritas and listened to the mournful strings of a strolling guitarist.

The day they met, Cyrus decided that Kyna was the most beautiful woman he had ever seen. Now, in that soft, flickering light, she looked positively enchanting.

"You look positively enchanting," he said.

She smiled. "You look pretty good yourself."

"I think I love you."

Kyna dropped her eyes. "It's the margaritas."

"No. It's you. You've always been beautiful, but you've

268

changed on this trip. You're so . . . real now.''

''Come on.''

She took his hand and led him to the dance floor, where she allowed Cyrus to amaze himself by making it through two songs without once stepping on her feet. They returned to the table and ordered hand-rolled enchiladas and chicken tacos smothered in a tart cheese sauce. For dessert Kyna had flan and Cyrus chose Navaho fry bread sprinkled with cinnamon and smothered with honey. Later, they wandered through Old Town with its Spanish town square, bandstand and Churrigueresque cathedral. Holding hands and occasionally walking single file, they explored the cramped streets. It was an unseasonably warm night and most of the shops were still open, the smiling entrepreneurs standing in the doorways smoking their illegal rolled Havanas and keeping an eye peeled for the stray tourist dollar. Kyna remained pensive. She paused at several jewelry stores but couldn't work up enough enthusiasm to buy. When she came out of the last shop, she found Cyrus talking to a wrinkled old Navaho woman pushing a street cart full of kachina dolls. Between spitting gobs of tobacco juice into the gutter, the old woman was trying to press one of her dolls into Cyrus's hand. The doll had a wolf's head and a chest covered with a rainbow-colored bead vest. Cyrus kept glancing from the doll to the old woman and shaking his head.

''Ten dolla','' the old peddler said. Cyrus shook his head. She spat. ''Five dolla' . . . three dolla'.''

''No. No. No!''

''Cheapskate!'' The old woman sent a blob of juice to the ground next to Cyrus's foot and then went on her way up the street toward a young couple trying to ride herd on three chocolate-covered little girls.

''You sure do attract the women,'' Kyna whispered.

''Did you see that doll?''

She nodded.

''What is it about me? Do I smell like a wolf? Is my tail showing? What?''

269

She just shrugged and took his arm. "I thought you said it was going to be cold."

"It will be. I can feel it in my bones. A change is coming and it's going to be a doozy. Snow maybe."

"Yeah, yeah. Thank you, Willard Scott."

"So what's on for tomorrow?"

"I've come to a decision," Kyna announced. "I'm supposed to meet Bryan tomorrow night to turn over the cash. The money from the last shipment, the one for Santa Fe, is supposed to be my payment. I'm going to give him money and flush the rest of the stones down the toilet. But after that I've got to disappear."

"No problem. We'll go on the lam together."

She squeezed his hand. "That's sweet, but I can't let you do that. You have a life."

He shook his head and kissed her hand. "The life I had before is gone. Can you see me hanging out at some bar asking some blond coed what her sign is?"

"But what would we do? Where would we go?"

"One thing at a time, remember? Let's settle up with your boss and then see what happens. I still have a little cash in the bank. We'll get by. But that's down the road. About tomorrow, if we have to go into hiding, fine. But let's make the best of the time we've got."

Kyna walked along staring at her feet for a moment or two, then looked up. "Okay. You know how much I like Indian stuff?"

He chuckled. "I've heard rumors to that effect."

"Well, there's a place near here that has some really neat petroglyphs and a bunch of Anasazi burial mounds. There are a lot of good hiking trails and in the summer they have a store that sells Indian jewelry, though I guess it's closed now. It's one of my favorite places in the whole world."

"Is it far?"

"Oh, ten miles or so."

"Maybe we should stick close to town."

"Why?" Kyna asked. "Bryan won't be in till tomorrow

night, and from what Paula said, this witch doctor can come at us anywhere.''

''I don't know. An isolated hiking trail? I don't want to make it too easy for him.''

''Would you rather have an audience if you have to change?''

Cyrus nodded. ''Point.''

''We'll have to dress warm. It gets awfully chilly up there this time of year.''

''Where is this place?'' he asked.

''Come on, let me show you.''

She led him to a public parking lot behind the rows of abode shops and pointed. In the distance, the silhouette of Sandia Mountain shot up into the night sky like the jagged point of a knife.

''There. That's Sandia Mountain. The peak is over ten thousand feet above sea level. I've skied it in the winter and hiked it in the summer. It's rugged and pretty and has a breathtaking view of Albuquerque and Santa Fe.''

As the peak's stark shape imprinted itself upon Cyrus's mind, the marrow in his bones slowly turned to ice.

''Sandia Crest,'' he whispered.

It was the mountain in his dreams.

''What's the matter?'' she asked.

''Nothing.''

But the night no longer seemed friendly. The paper jack-o'-lanterns and black cats, the ghostly sheets tied and hanging from the posts outside the shops, the straw witches in their peaked hats and all the other gay Halloween decorations that only moments before had seemed so charming, suddenly gave Cyrus a cold, sinking feeling in his gut.

Kyna had long since given up trying to interpret Cyrus's sudden bouts of silence. She didn't know whether he had always been moody or if it had something to do with being a part-time wolf. All she knew for certain was that the wind had suddenly turned mean and that his body was vibrating like a supercharged voltaic cell.

271

Turning up the collar on her coat, she took his arm. "Come on. Walk a lady home?"

The walk back to the motel was hell for Cyrus. Old Town was honeycombed with narrow, lightless alleys and recessed doorways. To preserve the illusion of an Old West town, most of the lighting came from electric candles atop old-time lampposts or torches. On the walk over, this mood lighting had seemed romantic, but now it only served to make the shadows more pronounced. At any moment, he expected some maniac with a sword to come charging out of the dark and take a swing at him. He wished he could change—Kyna could pretend she was walking her dog—but there were enough people out and about to make that dicey. Instead, he reached out with his senses and almost jumped out of his skin every time a piece of paper blew across the sidewalk.

Kyna was satisfied to walk along with her head resting on his arm. She kept silent, knowing well that his behavior was caused by his concern for her. When they got back to the room, he checked inside, and after he had double-locked the door and put on the chain, they undressed in silence and went to bed. Kyna looped Cyrus's arm over her waist, molded her body against him and closed her eyes.

"I love you," he whispered.

"I know."

It was an unusual dream, which in Cyrus's case was somewhat redundant. It was unusual because he knew it was a dream—a sensation that was disconcerting and that filled him with a sense of dread.

Another odd thing: He wasn't a wolf.

The mountain was the same—same peak, same rubble, same spooky forest, but he was just a man: two arms, two legs, one rather confused head.

As he walked down the now familiar path, he heard someone calling his name. Rounding a stand of fallen trees, he saw that it was Paula and that she was nude, which struck him as odd until he looked down and saw that he was naked too.

Why is it people are always naked in dreams? *he asked her.*
Is it Freudian?

Instead of replying, Paula waved him on. When he was closer he saw that she was standing in front of the entrance to a cave at the base of the peak.

Cyrus! Cyrus! Can you hear me?

He walked up and stopped right in front of her, then Kazie came floating out of the cave and hovered at the witch's side. The old man's face was covered with snowy-white fur, and a set of yellowed but exceedingly long fangs hung down over his bottom lip.

Hey, Kaz. What are you doing in my dream?

I needed his help, *Paula said.* I have been trying to reach you for several days and Kazie's new powers have allowed me to get through.

Gee, Paula, did you ever think of just dropping a quarter in a phone?

Listen to her, young son, *Kazie said.* A shit storm is coming and you got to get yo' mojo working.

I don't have much time, *Paula said.* He's been blocking me, but even such a foul creature must sleep.

What's so important?

You see the cave behind me?

Cyrus looked. It wasn't much of a cave. From what he could see, it was little more than a flaw in the bedrock. Yeah. So?

The answer lies there.

Answer? Answer to what?

I do not know.

So I'm supposed to go in there and look?

I cannot say. The cave may be a sanctuary or a trap.

That's a big help. What am I supposed to do?

Paula shook her head. I cannot tell you. When the time comes, you must use your senses. You will know what to do.

How will I know?

Paula and Kazie began to fade like black-and-white images on a cracked projection screen.

They will help you. Listen to them.

Who? *Cyrus shouted.* Listen to whom?

273

Chapter Seventeen

October 31

During the night, as the temperature outside the motel dropped, Cyrus unconsciously wrapped his arms around Kyna to keep her warm. When he tried to untangle himself the next morning, she refused to let go.

"What's your hurry, sailor?" she mumbled, running her fingernails lightly across the flat of his stomach.

"Happy Halloween."

They made love. Not the way they usually did—like two sumo wrestlers in heat trying to pin each other—but slowly, carefully, lovingly, the way the Swiss make watches. Afterward they shared a shower and dressed for a cold day in the mountains: cord jeans, flannel shirts, crewneck sweaters, double socks and hiking boots.

Cyrus felt good. The vague unease that had plagued his thoughts the night before seemed to have washed away in the shower, and even Kyna seemed to be in a better mood. She was whistling and singing the lyrics to yet another of her favorite rock ditties. After breakfast they loaded the Lincoln with camera gear and water bottles, then Kyna got behind the wheel and took I-40 east out of the city. After exiting the expressway, she followed the main road for about five miles and then took a series of hairpin switchbacks that went up the back side of Sandia Mountain so fast that Cyrus's ears popped. On the way up, they passed the entrance to a fashionable restaurant and ski resort and miles of dark, deserted forest. Just when Cyrus was beginning to think he was going to need an oxygen mask, they rounded a bend in the road, passed a series of terraced parking lots and stopped beside a dark green park service truck. At the end of the parking lot was an outdoor bathroom and past that—perched on the edge of the crest's steeply sloping face like one of the weather-beaten gargoyles atop Notre Dame Cathedral—was a multilevel general store and restaurant. Across the road in the other direction was a steel electrical tower and a large wooden sign.

"Here we are," Kyna said.

Cyrus stepped out of the car and was nearly bowled over by a forty-mile-per-hour wind.

"Jesus!" he exclaimed. "You said cold, but you didn't say anything about the frigging hurricane."

"It does get a bit brisk up here. It'll be warmer once we get into the trees."

They surrounded themselves with scarves and jackets and mittens and walked across the lot toward the general store.

"One more pit stop before the death march," Kyna said, slipping through the bathroom door.

Cyrus kept going. The general store was a narrow building made from rough pine planks held together by about a zillion pairs of graying deer antlers. He had to go down a set of concrete steps to reach the front door, and when he tried the knob, it refused to turn. In the window was a faded sign informing anyone who cared to look that the place would be closed until spring.

"Well, crap!"

Pulling his collar up tight against the wind, Cyrus walked down a long flight of wooden steps to the observation platform. Albuquerque was spread out below him like a matchbox town for a kid's model railroad. The city appeared so tiny that it was hard for him to believe he wasn't staring down from a satellite in deep space.

"Quite a view, huh?" Kyna shouted in his ear.

Cyrus nodded.

She grabbed his arm. "Come on. The sooner we start hiking, the sooner we'll warm up."

The trail started beneath the electrical tower on the other side of the parking lot. Kyna paused to study the map posted on the signboard and Cyrus read over her shoulder.

"People have actually been in New Mexico over ten thousand years?" he asked.

"That's what it says," Kyna replied.

"I went to Detroit one time. It felt like I was there that long."

"The Anasazi, or Ancient Ones, got here about nine hundred A.D. and flourished until sometime in the thirteen hundreds when their descendants were thought to inhabit land along the Rio Grande. They were basket weavers and pottery makers, magnificent craftsmen."

"And they make all that silver and turquoise stuff you like?"

"This stuff?" Kyna held up her wrists, showing off two Navaho bracelets. "These are Navaho."

"Probably made in Taiwan," Cyrus mumbled. "What happened to the Anasazi?"

"Depends on who you ask. Some say a drought did 'em in. Others say more aggressive tribes—maybe the Apaches. They left behind burial mounds, beaucoup cliff and cave dwellings and thousands of unanswered questions."

Cyrus was still peering at the map on the board. "How long is this trail?"

"About twelve miles, round-trip. The first six or so are all downhill. Which makes the trip back something of a challenge."

Cyrus traced the red line that denoted the trail on the clear plastic overlay.

"It follows the crest to this point." Kyna pointed to the tiny knob on the map that represented Sandia Peak. "From there you can see both Albuquerque and Santa Fe. Then it goes down this way and winds up at that restaurant we passed on the way up. We can have lunch there and then hike back."

The well-worn path started between a pair of tall fir trees and vanished down into a grove of aspens and poplars. Most of the trees had already shed their foliage and the few leaves still clinging to the branches looked like they had been gilded in eighteen-karat gold. The barren limbs cast overlapping patterns of shadow and light that played tricks on the eye and made the landscape appear unnaturally gloomy. Cyrus scuffed the ground with the toe of his boot.

"What are you looking for?" Kyna asked.

"Bread crumbs."

"Come on. It isn't that bad. I think it's kinda pretty."

Kyna started off at a leisurely pace. They cleared the first grove and turned sharply up toward the rim of the crest. As long as they were in among the trees the wind was tolerable— cold, but the forest cut the velocity in half. But each time they came out on the exposed face of the cliff, the wind sliced through their clothing like it was made of cardboard. The path was easy—mostly dirt and leaves, but they had to take care. Hidden beneath the dry foliage were loose pinecones and stones, lying in wait to catch the casual ankle.

A mile from the start, the path dipped down into a deep grove of aspens on the leeward side of the crest. Scattered around the grove like a set of building blocks were half a dozen or so lichen-covered granite blocks.

"Take a look," Kyna said.

Most of the blocks contained ancient renderings of four-legged animals that could have been either buffalo or horses with scoliosis, stick men on stick horseback shooting arrows, and squiggly lines that Kyna interpreted as meaning cultivated fields.

"Not exactly Picasso," Cyrus said.

"You try doing that with a sharp rock."

"I couldn't do that with a computer and five hundred dollars' worth of CAD software. I'm just saying it looks kind of . . . childish."

Kyna shook her head. "Philistine."

They sat on a fallen tree to catch their breath and enjoy the welcome respite from the wind. Here in the grove, protected by the mountain, winter was still just a threat and the trees were thick with rainbow-hued leaves that held back the sun. The stillness pressed down like an invisible hand and the silence was loud enough to raise the hairs on Cyrus's neck.

"Spooky back here," he said.

"Yeah. Nice to be out of the wind, though."

All at once Kyna jerked the zipper on her jacket down and began fumbling with the catch on the necklace. She took it off, placed it in her lap and rubbed the back of her neck with her hand.

"What's the matter?" Cyrus asked.

"I don't know. Every now and then this thing feels like it's burning a hole in my neck."

"What is it?" he asked, lifting the strap with one finger.

"If I tell you, you promise not to go all male on me?"

Cyrus let the necklace drop and wiped his hand on his trouser leg. "Who, me?"

"Bryan gave it to me."

"Oh. Well, it's easy to see why you two had such a special relationship."

"Don't be crass. I think he was trying to be nice. He knows how much I like Indian jewelry."

"Funny, it doesn't look Indian. It looks kind of . . . dumb." When Kyna rolled her eyes, he looked back up the trail and said, "How far—" Then he abruptly fell silent and Kyna jumped.

"What is it?"

Cyrus stared at the top of the rise until his eyes watered. After two minutes he shook his head and replied, "Nothing. Shadows. You know how the light plays tricks in the woods."

He gave Kyna a smile that masked the fact that all of his special senses had suddenly gone on full alert. As she continued to extol the virtues of the Anasazi, the woods, the sky and nature in general, Cyrus did his best to appear relaxed and interested. At the same time, he used his ears as twin directional microphones to carefully scan the trees back where the trail began its downward slope. He could almost swear that he had seen something moving up there. A tall, thin silhouette that ducked behind a tree when he turned. Yet now all he could hear was the rustling of leaves and a creaking like old bones as the tree limbs rubbed against one another.

"Are you listening to me?" Kyna asked. "I was telling you about why the trees back here still have their leaves."

"Every word. Thoreau couldn't have said it any better."

She punched him on the arm. "Ready?"

They hiked up and down the backbone of the crest, passing through glades where cascading rays of sunlight turned a sea of drifting dust motes into rivers of gold, and along the edges of precipices where one careless step would have sent them tumbling through thousands of feet of empty air. Along the way they passed dozens of small earthen knolls that Kyna claimed were Indian burial mounds and more of the ancient rock art galleries than Cyrus cared to shake a stick at. And Kyna stopped and took a photo of each and every one of them.

An hour later they came to a fork in the trail. The left branch curved up toward the summit, but they took the right path, the one that the trail marker indicated led down to the ski lifts.

And indeed, the trail did take them down. In three miles it dropped over two thousand feet. Before long they cleared the back side of the forest and found themselves traversing a field of thick, shin-high brambles that had been stunted and weathered by the thin mountain air. A little after eleven-thirty they reached the ski-lift parking lot and a few minutes later joined five couples that had driven up from the city to have lunch in the lodge's dining room.

The restaurant was one huge banquet room that had been built by skiers for skiers. The walls were hung with crossed skis, snowshoes and posters of sun-bronzed Nordic giants in Day-Glo snowsuits and five-hundred-dollar antiglare snow goggles wedeling down over an endless series of moguls. A waitress with enormous hair seated them at a table with a fantastic view of Santa Fe—forty-four miles to the northeast—and shoved menus in their laps. Cyrus asked for a double helping of quiche and Kyna had shrimp salad and a diet soda. When the waitress brought the check, Cyrus asked how long it should take them to make the return trip to the crest.

"'Bout five or six hours, I guess," the woman replied. "I never done it myself. You best be careful, though. Supposed to be a storm coming and you don't want to get caught up there in a blow."

Cyrus thanked the woman, tipped her 19 percent more than she was worth and helped Kyna bundle up for the trip back. The moment they stepped outside, they could see the clouds building to the south.

"Told ya," Cyrus whispered.

"Yeah? Well, even you have to be right sometime. We better not screw around. Let's go for the record."

"What's the record?"

"Safe to say, if we don't make it to the car before the storm hits, we didn't break it."

Kyna set off at a back-breaking pace, swinging her elbows like pistons and pushing hard with her legs. Before they even reached the field of brush, the sun had been swallowed up by a tide of angry clouds and the sky was streaked with dark purple bands that resembled leprous skin. The wind rolled down from the top of the mountain in waves that flattened the brush and threw leaves in their faces. Fighting the uphill slope was hard enough, but the wind made it a real chore. By the time they reached the forest, their bodies were bathed in clammy sweat and Kyna was puffing like an old plow horse. Just inside the first line of trees she stopped and braced herself on a rock.

"You okay?" Cyrus asked.

She nodded but she was working hard to pull in oxygen. After a few moments she said, "If I'm going to have a heart attack, the least you could do is break a sweat."

Cyrus laughed and shook his head. "I *am* sweating. Here, feel."

He unzipped his jacket and pulled up his sweater. She swiped her fingers over his chest.

"See," he said. "My shirt is soaked too."

280

"Then would you do me a favor and breathe hard? It looks like I'm doing all the work."

"Can I help it if I'm the perfect male specimen?"

"Yeah, right. I can run circles around any *normal* man. Come on."

As they neared the place where the trails converged, the first drops of rain began to fall. Cyrus held out his hand and his palm was peppered by a barrage of fat raindrops.

"We better find shelter," he said.

"Got any ideas?"

All at once the dream from the previous night came back to him and he remembered the cave and Paula's warning and his mouth was suddenly dry. "I think we can make it to the car."

No sooner were the words out of his mouth than the sky opened up and the rain came down like it was shot from a water cannon.

"Any other bright ideas," Kyna shouted over the roar of falling water.

In his earlier dreams, he remembered a rocky overhang at the base of the peak that overshadowed the entrance to the cave. He didn't remember seeing it on the way down the mountain and he wondered if it could be somewhere along the upper trail.

"Let's try the path up to the crest. There might be some caves up there."

She gave him one of her looks where one eyebrow turns into a question mark. "And what leads you to that conclusion?"

He shrugged. "What do we have to lose? If I'm wrong we're not gonna get any wetter."

Kyna sighed and pushed on with her shoulders stooped against the rain. When she reached the fork, she turned and looked back. Cyrus nodded and they set off toward the stand of firs that ringed the top of the mountain.

As soon as they started up the new path, Cyrus began to see things he recognized: the fallen tree where he had found the den of an old gray fox, the bush where he had spooked a large brown rabbit. It was like returning to a house he had once lived in, a place replete with both good and bad memories.

"Which way?" Kyna's voice jarred him back to the present.

The trail forked again. One branch led down into yet another stand of nearly bald aspens while the other went off to the left through thick brush.

"The left fork," he replied.

It was raining so hard that this time Kyna didn't bother to question him. She put her head down to keep the water out of her eyes and trudged on through ankle-deep mud and branches that scraped at her legs like dead fingers. As they approached the crest, the forest thinned and they could see that the clouds had completely blotted out the sky.

"Good place to be attacked by a werewolf," Kyna yelled back over her shoulder.

"Nobody likes a smart ass. Listen, when we clear the trees, follow the path to the right and around the big boulder."

Kyna stopped just inside the tree line. The top of the mountain with its garden of black and gray granite was being pounded by the storm.

It looks different in the daylight, Cyrus thought.

But not all that different, for the cloud cover had almost succeeded in turning day into night.

"Even I haven't been to this part of the mountain," Kyna screamed. "How did you know about the boulder?"

"Do you believe in dreams?" he called in return.

"Since you asked, I'll tell you my new philosophy on life. Anything anybody tells me, I'll believe. The things I've seen on this trip . . ."

Cyrus laughed. "Keep going. The overhang is just beyond this field of rocks."

They ran bent nearly in two, slipping occasionally as the wind cuffed them about. Cyrus recognized the round boulder where he had made love to the she-wolf.

"There!" he shouted.

Kyna saw the wide overhang at the base of the peak and redoubled her efforts. Another fifty yards and they were in the lee of the mountain and under the shelf. Lost in the shadows at the back of the recess was a narrow opening.

"Hold on a sec," Cyrus called. "Let me check it out."

The opening was as narrow as some Republicans' minds and totally black. He had to crouch and turn sideways to get his head and shoulders through, then he paused and willed his eyes to adjust. He didn't know what he had expected—skeletons hanging from rusty chains, a man in a black hood, a rack, an iron maiden, maybe the whole set from a medieval torture chamber. But the cave was little more than a large closet with a high roof and a dirt floor. On the far side, where the cave walls narrowed and the ceiling dropped down, was a small cairn under an umbrella of dusty cobwebs. He sniffed. The place smelled of dried leaves and twigs and badger glands.

So much for dreams, Cyrus thought.

He squeezed the rest of the way through the cleft and held out his hand to guide Kyna in.

"Stinks in here," she stammered as she molded her body against his.

"I think we just evicted the former tenant. Come on, relax. We may be here awhile."

They sat with their legs intertwined in order to see out the narrow opening in the rock. The rain gave no sign of letting up, and Kyna's teeth were chattering hard enough to shatter. Cyrus reached over and began briskly rubbing her shoulders.

"I've never b-been so c-cold in my entire life," she stuttered.

"I'll make a fire."

He walked to the back of the cave, then got down on his hands and knees and crawled to the pile of stones. The idea was to find dry wood, but he first had to wave the cobwebs away in order to see anything.

"I found the badger's nest," he called. There was a large

mat of dried leaves and he began moving the rocks around to see if he could find any twigs.

"Hey!" he said. "Look at this."

He crawled out and handed Kyna a piece of broken pottery. She turned the shard over in her hands.

"Look," she whispered. "You can still see a faint design."

"What do you think it was?"

"From the shape, probably a water pot. Are there any more back there?"

"There's stuff all over the place."

"Let me see." Kyna dropped to her knees.

"And spiders and about two years' worth of badger poop."

"Oh." She sat back on her heels.

Cyrus made three more trips to the rock pile. When he had accumulated a nice mound of kindling, he surrounded it with rocks and tossed in a few pieces of dried dung.

"Is that what I think it is?" Kyna asked.

"Yep. Makes for a good fire."

"Is this where you start rubbing two sticks together?"

He pulled a matchbook out of his pocket. Scrawled across the cover was the name of the ski lodge where they had eaten lunch. Seeing her expression, his face reddened. "I collect souvenirs. So sue me."

On his last trip back from the rock pile, Cyrus noticed a good-sized stick at the bottom of the pile. He grabbed hold of it and pulled and the whole top of the pile came rolling down, raising a cloud of dust and freeing an icy blast of air that hit him in the face like a two-by-four. Crouching down flat, he saw a black hole in the back wall that had been hidden behind the pile of rocks.

Oh shit! he thought, and he quickly began replacing the fallen rocks.

Scurrying back to the fire, he dropped the stick into the flames, then crawled over to the entrance of the cave.

Kyna muttered, "You know, sometimes living with you is like living with a freaking bird dog."

The stench from the opening had been as bad as anything

he had ever smelled. He wanted out—out of the cave and off the mountain, but the rain was still coming down like silver buckshot and at any second he expected to see some old guy with a beard come by collecting animals two by two.

"I guess I don't like small spaces," he replied.

The sun was going down. With the overcast, no one else would have been able to tell, but Cyrus could feel it and rain or no rain he longed to escape the confines of the cave and run in the forest. Kyna would be safe in the cave. The opening at the back was no threat. All that lay beyond it was a lot of old dead things.

"You hungry?" he asked.

"I could eat a horse, raw."

"You may have to."

Cyrus got to his feet and began struggling with his wet clothing.

"What are you doing?"

"I'm going to see if I can find us something to eat."

He had to sit on the ground to get his jeans off and by the time he was undressed, his body was one big goose bump.

"That's nuts," she replied. "You'll drown before you get ten feet."

"I don't have time to argue. I've got to change before I freeze to death. Now, as soon as I leave, throw some more wood on the fire and get out of that wet jacket and sweater— try to keep warm. I won't be long."

"Yes, Mother. What do you think you're going to find out there?"

He scratched his head. "Well, it's not going to be Caesar salad, that's for danged sure."

"Don't you dare bring me anything with fur on it."

"Right. One owl sandwich, coming up."

Kyna punched him on the arm, but at the same time little tears formed at the corners of her eyes. Against her pale skin they made her seem so very young and fragile. Cyrus hugged her to him and pressed his lips to hers stealing some of her warmth and vitality. Then he held her at arm's length.

She whispered, "I love you, Russ."

"I love you back."

"Don't take any chances. Grab the first bunch of berries you find and come back."

He looked through the opening. Coarse brown hair began sprouting from his arms like worms fleeing oversaturated ground. This time he had no trouble picturing the mountain in his mind.

Kyna followed his progress until he was swallowed up by the storm. "It's like living with Lassie."

She turned back to the fire and added another stick with a secret smile tugging at the corners of her lips. "I bet he comes back with Bambi's mother."

Amazement was the only way to describe the way she felt. To be in a relationship with a man . . . Well, okay, to be in a relationship with anyone she actually trusted.

"What an odd sensation."

The one thing she knew for certain was that from now on, her life would never be dull.

The pile of kindling was getting low so she crawled to the back of the cave to look for more wood. While shifting the rocks around, she uncovered a few pieces of broken pottery buried among the detritus and began scraping away at the dirt and leaves with her fingers. When she moved one particularly large stone, the entire cairn began to wobble and then it collapsed like a house of cards. Kyna sneezed several times and then noticed the sudden brush of chilled wind that caressed her cheek.

"Hello!"

She waited until the dust settled and then saw the opening and her eyes widened. "Oh, wow!"

She scrambled over the rubble and stuck her head and shoulders into the hole.

It was almost like waking up blind. She could hear a stiff wind whistling past her ears. A wind that carried a dry, musty fetor that made her want to take a bath, but she couldn't see so much as the nose on her face. The hidden cave could have been as small as a pantry or as large as the Superdome—it was impossible for her to tell. Pretty sure that Cyrus would kill her if she went any farther, Kyna reached out with one arm and walked her fingers out as far as she could. The ground on the other side of the opening was flat and damp and seemed to slope downward.

Certain now that she had discovered the American equivalent of Tutankhamen's tomb, Kyna was just about to go back and make herself a torch when she heard footsteps behind her.

"That didn't take long," she said as she spun around.

The two men were strangers. And yet Kyna had a pretty good idea of the identity of at least one of them. The first man was thin and nervous with a neatly trimmed goatee and a dark green raincoat that covered his lanky frame like a circus tent. He carried a battered brown leather suitcase in one hand and a short broadsword with a curved blade in the other.

The second man was a giant, with skin as black as coal and a tattooed face that still played a major role in her nightmares. Around the giant's shoulders was a rain-soaked cape of blue, black and red feathers that gave him the appearance of a rather awkward bird of prey.

"Ah, Ms. Rand. At last we meet face-to-face—so to speak."

Stall, she thought. *Cyrus will be back at any moment.*

As if reading her mind, the Dark Man glanced around the cave. "No Mr. Trigg? Don't tell me he ran off and left you?" He clucked his tongue and shook his head. "Well, you know how young men are today. My own son was less than reliable at times."

The Dark Man turned to his assistant. "Prepare the ceremony."

The man with the goatee took a small cotton cloth and several vials from the leather case. The cloth was the size of a Motel 6 bath mat and decorated with occult symbols. Next, he removed several jars, a long knife with an ornate handle, a three-legged clay bowl and several skin pouches and set them on the ground around the cloth.

As soon as the preparations were complete, the Dark Man said, "Keep your sword handy. You never know, Mr. Trigg may change his mind and decide to become a martyr."

The goateed man took the falchion and tiptoed around the cave. Every few steps he paused, jabbed at a rock or a shadow and then jumped back as if he expected the Devil himself to come charging out. The Hungan watched his assistant's performance for a moment, then shook his head sadly.

"I should have been a Catholic. They would make me a saint."

The Dark Man walked slowly toward Kyna. She gave ground until her back was pressed up against cool rock. She did her best not to shake. He towered over her, looking down with the coldest eyes she had ever seen.

"You are very beautiful," the witch doctor said. "I have a way with beautiful women, if I do say so myself. I mean, to look at this face"—the tips of his fingers gently caressed the tattoos—"you might find it hard to believe, but many women find me irresistible. Many have offered themselves to me . . . truly. Some have even crawled naked across the floor and tried to kiss my feet. And do you know why? They wanted something—don't they all? Do you know what they wanted? The simplest things are often the most precious. They wanted to die."

The Dark Man's hand snaked out and ripped the front of Kyna's blouse open. When she tried to cover herself, he backhanded her across the face and his steely eyes locked on the talisman.

"Ahhhh."

Slowly, his hands went around behind Kyna's neck. At his touch, her skin crawled as if a fat slug had oozed down her back. It took everything she had to keep from screaming.

Gently—almost reverently—he unfastened the clasp and pulled the necklace off.

"You have no idea what this is, do you?" he asked, holding the talisman in front of her eyes.

Kyna gasped in pain and put her hands to her face.

"Ah, yes. One of the little benefits of the talisman you stole. It has certain medicinal properties. It can ease pain." The Dark Man unwittingly flexed his knee. "I see in your case it also worked a few cosmetic wonders as well. But, it has its price."

Where before Kyna had had a few tiny lines around her mouth and eyes, she could feel the wrinkles popping up like ruts in a corrugated tin roof and finger-wide streaks of solid silver ran like bolts of lightning through her hair.

"It was a gift," Kyna managed to whisper. "I didn't steal it."

The Dark Man threw back his head and laughed. "Did you hear that?" He turned to the goateed man standing stunned next to the fire. "She didn't steal it."

The goateed man stuttered, "Master? The Butcher's Broom? How . . ."

Laughing all the more, the Dark Man shook his head. "Later." He let the feathered cloak slide to the floor and slipped the talisman around his neck. As he fastened the clasp, he closed his eyes and sighed.

"That's what all this was about?" Kyna spat. "Some stupid piece of costume jewelry?"

"You have no idea how wrong you are. This"—the Hungan ran his fingers lightly over the stones in the necklace— "is the key to the universe. Let me give you a little demonstration."

Without warning, he levitated straight up into the air. A split second later, Cyrus flew through the cave entrance and landed in a flurry of flashing teeth and claws in the exact spot that the Hungan had been occupying the moment before.

"An impressive entrance, Mr. Trigg," the Dark Man said as he floated to earth a few yards away. "But as you can see, any slight chance you may have had before is gone."

Cyrus stopped dead in his tracks and cast a cautious glance at the necklace. Caution wasn't easy for him, for the sight of Kyna's torn blouse and bleeding lip made the wolf inside his head howl. The urge to rip and tear his way into the witch doctor's steamy guts was like the bitter taste of dirt in his mouth. Yet the human part of Cyrus sensed danger in the dark giant's equanimity, and for the moment at least, the human part was still in control.

Cyrus lowered himself down on his haunches and forced himself to scrutinize the Dark Man and his companion—paying special attention to the way the witchman was fingering that strange talisman.

"I see you have learned to control your animal," the Dark Man said. "If only my late assistant had had the same good sense, you and Ms. Rand would be dead now and I would not be standing here on this accursed mountain. But that's neither here nor—"

A massive bolt of blinding green energy exploded from the crystal in the center of the Hungan's amulet and struck Cyrus in the chest with the force of a runaway tractor-trailer, hurling him backward through the air. He slammed into the wall and landed on his back more than a dozen yards away.

Rolling painfully to his feet, Cyrus shook his head back and forth and quickly moved between Kyna and the dark duo. His chest felt like it had just been stung by the universe's largest wasp, and the fur where the thing hit smelled like a scorched mattress. He saw the sword ready in the goateed man's hands and bared his fangs.

"See," the Hungan said to his apprentice. "I told you he was strong. That blast would have killed any normal beast."

The goateed man tried to appear relaxed, standing with his feet wide apart and his expression neutral, but it was obvious from his smell that he was terrified.

"Why do you hesitate, Mr. Trigg?" the Dark Man asked. "I can feel your rage. You're not afraid of a little piece of steel, are you?"

Feel my rage? Cyrus muttered silently to himself. *How 'bout feeling the pain in my chest?*

The Dark Man continued to sneer and regale Cyrus with insults, but Cyrus held himself in check by using his old karate coach's instruction to shout down the beast: "Think!" his coach used to scream at him across the dojo. "Don't react! If you think, the initiative is yours. If you react, the initiative is your opponent's."

Careful always to keep his body between the Dark Man and Kyna, Cyrus began to pace back and forth.

"Ah, you see how he protects her?" the Dark Man muttered. "How he protects the bitch that murdered my son?"

That's it!

Cyrus charged, sweeping in from the right to use the black giant's body as a shield against the goateed man's sword. But the apprentice was ready and he leapt in front of his master, carving a figure eight in the air with the point of the sword.

Cyrus put on the brakes, turned and circled back.

The Dark Man stood calmly staring straight ahead, apparently unmoved and unconcerned by the soap opera unfolding around him. Cyrus lifted his nose to the wind. The goateed man's fear reeked like cheap booze, but all Cyrus got from the Dark Man was the rather pleasant odor of bitter herbs.

Does the man not have a nervous system? Cyrus fumed.

"Come, Mr. Trigg," the Dark Man sighed. "I grow weary of this game. I have business with Ms. Rand."

The witch doctor's constant chatter was an obvious ploy to distract Cyrus and provoke him into making a rash move—so far it had worked pretty well. The thing Cyrus had to keep reminding himself of was that as painful as the blasts from that talisman were, it was the sword that he had to worry about.

It's the sword, stupid, he told himself. *Ignore the Dark Man for now and take care of Mr. Goatee.*

"You cannot save her," the Dark Man said reasonably. "If you were the right sort of man, you wouldn't even want to."

Cyrus stared at the witch doctor. He could almost taste the bastard's blood in his mouth. It would be watery and as bitter as turned wine.

"Shall I tell you what I plan for her? No? I understand. She is very beautiful and you are infatuated. Well, you remember Ms. Rand's friend—Mr. Douglas? In his own way, a very handsome man—such pretty blue eyes—such a big heart.''

Cyrus's hackles slowly rose until they were lined up like punji sticks all the way down his back. His world had become shrouded by a thick red mist that threatened to smother him if he didn't do something.

Again the Dark Man's high-pitched, somewhat girlish laugh echoed inside the cave. "He stole from me and then had the gall to ask me for a favor. Of course I couldn't give him what he wanted, at least not right away. I had to get to know him better, to share his secrets. In the end he was very helpful. He—what is the expression you Americans are so fond of?— spilled his guts.''

Wait! Cyrus thought. *Not yet!*

"We formed such a special relationship that when the time came, I hated to see him go." He giggled again. "See him go!

"So I cut out his eyes and heart and saved them in their own jars in my portmanteau.''

That does it!

Cyrus lowered his head and ran straight across the cavern at the witch doctor. At the last possible moment, he wheeled and launched himself at the skinny assistant's throat.

But once again the Dark Man had outwitted him. The instant the wolf turned its back, he pulled a wicked-looking combat knife from the belt at his back and swung the blade at the animal's exposed neck. In mid leap, Cyrus's incredibly keen ears picked up the sound of the knife blade cutting through the air and he twisted his body violently to the side. In so doing, he was able to save his neck, but he couldn't avoid the blow. The blade bit deep into his right shoulder, slicing through fur, skin and bone. He crashed to the floor—hard, as his blood gushed from the wound like water from a ruptured fire hose. The torrent of gore splattered everything in a five-foot radius, dousing the black magicians from head to toe with a deluge of red rain. When Cyrus raised his head, the first thing he saw was his right foreleg twitching on the ground a few feet away.

The pain was immediate and unbearable—but he bore it. The blood spray had momentarily blinded his opponents—the Dark Man was frantically wiping his eyes with one hand and waving the knife like a deranged sugarcane cutter with the other, while the goateed man had dropped his sword and gone to his knees as he tried to clear his vision. Unfortunately for Cyrus, he was in no condition to take advantage of their predicament. Shock and blood loss had left him dizzy and as weak as a cub and his first priority was to get Kyna to safety. He hobbled over to her on his three remaining legs, but when he tried to push her toward the exit, the Dark Man shouted to his assistant, "Spread out! Don't let them escape!"

Kyna whispered in Cyrus's ear, "Come on! Follow me."

She ran to the back of the cave and began rolling the rocks away.

No! Cyrus thought. *Not that way!*

But before he could hobble over and stop her, she had disappeared through the opening into the dark beyond.

Chapter Eighteen

Cyrus stood guard in front of the opening to give Kyna as much time as possible. When it was obvious that the Dark Man and his companion were about to regain their sight, he slipped through the hole.

"Stop him!" the Hungan screamed.

Even with his night vision, the cavern was a place of perpetual twilight. It was a gigantic bell-shaped dome, hollow down the middle and full of dark niches and restless wind. Cyrus discovered that he was standing at the top of a narrow catwalk that hugged the cavern walls as it meandered back and forth down into the very bowels of the mountain. The bottom—if the cave had a bottom—was so far below that even Cyrus couldn't see it.

He took off down the path—still much faster on three legs than two—leaving a trail of blood that even a blind man could follow. When he reached the first hairpin switchback about fifty feet down, he leaned against the wall and threw up.

Fucking quiche!

On the way down, he passed dozens of dark niches. Each of the cool crevices had called to him to crawl into its warm darkness and rest. He threw up again—a viscous mixture of blood, cheese and bile—but he felt a little better. His shoulder was starting to crust over but it still felt like it had been worked over with a blowtorch. As much as he wanted to lie down, Kyna's scent was on everything and that helped keep him moving.

After about a mile he came to a level area in the midst of another switchback and found the first signs that Kyna was in trouble. The side of the cave wall had crumbled and the walkway was littered with small stones. The dust on the other side of the slide was churned up as if someone had fallen, and there were spots of fresh blood that carried her smell. He peeked over the side of the walkway. About two hundred feet below, the shelf leveled off into a platform wide enough to support several crumbling adobe buildings set flush against the back wall. Most of the dwellings were two or three stories high, but all had small, rectangular windows and doors and flat, terraced roofs accessed from below with rough-hewn, wooden ladders.

A rock whizzed past Cyrus's ear and he turned and looked up.

The goateed man's head was jutting out over the side of the walkway about a quarter of a mile back up the path. He was using a flashlight like a light saber to cut the stygian darkness. Cyrus guessed he had about twenty minutes on them and pressed on down the trail as best he could. When he reached the hairpin above the village, he dropped to the roof of the closest building and peered down into the street below.

There wasn't much to see: a lot of dust, a cube-shaped box that the Anasazi had probably used as a kiln, a few pieces of pottery around a few blackened fire pits now as cold as Jimmy Hoffa. And Kyna, huddled in a tight ball up against the side of the building next door, shivering and holding on to her knee with both hands.

The buildings were so quiet that Cyrus could hear himself think. It was as if the whole village got up one morning, went out for a pizza and never came back.

When Cyrus limped into view Kyna moaned, "Dear God! You're a mess."

He eased down next to her and rested his muzzle on her thigh. Injured as he was, he was afraid to think what was going to happen when he tried to change back, but one look at Kyna's knee and he figured he didn't have much choice. The moment his body started to reform, he passed out.

* * *

When Cyrus woke he was more or less human again. His head was resting in Kyna's lap and her tears were dripping down into his face.

"Is it my imagination?" he mumbled. "Or is there light coming from somewhere?"

"It's not your imagination. It's fox fire. Look, up there on the wooden beams."

Cyrus glanced up and saw globs of softly glowing material that seemed to be growing on all the wooden support beams. "What the devil's fox fire?"

"A phosphorescent glow produced by certain fungi found on rotting wood."

Cyrus raised one eyebrow. "Oh? And when did you turn into Mr. Wizard?"

"You try living out of hotel rooms for months at a time with nothing better than the Discovery Channel to watch."

"How'd it get here?"

"My guess is, it's the Anasazi version of street lighting. Pretty crafty, those old Native Americans."

Cyrus chuckled, then moaned. "Don't make me laugh." He glanced at her knee. "What happened?"

"I zigged when I should have zagged."

Squinting, he glanced at his right side like a kid afraid to look at a skinned knee. His shoulder was a mass of scabs and blood, but the wound—although stiff and still very painful—had already closed. The knobby end of a new humerus was growing like a cornstalk from the mangled shoulder socket, and as he watched, new tendons and muscles were regenerating around it. New veins and arteries slithered around in the meaty flesh like pale worms and new layers of fresh pink skin were inching down from his neck. It was like watching a time-lapse film of a human arm being eaten away by acid—in reverse.

"All the amazing things I've seen you do," Kyna said in a hushed tone of voice, "and it's only now—seeing this with my own eyes—that I really believe what you are."

"What happened to you?" Cyrus asked again to take his mind off the pain.

She looked at her knee, then reached down and squeezed her ankle.

"It's my own damned fault. I couldn't see shit, but I was in such a hurry I twisted my ankle coming down the trail. Then, not long after that, I slipped on some loose rocks and took a chunk out of my knee. I didn't think it was too bad until it started to swell. I had to crawl the last few yards here like some kind of animal. . . . Sorry."

She was quiet for a moment as she watched his arm heal.

"Uh, Russ? Where are they?"

He snorted angrily. "In a display of my own amazing tactical skills, I not only managed to lose my arm, but I had to slink off before I lost my head too."

"Why do you always run yourself down like that?"

"Jesus, Kyna, look at me! If by some miracle my blood hadn't sprayed in their faces we'd be dead now."

"Maybe that's what I deserve."

"Cut the crap," he snapped. "Come on. We can't stay here. How long was I out?"

"Just a couple of minutes. Your arm had started to grow back even before you fainted."

Cyrus pushed himself to his feet with his good arm. "Well, the head honcho—no pun intended—and his sidekick were right behind me and I don't think I'm much of a match for them right now. Time to boogie."

"I can't walk, Russ. I can't even crawl." Kyna pointed to her swollen ankle.

"I don't want to hear it, Kyna. Off your ass and on your feet."

She began to sob again. "I can't. Don't you think I tried? I didn't know who was going to be coming down that path. I can't walk and yelling at me isn't going to change anything."

He dropped to his knees and pushed his face so close to hers that she could see the veins in his eyes.

"Didn't you hear what our friend has in that little leather

suitcase of his?'' Cyrus asked in a controlled scream. ''You want me to remind you?''

Kyna shook her head so hard that the tears flew like water from a lawn sprinkler. ''Why are you doing this to me? I hate you!''

''Good! Use that hate to get yourself moving. If you don't, your head just might end up as a trophy over that asshole's fireplace.''

She was blubbering too hard to reply.

''Come on, try!'' Cyrus insisted.

She tried to catch her breath. ''Go on . . . leave me.''

''I can't do that, and I can't carry you. I don't think he's going to wait until my arm heals and I don't stand a chance against him this way.''

''Leave me, dammit!''

''There's no way to sugarcoat it—if you don't get up right this second, you're dead. And I don't think it's going to be very fast or pleasant either.''

Cyrus grabbed the back of her jacket with his good hand and pulled her to her knees.

''Oh shit!'' she moaned. ''That hurts!''

''Come on!''

Kyna made it up on one leg before collapsing.

''I know what we can do,'' she said. ''Come on!''

She crawled through the doorway into the adobe house and scurried over to the darkest corner. Cyrus stood in the doorway and looked at her with eyes as warm as congealed blood.

''I'll hide here,'' she said. ''You go back to the restaurant, get help and come back. If you hurry, you can get here before he finds me.''

Cyrus let his eyes wander over the room—over the dust, the abandoned pieces of pottery, over the cold, soot-streaked fire pit. There were no skeletons or rotting clothing but the place stank of death. He didn't have to be a wolf to smell it. It was a city of the dead.

''That's it?'' he hissed. ''That's your master plan?''

"Then you come up with something, Mr. Asshole Were-wolf!"

He snatched Kyna up by her hair. "I will, Goddamn it! I'll drag your—"

The floor beneath them began to tremble and the room filled with the sound of a thousand eggshells cracking. Cyrus had just enough time to hug Kyna to him before the floor gave way and they plunged down into the darkest heart of the mountain.

"They won't get very far," the Dark Man said.

The goateed man and his master were following the trail of Cyrus's blood—a trail that had started out as a flood but was rapidly dwindling to a trickle of maroon spots in the dust of the walkway. Because of this, the goateed man held the sword ready in one hand while anxiously probing the darkness with the flashlight in his other hand; he didn't respond to his master's rosy prediction.

The Dark Man followed a few feet behind. Because his assistant's hands were busy with the sword and the flashlight, he was forced to carry the suitcase as well as his own light and he wasn't happy about it—the case was heavy. To take his mind off this temporary aggravation, the Dark Man entertained himself by creating and then discarding a series of dark mental scenarios starring Kyna and Cyrus.

"Do not worry," the Dark Man said, accurately interpreting his assistant's stony silence. "Trigg will not be able to regenerate before we find him. And once he is disposed of, the woman will be easy."

The goateed man smiled and nodded, but he wished his master were just a little less sure of himself.

The sorcerers were covered with dried but still sticky wolf's blood, and if that wasn't bad enough, the cavern was as cold as a meat locker and was bombarding them with icy condensation. This "false rain" made the trail slippery in places and it took all of the goateed man's concentration to maintain his balance while juggling the flashlight and the fifteen-pound sword. He suddenly stopped at the bend at the top of a steep slope.

"Ah!" the Dark Man purred, looking over his apprentice's shoulder. "It looks as if someone has had a tragic accident."

The goateed man's light shone over a set of skid marks in the dust made by sliding feet, and a little farther on was a small pool of blood.

The Dark Man glanced over the side of the walkway and slowly scanned the village. "I think Ms. Rand may be injured." He put the suitcase down and pulled the combat knife from the hidden pocket in his cape. "Down there. That first building. I believe we have our quarry."

The goateed man led the way into the dwelling, shining his light around the dust and desolation.

"Careful!" the Dark Man hissed, aiming his flashlight beam on the gaping hole near the back wall.

"Where did they go?" the goateed man asked.

The Dark Man stared into the hole and replied with a string of curses. "Go get the case. They will not escape me even if they are dead and I have to drag their souls all the way back from hell."

"Are you okay?" Kyna whispered.

They had skidded, rolled and tumbled down through a maze of ancient lava chutes, finally coming to a stop when they slammed up against a tall stalagmite on the floor of a vast underground chamber. Cyrus had used his body to cushion Kyna as much as he could and he had to wait until she disentangled herself before sitting up. He was having a bit of trouble coaxing air back into his lungs.

"Fine," he gasped. "I'm fine. You?"

"A few more cuts aren't going to kill me. Where are we now?"

"Give me a minute."

Concentrating on just his eyes, Cyrus was able to control the change. In a matter of seconds he stood up and looked around the cave.

"I'm getting pretty good at this."

"Pat yourself on the back later. What do you see?"

"You sure you want to know?"

"What could be worse than what we've already been through?" Kyna asked.

He took the book of matches from his pocket and set fire to the torch sticking out at an angle from a hole in the wall.

"Oh shit!" she whispered.

The cave was an immense crypt. The walls were covered with thousands of hand-carved petroglyphs and the ceiling was streaked as black as the night sky with the soot from an untold number of torches. Some of the ancient murals and been tinted with plant dyes that time had faded like the pages of an ancient comic book, and down the center of the cavern was a depression made by the passage of thousands of bare feet. On either side of this depression, as far as the eye could see, were hundreds upon hundreds of raised burial platforms made from saplings that had been lashed together with hemp and raised aloft on four wobbly poles driven into the bedrock. Most of these ersatz catafalques were decorated with eagle and hawk feathers; others were draped with disintegrating animal hides or ancient weapons. Hundreds of the platforms had collapsed under the weight of the years and Anasazi corpses, scattering heaping piles of bones, skulls and teeth three to four feet deep upon the chamber floor. The place stank of dry rot, dust and time, and it was so quiet that the flame on the torch sounded like sheets of plastic wrap being crumpled.

Cyrus lit a second torch from the flames of the first and walked over to the first body.

What is it about death that fascinates us so? he wondered, staring down at the remarkably well-preserved face.

"Look at those cheekbones, that marvelous forehead," Kyna said. "Who do you think he was?"

"You know more about this stuff than I do. But from the jewelry and bone vest, I'd say he was probably a medicine man."

"Medicine man? You mean he's another witch doctor?"

As if hearing the words to a magic incantation, the dead Indian's head began to turn. The desiccated muscles in his neck creaked in protest as the man looked up at Cyrus and Kyna through eye sockets that were as dry and empty as a desert well.

"Oh shit!" Kyna moaned. "Here we go again."

The corpse climbed to its feet in agonizing slow motion, its bones and stringy tendons popping like microwave popcorn. At last it stood upright for the first time in centuries, swaying drunkenly like a candle flame in a strong wind.

"I think I saw this in a Ray Harryhausen movie," Cyrus mumbled.

A second and then a third body began to stir and then joined the first as behind them more and more of the dead rose like decaying flowers stretching valiantly to reach the sun until they ringed Kyna and Cyrus inside a wall of petrified flesh. A man's voice exploded inside Cyrus's head and reverberated around inside his skull like the tolling of a Chinese temple bell.

"We mean you no harm."

Kyna was just turning to run when Cyrus grabbed her arm. "Did you hear that?"

"Hear what? Let go of me!"

"Wait."

None of the corpses tried to approach Kyna or Cyrus; they merely stood with their arms at their sides—those that had arms—like they were waiting for the crosstown bus.

"What do you want?" Cyrus asked.

The first Indian raised his arm and pointed at Kyna. "We have come to speak to her."

"Why is he pointing at me?" she whispered.

"I think they want to powwow," Cyrus whispered in reply. "What do you want?" he asked in a normal tone.

"In life, my name was Pablo Morales."

"Funny name for an Indian."

"What is?" Kyna asked.

"He says his name was Pablo Morales."

302

Kyna's hand went to her throat. "Oh my God! You remember, Russ. The guy in Miami—the guy that passed me the necklace."

"The guy in Miami was an Indian?"

"This is not my body," Morales said. "My wife and my child and I have reanimated these vessels to speak with you."

"Oh. What about these others?" Cyrus swept his arm around the circle of the dead.

"What's he saying?" Kyna whispered.

Cyrus cast her an irritated glance. "Listen, Mr. Morales, is there any way you can make Kyna hear you? We're kinda on a tight schedule here."

"We know why you run, and we know who it is you run from. We are all here because of Macumba's disciple."

"There, you lost me again."

"What's he saying?" Kyna said, tugging on Cyrus's arm.

"Ask the woman if we may touch her."

"Okay."

Kyna punched Cyrus's arm. "Dammit! What's he saying?"

"He said, 'Ask the woman if we may touch her.' "

"Touch *me?*"

"I don't think he meant me."

"The woman, huh?" Kyna said, wincing as she stared at the Indian's rotting face.

"His words, not mine."

The body that Morales had inhabited shuffled forward and placed a hand on Kyna's shoulder. At the touch of those cold, bony fingers, she cringed.

"Kyna Rand!"

Kyna's eyes grew as round as dinner plates.

"You hear him?"

She nodded, but didn't even consider trying to speak.

"Time is precious to us as well," Morales said, "so I will try to hurry. We are here because of one man—the monster that even now haunts your shadows."

"The witch doctor?" Cyrus asked.

"He is much more than a mere backwoods dabbler in the

black arts. Over the years he has caused the deaths of many people—some of their spirits stand before you in these borrowed vessels.''

''And now it's payback time,'' Kyna hissed. ''Well, that's fine by us. Go get him.''

The corpse just stared.

''What's wrong?'' Cyrus asked.

''This *was* to be the night of retribution—the night some of us have been waiting on for decades.''

''What the hell happened?'' Kyna asked.

''You allowed him to recover the Butcher's Broom.''

''There you go again,'' Cyrus muttered.

''The talisman,'' Morales said. ''The necklace!''

Kyna slapped the Indian's hand away, but the arm broke off at the shoulder and spun off into the darkness.

''Morales, you were an asshole and a creep when you were alive!'' she hissed. ''And being dead hasn't improved you any. I didn't *let* him do any damned thing.''

The Indian's other arm came up as Morales tried to reestablish contact, but Kyna backed away. Cyrus placed his hand gently in the middle of her back so as not to spook her and whispered in her ear, ''Maybe now isn't the right time to rehash old grudges.''

Kyna closed her eyes, took a deep breath and let it out loudly through her nose. Opening her eyes again, she asked, ''What do you want?''

The corpse shuffled forward and placed its remaining hand on her shoulder.

''Hurry!'' the Dark Man urged. ''They mustn't escape.''

''Where could they go?'' the goateed man asked, playing his light along the dank walls of the hidden tunnel.

''This passageway was here, wasn't it? There may be others that lead to the outside.''

The tunnel led down—ever down. The dark was as total as any the goateed man had ever experienced. He was no longer a Christian, but any second he expected to come face-to-face with a demon wearing horns and a pointed tail and carrying a pitchfork.

"Halloween!" he whispered.

"What is that you're mumbling?"

"Nothing. Master, you have recovered the talisman. Why not let them go?"

As he often had during this quest for the talisman, the Dark Man wondered why he had ever selected the goateed man for his apprentice. The man had the backbone of a jellyfish.

"You mean overlook the woman's involvement in Tomas's death?"

"Well . . ."

"You are right. Tomas's death has little to do with it. At the best of times he was an irritant and a disappointment. His powers bordered on the nonexistent—else, why would I have selected you?"

Thanks a lot, the goateed man thought.

"No, what you must always remember is that the Guédé are like a pack of ravenous beasts. And if we do not feed them, they just might turn on us."

"Like the spirits of the dead we have sacrificed?"

Silent, as he watched the flashlight beams dance over the dripping walls, the Dark Man felt the creep of cold flesh up the back of his neck. At last he replied, "Yes . . . I admit to some small measure of concern. But that was before I recovered the talisman. And that is why we must prevent these two from escaping. I had to promise their souls to our dark lords for their assistance—and to the Guédé, a promise is a promise."

The tunnel twisted like a snake. The sorcerers bypassed several blind offshoots and ignored storerooms full of moldy corn. After what felt like hours, the Dark Man suddenly hissed, "Stop!"

The goateed man paused and looked back over his shoulder.

"Turn off your light."

In the midst of all that blackness, the Dark Man closed his eyes. Reaching out with his mind, he touched a concentration of psychic power unheard of in the annals of occult lore.

"What is it, Master?"

"Power."

"I do not understand."

"Nor do you feel. Go slowly, we are close."

The duo felt their way along, for the first time feeling the cloying presence of the mountain over their heads in the oily condensation that seeped into their fingertips and the oppressive humidity that clung like parasites to their lungs. The only sounds were the wind whistling softly through the narrow passageway, and their labored breathing.

"Stop!" the Dark Man hissed. The water running down the walls was sparkling like a million tiny fireflies. "There is light ahead."

Rounding a right bend in the corridor, they entered the huge subterranean cavern. The Dark Man took note of the burial platforms and the lighted torches. "She is here."

The goateed man whispered, "She? What of the man?"

Grasping the talisman tightly in both hands, the black giant searched the vault with his mind. After a moment he uttered a single word: "Seek!"

The necklace emitted a low hum followed by a burst of weak light that shot to the top of the cavern and hovered there for a few seconds before gradually fading into nothingness.

Frowning, the Dark Man turned to his assistant. "The woman is at the other side of the cave, but the man is gone."

"Where could he have gone?"

"Another secret passage, perhaps. We will find him later. First, the woman."

The goateed man put his hand on his master's arm. "Could it be a trap?"

The Dark Man looked down at the goateed man's hand as if it were some loathsome insect. "If it is, Mr. Trigg will be very sorry."

The Dark Man stepped cautiously into the cavern, holding the talisman out away from his neck like a diving rod. Despite his confident words, he was worried. Locating the Rand woman had been almost too easy; her aura stood out among the dead like a beacon. But when he had tried to locate Trigg, all he'd received for his efforts was an incessant high-pitched buzzing in his head almost like the static on an AM radio during an electrical storm. Then, when he had used the talisman to try and locate the origin of the static, the psychic seeker had just dissipated, indicating that the source of the disturbance was too widespread to isolate. He suspected that the cave had trapped all kinds of psychic energy from the dead Indians—that might explain it. Only . . .

"I don't like this place," the goateed man whispered.

They were literally walking over the bones of the dead that had spilled down into the central aisle. In some places the skulls were so thick that it felt like walking over a cobblestone road.

"Not much farther," the Dark Man replied.

The duo had just about reached the center of the crypt when Kyna hobbled out into the aisle.

"Why are you doing this to me?" she shouted. Her words echoed hollowly: *to me . . . to me . . . to meee.*

The Dark Man's face split in a huge grin, but he quickly recovered his senses, and his glower. Releasing his hold on the necklace, the Hungan called out, "Nice to see you, Ms. Rand. We've had a good game of hide-and-seek, but I am afraid you will not be 'home free.' "

He drew the combat knife from his belt and let it dangle at his side. "Time to join your friend Bryan."

As he took the first step toward her, his mind already anticipating the pleasures he was going to derive from her agony, a skeletal hand came up out of the mound of decaying bodies and grabbed hold of his ankle. The witch doctor nearly fell, then looked down. When he saw what had happened, at first he was too stunned to speak.

"Master!" the goateed man cried as two skeletal scarecrows began clawing their way up his legs.

"How dare you!" the Dark Man screeched, and swung the knife, severing the offending hand at the wrist.

"Master!"

"Use your sword, idiot! They can't hurt you."

"What are they doing?" The goateed man had dropped his flashlight and was holding the sword in both hands, hacking away at the dead until their bones flew through the air like tall grass.

"Just some old friends dropping in for the holiday. Ignore them."

But that was easier said than done.

Dead Anasazi were rising from their graves like it was the Second Coming. Headless bodies, armless torsos, men, women, petrified little children—husks of human beings that were more gristle than substance. The corpses with legs climbed up and tried to walk. The ones without legs dragged themselves over the bones of their ancestors on skinless hands. Those without hands or arms wiggled like spiders that had taken a blast of insecticide right in the snout.

"Why are you doing this?" the Dark Man shouted as he swung his arm back and forth in great sweeping arcs.

Body parts filled the air like chaff blown before a hurricane wind, but still the dead rose, clutching and clawing even as the blades snapped their bones like green sticks and bit deep into their desiccated flesh. Sweat ran in rivers from both the Dark Man and his assistant. Their arms grew weary, but still the dead came. And all the while, Kyna shouted encouragement to the Anasazi and insults at the Dark Man and his assistant.

"Yo! You skinny bags of bones! How's it feel to have the dead tell you to kiss their asses?

"Hey fuzzface! Your buddy scarface is going to get you killed!"

"Master," the goateed man panted. "I can't keep this up."

"You stop and I'll kill you myself." The Dark Man's eyes blazed with fires of madness as he screeched at the spirits of his enemies, *"You'll pay for this! By the dark lords, you'll all payyyy!"*

The goateed man didn't shout anything—he couldn't. He

was swinging the sword like his arms were made of rubber and wheezing as if his lungs were about to explode. The debris of the slaughter was piling up around them like cords of wood. The new legions of dead troops climbed over their dismembered comrades like Pickett's men storming the ramparts of Little Round Top—and their fate was the same as Pickett's. To avoid being buried under an avalanche of skulls and rib cages, the Dark Man and his goateed apprentice had to keep scrambling higher and higher up the pile, until finally they found themselves standing alone atop an eight-foot mountain of bones. The Dark Man raised his sword over his head and let out a blood-chilling howl, "You'll never beat me! *No one can beat me!*"

In the midst of his moment of triumph, the mound of bodies began to sway. Skulls rolled down the sides like bowling balls, only to shatter like eggshells at the bottom. The Dark Man lost his grip on the knife when he instinctively threw out his arms to maintain his balance. "What the—"

Cyrus erupted from the hiding place the dead had prepared for him underneath their own bodies—a pocket they had formed in their midst and shielded from the dark fiend's probing mind with a wall of psychic white noise. Before the mad witch doctor could even blink, Cyrus ripped the talisman from the man's neck and hurled it away into the darkest corner of the cavern. Then he grabbed the Dark Man by his shoulders and lifted him straight up—up into the baleful glare of his yellow eyes. His transformation had begun. And the werewolf didn't care much for what it saw.

For the first time since the desert, Cyrus completely relinquished control.

Go ahead, he thought as he let his mind retreat, *just this once. Make him pay.*

And his mind was swept away by a tidal wave of primitive blood-lust. It was like watching a train wreck in freeze-frame. The lower part of his jaw unhinged like the mouth of a snake and he sank his fangs into the Dark Man's cheek, piercing the man's right eye like a rotten grape. The witch doctor's scream kept rising and rising until the very roots of the mountain threatened to crack.

Behind them, the goateed man stood as still as a concrete statue. He had never heard his master—or any human being, for that matter—scream like that. At that point the wolf released its hold on the witch doctor's face and the Dark Man turned and looked back over his shoulder. His face was hardly recognizable anymore. Gore from his mutilated eye oozed down over the tattoos like tears on a dirty window. A huge flap of skin hung down from his right cheek like a piece of bloody caul. The man's remaining eye swept the cavern until it found his apprentice.

"Ricardo—my friend—help me!"

The goateed man couldn't reply; he could hardly believe his eyes. His invulnerable master was being devoured by a demon and he was too terrified to remember a single charm or spell of protection. His eyes went to the sword in his hand and he dropped it like a leper's handshake.

"Ricardo!" the Dark Man screamed. *"Please!"*

Then the wolf snarled—a horrible, grating noise like two boulders grinding against one another—and sank its teeth into the Hungan's neck, burrowing and ripping into the soft flesh under the man's chin. The Dark Man shuddered once, then twitched and moaned until at last, as if tiring of the human's puny struggles, the wolf ripped open the man's chest and plunged its snout into it. After a few seconds of snorting and rooting around like a pig hunting truffles, the beast came out with the man's black heart clutched in its teeth, tilted its shaggy head back and swallowed the organ whole.

At this, the goateed man pulled his father's gun from under his coat and started backing away.

The wolf dropped the Hungan's body. And turned to the Dark Man's assistant.

The goateed man froze.

The burning gaze of the werewolf was deep and cold and full of menace. It didn't threaten painful death, it promised it. In a place of the dead it was the face of death.

''Keep away from me,'' the goateed man said. He had the gun in both hands, but the barrel was shaking so badly it looked like a conductor's baton.

The wolf took a step.

''Stay back!''

The wolf's mouth twisted into what looked almost like a human smile.

Wait a minute! Cyrus screamed silently from deep inside his mind. *This wasn't part of it. Let him go!*

But the wolf took another step . . . and another.

The gun exploded and Cyrus staggered as the bullet passed through his shoulder. The pain was immediate and exquisite, but it freed him from the beast's hold.

The goateed man fired again and again and kept firing until the hammer fell on a spent cartridge. Even then, he kept pulling the trigger until Cyrus, leaking blood from half a dozen places, stepped in front of him and stuck his claw in the muzzle of the gun barrel.

Click! Click!

What Cyrus longed to do was rip the man's goatee off and his face along with it and have them both for lunch. But six bullets—three of which had passed through his stomach— were enough to dampen even his appetite. Instead, Cyrus merely bared his fangs and growled.

The goateed man dropped the revolver and ran. Cyrus watched him slipping and sliding over the obstacle course of body parts. He fell twice and bounced back up before finally vanishing into the secret tunnel.

Phew! What the devil happened? Cyrus wondered as he began to resume his human form. His mind was still spinning. It wasn't just that he had lost control, it was almost like being possessed. He only hoped Kyna hadn't been watching.

Kyna!

He spun around.

Kyna was lying slumped across the hollowed-out torso of a young boy. One of the bullets that passed through Cyrus had struck her high in the chest. He fell to his knees to examine the wound and breathed a mental sigh of relief. It wasn't that bad—a small ragged hole about the size of a nickel just above her breast. He gently turned her over.

Sweet Jesus!

On its way out, the bullet had left a hole the size of an orange. Kyna's sweater and the yellowed bones underneath her were covered with red blood. Cyrus cradled her head in his arms and began rocking slowly back and forth.

Oh, God. Oh God, please no!

Her body was already starting to grow cold. He put his fingers to her throat and felt for a pulse. It was there; a tiny spasm so weak it took all of his powers to find it. Then he put his hand over the wound and tried to will it to close.

Her eyes fluttered and squeezed open.

"Don't look at me." Her voice was so tiny. "I look so old."

He had to get to a telephone—he had to get help!

But reality told him that even if there were a phone somewhere on the mountain it was going to take at least an hour for help to arrive. The way Kyna was losing blood, she had five minutes at best.

She couldn't die! She just couldn't!

Paula! he cried out with his mind. *Paula, can you hear me? Kazie! Someone, tell me what to do.*

"Don't be upset," Kyna whispered. "I've always been afraid of growing old, of the pain."

But the answer was right there in front of him.

Cyrus pulled his hand away—it was sticky with her blood. Holding the hand up, he turned it slowly in the light from the torches. It was like no hand he had ever seen: the coarse hair, the needlelike claws jutting from the tips of humanoid fingers. His eyes came to rest on the hole in her chest. It was still oozing blood, but slowly now. A spurt . . . another . . . Slow-motion death. There was so much blood! The coppery fetor filled his lungs like nitrous oxide and made him dizzy. Her pain reminded him of Kazie, for the smell of dying, fast or slow, was nearly the same. But could he do it to Kyna? Could he do to her what was done to him? Did he have the right?

Love gives you the right, his tortured brain insisted. *She's going to die if you don't. You can't just sit here and watch her bleed to death! She would want you to.*

Easy now! Just a kiss. A kiss to wake the sleeping princess.

He lowered his fangs to her throat.

SPREE

J. N. WILLIAMSON

Mix equal parts Charles Starkweather and Bonnie and Clyde and you've got Dell and Kee, a couple in love and out for fun—their kind of fun. When Kee casually suggests they murder her parents, that's just the beginning of their grisly road trip. After all, there's a long highway in front of them... and a lot of people to kill before they're through.

___4370-X $5.50 US/$6.50 CAN

BRASS

ROBERT J. CONLEY

The ancient Cherokees know him as *Untsaiyi,* or Brass, because of his metallic skin. He is one of the old ones, the original beings who lived long before man walked the earth. And he will live forever. He cares nothing for humans, though he can take their form—or virtually any form—at will. For untold centuries the world has been free of his deadly games, but now Brass is back among us and no one who sees him will ever be the same . . . if they survive at all.

___4505-2 $5.50 US/$6.50 CAN

B|TE RICHARD LAYMON

"No one writes like Laymon, and you're going to have a good time with anything he writes."
—Dean Koontz

It's almost midnight. Cat's on the bed, facedown and naked. She's Sam's former girlfriend, the only woman he's ever loved. Sam's in the closet, with a hammer in one hand and a wooden stake in the other. Together they wait as the clock ticks down because . . . the vampire is coming. When Cat first appears at Sam's door he can't believe his eyes. He hasn't seen her in ten years, but he's never forgotten her. Not for a second. But before this night is through, Sam will enter a nightmare of blood and fear that he'll never be able to forget—no matter how hard he tries.

"Laymon is one of the best writers in the genre today."
—Cemetery Dance

HUNGRY EYES

BARRY HOFFMAN

The eyes are always watching. She can feel them as she huddles there, naked, vulnerable, in an iron cage in a twisted man's basement. Someday she will be the one with the power, the need to close the eyes. And she'll close them all.

___4449-8 $4.99 US/$5.99 CAN

Dorchester Publishing Co., Inc.
P.O. Box 6640
Wayne, PA 19087-8640

Please add $1.75 for shipping and handling for the first book and $.50 for each book thereafter. NY, NYC, and PA residents, please add appropriate sales tax. No cash, stamps, or C.O.D.s. All orders shipped within 6 weeks via postal service book rate. Canadian orders require $2.00 extra postage and must be paid in U.S. dollars through a U.S. banking facility.

Name_____
Address_____
City_____ State_____ Zip_____
I have enclosed $_____ in payment for the checked book(s).
Payment <u>must</u> accompany all orders. ☐ Please send a free catalog.